D0056331

The Yokota Officers Club

The Yokota Officers Club

A NOVEL BY

Sarah Bird

ALFRED A. KNOPF
New York 2001

THIS IS A BORZOI BOOK

PUBLISHED BY ALFRED A. KNOPF

Copyright © 2001 by Sarah Bird

All rights reserved under International and Pan-American
Copyright Conventions. Published in the United States by
Alfred A. Knopf, a division of Random House, Inc.,
New York, and simultaneously in Canada by
Random House of Canada Limited, Toronto.
Distributed by Random House, Inc., New York.

www.aaknopf.com

Knopf, Borzoi Books, and the colophon are
registered trademarks of Random House, Inc.

ISBN: 0-375-41214-X
LCCN: 2001089763

Manufactured in the United States of America
Published June 27, 2001
Reprinted Twice
Fourth Printing, August 2001

For my father, John Aaron Bird, Lt. Col. USAF, DFC

My mother, Colista Marie McCabe Bird, R.N., Lt. US Army

My brothers, John Aaron, Thomas Cameron, and Steven Michael

My sisters, Martha Lynn and Mary Katherine

Warriors all.

I imagined that all of us could meet on some impeccably manicured field, all the military brats, in a gathering so vast that it would be like the assembling of some vivid and undauntable army. We could come together on this parade ground at dusk, million voiced and articulating our secret anthems of hurt and joy. We could praise each other in voices that understand both the magnificence and pain of our transient lives. . . .

In this parade . . . our fathers would stand at rigid attention. Then they would begin to salute us, one by one, and in that salute, that one sign of recognition, of acknowledgment, they would thank us for the first time. They would be thanking their own children for . . . enduring a military childhood.

—Pat Conroy, from the introduction to *Military Brats: Legacies of Childhood Inside the Fortress* by Mary Edwards Wertsch

He stretched his arms towards his child, but the boy cried and nestled in his nurse's bosom, scared at the sight of his father's armor, and at the horse-hair plume that nodded fiercely from his helmet. His father and mother laughed to see him, but Hektor took the helmet from his head and laid it all gleaming upon the ground. Then he took his darling child.

—Homer, *Illiad* (trans. Samuel Butler)

The Yokota Officers Club

White House
Washington, D.C.

Dear Dependents of the United States Air Force:
Welcome to your new duty assignment, Kadena Air Base, Okinawa.

Okinawa is the principal island of the 160 islands that make up the Ryukyu archipelago. Only 67 miles long and from 2 to 17 miles wide, Okinawa is often referred to as the "Keystone of the Pacific" because of its strategic Far East location roughly 900 miles from Tokyo, Manila, Seoul, and Hong Kong.

Originally an independent nation, Okinawa has endured long periods of both Chinese and Japanese domination. After World War II, the island remained under U.S. military control. The United States will continue its custodianship as long as conditions of threat and tension exist in the Far East.

Bear in mind as you begin your tour that the serviceman's family is just as much a representative of the United States Government as the serviceman himself.

Your President and Commander in Chief,
Lyndon Baines Johnson

*O*n the map at the back of the pamphlet, Japan resembles a horned caterpillar rearing up in the middle of the Pacific Ocean. My destination, the Ryukyu Islands, trails behind like a scatter of droppings. We've been in the air for seventeen hours. Sheets of rain snake across the plastic pane of the window next to me. A light on the wing blinks red in the night. Lulled by the drone of the jet engines taking me to join my family at Kadena Air Base, I slide back into the anesthetized stupor that travel always induces.

Phenobarbital, that was my mother, Moe's, drug of choice for traveling with six children packed into a station wagon when we PCS'd—Permanent Change of Station—six times in eight years. We, her children, took the drug, not Moe. A nurse, she administered the meticulously titrated doses in tiny chips that floated like specks of goldfish food in our cups of apple juice.

"How else was I supposed to keep you from murdering each other?" Moe had answered when I inquired about the peculiar lassitude that always seemed to overtake us upon departing Maxwell Air Force Base, or Travis, or Harlingen, or Brooks, or Kirtland, or Mountain Home Air Force Base. Especially Mountain Home. All I remember about leaving that base was pulling out of Boise, Idaho, with my breath freezing in the predawn mountain chill and regaining consciousness outside of Tonopah, Nevada, with a bib of drool and my nasal linings dried to corn flakes.

"You drugged us? Your children? You drugged us?"

"I thought about running a hose in from the exhaust pipe. That really would have quieted you down."

"You drugged us?"

"Think about it, Bernie. Six kids, two of them in diapers when we transferred out of Japan, crammed into a station wagon with the luggage strapped on top and a maniac behind the wheel who wouldn't stop unless you put a gun to his head. Me passing around the bologna sandwiches and the potty chair, sprinkling the cars behind us when the potty can got full. And the whole time I'm wrestling with a map the size of the Magna Carta and trying to navigate for a guy used to getting directions off a radar screen who keeps barking at me to do something about *my* children. No, I didn't have a lot of patience left to deal with Kit screaming about you 'breathing' on her or you screaming about

Kit 'looking' at you or the twins hammering monkey bumps and noogies and X no-backs into each other and Bosco wailing about whatever hamster or turtle or corn snake she had to leave behind at the last base and Bob reenacting entire episodes of *Clutch Cargo* and someone, usually you, barfing."

"Yeah, but what if you've turned us all into junkies?"

"Well, if I have, all I can say is that I did the best I knew how and you lived to tell the tale. That's all I can say."

It was during an unmedicated moment on the long hot drive to Harlingen, Texas, that we all, all us sibs, realized we hated our ultra-Hibernian Catholic names. No one else at our new schools would be named after saints famous for being enucleated or having their tongues plucked out with pliers. We wanted regular names. So, as Moe passed around the potty seat, we rechristened ourselves with the most normal, most American names we could each think of. The twins, Frances Xavier and Bryan Patrick, chose Buzz and Abner. Joseph Anthony, just three at the time, selected Bob, since it was not only a great name and easy to spell but also his favorite aquatic activity. No one wanted me to change Bernie. Mary Colleen, our youngest sister, declared that henceforth she would be known as Nancy, her book-loving soul released in ecstasy at the thought of sharing Nancy Drew's name.

"Nancy?" We'd all hooted in unison. We'd already given her the perfect name, Bosco, when she was two and loved Bosco Chocolate Syrup, and we weren't swapping it for some girl detective in a roadster.

"Okay," Bosco had agreed. "But in my mind I'm still calling myself Nancy, and you can't stop me."

"The name represents the self," my father said from the driver's seat, flicking a white Tums out of a foil roll into his mouth. "A rejection of the name represents a rejection of the self. You all hate yourselves."

We exchanged fiendish looks and had to agree. "Yeah, we all hate ourselves."

"Eileen is the only one showing any sense."

But it wasn't sense my middle sister was showing; it was concentration. She glowed like a full-immersion Baptist bursting to the surface of the tank when she finally revealed, "My new name is Kitty."

"Kitty?" Moe echoed.

"Okay, Kit. Kit Root."

As Moe dealt out Sioux Bee honey and peanut butter sandwiches, I glanced at Buzz, Abner, Bob, and Bosco and wondered what we'd unloosed. It was clear that Eileen wasn't getting the joke. Worse, with her platinum-blond hair and Siamese-cat blue eyes, the name Kit fit her too well.

At our new schools, we all registered under our real names and only called one another Buzz, Abner, Bob, Bosco, and Bernie at home. But Eileen died that day and never again answered to anything, anywhere, except Kit.

Maybe it was the phenobarbital; still, even without chemical amendments, moving, the part after the packers left but before I became the new girl, a spot I tended to occupy until the packers came again, was always the coziest time in my life. Just me and the sibs and Moe, sealed up in our mobile incubator hurtling down the highway, stuck to the vinyl seat covers, glued to one another with sweat, everyone oozing together, breathing the breaths a sister or brother had exhaled a hundred miles ago. Just us. No outsiders. Outsiders—which is to say, anyone that Moe had not brought into this world—and my family did not mix. We'd only allowed an outsider into the family once.

Fumiko. Of course I'm thinking about Fumiko again. The first time I crossed the Pacific I was six years old, twelve years ago, and heading for the horned caterpillar itself, not the droppings. Fumiko became part of our family the day we landed in Japan and was one of us for four years. Bob hadn't even been born when we PCS'd out of Japan eight years ago, and Bosco was barely two, so they don't remember Fumiko at all. The twins, who'd hung on to her like orangutan babies for the first three years of their lives, have no memory of her either. Kit probably does, though it's hard to tell since Kit speaks to me as little as possible and Fumiko's name was never mentioned again after we left Japan anyway.

But I know Moe remembers Fumiko, and our father, and me—of course, me. Of course I remember Fumiko.

The Okinawa-bound plane hits an air pocket and belly-flops a few hundred feet. My seatmate, Tammi, grips my arm, digging her pearlized pink nails into my flesh. Tammi looks only slightly older than my sister Kit, who is seventeen. But Tammi is on her way to Okinawa so that her baby daughter, Brandi, can meet her father for the first time. The cabin lights flicker, and Tammi and I look to the front of the plane to see if the stewardi are freaking in any manifest way.

"The pilot just rotated out of Nam." Tammi has made this observation every time the plane wobbled for the past seventeen hours since we left Travis. The implication is that if a pilot is good enough to survive Vietnam, surely he can get a planeload of dependents, mostly wives and small children traveling Space Available, delivered safely to Okinawa.

Tammi looks the way my two sisters and three brothers, certainly my parents, expect me to look. A year ago, they'd left me behind at the University of New Mexico when my father was transferred to Kadena Air Base on Okinawa. They'd said goodbye to a sister, a daughter, who set her Breck-washed hair into a flip on pink foam rollers. Who wore Villager blouses with coordinating pleated kilts held closed with an oversize gold pin above the knee. Who had a pair of tortoiseshell cat's-eye glasses correcting her vision, a white-cotton circular-stitched brassiere shielding her breasts, Weejun loafers covering her clean feet, and Heaven Sent cologne perfuming her thoroughly deodorized and depilated self.

When I stepped off the plane they would behold a vagrant in Levi's with peace-sign patches stitched to her ass and hems frayed to a dirty fringe from being trod upon by a pair of water-buffalo-hide sandals held on by one ring around the big toe. Who parted her straight hair in the middle and left it to hang lank as old drapes on either side of a groovy new pair of John Lennon wire rims. Who'd substituted patchouli oil for Wind Song perfume and had discarded deodorant, depilation, and undergarments altogether.

For the past year, I had breathed civilian oxygen for the first time in my life. It caused me to forget that I was the daughter of Major Mason Patrick Root, just as much a representative of the United States as the serviceman himself. It caused me to join an antiwar group on campus, Damsels in Dissent.

I started to remember who I was at Travis Air Force Base, where I had to hang around reading *The Confessions of Nat Turner* while my request for a Space A flight worked its way through MATS. Just the acronyms for Space Available and Military Air Transport System were enough to resuscitate me with the air I'd inhaled for the past eighteen years. I was returning to a world where officer fathers lost their jobs when sons didn't mow the lawn, when daughters dated GIs, or when mothers misbehaved too often at Happy Hour. Who knew what happened when offspring allied themselves with groups that advised draftees to swallow balls of tinfoil and put laundry detergent in their armpits to fool induction center doctors?

As we fly deeper and deeper into a world that is entirely military, I push that question out of my mind even further than I bury the memory of Fumiko. I've long since finished with Nat Turner and, desperate for the narcotizing effect of moving my eyes across print, I start on the pamphlet again. I don't get very far before lightning flashes outside the window. Almost simultaneously, thunder booms. Baby Brandi trembles, sucks her lip in, and wails. A crack of lightning explodes, and the clouds outside are illuminated in a battlefield flash of pale violet and gray.

Finally, the clouds part, and far below there is, at last, something visible in the darkness. Like a handkerchief tossed onto an endless field of mud, the island of Okinawa appears in the galaxy of black that is the night and the Pacific Ocean.

It seems impossible that they are all down there: my parents; Kit; the twins, Buzz and Abner; my little sister and brother,

Bosco and Bob. It seems even more improbable that this plane is going to land on such a minute button of light.

Abruptly the plane slews to the side so violently that luggage bins pop open and diaper bags and duffels shoot into the air. All the babies and children cry. The stewardesses at the front are ashen-faced and stare at each other, wide-eyed, stricken. The smell of vomit, dirty diapers, and fear spikes through the cabin.

The older stewardess speaks into a microphone. "Remain in your seats with your seat belts fastened." She has on chalky lipstick that makes her teeth look yellow. She tries to get the younger stewardess up to help her stuff bags back into overhead bins, but the younger one shakes her head and tightens the belt holding her into her seat facing us. Seeing open fear on a stewardess's face ignites panic in the cabin. The older one crimps her lips in disgust and wades into the aisle.

Lightning flashes continuously on all sides. A bolt crackles against the plane. Women scream as the thunder explodes. The older stewardess tries to speak through her microphone, but a roar of static is all that comes out.

Mascara-blackened tears streak Tammi's cheeks.

The woman behind me begins to pant as if she were giving birth. Another woman sitting on the aisle turns in her seat and tells us in a weirdly conversational tone, "Pray, everyone, okay? Just pray to Jesus."

But I am already praying to the Blessed Virgin Mary. She's much more likely to be interested in a plane filled with mothers and children.

The plane bucks violently and the brave stewardess is thrown to the floor. The panting woman behind me screams like a sleeper trying to wake from the nightmare of her own death. Full-scale panic breaks out, with all the dependent wives and all their children sobbing and ululating like Berbers.

Tammi turns to me and, in a voice as calm as if she were reporting how much apples were selling for at the base commissary, tells me, "We're going to die."

On the plane, all noise and all smells stop. Next to me, Tammi's face is red and squinched up from crying, but all I hear is the roar of an airplane's engine. I look around and see the experienced stew fight to get to her feet and the woman who wanted us all to pray to Jesus snatch at her so she falls down again, but I hear nothing.

Once again, I am the overwrought, unhealthily imaginative child prone to nervous attacks and stomach disorders with a neurotic attachment to my mother and a dangerous dependence upon sugar that I was on my first trip over these waters, and I understand that we are seconds away from going down in a storm over the East China Sea.

Then all I am aware of is my longing to be back with my family, and in return I am suffused with the depth of their wounded longing for me.

They left me behind when I was seventeen, and I was not ready. I was a pupa in the world without the exoskeleton they had always provided. I long for them, especially Moe. Always Moe. I grip the pamphlet about Okinawa in my hands and stare at it. But all I see are the words of the pamphlet I read that first time twelve years ago.

White House
Washington, D.C.

Dear Service Men and Women and Dependents:

As members of our Armed Forces stationed overseas, you and your dependents are representatives of the American people with the essential mission of building goodwill for our country.

Service men and women are the largest group of official U.S. personnel stationed in foreign countries. As a result, people form their personal attitudes toward our country and our American way of life to a great extent by what they see and hear about American service personnel and their dependents.

As you serve abroad, the respect you show foreign laws and customs, your courteous regard for other ways of life, and your speech and manner help to mold the reputation of our country. Thus, you represent us all in bringing assurance to the people you meet that the United States is a friendly nation and one dedicated to the search for world peace and to the promotion of the well-being and security of Nations.

Your President and Commander in Chief,
Dwight D. Eisenhower

"*B*ernie, put that down. Reading will make you start throwing up again."

"I've got to. It's required."

"You don't *got* to do nothin', kiddo." My mother snapped the pamphlet entitled "Welcome to Yokota Air Base" out of my hand

and flopped onto the lower bunk next to mine. She untied the strings on her navy-blue gabardine skirt that held up the flap of cheap black cotton covering her pregnant belly and squirted on a fat pink plop of Baby Magic lotion. Red stretch marks ran like lava down the white mound heaved up by her third child.

"Jesus, Mary, and Joseph." She huffed out a sigh and slathered the lotion around, covering acreage with the slapdash efficiency of a wallpaperer spreading paste. "This has got to be either twins or a baby mastodon. I sure wasn't this huge with you or your sister."

Moe glowed golden in the drizzle of illumination cast by the reading light embedded in the cabin's riveted metal. Her hand described a Great Circle around her belly like the one we were following around the globe from San Francisco to Japan. In the boiler room next to our cabin on the S.S. *President Wilson*, pistons boomed loud as a Victorian factory. My stomach heaved in time to the rise and fall of the great ship on the midnight blue waves. I sat up, panting, saliva flooding my mouth.

"Moe, I don't feel so good." I never called my mother Mom or Mama. Like her friends, I always called her Moe, short for her maiden name, Mohoric. She called me Bernie, short for Bernadette.

"Here. Sip." Moe reached across the narrow aisle separating the bunks to pass me a glass of warm 7UP, bending the accordion-crimped neck of the paper straw to my lips. As I sipped, she crushed a couple more Dramamine tablets between two spoons, added most of a packet of sugar, wet it with a few drops of 7UP pipetted up with the straw, and spooned it into me.

"It's all that reading. You're too young to be reading so much. You should be out playing with other kids, exercising some muscle beside your brain."

"Actually, the brain is not a muscle."

Moe shook her head, then sagged back onto the bunk with a long sigh.

The trip had started with such promise. Our first night on board was spent bobbing peaceably in San Francisco Bay. We were summoned to dinner by a crewman in a white jacket tapping out three notes on a miniature xylophone. Our father was handsome in his white mess dress jacket, a Morse code of colored ribbons pinned on his chest, his hair dark and shiny as Dean Martin's. Moe's dark hair was pulled back by the silver combs he had bought her on their honeymoon in Cuba. The combs had shown off the slight droop at the top of Moe's right ear where, when she was a premature baby, a stupid nurse laid her in the incubator wrong and her soft, unformed ear had creased forever. But the flap of turned-down ear is like a mark in a book, a page creased to call you back to the best part, which is Moe's face. My mother is beautiful.

That night, the first night of our trip, as we sat in the dining room, Moe had been especially beautiful, her cheeks rosy with excitement. That the Air Force was sending her family, headed by a captain, overseas on a presidential luxury liner was a windfall she wanted us all to take full advantage of. "Order the sea scallops and parfait," she'd told Kit and me.

My little sister, Kit, just turned five, exactly eleven months younger than me, had shaken her head no, whipping the long springy coils of blond hair against her cheeks to reject, as usual, any suggestion made by my mother. She'd insisted on mashed potatoes. Period. No gravy. No butter.

"Get the kid what she wants," my father intervened.

Utterly seduced from the beginning by my mother's vision of what life ought to be, I ordered the scallops and parfait. Moe and I shared conspiratorial glances with each bite.

Then, that night, the S.S. *President Wilson*'s mountainous boilers shuddered to life. The tendrils of paper streamers we'd thrown overboard to the crowd on the dock far beneath us snapped as the colossus slid, implacable as an iceberg, away from land. The instant the ship commenced teetering on the waves beyond the harbor, up, then down, I turned into a human snow globe. My contents swirled nonstop for the entire twelve days we were at sea.

Kit, pronounced "a born sailor" by our father, loved it. The long voyage that debilitated me left her in rampaging health. Like our father, she fed on everything that sickened me: motion, change, attention, people. She rampaged through shuffleboard tournaments, splashed in the saltwater swimming pool that sloshed from side to side, rolling in time with the dark waves. She ordered Shirley Temples with extra cherries from the deck steward, Bunny-Hopped with our father, watched magic shows, and sat at the officer's table while I lay in bed, the boiler hammering at my head, nibbling crackers and flat 7UP, struggling to keep peristaltic action moving downward.

I was indescribably grateful to my trampoline stomach.

Each time my sister burst through the oblong-shaped door into our dark room to throw down the ribbon she had just won for leading the longest Bunny Hop line or cannonballing the most water out of the swimming pool, then raced back out to win the Best Smile contest, I breathed a deep sigh of relief and nestled more deeply into the sodden sheets. Not only had seasickness brought me to this paradise of unlimited time alone with Moe, it had won me a temporary reprieve from strangers, from outsiders. As a daughter of the military, it would not last long. All too soon there would be classrooms, buses, playgrounds, neighborhoods filled with strangers. There would be teachers who might be kind, might be cruel, would probably simply be perplexed by the new girl who would only stop crying when she was reading while her sister—nearly a whole year younger!—would have five little girls fighting to be her best friend before *the bus, the bus, the B. U. S.*, had even halted at their stop the first day.

"Here, give me a tug." Moe propped herself up on her elbow, pivoted around, and stuck her toe out to me. I helped her pull off the rubberized tube of support stocking. Puffy purple worms of varicose vein throbbed on her leg.

Moe's smell filled our cabin. I concentrated on picking out the odors to keep from throwing up: Baby Magic with its scent of celery and babies. An ammonia tang from the permanent she'd given herself back at the Travis Air Force Base BOQ, where we'd stayed before leaving. The funk of body-warmed rubber. Slung beneath all that was the hammock of her regular smell, the smoky mint odor of Kool menthol cigarettes, a light pretzelly sweat scent, and Joy perfume.

"Moe, what did you look like when you were a little girl?"

Moe pulled the flap of her skirt back up and studied me for a long moment before answering. "Me? Oh, I was a funny-looking runt. Like a wormy pup with my big tummy and spindly arms and legs. And my knees! What a mess! Covered in scabs because I couldn't walk a foot without falling."

"Look!" I pulled my spindly leg out from under the damp sheet and pointed to the bumper of scab on my knee.

"How about that?" Moe shook her head at the coincidence.

"What else?" I prompted eagerly.

Moe angled the reading lamp until its light fell on my face. "Oh, dark circles under my eyes, from too much worrying and reading and not enough sleeping. And my hair! Had a mind of its own. Like a black cat caught in a rainstorm."

This was miraculous information! Moe had looked just like me when she was little. I wanted to believe this so much I didn't ask how spiky cat fur hair like mine could have ever turned into heavy Cleopatra hair like hers. Or how my raccoon-shadowed eyes could possibly have evolved into her dark-lashed wonders. Then I remembered and touched my badge of shame. "Yeah, but you didn't have this."

"I don't see why you hate your widow's peak."

"Because it makes me look like Dracula."

"You do not look like Dracula. It gives your face a wonderful heart shape. Vivien Leigh has a widow's peak. All the great beauties have them."

"So why did the kids back at Mather call me Dracula?"

"Because the kids back at Mather were congenital idiots."

With no warning, preliminary retching sounds issued from my throat.

"Oh, brother, here we go again!"

Moe lunged out of bed, grabbing the bowl on the floor. A bitter froth of Dramamine and bile came up. Even sitting up for that short a period caused my vision to drain downhill, leaving my head black. Moe grabbed me before I passed out and helped me lie back down. Her gray eyes passed across me, concerned, and for the first time I realized I was really sick. Not just faking it like I usually would to get out of the Bunny Hop and Best Smile Contest.

"You think this is crowded." My mother laughed and my stomach eased at her tone, jaunty and confiding, as if she were answering some snappily hilarious comment that I, her daughter, the shyest six-year-old in the galaxy, had just made.

"You should have seen our room on the troopship over to Casablanca. No bigger than this, crammed with sixteen nurses, and fourteen of us seemed to have our period the whole way over.

"Dotty Halpern, Mimsie Goldblatt, Becky Cohen, Jackie Friedman . . ." Moe lit a Kool and drew in, head tilted up, chin tipped out, in the movie-star way she had when she was inhaling memory. "Me and Caroline were the only shiksas in the crew."

I had no more idea what a shiksa was than a period, but if that was what my mother was I could only assume it meant glamour babe.

"What a crew." Moe laughed, shook her head, and, recalling the madcap group, made the clucking sound out of the side of her mouth that was her highest form of praise.

I rolled onto my side and snuggled in, slipping my hands in prayer position between my knees. This was my favorite position for my favorite activity, listening to Moe's nurse stories.

"Those gals could make the best of a tough situation. Sixteen women cooped up in a stateroom made for a honeymoon couple? Damp underwear hanging down everywhere like vines in a tropical jungle? Never knowing when a U-boat would decide that you were going to be that day's target practice? The unit that left just ahead of us was torpedoed. What a way to die: alone on the sea, engine oil flaming all around you."

She took a drag and waved both the smoke and the image

away, dismissing them with the words she used to take the curse off all vexations, *"Machts nichts."* I repeated the magical words under my breath. *Mox nix.*

"We put it out of our minds. Had our CARE packages open before we left harbor. Shared everything: halvah, butter cookies, sour balls. Of course, I had my fudge. It wasn't kosher, but that didn't stop anyone. It was wartime. That was when I first started admiring the Hebrew faith. Those gals knew we were all in it together and we might as well just make the best of it. What wisenheimers. And we were singing all the time. Bigger bunch of ninnies you never saw."

"Moe?"

"Yes, poopsie."

"Make designs, okay?"

"Sure, poops."

She turned off the light and painted patterns in the darkness with the orange tip of her cigarette. Tracers of ack-ack fire arced through the night, zipping about in roller-coasting slides of light that blurred as the Dramamine dazed me back toward sleep. I thought I said the word "Sing," but couldn't be sure, as Moe seemed to start crooning before I could open my mouth. She sang "Somewhere Over the Rainbow" and I saw her with her fifteen girlfriends perched about in a jungle of damp underwear, all singing, all in it together, as they crossed the Atlantic headed for Casablanca. My mother's throbbing, Judy Garlandesque voice and smell—earthy, rich with grown-up-lady pleasures and secrets—blended together. Her face was the moon, lit by comet flashes of a swirling cigarette, shining down on a perfect world.

The memory flashes past in seconds and I am again on a plane moments away from falling into the East China Sea.

"Boy, howdy." The sound in the cabin returns. "Tell you what, better get our shocks checked out." The pilot's casual, folksy tone mocks our noncombatant terror. "Got a little bumpy back there. Stewardesses, if you will, prepare the cabin for landing."

It takes the Jesus woman a second to unloose the death grip

she has on the older stewardess, whose face has turned the color of window putty. She straightens up and slings a few bags back into the overhead bins, slams them shut, and looks behind her. The aisle is clogged with disgorged bags. The veteran stew shakes her head and goes to the front of the cabin, where she sits stiffly next to her cowardly colleague.

My ears pop as we descend through shifting strata of clouds. Outside the window, Okinawa has grown only to the size of a white scarf and lightning still sizzles past the window. As we break through the cloud deck, though, my head fills with the smells of Baby Magic, Kool cigarettes, tangerines, caramelized sugar, honeysuckle, and Fumiko's Young Pinkoo lipstick, and I no longer have the slightest doubt that we will land safely.

Brasso

Within seconds the stark utilitarianism of the terminal at Kadena Air Base wipes out my entire past year of life as a civilian. Cinder-block walls are painted a dispirited tan. Standing ashtrays are made of hundred-pound bombs. Arrows stenciled in black on the walls order me unequivocally toward the reception area. Other signs bark out acronyms, squadron names, unit designations, the whole vast hieroglyphic that orchestrates every twitch of military life. Because I've been away for a year, because I've been in a society that contains as many women as men, I notice now what had always before seemed normal, the overwhelming hordes of young males everywhere.

Then, ahead in the waiting area, I see them—my mother, my three brothers, my youngest sister—bunched together beneath the flickering fluorescent lights of the low-roofed terminal. I pause for a second to absorb the shock of discovering that five members of my family have been kidnapped and replaced by a troupe of bad actors.

The actors impersonating my twelve-year-old twin brothers, Buzz and Abner, are too tall, too lanky. Instead of the boys I'd said good-bye to only one year ago, these impostors show impossible yards of bony shanks and knobby knees. The reedy boys with piping voices are now being played by jut-jawed youths, foreheads and cheeks spangled with acne, Adam's apples starting to poke out.

My youngest sister, Bosco, and brother, Bob, are unrecognizable. Intellectually, I accept that they're one year older now—ten and seven—but it seems impossible they could have mutated so thoroughly in such a short time. Bob was still a plushly padded little boy with golden ringlets when I'd left. He now looks like a junior version of my father and the twins, already turning gangly, his hair buzzed into the crew cut that our father calls the "cut of the young athlete."

Looking at Bosco, my bookworm sister, I see why Kit calls her Bernie, Jr. A new pair of plastic government-issue glasses dominates her pale, anxious face. She's already developed my trademark dark circles under her eyes, testament to too many nights sneaking out of bed after everyone is asleep to continue studying for the geography test because she suddenly can't recall the three major exports of Bolivia.

By far the most unconvincing member of this body-snatching troupe is playing my mother. For Moe, they should have gotten Elizabeth Taylor from sometime between *Cat on a Hot Tin Roof* and *Butterfield 8*. Instead, they've ordered up the bloated, blowsy Liz of *Who's Afraid of Virginia Woolf?* As if Moe has been stealing all her skinny children's food, she is easily forty pounds too heavy. Replacing my mother's sparkle, this glassy-eyed stranger has a stunned and stuporous mien. Even in the subtropical heat of Okinawa, though, Moe is wearing a girdle, hose, heels, makeup, and white gloves. Wives of majors who wish to make colonel wear heels and hose in public.

Someone is missing, and for just a sliver of a second it is Fumiko I expect to see waiting with my family. But, of course, Kit is the one who is not there.

And then they catch sight of me as I approach, and I see in my family's gape-jawed stares that I am the biggest impostor at this reunion. I reach them and no one says a word. The Okinawa heat presses on us, soggy and airless.

"Hey you, knucklehead." I rub Bob's bristly scalp with my fist. "Did you get your head caught in the lawn mower?"

"Hey, Bernie, sisterman, how's things back in the world?" Abner puts on his joke hip GI voice and shoots me a peace sign. "What's shaking stateside? What's the haps, baby?"

"Hey, Abner, brotherman, you haven't changed. Still dumb as a stump. I like that in a man."

"That and total lack of personal hygiene," Buzz throws in. "Don't forget his other big plus."

"Bernie," Abner asks, "can a person actually purchase a pair of jeans like those, or do they have to do like you did and just wait for the previous owner to die?"

I turn to Buzz. "Buzz-tardo, this one offends me." I point a languid finger toward Abner who twitches and cringes in terror. "Hasten demise, Buzz-tardo."

Buzz slips immediately into one of our favorite routines, Zombie and Bitch Goddess of the Underworld. Buzz's eyes glaze over, he holds his arms out straight, and shuffles toward Abner muttering, "Hasten demise. Hasten demise. Yes, O Bitch Goddess." As Buzz chokes his twin to death, it's like we've never been apart.

This seems to break the spell. Bob and Bosco leave Moe's side and crush me with sweet kid hugs that smell of Coppertone and caramel. All my siblings except Kit huddle up next to me like puppies in a litter. I feel as if a missing limb has been reattached.

Moe steps forward and the huddle breaks apart. She wraps me in a damp embrace that has the dense, overpacked feel of flesh compressed by a Playtex girdle and runs her hand along my back. "I see we're not wearing a bra." This is not the first thing Moe, the mother from the S.S. *President Wilson,* from the little house in Fussa, my *real* mother, would say to me after we'd been apart for a year. She would have known I'd almost died trying to return to her.

At that moment, the bathroom door swings open and the biggest surprise casting yet emerges. Kit is being played by Lolita. In one year, she has gone from a sixteen-year-old in braces to a voluptuary. Given that her last words, whispered to me on the morning my family left for the other side of the earth, were, "My prayers have been answered. Actually, I prayed that you would die, but this is good enough," I wasn't expecting much of a welcome.

I brace myself as Kit comes toward me with her arms spread

wide. As she crushes me in a hug, I notice that my little sister smells heavily of Tabu cologne and sloe gin. Kit whispers her own observations.

"You reek of pot. What were you doing, toking up all the way over here? Are you holding?"

"What are you talking about?" Pot-smoking was a campus activity I hadn't participated in, requiring, as it did, contact with outsiders.

Kit rolls her eyes. She is wearing a Villager outfit I'd handed down to her. The Peter Pan collar, knee socks, and oxblood Weejuns had emphasized my mousy bookwormishness. The same outfit on Kit makes her look like a baby porn queen in Catholic schoolgirl drag. All she needs is a big cherry lollipop and a pair of heart-shaped sunglasses.

"Holding?" I repeat, incredulous.

She pops her throttled eyes in exasperation. "Never mind. Coals to you know, that place where they already have a ton of coal. Why bother bringing some crappy Mexican pot to the drug delta of the universe?"

I have no answer to that question.

"Besides, only losers and noncoms smoke dope."

Kit was born finely tuned to the nuances of social ranking, a tendency that life as a military brat has exacerbated in interesting ways. I glance from my glassy-eyed mother to my glassy-eyed sister and add my own coda to her decree: *And Post Princesses drink. And their mothers take pills.*

"Oh, you girls are friends again," Moe coos, as if a year apart could change the fact that nine months in her womb are the only thing on this earth we have in common.

A bowlegged Okinawan man with a wobbly-wheeled cart overloaded with luggage teeters toward us. In the split second that my brain is occupied with worrying whether my Lady Baltimore suitcase with the giant daisy decal will topple off the top of the cart, I catch a flashing glimpse of knuckled hand, square nails, gold wedding band, aviator's watch, and the splinter of a memory enters my mind.

I am ten, the last year we lived in Japan, and I am wearing my Girl Scout uniform. My father kneels in front of me adjusting my merit badge sash before we enter the Father/Daughter Banquet held in the Yokota Air Base Teen Center.

"Hey, troop." He called all of his children "troop." It usually, but not always, meant he was joking. "Your Sharpshooter badge is crooked."

"Girl Scouts don't have Sharpshooter badges." I reach down and touch the badge. "See, that's for Pet Care."

He tapped my nose. "Made you look."

For that second, the smiling, loose-limbed man who joked and tapped my nose walks toward me leading the Okinawan luggage carrier our way. Then my father snaps his fingers with a crack like a rifle firing and the young captain he had been in Japan vanishes. At each crack, my father points from the twins to the luggage cart.

"Cut the happy chatter and go get your sister's luggage."

Unlike the rest of his family, my father looks precisely the way he did when they left a year ago. He stands ramrod straight in starched khakis, his hair in a crew cut, black shoes shined to a mirror finish, the smell of Brasso wafting off his polished belt buckle. It doesn't appear that his weight has fluctuated more than six ounces or his hair been allowed to grow an extra millimeter.

My father looks at me and blinks, clearing away, no doubt, the image of the Brownie he once knelt in front of. He gives me a quick hug and asks how the flight was. I think about the lightning sizzling past my window, about believing I was going to die, but all I can say is, "Fine."

The twins start pretending to strangle each other and droning "Hasten demise" in zombie voices until my father barks at them. "Cut the wise-assery."

He hates the "wise-assery" that is our main mode of interaction, even though we learned all the basic tropes from him.

"Get your sister's luggage."

"Which ones are hers?"

"They're the ones with the—uh, big daisy decals." I point to the suitcases, carefully selected from the BX for my high school graduation present, now covered in stick-ons.

My father looks dubiously at me before he moves the twins out. My family is not good at public appearances and, for a military family, every time you set foot out of the house is a public appearance.

He turns to Moe. "Get your daughter into some slacks where her ass isn't hanging out. She looks like a peace puke."

With two more cracking finger snaps, my father gets our attention, then hacks the air with a finger pointing toward the exit. Without a word, we all form up and follow him out of the terminal.

Outside, the subtropical Okinawan air is unbreathably humid. It halos the lights in the parking lot like fog. I spot Frenchie, our Oldsmobile station wagon, named for its dung-hued mustard color. My heart leaps. Frenchie is as close as we ever came to the family dog we've all lobbied for but could never have because we move so often. My father drops my suitcase beside our car and turns to me. He has his hand extended out like a Roman senator about to deliver an oration. "Time?"

"Dad," Abner starts to groan, but my father silences him with a look and Moe, my brothers and sisters, even Kit, glance down at their watches and pincer out the stems. Then my father notices me.

"Where's your watch?" he asks. My lack of undergarments pales in comparison to this absence. Quickly, I dig my silver Seiko with the black grosgrain band, bought in Tokyo when I was ten, right before we left Japan, out of my leather-fringed shoulder bag. I haven't worn it for the past year. Love beads and Seiko watches do not go together.

The watch is our family totem. Kit has a Seiko exactly like mine except that she's traded the band in for a silver mesh type. The twins both have on the new thing—quartz watches with twisty gold bands and the time broadcast in chunky numbers in a window on the face. Bob, who worships his big brothers, wears the same kind except that, even tightened as far as the band will go, the watch still looks like a handcuff on his spindly wrist. It slides down to his elbow when he raises his hand. Bosco has on a pink plastic Hello Kitty model. My mother wears her dress-up gold Longines with a face no bigger than a fingernail that had been my father's fifth anniversary present to her. Her everyday watch is her "nurse's watch," a man's Timex with a sweep second hand for taking pulses.

My father wears the aviator's watch he'd been issued at flight school at Kelly Air Force Base in San Antonio, the watch he wore while he copiloted planes through World War II, the Korean War, the Cold War. Once a month, with ceremonial gravity, he calls the atomic clock to nudge the instrument one or two seconds into keeping with Greenwich mean time.

"Synchronize."

We all bend our heads over our watches.

"Synchronize."

I pull out the stem on my Seiko and wait until my father announces, "I make it twenty-three hundred hours and thirty-three minutes in . . ."—we all move the minute hands of our watches to that position—"five, four, three, two, one, now!"

All eight of us snap our stems down on the same exact second. I set my watch and fall back into time with my family.

Diesel

"Hey, Joe, you want short time? Fi'e dollar, I be you girl-friend. You want three-holer? I do three-holer." We are trapped in a late-night traffic jam in Koza, the Okinawan town outside Kadena's Gate Three. The station wagon fills with the diesel and open-sewer smells of a Mexican border town.

"Whose bright idea was it to come into the ville?" my father asks in tones etched in acid, even though he knows it was Moe's idea. "We had to show Bernadette the ville tonight. It had to be tonight. What? You think she should apply for a summer job here?" He reaches over the seat and, with furious turns, rolls up Abner's window so quickly that the prostitute sticking her face in bumps her beehive trying to keep from being guillotined.

"Mace, come on." A year away makes me notice what no one else hears, the note of hopelessness in Moe's supplicating tone.

All around our station wagon, tiny Japanese cars honk. The prostitute, a petite Okinawan woman in short shorts, halter top, and platform mules waves at Abner. When she has his attention, she turns around, bends over, and shakes her ass at him. All of Abner's face turns as red as his pimples.

Outside, the whore and her papa-san, a tough pimp in rubber zoris and a T-shirt with the inscription I MAY NOT GO DOWN IN HISTORY, BUT I'LL GO DOWN ON YOUR LITTLE SISTER! roar with laughter. Koza is like a low-rent tropical Bourbon Street populated by roving groups of GIs. The white boys are un-mistakable in their newly plucked haircuts, JCPenney Dacron shirts and trousers, and the twitchy air that comes from their effort to channel homesickness and vulnerability into swaggering machismo.

Pawnshops, tattoo parlors, tailor shops, and optical, electronics, and T-shirt shops are scattered among the bars: Ace High, Okay Joe, New Pussycat No. 3, Gentilemans Club, Stateside Bar. Promises of SEXY FLORR SHOW! or GIRLS! GIRLS! GIRLS! or GO-GO SHOW! are illustrated with posters of dark-haired girls—either totally naked or encumbered only with go-go boots, pink baby dolls, and a whip—thrusting out perfect breasts.

Moe turns to face me. "Koza's not usually this—*ahem*—lively when we're here."

"Lively?" My father catches my gaze in the rearview mirror. "Tell your mother she doesn't know what she's talking about. This is the decline of Western civilization passing in review."

Again, no one but me seems to notice our parents' habit of talking to each other through us. I try to remember when it started. I know they spoke when we were at Yokota. They spoke, they danced, they shared "loving cups" and "togetherness."

A group of black servicemen in locally tailored suits of lavender, lime green, coral, and electric blue strut past. Bar girls flood out of the Harlem Club. My father watches the girls tug the men inside.

"There's your American fighting man. There's your sentinel of liberty."

For a second, my heart clutches, and before I can figure out why, my head fills with the burnt sugar and citrus smell of the candied tangerines Fumiko made for me when we lived in the little house in Fussa. Lounging against a light pole is, I'm sure of it, Fumiko. Her back is to us, but I recognize the high ponytail she took to wearing after she abandoned her kimono in favor of sweaters, pedal pushers, and bobby socks.

"Oh, my God! There's—" I pivot, following my pointing finger as we drive on. I can't say her name. It hasn't been mentioned since we left Japan.

"There's who?" Moe cuts me off. In her tone is a warning to me to leave well enough alone.

Then I see the woman's face. She doesn't look anything at all like Fumiko. "No one." I sag back into my seat, as disappointed as I am relieved.

We drive on in silence, broken only when Bob asks, "What's a three-holer?"

Grass

We come to a halt in front of the Gate Three guard hut, one of the few breaks in the miles of barbed-wire fence that encircle the base. Ahead of us, an Air Policeman wearing a white helmet with AP stenciled on it examines a load of pineapples being ferried on-base by an Okinawan native driving a three-wheeled truck. A white webbed strap crosses the AP's chest; his khaki pants are neatly bloused into laced-up combat boots.

When he steps around to the back of the miniature truck and comes close to the station wagon, Bob squeals, "Oh, no, the Apes!" and ducks down. Apes are the agents of potential destruction, destroyer of worlds, for all military brats. They stand sentry at the entrance to our neighborhoods, and they patrol them, seeking out bad kids whose infractions—graffiti, broken windows, drinking, vandalism of government property—could get their fathers RIF'd, fired.

"Pass, pass?" the guard asks the pineapple man.

The Okinawan answers with a gush of Japanese.

"Okay, pull over there. Over there. To the side." The guard tries to wave the man aside, but, smiling all the while, the Okinawan insists upon his right to deliver the pineapples.

"Oh, my sweet Aunt Fannie!" My father pounds his palm on the steering wheel, irritated out of all proportion to the inconvenience. He slams the glove compartment with his fist several times, but it doesn't open.

"Okay, Mace, okay." Moe speaks like the leader of a squad sent to defuse a bomb. She pushes the button on the glove compartment and it falls open. Without looking at her, my father snaps his fingers and holds his palm up, jiggling it impatiently until Moe pulls out one of his many rolls of Tums and flicks two into his palm. He keeps jiggling his hand and Moe flicks in two more.

While we wait for the pineapple man, I have plenty of time to study the sign in front of the guard hut that declares Kadena Air Base to be the HOME OF THE 313TH AIR FORCE. The base seal sits on a background that depicts a pagoda floating above an outline of the island, both floating on a field of red and white stripes and blue stars. The seal itself features a black rooster on a gold shield with a jet streaking across its wattles. Next to the rooster is inscribed in Gothic script:

Our Mission:

To defend U.S. and Japanese mutual interests
by providing a responsive staging and
operational Air Base with integrated,
deployable, forward-based
Air Power.

Beneath the shield a scroll unfurls reading *Unguibus et Rostro.*

"Ugly Butts and Roosters, nowhere else but Oki," my father jokes grimly. "Well, here you are, Bernadette, Kadena Air Base, the elephant graveyard of the Pacific. Where military careers come to die. Where the deadwood is farmed out to rot away." My father worries about being RIF'd because he's been in almost twenty years and is still only a major.

Moe catches my eye in a glance that says she's heard this way too many times.

I turn to Kit, hoping for a sign from her about how things are between our parents. She turns away from me. Bosco huddles closer against my side and, from the anxious look pinching her face, I gather they are pretty bad. Our father believes the assignment to Okinawa to be the death knell of his career, a dirge that started playing at a point so long ago I can no longer pin it down. No details are ever offered, but, as in most marriages, 90 percent of all communication is carried by tone, and his, when he does speak to Moe, is accusatory. For reasons I can't fathom, it seems my father holds Moe responsible for the downward trajectory of his career. But now, listening to a symphony of exasperated gasps and curses at the holdup, it seems my father also believes that the pineapple man has it in for him.

The three-wheeled truck is finally waved on and we creep forward. The guard snaps off a crisp salute, we drive through the gate, and I am back on every base we've ever lived on, breathing in the watermelon smell of new-mown Bermuda grass mixed with the tang of jet fuel fumes wafting in from the runway. On either side of the broad main avenue is a prairie of a parade ground that rolls on into a tundra of runways. Though vast expanses of open space—runways, golf courses, parade grounds, parking lots, immense yards—characterize every base I've ever set foot on, coming now from the claustrophobia of Koza, I notice this profligacy for the first time. An American flag snaps in the breeze above it all, its tether clanging against the metal pole. Signs everywhere urge personnel to contribute to the Red Cross blood drive, take salt tablets, observe the speed limit, know the typhoon warning system, update inoculations.

We pass the base theater and I recall the start of every movie I've ever seen on every base we've ever lived on. That's when it finally, fully, hits me that I am back in a world where the National Anthem is played before previews of coming attractions and if you aren't standing you'd better have at least one leg in a cast.

Wedged between my parents in the front seat, Bob laughs and repeats, "Ugly butts and roosters."

My father raps Bob's forehead with his middle finger like he's testing a melon. "Cut the comedy."

We drive home in silence.

Herbal Essence

My first night on Okinawa, I dream about Eileen, before she became Kit. I dream about the moment after we landed in Yokohama Bay and she ran down the gangplank of the S.S. *President Wilson* into a calligraphic world of people all drawn in black: black hair, black eyes, black clothes.

The sea of black closes in around Kit until the flame of her white hair is extinguished. My father holds me. My mother stands by his side. But when I turn to look at them, I am back in the backyard of the house in Fussa. Fumiko stares at me. She wears a kimono printed with bamboo brush drawings of Mount Fuji. Two of the perfect cones float above her breasts.

Then Moe screams, "Come on, girls! Let's go! Get dressed! They're coming! Move! Move! Move!" and the OSI officer appears to take Fumiko and me to prison. Even after I wake up in a dark bedroom in a house on Kadena Air Base, it takes me a moment to realize that the OSI officer was in my dream but the yelling is not. My mother is standing in the middle of our room, her eyes wide open, glittering, Bob by her side, ordering us to get up.

"Mom, wake up." Kit's voice, sleepy, irritated, pulls me away from Fumiko. "You're having that dream again."

"Don't argue with me, Kit! Not now. We've got to go! Now! They're coming! Get Bosco!"

In the dim glow cast by Bosco's Huckleberry Hound night-light I can see the terror on my mother's face.

"Moe, what is it?"

She stares blankly at me. She's wearing the pink nylon nightie I gave her for Christmas the year we lived in Harlingen, Texas, and it never got cold enough to wear the heavy wool jackets and thick sweaters we'd brought from Japan to grapefruit country.

I get out of bed and put my arm around her shoulders. "Moe, it's okay. Wake up."

My mother blinks, recognizing my voice but not my face.

"It's me, Moe: Bernie. I'm here."

My mother wakes up and bursts into tears, hugging me. I bury my face in her neck. She smells like my mother, but I have to make sure. I run my hand down her back.

"I see we're not wearing a bra," I tell her.

For a second Moe stiffens back into the girdled stranger who'd met me when I'd landed. Then she laughs and she's finally Moe, finally my mother, again. "You sassy brat, you're gonna end up with boobs like a hound dog's ears."

"Is it a school day?" Bob wakes up. "Is Miss Delgado still my teacher? What room am I in?"

"No, baby, school's out for the summer. Back to bed." Moe turns him around toward his room and marches him out.

I crawl back into bed and survey the room. It is pure military. A bunker of poured concrete with a slit of a window set too high to see anything but a slice of the tropical night sky. A bunk bed stands against the other wall. I'm back in the girls' room. Six children. The inevitable three bedrooms in a base house. We always had a girls' room, a boys' room, and a parents' room. Bosco snuffles softly in the top berth. From somewhere in the darkness comes an odd sound, like a cross between a chirp and a delicate burp. Before I can identify it, Kit, in the bottom bunk, heaves a sigh.

"Shit, I thought she'd be okay once *you* got here." In her tone is the familiar accusation that Moe likes me best.

"What do you mean?"

"Wait till you see the house in the morning."

"What about the house?" I'd been too exhausted to notice much last night, walking straight back to the girls' room where I'd fallen into bed in my clothes, too tired to even open my suitcases.

I'd assumed that the house was arranged the way every house we'd ever moved into had been arranged, in accordance with Moe's philosophy that "Even if you're only going to be somewhere for three weeks, you should set the place up like you're going to be there for three years. We're not Bedouins," she'd protest, hammering nails into the walls of whatever base house we'd landed in in order to hang up her giant wooden fork and spoon from the Philippines or the framed set of fans she'd brought back from Japan. Those and all the other spoils from a military life—the camel saddle, Hummel figurines, Toledo sword, coconut pirate heads, geisha dolls in glass cases—they were Moe's first line of defense against the charge that her family were nomads. Once she had erected that line in a house where floors were mopped and waxed weekly, where dust never settled, and all the beds had hospital corners, then she could relax.

That, I assumed, was how this latest in the long line of houses Moe had settled her family into would be arranged. I asked Kit again, "What about the house?"

"You'll see."

"Come on, just tell me."

"No, I don't want to spoil the surprise."

"Kit, it's not absolutely required that you be a total bitch to me all the time. You can, like, take a night off or something."

"Fuck you, Bernie. Listen, you haven't been around here for this last year in paradise."

"What's going on? Why didn't you write me? Or call?"

"Oh, right, call. Roger that," she says sarcastically.

Phone calls with my family for the last year had been placed through MARS, some military operation, because normal phone lines don't reach Okinawa. My father had to requisition time on the service in advance. Then our few calls, placed on lines that hissed and roared with static, were relayed through a radio operator and you had to say "over" when you finished talking and "roger" when the other person finished. Having an outsider listen in, then relay our words, had frozen our few conversations to abrupt stilted telegrams.

Kit rolls over and pulls the sheet up to her ears. She still has a genius for willing herself into deep and instantaneous sleep.

I can tell from the lump-and-divot pattern beneath me that I'm lying on the single mattress that has been mine for most of my life. I snuggle into its familiar hammocky contours, close my eyes, and try to sleep in spite of the odd chirping that creeps closer to my bed.

Not enough hours later, I open my eyes to find Bosco and Bob crouched above me like a pair of Lilliputians gloating over their gigantic Gulliver find. Bob wears Mighty Mouse underpants that highlight his spider-monkey body, while Bosco resembles a loaf of French bread in her two-piece swimsuit. The radio is playing.

You're listening to Armed Forces Radio, the voice of the Keystone of the Pacific. Temperatures will be climbing into the high nineties with winds out of the northeast at thirteen knots per hour. Sunset at eighteen twenty-three hours. Sunrise at oh six hundred hours. The Thomas Crown Affair, *with Hollywood stars Steve McQueen and Faye Dunaway, is playing at the General Curtis LeMay theater at nineteen hundred hours.*

"Why is there a mirror under my nose?" I inquire.

"To see if you're dead."

"I'm not."

Bob takes the mirror away from my nose. "There wasn't any smoke coming out of your nose."

"Condensation." Bosco corrects her little brother. "Just carbon dioxide and breath stuff."

"Oh." Bob notes the correction without further comment. It's understood that if Bosco says it, it's right. Everyone in my family has one thing that no one else has. Bosco's is that she is never wrong about a fact. It's a big thing—bigger than Abner's ability to do his age in sit-ups times one hundred, or Buzz's rubber-limbed talent for putting both his feet behind his head and swinging on his arms like a gorilla, or Bob's capacity to recite, line for line, ka-blooey for ka-blooey, every cartoon he's ever seen. Kit's one thing is big too. We all recognize that Kit can walk into any new school on any base in the world and become the most popular girl inside a week. My one thing is dancing.

There is a common belief about military brats that all the moving around makes us very adaptable and we end up becoming sort of social geniuses. The only person in our family that this is true for is Kit. The rest of us are class-A social retards. The best we can hope for is not to be noticed, to survive the purgatory that is any place outside our front door.

Kit is just the opposite. She would rather be anywhere except home, which is the only place the rest of us can take a full breath. Kit's ability to relate to humans outside of our family awes us. Still, Bosco's thing of never being wrong is pretty good too. We suspect a photographic memory, but Moe forbade us to utter those words.

"I don't want your sister feeling she is unusual in any way," she warned me. This is mostly because Bosco is already "unusual" in far too many ways.

"So, does this mean I'm dead?" I ask.

Bob raises his skinny shoulders to his ears until the blades stick out like the buds of angel wings and shrugs as if to tell me to face the evidence and deal with it. It is out of his hands. He glances at the big watch on his wrist—"Oh, no! *Road Runner* already started!"—and darts out.

Overly bright tropical light slices into the room through the high window. The major decorating motif in Bosco's sector is equine. Shelves of resin horses line the walls above her top bunk. Color drawings of particularly lustrous horses are taped everywhere. From her extensive letters I knew that my little sister has achieved satori here on Okinawa through actual horse ownership. The beast in question, a gelding named Hickory, is well represented. Taped to the wall above Bosco's pillow are snapshots of a swaybacked, dwarfed creature with a fuzzy coat like the lining in a cheap jacket.

"He's descended from Genghis Khan's horses."

Indeed, the stumpy Hickory would not look out of place with

one of the Mongol horde on his back. Bosco sticks another stack of photos in my hands.

"These are newer. Sit here. The light is better."

I sit on the stool in front of Kit's vanity. As I sort through the photos, the urge to curry overtakes Bosco and she brushes my hair.

"He's really happy there." Bosco touches the photo. "He's sad in that one." I flip through a dozen more photos with accompanying commentary on the many moods of Hickory the Horse, though the only emotional state I can discern seems to be digestion.

I feel stuporous, lulled by jet lag and the uniquely narcotizing sensation of having soft little-girl hands brush and pat my hair into a side ponytail with swizzle sticks poked into it for a saucier effect.

"Don't move," Bosco orders me.

Kit's vanity is covered with enough cosmetics to stock a Las Vegas revue. Tubes of iridescent Mary Quant lipstick. Pots of strawberry-flavored Bonne Bell lip gloss. Cakes of sparkly lavender Yardley eyeshadow. Tubs of Dippity-Do. Spider's legs of false eyelashes with clumps of glue covered by strips of vinyl eyeliner. Spray bottles of emerald-green Emeraude and amber Tabu cologne.

Then, out of the corner of my eye, I see a flash of motion skitter up the wall next to me. I shriek and jerk, causing Bosco to ram a swizzle stick into my temple.

"I *told* you not to move."

"What is that?"

"Oh, that. That's Lucky, our gecko. Geckos are lucky. Plus she eats cockroaches."

Lucky the lady lizard seems to have been startled by my shriek. She does delicate little push-ups, her tiny gumdrop feet suctioned to the ceiling above my head, the pink bubble at her throat inflating and deflating with each breath.

"You scared her."

"*I* scared *her?*"

"Wait here and don't move. I've got to get something." As Bosco leaves, Bob bursts in and takes her place at my side. He can barely breathe, he is laughing so hard. "Bernie, you should see. Wile E. Coyote runned after Road Runner and then Road Runner runned over the clift and Wile E. Coyote runned after him, then—" Bob loses control, overcome by the indescribable hilarity of it all, and tries to pantomime the rest for me. Wile E. Coyote's futile backpedaling in midair. Road Runner's triumphant *beep-beep* as he zips back to the safety of the cliff ledge. Coyote's weary resignation before his inevitable plummet to the earth below.

Bob's rendition is funnier than any cartoon ever made. I crack up as he does Wile E. bonking his head and stumbling around in drunken loops. He gets so worked up that his asthma kicks in and he begins wheezing slightly. The sound of a maniacal cartoon laugh echoing from the living room—"Heh-heh-heh-*heh*-heh Heh-heh-heh-*heh*-heh"—effects an immediate cure, however.

Bob holds his wrist up to check the time, but the jumbo watch slides down to his elbow. "Woody Woodpecker!" A puff of air whooshes behind him as he runs out of the room, trampling over Bosco coming back in.

"Knock me down, why don't you?" she calls after her little brother, before turning to me, holding out a pair of red lacquered chopsticks inlaid with mother-of-pearl. "Look what I found."

"You shouldn't be using those."

"Why?" Bosco pokes them into the do she has created for me.

The year out of the self-contained system of my family loosens my tongue enough for me to say the name that hasn't been mentioned since we left Japan. "Fumiko gave them to Mom."

"Who's Fumiko?"

That question opens a vault containing all the other questions I haven't asked for the past eight years. Eight years when a child's memories faded and were replaced by unspoken family credos.

"She lived with our family for four years. She was the first person who held you when you came home from the hospital."

"Before you?"

"Before me."

"She did not live with our family for four years or there would be pictures of her in the trunk."

Because she always is, I accept that Bosco is right about there being no photos of Fumiko in the trunk. It's been years since I pawed through the trunk full of photos that Moe intends, one day, to put in albums. But I know that at one time there were photos of Fumiko. I remember Girls' Day when I was nine, smiling into Moe's Brownie box camera, Fumiko and I wearing matching pink kimonos with yellow chrysanthemums, holding the chalk-faced doll Fumiko had given me. I remember another photo of Fumiko. Black and white. Fumiko is wearing the gray mouton coat Moe gave her, standing outside in the snow, holding Buzz in one arm, Abner in the other.

Bosco stops brushing my hair and leans close to my ear. "I know a secret about Kit. Want me to tell?"

I hold my breath and am certain that Kit's secret is that she is pregnant.

"She's going to enter a dance contest and win an all-expenses-paid trip to Tokyo."

Now I wish that something even worse than pregnancy was happening to Kit. Dancing is *my* one thing. Moe assigned it to me back in the days when she and I and Fumiko used to clean the house together, singing and dancing to albums. "Bernadette Root," she'd told me, "you've got rhythm. You are going to be our family's dancer." And though my most constant partner had always been the mirror in the girls' room, I was good. I couldn't sing. Never really got the knack for making friends. My thighs are heavy, lips thin, hair lank. But dancing, dancing is mine.

Bosco checks her watch and drops the brush on Kit's vanity. "Hurry up! Put your swimsuit on. You'll miss it. Bring shampoo," she orders, running out of our room.

The disc jockey's voice seems louder in the sudden silence that follows Bosco's exit.

That was the Chairman of the Board's daughter Nancy, with "These Boots Are Made for Walking," here on Armed Forces Radio, the voice of the Keystone of the Pacific.

It is a shock to hear a straight disc jockey after a year of listening to the stoned cynics on FM radio who could barely be bothered to tell you the title of the last Hendrix or Doors cut they just played, though they might go on at length about how very, very trippy the selection was for them. The hyperkinetic Armed Forces Radio voice comes from the very near yet irretrievably lost past. It is a past that lives on, here on Okinawa, the keystone of the Pacific.

Run for cover! the disc jockey advises in his jokey Casey Kasem voice. *Cuz them raindrops are gonna be a-fallin' on yo' head!*

As B. J. Thomas croons that he has just done him some talking to the sun, Okinawa begins to seem like a *Twilight Zone* episode with all the massed forces of the military combined to maintain the illusion that the America I just left has not changed forever. That the country everyone on this tiny island has been sent to defend is still back there, everyone listening to the same happy tunes. I snap the radio off the instant the Fifth Dimension begins crooning "Up, Up and Away."

The eight-inch-thick poured concrete walls and typhoon-proof windows give the house a dead, airless feel. In the hall, on the floor beneath the spots where, I guess, Moe wants to hang them, is the set of three framed fans that have hung on the wall in the hallways of all the houses we lived in since Fussa.

I pass by the closed door to my parents' room and assume that Moe has taken the station wagon to the commissary. I imagine her return and the familiar ritual of unloading several dozen brown paper bags containing multiple bags of Oreos, blocks of frozen peas, planks of frozen steaks. A crate of frozen orange juice. A pallet of milk.

At the door to the boys' room, I stop, stunned by the disorder. For all the years of my growing-up, the boys' room under Moe's strict guidance had been a miniature barracks, with beds made the instant they were evacuated, sheets and blankets tucked in under the mattresses so that the entire waxed and gleaming clean bare floor was visible. I now behold a hobo's camp of dirty pants, socks, underwear, hand grips, barbells, jump ropes, Boy Scout manuals, books by Isaac Asimov, Harlan Ellison, and Ray Bradbury, various hand tools, a clarinet, a bolt cutter, a snorkeling mask, three swim fins, the remnants of a Lego tower, and wrappers from Slo-Pokes, Sugar Daddies, Chicken Bones, and Pixie Sticks. Above this disaster, the twins have suspended their model airplanes from the ceiling with clear fishing lines. The collection includes the planes our father once flew. The B-17 soars upward. A B-25 bears down on it. An RB-50 flies above them all, doing reconnaissance.

The living room looks like my brothers had a slumber party for a platoon of derelict scouts. Clothes, pillows, sheets are strewn about amid old copies of *Stars and Stripes.* Several chairs are overturned and covered with blankets to make a fort. Used cereal bowls are shellacked to the coffee table in a ring around several open boxes of Cap'n Crunch. Packing boxes, still taped shut, are stacked in the corners of the room. I read the labels: "Camel Saddle," "Geisha Doll," "Fork & Spoon."

The kitchen is worse. Cockroaches scuttle in and out of an open garbage can. Dishes are heaped in the sink. The refrigerator door is open. Two half gallons of milk and a pitcher of grape Kool-Aid sweat next to several curling slices of bologna and an open jar of mayonnaise. The only other item is a large plastic bag filled with damp khaki uniforms kept refrigerated so they won't mildew before Moe has a chance to iron them. I throw everything out except the uniforms and close the door.

On the front of the refrigerator a duty roster is attached by a couple of shell-people magnets. It has FEBRUARY written on the top. There are only a few sporadic checks on it. My father started posting duty rosters eight years ago when we left Japan and reentered an economy that did not subsidize domestic help for Air Force captains. Each month he would sit at the old Underwood typewriter he'd once used to type papers on when he was a philosophy major at the University of Michigan and divvy up KP. Most of the assignments were framed in terms of policing.

> Bernadette: Police latrine.
> Eileen: Police kitchen.
> Bryan and Francis: Police trash.

Our father always uses our real names as if use of our nicknames signifies entry into a club he doesn't want to join.

I stare at this duty roster, four months out of date, the wreckage of the kitchen, and Donna Ingram comes to mind.

Donna Ingram got her family RIF'd. Her family lived at the end of the block on Mercury Drive on Kirtland Air Force Base. Her brothers let the lawn grow into a field of dandelions. The wash on the back line stayed out through several downpours and a dust storm until the undershirts and panties dried into stiff, gray disks. Their dog, Mr. Sniffer, ran loose until Mrs. Detwiler, the president of the Officers' Wives Club, found him in her backyard locked up with her bichon frise, Snowball. Then, when Colonel Detwiler dragged Mr. Sniffer on a rope back to the Ingrams, he discovered that Donna hadn't been doing the dishes and had left her mother's Harvey Wallbanger glasses all over the house.

One day Donna Ingram was sitting next to me coloring in the route Vasco da Gama discovered to the New World, and the next she was gone, RIF'd. RIF'd was one of those terms like "reconnaissance" that we knew for years before finding out their meaning. We always knew that reconnaissance meant something you weren't even allowed to ask about, and we knew that RIF meant your father lost his job because of a bad family. Learning later that the letters stood for Reduction in Force added little to our elemental understanding that if the lawn wasn't mowed every week the life we knew would end in the time it took the Housing Officer to report our transgression. I think of Moe's blank expression and, for the first time, realize that the Harvey Wallbangers must have had a lot more to do with Donna's disappearance than the glasses they were served in not being washed.

I run to the kitchen window. As I try to calculate if the occupants of the house across the street can see the mess, I notice that Frenchie, the Oldsmobile station wagon, is parked in the carport, which means that Moe is *not* up and *not* at the commissary. I jerk the curtains closed and hurry back to my parents' room.

Moe is asleep on the four-poster mahogany bed they bought in Japan. Her mouth is open slightly and her head tilts back into the pillow as if she were about to do a back bend. A stripe of gray on either side of her part pushes away the rest of the hair that is dyed chestnut. Aside from three miscarriages, I can't ever recall seeing my mother in bed. Not during the day. She was always up before anyone except my father. Always out in the kitchen flipping pancakes or spooning pablum into a baby in the high chair or chopping cylinders of frozen orange juice into cubes so they would melt faster in a pitcher of water. Then she would stay up late at night dyeing coconut green for an Easter cake or sewing a costume for one of Kit's tryouts or courts or squads.

I think about the sheer draft-horse labor of raising six children. Of simply keeping eight people fed. I try to remember when Moe stopped singing through it all, and my head fills with the songs she did sing back in Japan when Fumiko helped her carry the load. *And the wayward wind is a restless wind. . . . I'm an old cowhand from the Rio Grande. . . .* And the one Fumiko loved. The one she would shyly ask "my dam" to sing as they mopped or dusted or vacuumed side by side. *Somewhere over the rainbow . . .*

"Come on, you'll miss it." Bob pulls on my hand, tugging me outside, away from my mother's door.

In the backyard, I take my first good look at the island. Our house is one in a line of identical reinforced concrete boxes built on top of a high hill that might have been drawn by Dr. Seuss. A far-off ravine at the base of the hill, clotted with a tangle of vines and low-growing jungle vegetation, separates the houses from the rest of Kadena Air Base sweeping out below. I recognize, in the distance, the comfortingly familiar bulk of a commissary, the BX, the endless stretches of runway sweeping out to the sea.

"See that big bare spot over there." Bosco points to a distant hill. I squint and can see that it is honeycombed with craters and mostly gray beneath patchy vegetation. "That got bombed out during the Battle of Okinawa. There's still so many chemicals from bombs that nothing can grow. One time a kid blew off his leg because there was a mine that hadn't exploded. The Battle of Okinawa was the most costly naval battle of the war in the Pacific." Bosco's voice takes on the droning quality it does when she reads the pages that appear in her mind.

"More than twelve thousand American and one hundred ten thousand Japanese and Okinawan soldiers lost their lives, along with seventy-five thousand civilians, many of whom committed suicide." In her normal voice, Bosco explains, "I did my Geography book report on Okinawa. Mom says it's stupid to come halfway around the world and then do your Geography book report on Switzerland."

"Mom's right."

The *thump-thump-thump* of a helicopter's rotors catches my attention. It hovers above our house close enough that I can see the dog tags swinging around the necks of the three Marines leaning out the open doors on the side.

"They're from Camp Hansen," Bosco explains. "They're here for her."

I follow Bosco's finger to the roof. Kit perches on a towel on the flat pebbled roof, rubbing baby oil with globules of iodine floating in it on the inside of her thighs.

"Christina Kelso's mother says that Kit is just a big P.R.I.C.K. tease and that she's going to get into more trouble than she bargained for if she doesn't cool her jets and that the only reason

Kit got head cheerleader at Kubasaki instead of Christina's sister is that Kit showed *everything* at tryouts, and anytime you waggle *that* in front of any male they'll go crazy and it'll look like someone's popular when it's really just the testosterone talking and Moe should do something about her before it gets any more out of hand or Daddy'll end up getting RIF'd." Bosco gulps in a big breath.

"Gosh, Christina's mother must not have much to worry about."

"Nobody does. Not here. Mom says that's the problem. That's exactly why she hates living on-base, and it's ten times worse here than any other place we've ever lived, and the officers' wives are the cattiest bunch of bitches she's ever seen, and the less we have to do with any of them the better. That's why she hates it so much and never gets up. She sleeps all day and Dad goes to his Community Liaison Officer job and says a monkey with a pencil stuck up his ass could do it—but what is it? What does he do that a monkey with a pencil stuck up his ass could do?"

I'm so unused to questions about what our father does that I just stare at Bosco. It had been odd in the dorm during my year as a civilian to meet new people and have them ask what my father did. To overhear them talking about their fathers being lawyers, CPAs, store managers, art teachers, construction foremen. No one on any of the bases where we'd grown up had ever asked me what my father did. The question wasn't needed; the answer that I gave to the girls in the dorm—"He's in the Air Force"—was the very ground all dependent lives were built on.

"Kit! Kit!" the boys in the helicopter yell. "Take off your top!"

Up on the roof, my sister shoots them the bird and the three Marines hoot and slug each other. Pebbles from the roof skitter down on us when Kit rolls over. I wish I had a gun. I'd have fired off a few rounds at the helicopter jerks when they started making humping motions in the direction of my sister's backside.

"Can you stop her, Bernie? She's gonna get us RIF'd." Behind her glasses, tears pool in Bosco's eyes.

I am about to scream for Kit to get down when a solid wall of gray clouds rolls in. Like turning on a faucet, the clouds pour rain as evenly on runways, highways, bombed-out hillsides, and parking lots as they do on the mat of green fighting to reclaim the island. Kit stands on the roof in the sudden downpour and wraps the towel she was lying on around herself like a sarong. The rain makes it hard for the helicopter to hover above our roof, and it lifts and peels away.

Bosco and Bob stand beneath a spout that drains the roof and rain waterfalls over them. Bosco has on a two-piece suit made of stretchy navy material with a band of lime green where her waist will be one day.

Kit drops onto the top of the air-conditioner compressor and takes up a spot at the rain spout on the other end of the house.

"Hurry! Hurry!" Bosco waves me over and I crowd under the stream with her and Bob. The water that pours onto me is a substance I've never experienced before, so pure it tingles on my skin. I open my mouth and rivulets stream in, sweet and clean. Bosco hands me her bottle of Herbal Essence. I squirt on the piney-smelling stuff, close my eyes, and suds up. When I open my eyes again, three identical redheaded boys of only slightly varying heights stare at me. They are so pale that albinism seems a possibility.

Bob steps up to the tallest one. "I told you my big sister was coming from Alvinturkey."

The boys gape at me.

"Do you live around here?" I ask.

The tallest one points to the house across the street.

"Oh." I smile to show my benign intent to this tiny tribe.

Bosco glances up at the sky and orders me, "Finish quick."

I rinse the shampoo out of my hair, and a minute later the last of the gray clouds rolls away, the faucet of rain is turned off, and the sun explodes, hotter than ever.

The three little boys look at one another with alarm, then run single-file up the hill to their house.

"They're not allowed to be out in the sun," Bob explains. "They can die."

"Their father is a butt smoocher of the first water who only made colonel because he's got his head buried up McClintock's ass." Bosco quotes my father so accurately she even duplicates his chopped cadence.

"Who's McClintock?"

"You mean old Bubble Butt?" I recognize my father's gift for characterization. "Colonel McClintock is the overseer of this elephant graveyard of military careers. Final resting place for all the deadwood who fail to kiss the right asses and get sent to Command and Staff College. Bubble Butt is not command material. Never was. Never will be. Hasn't flown since Orville and Wilbur bumped their heinies at Kitty Hawk. He just knew the right butts to smooch, that's all." It's unsettling to hear my sister channel our father so perfectly. "Bubble Butt is part of the whole power elite, the pointy-headed Academy pukes who made Dad a ground pounder."

It occurs to me that my father lives in a more vivid world than most, where each day is a series of agonistic encounters against a host of enemies, from the pineapple man to Bubble Butt to—I had to admit it—Moe, all bent on his destruction.

"Look! It's Mama-san!" Bob waves wildly at an Okinawan woman toiling up the steep hill leading to our house on an ancient black bicycle so heavy she must stand on the pedals to inch forward. She reaches our house and springs off.

"*Mama-san, ohio goziamasu.*" Bosco bows.

Mama-san is a garden gnome come to life. Barely taller than Bob, no more than four and a half feet, she is as stringy and weathered as a piece of beef jerky. Though her leathery skin looks at least sixty years old, her brilliant big-toothed smile and matte-black hair permed into a crispy frizz belong to a woman in her twenties—a very fit woman, one who can pump a bicycle made of cast iron up a roller-coaster hill. The toes of her bare feet grip the earth.

Mama-san bows several times and speaks in what I take to be rapid-fire Japanese. I bow back and put my hand out to shake hers. Laughing behind her left hand, she extends her right and shakes mine, acting as if this were the most outrageous act of her life. Still laughing, Mama-san goes to the carport and comes back out pushing a hand mower.

Mama-san follows the mower in a straight line down the steep hill, her ropy arms straining to keep the ancient machine from breaking away. The smell of cut grass fills the air with a fragrance like watermelon. At the bottom of the hill, she turns and pushes the mower back up the hill, cutting a strip of grass exactly next to the first.

"Moe tried to tell her that the twins would cut our grass, but she just kept coming anyway. The albino boys' parents told Moe she came with the house."

"Just like Fumiko." The words slip out.

"Fumiko who held me even before you did?"

I nod and am about to tell her more when I see what I have been waiting for. Kit goes inside. I rush to follow her. The house seems dark and quiet after being outside.

"Kit, I need to talk to you."

"I gotta get this gunk off." Kit waves her hand at her oil-slicked midriff and starts to leave.

"Kit, wait." She doesn't turn to face me, but her shoulders sag with exasperation. "What's going on around here?"

"What do you mean?"

I point to the cereal bowls, the general chaos. "This?" I gesture toward our parents' room. "Moe?"

"What about Moe?"

"That's what I'd like to know."

"How should I know? You're the one she likes."

"Look, this place is a wreck. It's"—I am stunned when I locate the starburst clock that usually hangs above the television propped up on top of the set and discover the time—". . . after three in the afternoon and she's still in bed! I have no idea where the twins are—"

"The lapidary shop. They buy opals and settings cut rate from Dependent Services, make jewelry, and sell it at the Officers' Club pool for a big profit."

"Oh, great. Does Dad know about this?"

Kit shrugs and makes a face reminiscent of a cow chewing its cud. In that one expression is communicated an entire lifetime of dismissal, and in spite of my resolution not to let Kit get to me, she does. A sound like rushing water fills my head. "What did I ever do to make you hate me so much?"

Kit glares into my face. Her eyes, usually a swimming-pool aqua, redden until the irises look yellow.

The phone rings and, even as we glower at each other, Kit picks up the receiver and answers the way we have been trained to answer since we started talking: "Root residence. Kit speaking." The call is obviously for her. She turns away and purrs, "Mikey," making the name into a two-syllable seduction. This ability to shift from snarling rage to honey-tongued coquetry has always baffled me. I could never figure out which was real, the rage or the honey.

"Just a min, Mikey." She covers the receiver, turns, and pops her eyes at me to ask why I'm still standing there.

I shake my head to stop the roaring. "Look, could we just declare a truce? I'm only going to be here a few weeks."

"Don't worry. I'll be gone most of the time anyway."

"The all-expense-paid trip to Tokyo?"

"God. Bosco. It's like living with a fucking parrot."

"Uh, you want to help me clean up a little?"

"Fuck that. What do you think I've been doing for the last year here in paradise? Just because Moe refuses to have a maid doesn't mean I'm going to become the house slave."

"Moe refuses to have a maid?"

"Everyone else here does, but she won't allow it."

"Why?"

Kit rolls her eyes and gasps with exasperation. "What do you think?"

"I don't know. Tell me."

"Obviously because of what happened last time."

"What?"

"You're the brain. Figure it out." Kit turns her back to me, picks up the phone, and walks out to the kitchen as far as the cord will go.

My head throbs and I have to breathe through my mouth until my heart stops pounding. Outside, Mama-san incises a neat strip of pale chartreuse straight up the green hill.

Jungle Gardenia

At three the next morning, I sit up in bed, wide awake. Lucky is chirp-burping softly. Bosco snuffles in her sleep. She's supposed to take Actifed for her allergies before she goes to sleep but usually forgets. Traces of iridescent makeup left over from her date the night before give Kit's tanned face a phosphorescent glow. Even when she is sleeping, her beauty and hostility radiate dangerously. Suddenly, the little room is too hot in spite of the chilled air blowing in. I throw the covers off and leave.

Out on the back patio, Moe reads a thick hardcover book by the dim yellow light cast by a bug bulb. She stubs out a Kool in an ashtray already crowded with butts and looks up when I slide the door open.

"So, your clock's not reset yet?" she asks, as I scrape a web-strapped lawn chair across the concrete and sit down next to her.

"I guess not."

A constant ocean breeze sweeps up the long hill, cooling off the humid night. I pull my knees up to hug them to my chest and cover them with the stretchy expanse of my nightie.

My mother lights another Kool. "My clock never has really reset."

"You've been here a year."

"Is that all? It seems like ten. So, tell me about college."

"Oh, you know, big rooms filled with sullen young people napping and doodling."

"You sassy brat. Did you make many new friends?"

I hate the strain in Moe's voice as she tries to sound casual, as if the subject of Bernie having no friends has never come up before.

" 'Make any new friends?' You mean, like, construct them in biology lab?"

"Hah-hah."

"Oh, okay, friends. God, Moe, the tiaras I collected. I had to leave most of them in storage. Jeez, it got embarrassing. They were always electing me queen of something or other."

The air-conditioner compressor cuts off, and in the silence the deep bass hum of a jet engine thrums.

"So, no friends," Moe concludes.

"Nary a one. They said it was a record for an incoming freshman to make it through an entire year without speaking to anyone except the ladies at the cafeteria line. Got some great tips on hair nets."

"What about your roommate? Surely you had to speak to her."

"Ditched out on me the first week. My personal charisma was so intense that she told the Dean of Women she was pregnant to get out of her contract and moved in with her boyfriend. Had the place to myself the whole year. Thank God. No outsiders."

Moe heaves a big sigh that signals she is worrying about me being a pariah.

"Face it, Moe, you are breeding a race of social misfits unlike any the world has ever seen. Except Kit, of course."

A second later, she issues her all-purpose benediction. "Ah, well, *machts nichts,* eh, bebby? We'll always have each other."

On the distant runway, a jet takes off. The bawl of its engines rises to a higher and higher whine until the red taillights disappear in the dark sky.

"C-one-forty-one." Moe points the orange dot of her cigarette toward the departing plane. "They take off and land all night long. Cargo planes going to Vietnam."

A minute or two later, another plane takes off.

"B-fifty-two. Can you hear the difference?"

I shake my head no. "They sound the same to me."

Moe holds up a finger and tilts her head as if listening to a celestial symphony. "No, no. A different timbre. More bass in the one-forty-one." Moe reaches behind her and flips off the bug light. The darkness is a relief.

I listen to Moe's long exhalations and wonder if she is staring at me, studying my face and worrying about me the way she usually does. Then my eyes adjust to the darkness and I see that she's not looking at me at all. In fact, she seems so unaware of my presence that it takes my breath away, like peering into the one mirror that ever reliably reflected me back and seeing nothing. I wish she'd go back to worrying about me having no friends. I don't expect to lead singsongs for my nurse pals or anything, but she could give me some advice for making contact with humans whose last name isn't Root. But I seem to be the last thing on my mother's mind.

"A plane takes off every three minutes. Do you realize how much fuel that is? A million gallons every day. A million." Her voice sounds overwhelmed, defeated, as if she were telling me how much water washes up onshore each day, letting the number alone show us both how little anyone can do to change it.

"Moe, what's wrong?"

"What's wrong?" Her question is an answer that asks, What's right? For a long time neither of us speaks. Then Moe lets out a long sigh. "God, what I wouldn't give for a fresh strawberry. You come to a tropical island, you think they'd at least have decent fruit. Have you seen the produce at the commissary? Some mingy cold-storage apples. Pears hard as hand grenades. Strawberries. A big, juicy strawberry. I smell them in my dreams."

The burned menthol scent of her Kool fills the air.

"I thought you quit. You quit in Mountain Home. You were a bitch for months."

"Mosquitoes. I had to start again. And I don't like that language."

"Had to?" I am peevish, impatient with my mother for not doing her job.

"Do you remember how you and Kit used to beg me to do this?" she asks, tracing the glowing coal of her cigarette through the night, making designs in the dark, as she spells out my name the way she would do after stories were read and the lights turned out. But it was me; I was the one who always begged her to "make designs." Moe would only have to spin out the loops of Kit's name once or twice before she was sound asleep. But I, fearing the moment when she would leave, kept begging for more words, for starbursts and loop-de-loops and roller coasters to slice the dark into safe patterns. If I was lucky and the twins didn't cry, Moe would stay and tell another piece of the long story she started telling me before I could remember.

Her Kool glows in the dark. She stops and holds the burning butt out as if she was trying to figure out what it is. "Damn those Tunisian mosquitoes."

In spite of myself, I snuggle into the lawn chair. I love this part of the story, How World War II Made Me Start Smoking.

"What Tunisian mosquitoes?" I prompt.

"Little tiny ones. Couldn't see them, but, God, they were deadly. We had movies every Thursday night. A couple of the corpsmen would back a troop truck around and tack up a bed-sheet across the back, and that's where they'd show the movie. I think it was the projector light that drew those mosquitoes in from off the desert. Plus the feast *we* were laying out for them. Big bunch of fat, juicy American nurses.

"Either that or Minnie Kravitz's perfume. I don't know how she managed it, but Minnie had a steady supply of Jungle Gardenia through the entire war. We banned her from wearing it on the troopship going over. But the longer we were over there, the more I came to love that Jungle Gardenia. Anything that didn't smell like carbolic acid, or Pine-Sol, or men."

Moe sucks on her cigarette and I fill in the other World War II smells she has described before. The sweet rotting-fruit odor of gas gangrene. The loamy, mushroomy scent of a wound about to go septic. The acrid burnt-metal smell of a bone saw cutting through a femur.

"Jungle Gardenia." She concludes her reverie. "Came to love that Jungle Gardenia. But if I sat anywhere near Minnie, I'd have to have a smoker on the right side and a smoker on the left or I'd get eaten alive. So I just gave up and started myself. For years after the war, a movie didn't look right to me without a haze of cigarette smoke twining up through it. Bogie'd be up there smoking on-screen and we'd all be puffing our lungs out right along with him. Smoking then was *good* for your health, I promise you! Kept those damned Tunisian mosquitoes away. The ward I worked on was filled with boys, young boys, shipped back with malaria or, worse, dengue fever that they'd gotten from those damn mosquitoes. Bonebreak fever, we called it, because those poor guys'd seize up so badly they literally broke bones.

"I remember walking up to the ward on the third floor, and you could hear them before you reached the second. It sounded like they were jumping on pogo sticks up there. When the fever got really bad, those poor guys'd thrash around on those metal cots until they got them jumping around the floor. Hilda Heinz was the charge nurse on Three. Big farm girl from Wisconsin. She fell in love with a major, Howard Patterson, who neglected to tell her he was married. Broke Hilda's heart. She came from a family of thirteen kids and wanted a baby more than anyone I ever knew. Never married after Howard. The corpsmen called her Brunhilda. Big girl. She could lift a patient out of bed like he was a baby. But old Hilda, boy, she always had a joke for you. When the patients thrashed around like that she'd tell me when I checked in, 'They're off to the races again tonight, Moe.' "

Moe laughs. It's the first time she's truly sounded like herself since I arrived.

"You had to laugh, or you'd never stop crying. All those boys. Most of them younger than us, and us barely twenty. Babies, really. Scared, crying for their mothers or out of their minds with fever. I'd hear the beds bouncing as I started up to the second floor, and if I was really tired the tears'd just jump into my eyes. But that Brunhilda, boy." Moe makes the clucking sound at the side of her mouth that is her ultimate gesture of admiration. "She could always put the old snap back in your garters. I'd hit the third floor and there she'd be, her blond hair all braided up and wound around her head, and she'd say something to make me laugh, like, 'Well, they're off to the races again tonight, Moe.' Those beds jumping around like drops of water on a hot griddle, that'd just be the way it was and we were all in it together. Then she'd tell me to put Posey restraints on bed fifteen and I'd be surprised, because fifteen was a skinny kid from Erie, Pennsylvania, who looked like a plucked chicken, who'd said an entire rosary while he was delirious, and he was so worn out from the fever he didn't have the energy to thrash much anymore.

"So I'd go over with the sheets you needed to tie a patient in with, to do the Posey restraints, and the skinny kid from Erie's gone and a new skinny kid is in his bed and the fever would be new and fresh in him and he'd have that bed bouncing like you wouldn't believe. That was when, every time, you'd have to make a choice. Do you cry for the skinny kid who's gone or try to smile for the new kid? Maybe I couldn't always smile, but I'd look over at Brunhilda and we'd both sort of shake our heads like we were mothers watching our wild kids on the playground, and Brunhilda'd say something like, 'Musta had Mexican jumping beans for supper.' Oh, she was a sassy one, that Brunhilda." Another cluck of admiration, silence, and then: "So you start smoking in self-defense. The mosquitoes. Everything. What choice did you have?"

The silence stretches out until I ask, "What are you reading?"

She holds up the book. In the darkness I can make out that it has a big Star of David on the front. "Judaism has always fascinated me. There were lots of Jews in my unit, and I always admired them. I'm thinking about converting."

"Converting? Now? After you've turned six children over to the Whore of Babylon?"

"Don't use that kind of language to describe Holy Mother Church."

"That's what the Jehovah's Witnesses call Holy Mother Church."

"Yeah, well, they don't allow blood transfusions either."

"I think that's some other wacko group, unlike us enlightened Catholics, who believe in virgin birth and old guys in big hats never being wrong."

"Bernadette Marie Root, you *are* a sassy brat." I earn a cluck of admiration.

"So, you're going to convert?"

"The Jews, they just understand suffering so well."

I sense the old snap starting to sag. "Moe, look at us Catholics. We have such a keen appreciation of suffering we've taken up big chunks of the past two thousand years inflicting it upon most of the known world."

"Catholics aren't responsible for all the evils of the world."

"Oh, yeah, right, I forgot about the Mongol invasions."

Moe closes the book and puts it down on the patio. "Oh, well. Just a thought." She has that unstrung sound in her voice again. I pick the book back up and put it on her lap.

"Moe, no, I'm only kidding. Be a Jew." Desperate not to have her slump back into the stunned stranger who'd met me at the airport, I sing, "Be a Jew!" doing a really bad Ethel Merman, finishing with "Everything's Coming up Moses." Anything to put the old snap back in her garters.

But Moe doesn't seem to hear me. She takes a long drag on her cigarette. The glow is not as bright as it had been, and I realize dawn is coming.

In the house, I hear my father in the kitchen. He says he likes to go into work really early to get "a jump" on the day, but it seems like he simply prefers living in a different time zone from us, from his family, which is why he goes to bed to read at seven-thirty every night and leaves before dawn. I hear each noise of his familiar morning ritual in my head before he makes it. A cup of orange juice pouring into the blender. The rip of the three Knox gelatin envelopes he empties into the juice. The crack of the aluminum ice cube tray as he lifts the lever, freeing the cubes. The clatter of the blender as the ice cubes batter against the blades. The subsiding moan when the blender is turned off. A creak as the lid of the hi-fi is lifted. A clunk when the record album is released.

In the predawn light, I catch Moe's glance and we wait for . . .

"¿Cuánto cuesta una tarjeta postal para los Estados Unidos?" an ultra-suave Latino voice asks.

"So Dad and Ricardo Montalban are still dating," I say, and win the big prize. Moe puts her hand over her mouth and stifles a laugh.

"¿Cuánto cuesta una tarjeta postal para los Estados Unidos?" my father repeats. He has been studying Spanish for the past two years.

"Quisiera una camisa deportiva, por favor."

It didn't used to be my father's choice to rise before dawn, back when he was still flying and had to be at the Flight Line for early missions. Since we left Japan, he's gotten up to study whatever his current area of interest is. First, he filled a dozen thick scrapbooks with material from his Great Works of Art correspondence course. Using the stiletto-thin pair of scissors we kids were forbidden to touch, he would clip out *Guernica, Starry Night,* and various adorations of the Magi and paste them into one of the scrapbooks. Then he would study the notes that came with each painting, underlining significant details about the artist's life and distinctive characteristics of the work in question.

"Quisiera una camisa deportiva, por favor."

From there he moved on to an exhaustive survey of the Civil War. Every few weeks another massive tome would arrive at our APO address and my father would begin systematically working his way through all the campaigns of General "Little Phil" Sheridan or Stonewall Jackson.

The Civil War was abruptly abandoned when my father discovered a contest in my *American Girl* magazine to write a jingle for Chiquita bananas. The prize was a Duesenberg. Other contests followed. I woke up every morning to the clacking of the keys of his Underwood as he went from bananas to Noxema to catchy slogans for a new product that had just been introduced,

Fizzies. As a runner-up, he won a year's supply of effervescent tablets, and we all had grape-blue or cherry-red tongues for the week it took us to wipe out the entire supply.

"Me gusta el café pero no quiero café en este momento."

My favorite period came during the brief tour we all endured in Wichita Falls. Stranded in a house off-base surrounded by nothing but hundreds of miles of dustbowl landscape and neighbors who wouldn't allow their children to play with military brats, my father, in a fit of nostalgia for Japan, took up bonsai gardening. He filled our house with little wonderlands of combed sand and mirror lakes and torii and forests of tiny arthritic pines that, for a few moments, took away my homesickness for Japan. Then, one day, we got orders and all the bonsai were tossed out. I begged to save just one, promising to hold it on my lap all the way to the next assignment. Bosco was still in diapers and Bob was nursing, however, so I was destined to spend most of that trip with one of them in my lap.

"Me gusta el café pero no quiero café en este momento." My father turns the hi-fi off and goes back to shower and dress.

Moe heaves a big sigh.

"What?" I ask again.

"Nothing. Tired. Just so tired." She starts to hoist herself up, then sags back into the nylon webbing. "Do you remember those stupid wind-up toys we used to give you kids back in Japan? Little monkeys that, when you wound them up, they'd scoot around banging their cymbals together, or wind-up chicks for Easter that'd jerk around pecking away? And how, inevitably, someone'd wind them up too much and they wouldn't peck or bang their cymbals together anymore. That's me. I think I just got wound up once too often. One too many moves, that's all."

Moe touches my face.

"Don't worry about me. My little worrier. You always worried about things you shouldn't have. Things I should have kept to myself."

Things I should have kept to myself.

The deep rumble of my father's Corvette coming from the front of the house reaches us. Moe shakes her head and rolls her eyes. My father bought the Corvette in Albuquerque and acted as if he were having an affair with it, reupholstering, waxing, taking it on dates to see mechanics in white lab coats. He is the only one who has ever driven the "'Vette" and then only to work, where it can be admired by other men. Moe's feelings about the "'Vette" are well known and center on the twins needing braces that the Air Force won't pay for and we can't afford.

The low-pitched rumble of the powerful engine fades away. Moe sighs. "Oh, well," she says, as if concluding a long discussion that has ended, once again, in a hopeless stalemate. Her chair squeaks as she stands. She stares out toward the Flight Line for a long moment. "God, what I wouldn't give for a strawberry. Oh, well. *Machts nichts.*" She pulls open the patio door, and the house exhales a puff of air-conditioning before she slides it shut again.

Far off to the east, at the point where the island meets the Sea of Japan, a crack of salmon appears beneath the dark wall of night.

DoD Services Bulletin "Welcome to Okinawa"

HAZARDS SECTION

All personnel should be alert to dangers present on the island.

Climate

Okinawa's climate is subtropical. Dehydration and third-degree sunburn are hazards to be avoided by the ingestion of ample fluids, the wearing of hats, and avoidance of the sun. Remain alert for the signs of heatstroke, which include dizziness, disorientation, heart palpitations, clammy palms.

Snakes

Among the venomous snakes on Okinawa, the habu is the most deadly. Every year, approximately 500 people are bitten by habu snakes. The bite of the habu will cause paralyzing pain, swelling at the bite point, and internal hemorrhaging. The habu has a triangular-shaped head with a white belly. It averages two yards in length with a firm tail. It inhabits damp, secluded places like sugarcane fields, tombs, roadsides, walls, and caves.

Animals

Mongooses, imported from India to control the deadly habu, have become a menace in and of themselves. Frequent carriers of rabies, they become insanely aggressive if infected. Annually, they bite in excess of 400 people, who must then endure a painful course of rabies shots. They inhabit damp, secluded places like sugarcane fields, tombs, roadsides, walls, and caves.

Unexploded Ordnance

As the site of the costliest naval battle fought in the Pacific during World War II, unexploded ordnance still exists on the island. Do not handle such ordnance even if only shell casings, etc. Every year medical facilities throughout the island report over 90 phosphorus burns, lacerations, and trauma wounds from the handling of unexploded ordnance.

Insects

The *Anopheles sinensis* mosquito can transmit malaria.

The *Aedes albopictus* mosquito can transmit yellow fever and dengue.

The *Culex tritaeniorhyncus* transmits Japanese B encephalitis.

The *Culex quinquefasciatus* transmits filariasis (elephantiasis).

Flies are important disease carriers. The local use of "night soil" (human feces) for fertilizer makes it imperative to keep screens in proper conditions.

Especially be aware of termites. Okinawa's summers are very hot and humid. Termites, left unattended, will cause a lot of harm to government property.

Typhoons

Okinawa is in one of the major typhoon areas of the world. June through October is typhoon season. Various Typhoon Conditions require all personnel to take specific actions based on the current condition as identified by public information media. TC–1E (Typhoon Condition 1 Emergency) requires halting all outside activity and a return to quarters for all nonessential personnel until the AC (All Clear) is posted.

Tabu

I jerk awake, batting my nose against a newspaper clipping glued to a sheet of Big Chief notebook paper.

"What the fuck?" The forbidden word that was every other word at the university slips out.

Bosco, Bob at her side, puts her hand over my mouth. "Sh-h-h, don't talk or Moe'll know we're telling you."

"Telling me what?" I try to ask, but Bosco's moist palm sealed against my lips turns the words into wet, rude sounds that amuse Bob in ways only a seven-year-old boy can be amused by wet, rude sounds.

"Will you not talk?"

I nod agreement and Bosco removes her hand.

"What is the deal here?"

Bosco and Bob both panic. Bob runs to shut the door and I lower my voice. "Is it a custom on this island to wake people up by sticking things under their noses?"

"Moe told me not to tell you because you're our big worrywart."

"*I'm* our big—?"

Bosco clamps her palm back down on my mouth, leans in, and whispers, "Okinawa is going to sink! Look, it says so right here in the *Stars and Stripes*."

I read the clipping, which does, indeed, predict that this very summer Okinawa will "sink to the bottom of the Pacific Ocean in a cataclysmic firestorm."

"Jeane Dixon wrote this." I toss the clipping back.

"Yeah," Bob breathes, more convinced than ever. "Jeane Dixon."

Bosco, breathing hard, starts to unspool her vast memory bank. "'The Ryukyu Trench has been sounded to a depth of twenty-nine thousand feet. Mount Everest might be sunk in this vast sea crater without showing its peak above water.' That's deep, Bern. Really, really deep."

"Look, you guys, Jeane Dixon is nuts. She also predicted that Jackie Kennedy was going to marry Fidel Castro and World War Three would start in 1964."

"Did it?" Bob asks.

"No, dipshit," Bosco answers. "But that still doesn't mean that Okinawa isn't going to sink."

"'In a cataclysmic firestorm,'" I add.

"Right."

"Does Moe actually believe this?"

Before Bosco can answer, the twins burst into the room wearing ski masks pulled down over their faces, tank tops, and polyester pants with jockey briefs worn on top. While Bob shrieks, Bosco requests wearily, "Don't loot us again."

But Abner is already unplugging Kit's clock/radio and Buzz is sweeping all the resin horses into a pillowcase.

"Fresh loot!" Buzz bawls out in a pirate voice as he unsnaps my footlocker and rummages for lootworthy items. My hair dryer and camera disappear into the pillowcase. Bosco runs out of the room and opens my parents' door.

"Mom! Tell them to stop looting us!"

I listen for my mother's answer as I check the time, past noon. Her voice is scratchy and not fully awake. She clears her throat and tries again. "Boys! Stop looting your sisters!"

"Cheese it! The coppers!" Both twins pretend to try and cram through the door at the same time, bouncing back and turning into sumo wrestlers. They hunker down and stomp their feet on the linoleum-covered cement floor. Then, in one lightning move, Abner lunges forward, grabs Buzz's jockeys, hurls him to the side, and slips out the door with Buzz and Bob in hot pursuit. Buzz has his arms out and is yelling in his zombie voice, "Hasten demise! Hasten demise!"

Bosco takes her horses out of the pillowcase and carefully sets them back up. "I hate it when they loot." Brightening, she looks up at me. "You promised you'd come with me to meet Hickory. Remember?"

I make a deal that I'll go meet Hickory the Horse if Bosco helps me finish cleaning the kitchen.

I tell Bosco to get started and slip into our parents' bedroom. Moe has fallen heavily back to sleep. I peek in her medicine cabinet. It is filled with bottles—Valium, Seconal, Vicodin, hydrocodone, Equagesic—all bearing Kadena Air Base Dispensary labels.

Out in the living room, Kit is dancing to a Monkees album in front of Moe's large brass serving tray. She has perched the tray on top of the buffet so she can see her wobbly gold reflection and is concentrating with the same ferocity she always applied to cheerleader tryouts. Kit catches a glimpse of me in the tray and turns her All-American smile on as if she hadn't wished for my death only the day before.

"Bernie, you're up!" She sashays toward me with both arms out, takes my hands, and pulls me toward the tray. "Show me the new moves from the States." I figure this must be about the dance contest.

As the Monkees advise sleepy Jean to cheer up and ask her what can it mean to a daydream believer and a homecoming queee-ee-een, Kit executes a few shoulder rolls and rotates her fists in front of her face in the sort of dance simulacrum that muscle-bound football players engage in.

"Uh, let's see if there's anything on the radio." I tune in just as a dj announces, "And here's The Association with 'Cherish'!" Kit closes her eyes and sways to the ominous opening chimes. I lunge to turn off the radio, shuddering at how close I came to hearing Cherish is a wu-r-r-r-r-rd. . . . I wonder if Okinawa is haunted by the ghost of all the songs I've ever hated and never want to hear again. The Oldies Undead.

"Is there anything else? You know, actual good dance music?" I ask, thinking of the great dance classics: "Little Latin Lupe,

Lu," "La Bamba," "She's Not There," "Land of 1,000 Dances," "Johnny B. Goode," "96 Tears," even the ur-dance tune that introduced Young White America to its pelvis, "Louie Louie." I flip through the family album collection. Aside from Kit's one Monkees album, all I find are Moe's old 78s: Harry Belafonte, Johnny Mathis, *My Fair Lady*, Peggy Lee. I put on Peggy doing "Fever" and break into a slow Jerk just to acquaint Kit with the concept of moving in time to the music.

You give me fever.

"Buh-bum-m!" I execute an emphatic spine snap to help Kit find the beat, but she's lost in a hitchhiking move, thumb twitching spastically in no apparent relationship to the music. For a second, she stops dead, bobbing her head as she tries to find the rhythm, then holds her nose and shimmies down, pretending to blow bubbles as she descends.

"The Swim!" she announces, pleased with herself.

"So it is," I answer, amazed that, with all her frenetic motion, she never manages to hit the beat once, even accidentally.

"Try this." I face her, move her hips with my hands, and help her find the back beat. Then for thirty seconds, a minute, Kit reflects what I'm doing and we dance together. For those few seconds, we sway in time like dandelions blown by the same wind and I want my sister to win. I'm proud that the most popular, most beautiful girl anywhere we've ever moved has always been my little sister.

Abruptly, she turns away from me and begins running in place, throwing in karate chops here and there at random moments, and I have to conclude once again that Kit and I always have and always will dance to the beat of radically different drummers. I also admit, as she drops to the ground and shoots out a series of burpees, that a complete lack of rhythm won't be any obstacle to Kit's winning a dance contest. In fact, as she jumps back up, her flushed cheeks even peachier than before, her platinum hair seductively tousled, her turquoise eyes glittering, I know that all Kit will have to do to win this or any other dance contest is walk in the room.

The front door bursts open. Abner leans his head in to yell, "Hey, Queen Kit, your subjects await you!"

"Oh, they're here!" Kit sprints back to our room and reemerges a few seconds later drenched in Tabu cologne, her lips sparkling an iridescent pink. She runs outside where a couple of girls almost as tanned but not nearly as beautiful, probably members of Kit's court when she was Queen of Homecoming at Kubasaki High this year, wait in a white Mustang convertible with the top down. Sprawled in the backseat is a guy who could have been king of Kit's court. He has the combination of bland good looks, enough muscle, and just enough intelligence to make a fine high school quarterback. Kit jumps in beside the boy.

Bosco takes up a place beside me at the kitchen window. "He's not even her main boyfriend."

Kit sits on top of the seat in the back of the convertible like she should be wearing a tiara and holding a bouquet of Rose Bowl roses. The grass in our front yard, untouched by Mama-san's mower, is ankle-high with dandelions sprouting in weedy clumps. Bob's yellow Big Wheel lies tipped over in the desic-cated remains of a flower bed. A screen hangs off one of the front windows. Seeing the disorder in full daylight stabs me with panic.

The twins, still in lootwear, slither along the sides of the car-port, their backs flattened against the concrete wall. The game has shifted now to Commando. Buzz is the leader. He hacks his arm down swiftly, pointing at the convertible. Abner receives his order, nods solemnly, an imaginary assault rifle held at port. In a lightning attack, Abner darts out, rolls, sprays the convertible with gunfire, pulls the pin on a Wiffle ball, lobs it into the con-vertible, and sprints away.

The quarterback rifles the ball back at Abner and manages to clip him in the eye.

"Pretty good arm," Bosco comments from our post at the window.

Kit looks on with supreme exasperation as her young brother dies a twitching, gasping death on the front lawn.

The convertible drives away. Hovering in the air above them

is the same Marine helicopter that peeped on Kit while she sun-bathed yesterday. As the wind whips her white hair back, Kit raises her right arm straight over her head and thrusts her middle finger into the air. Painted silver, her middle fingernail twinkles in the sun, much more invitation than curse. The Marines clearly interpret it that way and bank the helicopter in so low to the convertible that the girls' hair swirls in cyclones above their heads.

Moe squeezes in next to us and stays at the window for a long time after the convertible disappears from view. She has on her reading glasses. They magnify her eyes and give her a bewildered, goggling expression. "She never tells me where she's going anymore." Moe shuffles out to the kitchen, pulling shut the cotton kimono that hangs slackly about her.

I stare out the window and think about the time the monkey bit Kit when we lived on Yokota and wonder if that is when my little sister began to hate me.

Young Pinkoo

It happened right after we moved on-base. Moe predicted that leaving our little house on the alley in Fussa would be calamitous, and this was the start. Our father was gone on one of a long series of TDYs, Temporary Duty assignments. It was summer. Bougainvillea and hydrangeas nodded their heavy heads in the heat. The odorless flowers made me miss my honeysuckle vines back at the house in Fussa. The three of us, me, Moe, and Fumiko, sat in front of the fan set up at the end of the kitchen table to swivel around and blow air into our faces.

The twins and Bosco were taking naps. Kit was outside. Even the heat couldn't stop the worshipful gang of little girls who began beating on our door early in the morning demanding that Kit come out and transform them into a herd of wild mustangs that would thunder about her, their leader. Or into a corps of dancers who would writhe on the ground dying as Kit, the only caterpillar to live, would burst from her chrysalis into exquisite butterfly flight. It amazed me how, even that young, Kit had the power to convince her besotted playmates that it was the most fun imaginable to be a slave and build a pyramid for her, the mighty pharaoh. She could sometimes even get her acolytes— who included Lisa Wingo, Major Wingo's daughter, and the second most popular girl, as well as Debbie Coulter and Sheryl Dugan, daughters of other members of our father's flight crew— to play her favorite game, Elvis, and simply roll around on the grass screaming out adulation for her, the Queen.

That morning, Moe, Fumiko, and I finished the housework early, dancing through our dusting with Mahalia Jackson singing about God having the whole world in his hands. We were sitting at the table eating broiled bologna and cheese sandwiches with the crusts cut off and drinking Coke out of little bottles when Fumiko shared the secret with us for making Pink Cokes, the best Coke anyone ever drank. It was Shiseido's Young Pinkoo.

"Make your lips like this," Fumiko instructed me, stretching her own full lips over her teeth as she held her tube of Young Pinkoo beside her head like an artist with a brush. Young Pinkoo was the favorite lipstick among Japanese women for many post-war years. It was the color of cherry blossoms and had a scent with the warm, waxy appeal of my Crayolas, spiked with elements more sophisticated, grown-up, and dangerous but which, in the end, just smelled pink in the mysteriously contrived way of women while crayons and flowers and iced cookies smelled pink in a dismissably childish way.

I imitated her. Fumiko breathed talcum powder and rice crackers on me as she carefully applied the lipstick then handed it to Moe, who put it on herself, making the face of Tragedy like she always did to apply lipstick. Usually Moe blotted her lipstick thoroughly afterward, leaving fallen petals of rose-kissed Kleenex behind. But not this time. This time, we all looked at each other, our lips the color of Hostess Sno-balls, me dreaming that I'd grow up and be as beautiful as Moe, as Fumiko, then pressed the mouths of the Coke bottle against our own and drank the Young Pinkoo–flavored soda.

"My God, Fumiko," Moe said, staring at the squat bottle, its neck ringed in waxy pink. "You're right. That is the best Coke I have ever had in my life."

"Me too," I marveled. "Pink Coke."

Fumiko reddened with pleasure at our compliments.

"Fumiko," Moe said, draining her bottle, "let's get another treatment in before the twins wake up."

These "treatments" of Moe's were a major production that could only be done with Fumiko's help. Back in the parents' room, Fumiko quickly set up a machine called the Metabo-Liter that had arrived in a large, wooden crate last month. Moe stepped out of the bathroom, her hair wrapped in a towel turban, wearing only her bra and panties. Her tummy was soft and caved-in from having five babies, like a balloon blown up too much, then popped. Fumiko untangled a mass of wires that led from the heavy control box to banners of rubber. Moe wrapped rubber strips around her thighs, then another one around her tummy. Swaddled like a mummy in the flesh-colored rubber, she stretched out on the table. Fumiko attached wire leads to each long strip and plugged them all into the control box. She fiddled with the many dials on the control box, and a steady buzz hummed through the bedroom.

"A little bit more," Moe said, and Fumiko turned the dial up until the hum hit a higher pitch. "Ee-yow! You're electrocuting me!" Moe yelped, making Fumiko laugh out loud. It took Moe most of the four years that Fumiko was with us to get her to make a sound when she was amused, but she'd finally succeeded. Fumiko's laugh was startling, a horsy whinny unlike any other laugh I'd ever heard. Fumiko only laughed that way when she was alone with Moe and me. Her staccato whinny never failed to crack Moe up, so that she and Fumiko would end up laughing until one of them either wet her pants or cried. As their laughter subsided to odd snorts and titters, I studied the Metabo-Liter.

I didn't understand the exact scientific principles behind the Metabo-Liter, but the whole procedure of Moe yelping and electricity being shot through her flab bore a creepy resemblance to the *Bride of Frankenstein.*

"Hey! I get one too!" Kit, her pale hair clinging in a sweat-darkened frame around her face, flushed a sunrise pink, burst into the bedroom, pouting and holding one of the empty Coke bottles. At that exact instant, the twins, as they always seemed to, woke up together, screaming in stereo.

"Shit," Moe hissed, glancing at the rubber wraps it had taken ten minutes to girdle herself in. "Bernie, could you, please, take the twins to the playground before they wake up the baby?"

I pushed Buzz's stroller and Kit pushed Abner's through the heat. The walk to the playground took us out of officers' housing into the noncoms' area. Here families didn't live in their own houses; they shared two-story apartment buildings that looked like the barracks where the GIs lived. Each building squatted on flat land unadorned by trees and shrubs. Lawn furniture sat out front, along with bicycles dropped on the dirt, pull toys, and broken barbecues, debris unimaginable in the officers' section. A group of mothers lounged on webbed lawn chairs in their front yards, smoking and yelling at their children. A couple of the women even held cans of beer.

As we wheeled past, first the mothers, then the children, fell silent and stared at us. It wasn't because our faces were unfamiliar. New faces are the norm in military neighborhoods where a family can be packed up and moved away overnight if the assignment is urgent or the scandal great enough. No, we exuded an indefinable quality that marked us as officer's kids, alien outlanders in this neighborhood.

I wilted under the strangers' stares, particularly that of an obese woman whose upper arms swung with a pendulous heft as she stroked a gray cat on her lap. Face prickling with embarrassment, I leaned into the stroller and pushed harder, rushing to escape their attention, to reach the neutral zone of the school playground. As always, however, Kit, with her bone-deep conviction that she was welcome anywhere, blossomed under the attention. To my intense chagrin, she lagged farther and farther behind until a gulf half a block long had opened up between us.

"Hey," I heard her call out to the fat woman. "Is that a real monkey?"

I looked back to see Kit abandon Abner's stroller and walk toward the clump of noncom wives, who all sat up a bit straighter in their chairs and flipped the damp hair off the backs of their necks at the approach of this little princess. In that instant, for the first time, I realized that whatever group my sister stepped into would always rearrange itself into a party for her. In the same moment, what I had taken to be a cat stood up on the woman's lap and I saw it was a snow monkey, a fuzzy, big-eyed baby macaque from Kyoto.

Kit, believing that no primate could be immune to her charm, walked right up to it. With one shriek, the monkey launched itself off the woman's lap directly into Kit's face. The monkey, the women, Kit, Abner, and Buzz all screamed as the animal was peeled off Kit's face. Blood streamed from her lips.

The monkey was killed; Kit had to have a series of rabies and tetanus shots. All the noncom wives visited and brought her dolls, and boxes of the soft Japanese crayons that could be smeared for foggy effects, and coloring books with special pages that you could just paint with water and a hitherto invisible picture would appear. Moe cried every time she looked at Kit's bandaged face.

When the stitches came out, we witnessed a miracle. Kit had had what Moe called the Root Lip, an upper lip thin as a dog's. It was her only defect. The baby monkey's tiny front teeth had sunk in above Kit's lip at precisely the spot where the bow of an upper lip should have been and punched one in. Somehow, the shiny red scars never completely faded, so that Kit's upper lip ever after looked as plump and bee-stung as Fumiko's had the day she showed us how to make Pink Cokes.

Fries

Island-Wide
DANCE CONTEST!!
Win an all-expenses-paid trip to
Tokyo, Japan!!!
To accompany internationally renowned comedian
BOBBY MOSES!!!!
Far East Funnyman Three Years Running!!!
On his sold-out Fourth-of-July Tour
of the
LAND OF THE RISING SUN!!!

"Is this the thing Kit is going to win?" I ask, reading the flier taped to the outside wall of the neighborhood snack bar, the Scoop 'n' Skillet. Bosco and I stand next to the small, screened order window. A stream of chilled air blows out, carrying the smell of grilling hamburgers, fries, and fermented ketchup.

"She'll win. She wins everything she tries out for."

"She's never won Science Fair or a spelling bee," I remind Bosco.

"Oh, well. Those." Bosco waves her hand, dismissing the things she's won. The same things I'd won.

"Whuh you wan?" A Ryukyuan woman, her silver hair pulled back in a bun, appears at the window.

"Bosco, I'm treating. What do you want? Hamburger?"

Bosco's eyes widen in horror. "A hamburger? At the Poop 'n' Kill It? Are you crazy?" She turns to the woman. "One Nutty Buddy, please."

I get one too, and we continue on our expedition to the base stables to meet Hickory the Horse, following the broad sidewalks through the rolling green hills of officer housing. Maybe because for the first time in my life I've lived for the past year in a normal neighborhood, I notice what's missing in an overseas military neighborhood.

Of course, most obvious is the complete lack, during working hours, of any male over the age of eighteen. And no old people at any time, ever. Someone's grandparents coming for a visit is a major show-and-tell for the whole neighborhood. No mailmen, since your mail comes to an APO box and you pick it up. Outside dogs are as rare as grandparents. The occasional senior officer's wife might have her matched set of Pekingese or Japanese Chins, but regular old yard dogs are encumbrances that overseas military families live without. Besides, a misplaced pile of poop could go on an Officer's Efficiency Report as easily as any other infraction noted by the Housing Officer, who patrols regularly, noting whose lawn is overgrown with weeds, which family leaves Big Wheels in the flower bed, which house has screens hanging off the windows.

All of which explains why officers' housing on Kadena Air Base resembles a very well maintained golf course, with grass kept as trim as the occupant officer's own crew cut. No one, not even the base commander, has a fence around his yard, but around all the yards, around all the runways and parade grounds, are the miles of barbed fence that corrals us all.

At the edge of the housing area, Bosco moves a rock and exposes a hole dug beneath the fence. "This is my shortcut," she tells me proudly, slithering under, then holding the bottom strand of wire up while I squirm through. On the other side of the fence, Okinawa waits in all its chaotic, semitropical lushness.

We enter a wooded ravine overgrown with vines looping down from a profusion of scrubby trees. Sweat dries almost instantly in the shady ravine cooled by the constant ocean breezes. A damp, fungal odor saturates the air.

"Do you ever wish you knew when the last time for something was going to be?" Bosco asks me. I'm concentrating on the path, watching for habu snakes, mongooses, unexploded ordnance, burning phosphorus, *Anopheles* mosquitoes. I remain alert to the signs of heatstroke.

"Like, I walk through this ravine every day to get to the stables," Bosco goes on, as we thread our way around the thick vines that twine across the path. "But say I get a best friend and she hates walking through the ravine." This hypothetical discussion of a best friend makes me feel sad for myself and for Bosco, who is as buddy-free as I am.

"So we go around and stay on the sidewalk the whole way to the stable and I never walk through the ravine again. Then, one day, when I'm grown up, I remember the ravine and this smell"—she pauses to identify it—"sort of between a gagging sewer smell and a sweet jasmine smell, and how it was all cool and dark in there even when it was hot and still in the sun, and I just stopped walking through it. Stopped walking through the ravine. There was no last time. I just stopped and never noticed."

Bosco stares at me, distraught, burdened with the inevitability of this tragedy. Her voice rises as she goes on. "Think of all the last times that no one ever notices. You think you'll play with your troll dolls forever, but one day you get a horse and you never play with them again, and you can't even remember when the last time was because you don't plan to stop playing with them. You just do and then you move and your mom throws them away because you're over your weight allowance and you get to the new base and you don't have your horse so now you want to play with your troll dolls, but they're gone. They're gone, and you can't even remember the last time you played with them. They're just gone."

Bosco looks impossibly bereft thinking about her abandoned troll dolls.

"Look, Bosk, this is easy. You can control all these last times that are trying to gang up on you. When we get home, we'll play with your trolls."

"You don't understand. The whole day is probably filled with last times you never even notice. I mean, this, *this* may be the last time I'll ever eat a Nutty Buddy." She studies the soggy tip of the melting cone with a mixture of adoration and betrayal as if this, *this* Nutty Buddy will be the one to do her wrong.

"I don't know, Bosk. I actually see many Nutty Buddies in your future."

Bosco's face creases with woe. "Yeah, but sometime, someday, some Nutty Buddy will be the last."

It is clear that my little sister needs some of the old snap put back in her garters. "Here's a last for you, Bosco." I pluck the last melting bit from her fingers and toss it away as we step out of the ravine. "This is the last time we'll ever talk about Nutty Buddies. Okay?"

The sun pounds down, making sweat stream from my temples, between my breasts, armpits, spine. I even feel a trickle run down the back of my knee. A wall of what looks like very skinny bamboo or six-foot-tall Johnson grass appears on either side of the path. I whack at it with a stick.

"Don't do that!" Bosco grabs the stick out of my hand. "That's habu grass. Habu snakes live in there. Among the venomous snakes on Okinawa, the habu is the most deadly. Every year, there are approximately five hundred people bitten by habu snakes. The bite of the habu will cause paralyzing pain, swelling at the bite point, and internal hemorrhaging. The habu has a triangular-shaped head with a white belly. It averages two yards in length with a firm tail." Bosco stares at me, hyperventilating.

"They brought the snakes here to kill the rats. But the snakes killed the people, so they brought mongooses. The plural is mongooses, not geese." Bosco is talking fast and her eyes dart over my face, searching for answers even as she pours out her own. "But the snakes multiply too rapidly. The mongooses can't kill them all. There aren't enough of them. Besides which, mongooses, imported from India to control the deadly habu, have become a menace in and of themselves. Frequent carriers of rabies, they become insanely aggressive if infected. Annually, they bite in excess of four hundred people, who must then endure a painful course of rabies shots. They inhabit damp, secluded places like sugarcane fields, tombs, roadsides, walls, caves, and particularly their favored habitat—the habu grass field named in the snake's honor and that—" she snaps back into focus and points at the tall grass I am whacking at "—*that!*—is habu grass!"

"It's okay, Bosk. I wasn't going to go in."

"They're very aggressive. They're a very aggressive snake." Tears pool in her eyes. She marches off down the path before they can fall. I catch up with her and she runs away, disappearing as the path turns farther into the dense habu grass. Like clockwork, fat gray clouds bully their way in from the east.

"Bosk?" The only answer is the beat of distant helicopter rotors and a relentless roar from the Flight Line. A gathering wind whips the tall habu grass. The long blades tilt their silver backs to the darkening sun. No preliminary scattering of drops announces the rain. It falls in a torrent as drenching as standing beneath the rain spout. "Bosco!"

The tall grass gives way to open land, gentle hills covered in mossy green. At the top of a rise, Bosco stands next to an ornate concrete structure that resembles a miniature bunker embedded in the hill. The bulging top of the structure is nearly as tall as my sister. Rain streams down her face.

I put my arm around her shoulder. "It's going to be okay."

"How?" She is bereft. "Okinawa is going to sink. Do you realize that we are literally floating over the deepest part of the Pacific? Twenty-nine *thousand* feet. Do you know that Mount Everest could be underneath the island and it wouldn't even touch us?"

"Okinawa is not going to sink. I told you, Jeane Dixon is a crackpot."

Tears blend in with the rain coursing down her face. "Underwater is worse than on land, too! There are sea snakes and stonefish. Sea snakes have the deadliest venom of all. And stonefish. They look just like stones. And you could be wading and step on one and they inject you with a potentially deadly but always extremely painful poison. And there's nothing you can do to avoid them. They look like stones! How are personnel supposed to avoid all stones? . . . How, Bernie?"

"Bosco, Mama's going to be all right. She's just tired."

Bosco gulps several deep breaths before she can calm herself. "But she never gets out of bed. I thought she'd get up when you got here. Kit is going to get us RIF'd. Her best friend, Sandra Muller, they RIF'd her. She was taking drugs. She went up to the north end of the island with some GIs. I heard Kelly Kulchak's mom talking about it. OSI came and her whole family was gone overnight. Her hamster, Snerd, was in a cage in the carport and they just left him. He was mummified when the next family moved in and found him. And there are stealie boys. They took my troll house. I left it in the carport, and"—Bosco is overtaken by grief and sobs openly—"it was gone and it had my favorite troll still in it and she was my favorite even if I hadn't played with her for a while. I was going to."

I pat Bosco's back. In the silence I listen to the planes taking off and realize that Moe is right. I can tell the difference between the C-141s and the B-52s.

My sister cries until the rain stops. Then we walk on to the stable and take turns brushing Hickory the Horse.

Weed

"What is *their* problem?" Kit asks, as we drive out Gate Three. Flanking each side of the gate are dozens of Okinawan demonstrators sitting cross-legged beside the barbed wire fence encircling Kadena. Even though the sun is brutal, the men wear dark suits and ties, the women dresses. They hold banners written in Japanese and have white cloth headbands splashed with red characters tied around their foreheads and sashes across their chests. Amidst the scramble of kanji, I make out "B52" without the hyphen, repeated again and again.

"Just guessing, but they don't seem too happy about having hundreds of warplanes loaded with bombs crammed onto their island."

"Why do they care what we park here?"

Buried behind a picket of signs is one that demands NO NUCLEAR!

I start to ask Kit if this could be true. Are there nuclear weapons on the island? But the last people on earth who would ever know would be the families of the men stationed here. Besides, I'm flattered that Kit, who has had her license suspended, has asked me to drive her to the preliminaries of this dance contest she plans to win. It feels great to be out of the concrete house. I am determined I won't let Kit get to me.

HIGHWAY ONE, I read a sign beside the road as we head south.

"One and only," Kit sneers, as she flips on the radio.

That was "A Beautiful Morning" by The Young Rascals. No argument here! It is a beautiful morning here on the Rock. This is Private First Class Keith Delano, your Jock on the Rock! *Here's*

*The Fifth Dimension. They're gonna get up, up and away in their beautiful—oh, yeah—that bee-*yoo*-tiful bah-looon!*

We break free of the miles of runways and acres of concrete stacked with tarp-covered crates, and the East China Sea appears beside us. Towers of white clouds extend from the water high into a sky of dazzling blue. We spin along the coast on a day so beautiful even the corny music seems right. We're all floating, all of us—me, my family, the entire Department of Defense—we're floating on this beautiful balloon of an island where no one mentions nuclear weapons or Vietnam. Where troublesome teens and their families simply vanish overnight.

A convoy of camouflage Army trucks boxes us in. I floor the accelerator, and the sluggish station wagon surges ahead.

"All right! Pedal to the metal!" Kit whoops and, for one second of bad-girl glee, we could be buddies, girlfriends out cruising around. That is what the GIs in the trucks take us for. They honk and wave their caps as we pass. A boy on the passenger side of the lead truck opens his door and leans out, holding his arms open to us, pleading.

My beautiful, my beautiful bah-looon!

Heading toward Naha where the tryouts are to be held, we pass fields of sugarcane and pineapple. In one pineapple field, harvesters with baskets strapped on their backs hack fruit from the low bushes, then toss them into the baskets without a backward glance. I swerve to avoid a bandy-legged farmer in rubber zoris and baggy khaki shorts who leads a water buffalo beside the road.

"Hey, egghead, what time is it?"

I can't recall anyone in our family ever asking this question and check to see if Kit is kidding. She's not. She isn't wearing her Seiko.

"Twelve-twenty-five. Twenty-six. Somewhere in there."

"Tryouts start at two. We'll be too early. I want to be last. Last is always best. I always make sure I go on last. That way you leave a lasting impression with the judges. We've got some time to burn. Turn off up there." I take a left onto a road topped with crushed coral. It winds through sandy terrain, then heads steeply upward.

"So that's your secret?" I ask. "Going last?"

Kit sniffs at the insinuation that she needs to rely on trickery. "It doesn't matter when you go if no one's going to vote for you."

"Ah. And what *is* your secret then? In the event no one is going to vote for you?" I try to make it sound like I'm kidding.

At the top of the rise, a flatbed truck loaded with sugarcane hurtles directly toward us on our side of the road. Kit and I shriek like lunatics as I bump off onto the shoulder. Almost dying together seems to warm Kit up enough to really talk to me.

"You want to know the secret to making people like you?" She pauses for dramatic effect, then answers herself. "There's no secret. God, Bern, you're such a brain, I could never understand why you didn't want friends. I mean, it's the easiest thing in the world."

On the other side of the hill, the Pacific Ocean stretches out beneath us all the way to California. Instead of the hard granite black it was when we landed in Yokohama Harbor twelve years ago, the water pools in a lagoon below, turquoise and then cream where the soft waves splash to shore.

"It was never easy for me."

"You make it hard. All you have to do is give people what they want and they always let you know what that is in, like, the first three minutes after you meet them or something. I mean, like, you meet this girl and she's all worried about being fat, so you tell her she's not fat and she's your slave. And guys! Guys are so easy it's pathetic. You don't even have to bother listening to them. They *show* you how they want you to control them. They've got on their letter jacket, or they show you their Honda six-fifty or their comic book collection and they have the original Spider-Man or something, and you just act like that's amazingly cool and they love you."

"They love *you*. Guys never much care what I think about their Spider-Man comics."

"Because you never acted like you cared."

"It got kind of hard after the first half dozen or so moves, though, didn't it?"

Kit shrugs and I try again.

"I mean, growing up military sort of makes you a Buddhist from a very early age. Like, you have to detach. You know it's all transitory. None of it's permanent, you know?" I am so excited to have my sister talking to me that I throw in as many "likes" and "I means" as I can to keep her hooked.

Kit tilts her beautiful face toward me and I can understand every sappy guy who ever gave her his heart for just this much.

"Like, when we'd start at a new school, I could never believe how seriously everybody took everything. Like it really mattered who was in and who was out? Who was Homecoming Queen and who was going to the prom and who wasn't? It was already too late to care. I mean, I already knew that this particular microcosm I just happened to be inhabiting was being duplicated millions of times over all around the world. The same in–out, popular–outcast stuff was going on in Hap Arnold Elementary and General Chenault Junior High and Kubasaki High School. . . ."

Even listing a fraction of all the schools we've attended exhausts me, but it's thrilling to finally talk this way with Kit. To have her listen, her eyes now the exact same tender aqua as the water below, and believe that she is finally going to understand me.

"Anyway, I already knew going in that this arbitrary little system truly was not the center of the world. I guess I cared, but in the way a performer cares that the play they're in is well done, believable, successful. What I could never understand was how anyone could ever truly *believe* in such a totally fake thing? I guess that was my problem. I was always baffled by the ones who did. The climbers, the school-spirit people, the boosters. Didn't they know that other girls in sweaters with animals pasted on their breasts were yelling just as hard at millions of other schools? That they believed *their* quarterback was the hottest guy in the universe? Didn't they know other children believed their country was the best on the earth? I mean, even being a Catholic. How are you supposed to believe that it is the one true religion?"

Kit blinks and shakes her head. "Wow. You sound exactly like Bosco. Or she sounds like you, more like it. You guys are *so* weird. Did you ever stop to consider that there might be such a thing as thinking too much?"

"Yeah, okay, it was really good to open up to you like this."

Kit shrugs and points to a stand of pines where the coral shell road ends. "Park up there."

A dozen other cars are already clustered at the end of the road. They all have Kubasaki Dragons bumper stickers pasted on them.

We get out and I follow Kit to the edge of the cliff. We're on top of a coral outcropping hundreds of feet above the lagoon far below. The East China Sea surrounds us on three sides.

"It's beautiful."

"Yeah. Sometimes you can see Taiwan from here."

I squint hard into the opalescent glare.

"See that right over there?" Kit points to the other end of the horseshoe, across the lagoon from us. It rises to a column of coral, twisted and ventilated by the waves, that arches out over the jagged peaks at its base. "Suicide Cliffs. That's where all the enemy soldiers jumped instead of surrendering. Hundreds of 'em. Just . . . Banzai! and over the top."

She stares in silence at the black lip of coral jutting out above the waves, and for a second I am certain that Kit and I are remembering the same thing, remembering Fumiko telling us about her father coming home and giving her rock candy. I'm certain we are both imagining hundreds of men like Fumiko's father, trapped at the edge of the world, choosing to step off the black coral into the blue of the sky that will become the blue of the ocean. I'm certain we both see them falling through the air.

Their caps with a cloth in the back to shade their necks floating off their heads as the soldiers plummet toward the spiked rocks. Their moss-green puttees unwrapping from around their ankles to flap loose about their bodies like wings that will not work.

Then Kit says, "Crazy Japs," and I remember she had been asleep when Fumiko told me the story about her father; she doesn't remember it at all.

"Come on!" Kit is already scaling the hill behind us, grabbing at the gnarled roots of pines to pull herself up.

"Kit! Watch out for snakes! Habu!" But she's already out of sight. I scramble to catch up, following a trail of Pabst Blue Ribbon beer cans, Slim Jim wrappers, and empty Coppertone tubes. I catch a glimpse of Kit just before she disappears into a slit in the rocks.

Sweat is streaming off me by the time I reach the slit. It exhales cool, musty cave air. From inside, voices echo out. High-pitched female squeals peal out greetings to Kit. I don't hear what she says, but it elicits the deep rumble of a male laugh. I squeeze past the wedge of rocks and follow the voices and a flicker of light down a cramped and twisting passageway. The damp limestone walls narrow and I have to crouch down and inch through sideways until, abruptly, the mountain opens into a cavern where shadows cast by Coleman lanterns dance crazily upward for ten, twenty, fifty feet, flickering in and out amid an upside-down forest of stalactites.

The answering forest of stalagmites projecting up from the ground is inhabited by a platoon of young Americans lounging among the broken nubs. As always, Kit is at the center of this group of twenty or more. Half are high school kids, Kubasaki Dragons, the other half, in olive drab and camou, bad haircuts slightly grown out, are obviously GIs. The quarterback-looking guy from the convertible grabs Kit and kisses her, blowing a lungful of smoke into her mouth. She exhales it immediately—*pot is for losers and noncoms*—and dances out of his grip. Three girls cluster around Kit, whispering and shrieking. Beside them, a GI in a floppy olive-green hat and tank T-shirt holds the flame of a Zippo lighter under the wire mesh of a hookah as a girl in a Madras plaid blouse and a pair of clam-digger shorts inhales until the water burbles.

Disconnected bits of conversation ricochet off the limestone walls.

"This is some righteous weed, man."

"Like I give a shit. I'm short. I'm booking out in three weeks and counting. Stateside. Back to the world. So long, suckers, see you in the next cartoon."

"Carlene gave Matt his ring back."

"You lie like a dog!"

"If I'm lyin', I'm dyin'. Steffie told me."

"Travel light and carry a heavy bag."

"Roger that, bro."

"No, I told you. My dad is like royally PO'd. One ding and I'm, like, permanently grounded. Thank God he's TDY."

"Big sister."

I turn. A hawk-nosed guy with frizzy red hair picked out into as much of an approximation of an Afro as he can manage stands beside me, holding out a joint.

"I understand you get high." He tries to make his hookworm accent from one of the meaner southern states like Arkansas or Mississippi sound as black as he can. "Tha's what they tell me. They tell me big sister, she'll smoke herself a joint now and again." He laughs a stoned cackle that stretches lips so smeared by freckles that it's impossible to tell where they leave off and the rest of his pale, speckled face begins. Too much of his doughy skin shows beneath a GI undershirt. His dog tags hang atop a few sparse, carroty chest hairs. I wave the joint off and step away, searching for Kit in the hazy gloom.

The GI lopes after me, trying to imitate the loose-limbed grace and street savvy of a black pimp. "Big sister seems a mite freaked out." He takes a hit, chants as he exhales, "Hey, hey, LBJ. How many babies you kill today?"

I tell myself this idiot couldn't possibly know about anything that happened on the other side of the world, at the University of New Mexico. He couldn't possibly know about the Damsels.

"Oh, you met Ron. He's our friend in OSI." Kit puts her finger over her lips to give me the hush-hush sign and giggles a laugh that sounds more drunk than stoned. "You know. OSI? Office of Special Investigations. The ones who spy on us. Ron, tell her what's in big sister's file."

Ron quotes from my file. "Bernadette Marie Root. Height, five foot five. Weight, one-forty—you could stand to drop some L.B.s there, big sister. Eyes, hazel. Schools attended. Man, there's a shitload of them. Forget schools. Member of antiwar group Damsels in Dissent that disseminates information on illegal means of dodging the draft and generally undermining the United States military. Associates with known narcotics users. Active in protest marches. Oo-wee, big sister, you in a world of hurt that shit gets around. What yo' daddy gonna say?" He cackles because he doesn't care what my father would say.

My heart is pounding and the cave and everyone in it scares me. "I'm leaving, Kit. If you want me to drive you, you come now. Otherwise, stay here. I don't really give a shit."

The sunlight blinds me as I squeeze back out of the narrow opening. I sit in the broiling car for twenty minutes and my hands, suddenly gone icy, never warm up.

Kit finally comes out and gets in, but neither of us says anything until we're back on Highway One and the traffic has clotted up again as we head into Naha.

"Funny, isn't it?" Kit asks. "That you should end up being the one who could get us RIF'd. And you could, you know. Major's daughter telling guys how to get out of the draft. They'd nail him for that. At the very least, he'd never make light." Kit's habit of using military slang—*light* for lieutenant colonel—seems even more foreign and annoying than usual.

"What about you? Hanging out in caves, smoking dope with GIs. Like *that's* going to get him sent to Air Command and Staff?"

"Ron does all the filing at OSI. Any reports I want him to, he just loses. He'd never narc me."

"Was Sandra Muller a friend of Ron's too? Was he never gonna narc her?"

"Sandra had it coming. Sandra was smoking opium. She was a loser. Don't worry, I'm not Sandra." Kit grins at me, as stoned on the invincibility of her beauty and charm as she is on anything she smoked or drank. I want to knock her perfect teeth down her throat.

"You stupid idiot."

"Of course. How could I not be? You took all the brains before I even got here."

Right Guard

*N*aha, the island's largest city, looks and smells, initially, like five Kozas crammed together. Swarms of Daihatsus and Nissans and three-wheeled trucks eddy around the station wagon. It takes all my concentration to keep the wheels out of the *benjo* ditches that line the road on the outskirts of town. We cross over the Kumoji River. Below us, on the river, log rafts float past on their way to the plywood factory.

By the time we reach Kokusai Street, the commercial heart of the city, the open sewers have been paved over and the buildings rise up ten and fifteen stories above us. This isn't the strip-show pawnshop boomtown of Koza but an actual city where the main business is not the American military. A stream of diesel buses belches past, followed by a delivery boy on a bicycle balancing a tray of brass lunchboxes.

At a stoplight, a flock of schoolgirls in pigtails and black middy blouses wearing pastel-colored backpacks crosses the street.

"Hey, look." Kit points to two little Okinawan boys. One has scrambled up into a tree and is wiring pink plastic cherry blossoms handed to him by the other boy onto the tree's barren branches.

"Isn't that cute?" Kit laughs her pinging crystal laugh, and I realize that while I have been brooding since we left the cave, despairing over the future of our family, she hasn't given the incident a second thought. "Oh, turn right up here."

Tryouts are being held in the Kokusai Hotel, one of the few structures on the street with a sign outside in English. A Ryukyuan man in a straw pith helmet waves us officiously into a parking garage, where Frenchie bulges over both sides of the designated space.

A sign just in front of the reception desk reads DANCE CONTEST: *Fourth floor.*

The elevator creaks and groans on the way up. Kit works at the smoked-glass mirror. She tugs her lower eyelid down to line it in black, quickly rats up the top of her hair, then pulls out three lipsticks.

"You're putting on three different colors?"

"Of course. You've got to start off with your matte base coat." She applies a peach tone, then blots it off. "Hit eleven," she instructs when the doors open at the fourth floor. As we shudder upward, she continues her commentary. "Always add yellow. Makes your teeth look white." She twirls up a tube of yellow and smears that on top of the peach, turning to smile at me. Her teeth are so white, they look blue. "Then finish off with your pearlizer." She adds an iridescent topcoat and pushes the button for four.

The elevator stops on the seventh floor on the way back down and a Ryukyuan family—mother, father, two young boys in shorts, and an older girl in a school uniform—gets on with much bowing. Kit continues her toilette, whipping out a mascara wand.

"This is layer five or six for the mascara. Mascara doesn't get good until at least the fourth layer." The Ryukyuan family watches as if Kit were putting on a cooking demonstration. She finishes and turns to them with a smile.

They suck air in through their teeth and exclaim, "*Ah so, desuka. Utsukushii.*"

Kit gasses herself and everyone else with Emeraude. The Okinawan family all smile and bow when we get off at the fourth floor.

We follow a clump of American girls to a windowless, low-ceilinged banquet room packed with the dependent daughters of every branch of the armed services. It is obvious that no one has any clearer idea of what this dance contest constitutes than I do. A girl in a sequined drum-majorette costume warms up with a baton. Another one beats out a snappy rhythm with her patent-leather tap shoes. Yet another girl is draped in the billowing chiffon of a ballroom dancer. Most of them, though, are just ordinary girls who smell like coconut hair conditioner and look as if they stepped out of the Sears Junior Miss section three or four years ago.

Kit enters and slips behind a decorative screen where she surveys the crowd, appraising the frosted lips and blushered cheeks of the other contestants with the wary eye of a Secret Service agent. The banquet room crackles with the murderous competitive urges of several dozen girls all pretending they're not competing.

"Who's supposed to be in charge here?" a petite redhead with too much foundation covering her freckles asks.

"Yeah, they said two o'clock. It's almost three-thirty."

A swell of peevish murmurs ripples through the room that stops dead when a smiling Ryukyuan woman, a hotel employee in a crisp white Dacron blouse and navy blue skirt, hurries in on quick little bird steps, accompanied by a barrel on legs that I assume is Far East Funnyman Bobby Moses. In a chrome-colored sharkskin suit, Bobby looks like one of the Rat Pack guys, Joey Bishop maybe, if Joey had been soaking in a vat of pickle juice for the past decade, wrinkling and swelling up to an enormous size. Bobby must weigh three hundred pounds, not counting the pinkie rings. His face is pasty beneath the telltale orange stain of a QT tan. His thin hair glistens with Brylcreem and has the uniform flat black that comes with one too many applications of Grecian Formula. Bobby mounts a low dais and the Ryukyuan woman rushes to pull up a chair. He surveys the crowd with the seigneurial eye of a Las Vegas Mafia don, beckons the woman to him, whispers in her ear. She nods several times and hurries to the edge of the dais.

"Today, no dance. Onaree give name." She forms the girls into a line and has them pass in front of Bobby Moses. The first girl carries a baton and looks about eleven. Without a word, Bobby motions her to move on. Next up is a heavy-legged girl with bleached hair and too much mascara. Bobby holds out a card that indicates she's made the preliminary cut. She takes it and skips happily out of the room.

The line has dwindled to less than half a dozen by the time Kit emerges from behind the screen, but her entrance has a dramatic effect.

The girl nearest me spots her and groans to her mother, "Oh, shit, Kit Root. Why did we even bother coming?"

Kit wears the look that our father calls "owning the place" as she saunters toward the dais. Knowing they are defeated before they even try, the remaining girls file meekly, swiftly, past Bobby Moses, who doesn't so much as glance at any of them before they scurry off like peasants making way for the queen.

I trail behind Kit as she steps onto the dais. A cloud of Brut cologne, Sen-Sen breath mints, Dial soap, and Right Guard deodorant envelops Bobby Moses. He seems to have the obsessive concern with hygiene of many fat men. His small nails have been buffed and coated in a clear polish. He hands Kit one of the cards that are passes to the official try-outs. Kit gifts him with a dazzling smile, but Bobby waves her on without changing his expression.

"What about her?" he asks as I pass by. Bobby Moses's voice doesn't sound as if it could have come out of his ponderous body. It is a speedy New York voice, punchy and quick.

"Her?" Kit asks, amused. "That's my sister. She's not entering."

"Why not?" Bobby asks. "You crippled, sis? You don't look crippled. Here, take a card."

"But she doesn't want to try out," Kit explains.

"You dance?"

I nod.

"You dance but don't speak, huh?"

"No, I do both."

"She dances and she speaks. This we don't know about the other ones. Here." Bobby holds a card out to me but hangs on to it when I try to take it and nods at my jeans and dashiki. "You're not going to wear the Mau-Mau threads when you try out?"

"No."

He turns the card loose. "Good. Time and address are on there. Try to look like a member of the female species." He makes his thumb and forefinger into a little gun, shoots me— *"Kyew"*—then heaves himself to his feet and sails out of the Kokusai banquet room.

"You're not actually going to try out, are you?" Kit's question is equal parts threat and statement of obvious assumption.

"What does it matter? It's not like our father would ever in a million years let either one of us go to Tokyo with Mr. Pinkie Ring there."

"I can handle Daddy."

"There is no way, Kit. Not even you are going to get him to agree to this."

Popcorn

At first, the concussion is absorbed into the dream I am having of being back aboard the S.S. *President Wilson* with the great boiler clanging next to my head and the ocean heaving below.

Then Bosco's hot breath on my face wakes me fully. "We're sinking!" She clutches my nightie, pulls me out of bed. "Jeane Dixon was right! The island is sinking!"

Kit stands at our high window. Her face is orange. It reflects a pillar of flame that ascends so high into the black night that the full moon is lost in the blaze. I remember the sign protesting nuclear bombs and imagine Kit's hair blown straight back, her bones glowing like a cartoon skeleton's. In the boys' room, Bob sobs.

The twins come in, Abner holding Bob. We all stand, silent, at the window. Down the hall, our parents' voices rise. The front door opens and a scream of sirens penetrates the concrete house. The door shuts and the thick concrete walls again muffle all sound. Moe comes into our room.

"Where's Daddy going?"

Moe lifts Bosco up without answering. My little sister's face is glazed with tears and snot, and she's gasping in hiccupy breaths.

"Is the island sinking? Are we all going to die?"

"No one in my family is going to die."

Moe sounds as sure as if she is explaining gravity, and for that moment I stop wondering about nuclear weapons. In the next instant, however, my mind fills and refills with the luxurious image of a mushroom cloud billowing out at the base of the column of fire, ballooning toward us with an opulent languor that will liquefy even our house of concrete. It seems inevitable. It seems like the obvious ending to the story that started when Moe struck the match that lit her first cigarette in Tunis.

"It's a plane. A plane blew up on takeoff, that's all. The men in the plane will be rescued. The fire will be put out."

"Where's Daddy?" Kit asks.

"He went down to the Flight Line."

"Why? Why does a Community Liaison Officer need to show up for something like this?"

"Everyone pitches in during an emergency," Moe answers.

"In other words you have no idea," Kit snipes. "As usual, you don't know anything."

"Eileen Root, that will be all. If you don't have anything constructive to contribute, you can keep your mouth shut."

"Was it a B-fifty-two that blew up?" Bosco asks. "Like the B-fifty-twos the protesters at Gate Three want us to get rid of? The ones with nuclear bombs?"

"No one said anything about nuclear bombs."

"No one says anything about anything on this island. They just do it."

Moe hears Bosco's voice teetering toward uncontrolled panic and asks, "Who's for Sticky?" It is part of my mother's alchemical omnipotence that she can transform sugar into an antidote to any crisis. Sticky, a Cracker Jack–like combination of popcorn, peanuts, and caramelized sugar, is her big gun.

"Bernie, you and the twins pop the corn. Bob? Bosco? Whaddaya say?"

It scares me that Moe is working so hard at being casual.

The smell of sugar melting, then caramelizing in the black cast-iron skillet calms us all. At just the right moment, Moe tosses in a pinch of baking soda and the clear sugar magma fizzes until it has foamed into an opaque syrup that she quickly drizzles over the popcorn Abner, Buzz, and I have waiting in a stainless steel bowl. Moe tosses in peanuts before the aggregate cools.

We take our treat outside to the patio, where we stand,

gazing fixedly at the fire as we chomp Sticky with a mechanized fervor.

"It's just as big as it was before," Bob says.

Moe laughs in a way meant to sound gentle and lighthearted. "Oh, no, Bob, it's lots smaller. They are definitely getting it under control." Moe stuffs several quick handfuls into her mouth and stares at the fire as she chews. "Definitely."

"Is Daddy down there?" Bob asks.

"No, he's not anywhere near the fire," Moe answers. "He's directing the whole operation with a walkie-talkie up in the control tower behind six inches of plate glass." The twins look at each other, impressed by the calm authority of our mother's lie.

"He's down there because of the nuclear bombs we're not supposed to have here, isn't he? That's what 'Community Liaison' means, doesn't it?" Who knows what combination of photographic filing of random comments led to Bosco's question, but one look at Moe's face tells us all that our mother believes the same thing.

"Did I ever tell you kids about the time Caroline and I made fudge with Audie Murphy?" Moe asks.

"Who's Aw Gee Mercy?"

"Twerp." Buzz cuts Bob off. "Only the biggest hero in all of War Two."

It gives me the creeps to hear my brother mimic my father's pilot talk.

"He was in that cool movie, *No Name on the Bullet.*"

"A movie star?" Kit displays a rare show of interest. "You knew a movie star?"

I can almost accept Bob not knowing this essential part of our mother's history, but Kit? She must be joking. How could she not know that our mother made fudge with Audie Murphy? Then I realize that all those mornings back in Japan with Fumiko when Moe told us stories about her time as a nurse in North Africa, Kit had been outside playing Elvis or Pharaoh or just leading her herd of adoring girl-horses around.

"Oh, Audie wasn't a movie star then. This was when the unit was still in Tunisia and the Battle of Sicily was raging."

A boom that could be a piece of plywood falling or the detonator bomb that will ignite a nuclear explosion sounds in the distance. Moe's eyes dart to the tower of flame. I imagine her hair swept back by a nuclear blast. I imagine all of us incinerated, transformed in the blink of an eye from Moe, Bernie, Kit, Abner, Buzz, Bosco, and Bob into stair-stepped skeletons.

Moe laughs. Her imitation of insouciant amusement is so convincing I believe for a moment that there is nothing to worry about. "My gosh, I haven't thought about this in years. We had a lot of Colonial troops on the ward—Senegalese, French Foreign Legionnaires—and I went to check on this one fellow. Senegalese. Black as tar. Big, strong fellow with those fearsome tribal scars slashed along his cheeks."

Moe's story has made Bosco forget about nuclear weapons. Bosco still watches the fire, but she is now seeing the scar-whelped face of Moe's patient in Tunisia.

"Moamar, I believe his name was. I went in there with a bed-pan because the poor guy had both his legs in traction and what do I find?" Moe trills a laugh. "Damned if old Moamar hasn't cut himself loose. All that traction that it had taken me hours to rig up was just hanging around him like yesterday's wash. 'Hey, Moamar,' I said to him. 'What gives?'

"Oh, what a sweet smile that man had. Maybe it was just his skin being so black made his teeth look so white, but the instant he smiled, I couldn't be mad at him. So he rattled away at me in French. Guess he thought that since I was white, I must savvy the lingo, but all I caught was 'Pee-*pee*, pee-*pee!*'"

Bob, helpless before any mention of bodily functions, chuckles maniacally.

"Moamar had cut himself loose so he could go outside and sprinkle the daisies! Never did find out how he managed that one, with compound fractures in both legs, but people who could sit through sandstorms like the ones we had that left an inch of grit *inside* your jar of cold cream with nothing but the burnoose on their backs to protect them—*well,* those are some tough customers."

"The movie star," Kit urges. "Get to the movie star."

"Right, right. Audie. Anyway, by the time I got back to the charge desk after stringing Moamar back up, I was bushed. I plopped myself down and was just finishing up the charts when this little face pokes around the corner. I swear, my first thought was, Who the heck let a Boy Scout onto the ward? Because that's what Audie looked like." Moe looks at her sons, at their Boy Scout faces, and her voice falters, the flirtatious perkiness leaks out, and she sounds tired again. "This big war hero just looked like a boy." She stares at her boys long enough for Buzz, Abner, and Bob to become self-conscious. "A little boy."

"Hey, look, it's going down!" Buzz points at the blaze.

"No, it's not, twerp. It just looks that way 'cause the sun's coming up."

"Can't you boys ever call each other anything but twerp or twink or dipshit?"

"Mmmm . . . queerbait?"

Clouds of black smoke envelop the bright flame. Abner reconsiders. "Look, it *is* going out."

"Or is it just that you're"—Buzz yanks Abner's running shorts down to his knees—"not paying attention!" Abner whirls around and traps his twin in a hammerhold. Buzz breaks free and lets rip with a samurai shriek. Abner answers by squatting into a sumo crouch. They lunge, each grabbing hold of the other's running shorts, locked like battling rams, cartwheeling down the long hill. Bob runs alongside them, jumping and hooting loud as a howler monkey.

"Boys! Come on now! Someone's going to get hurt!" Since Moe is laughing so hard that tears are running down her face, the twins grunt and shriek all the louder. Bosco studies Moe's face nervously, trying to decide whether to believe in the tears or the laughter.

Before Bosco can get fully frantic, Buzz yanks down her pajama bottoms. Both twins run down the long grassy hill, waving their hands above their heads, shrieking in a terrified falsetto, as Bosco and Bob run after them.

"What retards," Kit says, but even she is smiling. We watch the four youngest members of our family careen about like demented lunatics until the sun comes up enough for the other officers' families to see us, then we all go inside.

Tide

By the time the sun is fully up, the fire, from my vantage point in the girls' room, has been reduced to an oily smudge clouding the far horizon and our father is home. From the living room comes what sounds like a rusty nail being pulled out of dry wood—the sound of the metal legs of the ironing board when Moe opens it.

I wander out to the living room. Moe yanks a damp khaki uniform out of the bag she's taken from the refrigerator. She shakes a little extra water on it from a Coke bottle with a sprinkler top, then batters the fabric with the hot iron. A cloud of steam rises that smells of Tide detergent, warm cotton, and the sulfuric pinch of my mother's anger.

"You're gonna ruin it." Only when she speaks do I notice Kit lounging on the sofa in her shortie pajamas eating a Pop-Tart.

"Then you get your little butt over here and do it yourself." Moe holds up the steaming iron.

"You know I can't iron."

"Well, it's high time you learned."

Kit rolls her eyes. The hiss of the iron as Moe bangs it onto the uniform punctuates her fury.

"He's leaving?" I ask. I can hear the sound of the shower running.

"Apparently." Moe mists the pants with a long spray from the starch can.

"Where's he going?"

"You know just as much as I do." Moe irons in silence for a few minutes. The shower stops running. "Here." She holds the iron out to me. "I know *you* have mastered the mysterious art of ironing." Moe glares at Kit. Kit shakes her head at the painful predictability of it all. Moe looks at me, Kit looks away, and the history of our alliances is chronicled in three glances. Moe leaves.

A warm cloud of steam hisses into my face. The water in the iron burbles and sloshes.

From the bedroom comes the rare sound of our parents speaking directly to each other.

Kit snaps her fingers at me and orders, "Stop doing that." She sits upright on the couch, listening intently.

I rest the iron on the board until the hissing burbles stop and I can hear Moe ask my father where he is going. He answers in a testy voice, "As I said before, T, period—got that? Am I going too fast for you?"

"Mace, don't be like that," Moe warns, but my father goes on, acting as if he were speaking to a retarded person.

"D, period. Y, period. Temporary duty assignment."

Kit stands beside me to hear better.

"I know TDY, Mace. I want to know where and for how long."

"That's classified."

"Is it because of the plane blowing up? Are you going to SAC? Were there nuclear weapons? *Are* there nuclear weapons?"

"Classified. Classified. Classified. And classified. Any other bright questions?"

"Mace, for God's sake, you're leaving your children on this goddamned island. Should I try to get us emergency leave?"

"Emergency leave? Emergency leave! Why don't you just send Ho Chi Minh a nice note and alert him to *all* of our strategic circumstances? No one is getting emergency leave."

"Mace, maybe you don't care about me, but if you care about your children, tell me: Are we safe here?"

"I don't have time for this crap. I have to get back to the Flight Line. I've got a hop out of here in twenty minutes."

Zippers rasp in the silence that follows as he opens his flight bag.

"Bernadette! Front and center!" I almost tip the iron over in my haste to answer my father's call.

In the bedroom, my father is hefting his B-4 bag off their bed.

I can feel Moe's anger in the air. My father tosses me the keys to his Corvette. "You're on deck."

"Bernadette," Moe says, her voice tight, coming from deep in her chest. "Wait for your father outside."

I leave the bedroom but linger in the hallway. Moe's voice is so quiet, I have to stop breathing to hear her say, "Tell me this. Do you not tell me anything because of the Air Force or do you stay in the Air Force so you won't have to tell me anything?"

"I doubt I'll be back for the rest of the month."

"Christ, Mace. A month?" Moe's voice is shrill. "You're going to be gone for a month? Why?"

"If you must know, my dear"—he pronounces the words "my dear" as if he were really saying "you asshole"—"the civilians are involved now. Everyone from the Joint Committee on down. They're talking reversion. Giving the island back to our yellow brothers. They need their *Community Liaison Officer* to peace them off."

As annoyed and generally irritated as my father sounds, the depth of loathing in his voice when he pronounces his job title, Community Liaison Officer, takes my breath away.

I tiptoe out to the living room, where I find Kit, beaming.

"Did you hear that?" she whispers gleefully. "A month! I'll be back from Tokyo before he knows I've ever left. I told you I'd handle Daddy."

Wild Root Creme Oil

"You're riding the clutch! Stop riding the clutch!"

I don't know what impulse possessed my father to allow me to drive his Corvette other than he doesn't want to leave it at the Flight Line for the next month, and since Moe is too mad to drive and Kit had her license suspended, I'm his only choice. Sitting behind the wheel of my father's beloved car turns me from a mediocre to a criminally awful driver. I jerk my foot off the pedal. The Corvette hiccups forward and dies in front of the Base Dispensary.

Without a word, I get out and trade seats with my father. He taps the tachometer, talks to me about RPMs, and tells me which numbers to watch for when I shift. I can't remember the numbers for any longer than it takes me to nod my head, pretending I understand. The sound of the engine fills the silence after this lecture. I glance at my father, at his graying crew cut, and try to recall when he stopped oiling his hair and cut it so short. When he stopped resembling Dean Martin. All I can remember for sure is that his friends back at Yokota used to call him Wild Root, for Wild Root Creme Hair Oil. For a second I remember his squadron commander, Major Wingo. Major Wingo had a Corvette. He had it shipped over from the States for what Moe whispered to me was a ruinous amount. My father mentioned that Corvette, "Wingo's heap," every day. Each time the overseas gas caused its engine to ping or the Japanese roads tore hell out of the shocks, we would hear about it, but in a way that was both gloating and loving and told us how much our father yearned to have "a heap" just like Wingo's.

"So, who are these Damsels in Dissent?"

The breath turns to concrete in my throat. In one glance, my father tells me not to even consider lying.

"Um, a . . . sort of . . . antiwar group."

"Bernadette, answer one question for me, will you?"

"Yessir."

"Bernadette, tell me what I'm supposed to think when some butt-sniffer from OSI comes in and puts a folder on my desk detailing my oldest daughter's subversive activities?"

"Subver—!"

"Tell me what an officer of the United States Air Force who has given his life—*his life*—to the protection and defense of this country is supposed to think about that?"

"I don't know."

"You don't know. Well, then, Bernadette, answer me this. Do you know what they're going to think in Hanoi when they learn that the children of the officers of this country's military are protesting the war? Do you think they're going to believe that America is committed to this struggle? Do you think they're going to *hasten* to the negotiating table to end this war you, apparently, object to?"

"No. Probably not."

"No. Probably not. What exactly are you damsels dissenting?"

I would like to write an essay. I could write an essay on this topic. But speak? My father's majestically peeved tone stifles the futile words. I shrug, utterly miserable. "The war?"

"*The war?* I'd gotten the general impression that it was *the war*. What *precisely* about *the war* do you object to?"

It's that word "precisely" that stops me, makes me abandon hope. All I want now is for this conversation to be over. "I don't know."

"You don't know. Before a young woman who has been housed, clothed, and fed her entire life by the United States government criticizes that government, wouldn't you imagine she should have an exceptionally clear, an exceptionally *precise* idea, of what it is she's protesting?"

"Yessir. I guess, sir."

"Toward that end, I'm going to supply a few legitimate gripes to help you fill in the blanks a little. Containment, that was Curtis LeMay's big theory after War Two. No country in the history of the world has ever exercised such restraint. Contain, not conquer—that was the mission after the war. That was the mission of the Thirty-eighty-first in Yokota. Do you think Germany would have been content with that if they'd come out on top? Japan? No, we got a pretty good glimpse in Nanking, Singapore, the Philippines of just exactly how Japan celebrates victory. We were it, Bernadette. The glittering edge of America's sword. Look where it got us."

I am astonished by everything my father is saying, by the tone of regret he is saying it in, but mostly by the simple fact that he is saying it to me.

"Would you like some ideas about what you damsels might want to dissent? Try this. The Vietnam War is the only war in the history of man where enemy territory is sanctuary. Where we systematically bomb our allies into oblivion, while the enemy's country is off-limits. What genius thought up those 'rules of engagement'?"

My father doesn't care that I don't answer. He seems to have forgotten that I'm sitting next to him.

"No one's ever fought a war like this before, where you hand the enemy your ass on a platter, then have to snatch it away and hit him over the head with it. The numbnuts in Washington think we're going take Charlie apart with preannounced saturation raids. Nebber hoppen, number-one daughter. What none of them wants to hear is that the North Vietnamese have created the most impenetrable ground defense in history around Hanoi and Haiphong. Berlin? Vienna? Tokyo? Piece of cake compared to what Charlie's got.

"It's a parody of warfare. An expensive half-ass intervention in the wrong cause in the wrong country in the wrong part of the world. You want an example? We have to have visual contact to shoot the mothers and they're launching Atolls and SAMS at us from anywhere they goddamn care to."

My father gives a comradely gasp of exasperation now that we both agree on how ridiculous this war is.

"Here's the good news. Here's what you can go back to college and tell your peace-puke buddies: We're not actually killing many humans over there. That much I can guarantee them. You know what we should do? Yeah, get the Damsels working on this angle. Put them on pensions. Every mother-loving one of them. Pay every man, woman, and child in North Vietnam what—thirty thousand? Forty? Hell, pay 'em fifty thousand a year for life. It'll be cheaper than what we're doing now.

"Ike, here's what I liked about Eisenhower. When LeMay came to him saying the Bolsheviks were gonna crawl up our heinie if SAC didn't get all the B-fifty-twos they wanted, Ike told him to pound sand. That you can build thirty-five—*thirty-five!*—elementary schools for what one strategic bomber costs and that good schools were going to keep America a hell of a lot safer in the long run than B-frigging-fifty-twos."

The guard at the Flight Line waves us through with a crisper-than-average salute. We are routed far around the site where the plane blew up. A plume of black oily smoke marks the distant spot.

My father backs into a parking space beside a hangar and puts it in neutral, warning me, "I don't want the last sound I hear before I get on that bird to be my reverse gear getting stripped out." He reaches behind the front seat and pulls out a briefcase, his attention already on the men gathering in the Ready Room. "So, you going to do this? Get the Damsels working on this pension plan?"

The sound of my father joking comes back to me like a lullaby from childhood whose words I can no longer remember, and only the tune floating far back in my head proves that I ever really heard it. "Sure," I answer.

"I'm telling you. Fifty thou a year will be a bargain. Save us billions of dollars and the lives of untold young men who—" He pauses while the trembling roar of a departing jet vibrates the earth beneath us.

"Bernadette, if this FUBAR of a war is still going on then, tell your brothers—" He looks around guiltily and finishes starchily, his eyes avoiding mine. "Advise them of the procedure."

For a fraction of a second, I can't believe that my father has asked me to prep his sons on how to dodge the draft. I nod, afraid to answer, to reveal that I might have misunderstood.

"Help your mother while I'm gone. This has been a difficult adjustment for her."

"Yessir, I will, sir."

My father slams the door and walks away. Heat shimmers pouring off the concrete runway make his image wobble. I remember other flight lines, other times, and it suddenly seems odd to see my father walking toward a plane wearing his regular uniform and not the flight suit of a pilot.

Spic 'n' Span

I dig rock and roll music.

The worst of all the bad rocklike songs that are Okinawa's sound track wakes me. Through sleep-filmed eyes, I watch Kit gyrating in front of the mirror, dancing to the clock/radio. It is almost two in the afternoon. I wonder if I'm falling into Moe's lethargy. Kit has her shoulders hunched up around her ears and appears to be doing an impression of a hyperkinetic dwarf digging for something. Perhaps his chestful of treasure. Her face is even squinched into a pruney dwarf expression. As she throws wee shovelsful of imaginary dirt over her shoulder, I marvel, realizing that it *is* possible for my sister to look unattractive.

I groan and bury my head under the pillow. I am so grateful for the sound of an electric drill that obscures any further proclamations of Peter, Paul, and Mary's passion for rock and roll music that it takes me a moment to wonder who might be driving a hole into the concrete hallway.

I emerge just in time to face my equally sluggish brothers gaping in wonder as our mother hangs the last of the three framed fans that have sat on the floor for the past year.

"All hands on deck. We're gonna snap to today."

Overnight, Moe has shed the logy, dazed look she's worn the entire time I've been here. She has the manic energy peculiar to TDYs I remember from our time at Yokota, when my father left on his mysterious temporary duty assignments and Moe was in charge of our family for weeks, sometimes months, at a time. Seeing that old animation is startling. It is as if she's been lying in wait for our father to leave so she could take over again.

Moe barges into the girls' room, where Kit is practicing a

sporty pirouette to "These Boots Are Made for Walking." Kit sees Moe and groans. "Oh, no, not the bags."

Moe has a webbed belt buckled around her waist with six bread bags tucked under it. As she shakes Bosco awake with one hand, Moe plucks Daddy's nail clippers off of Kit's vanity with her free hand and drops them into a middle bag that already contains the cuticle scissors and a bottle of rubbing alcohol. Clearly the Bathroom Bag.

After we PCS'd out of Japan and Moe returned to an economy where a captain's wife could not afford domestic help, she developed the bag system. With a bag for every room looped around a belt at her waist, Moe went about her day returning the objects her six children and husband scattered throughout the house to their rightful spots. I am delighted to see the bags reemerge. As Bosco begs to be left alone, Moe scoops up the carrot peeler and a box of matches that Kit has been using to melt together the remnants of old lipsticks and dumps them in the Kitchen Bag.

"Man your battle stations. We're going through this house today like shit through a goose!" At the word "shit" Bosco pops her eyes at me and starts to understand that the normal rules are off. Manicure tools clanking against the carrot peeler, Moe strides down the hall, yelling at Bob and the twins to "Look alive! You boys are on yard detail. Let's get this place shaped up and then go have some fun!"

Out in the living room, Moe cranks up the hi-fi with her housecleaning battle anthem, Rosemary Clooney singing "Come On-a My House."

I am grinning when I catch Kit's eye. She is the only one old enough to remember TDYs past, since they ended abruptly after Japan. Our father's absences back then were odd little grace periods when we all took a vacation from being in the military. Once the house was cleaned, Moe might decide to borrow a projector from Base Supply and let us stay up all night to eat powdered sugar doughnuts and enjoy multiple viewings of what she considered the choicest of all TDY films, *Little Women*. Then we would sleep all the next day and have ice cream for dinner. On one of the last TDYs before we left Japan, Moe and Fumiko took me, Kit, the twins in their stroller, and Bosco in Moe's arms off on a trip that included a visit to the Kamakura Buddha, a glimpse of a bathtub made of pure gold in the shape of a fish, and the discovery that sweet potato tempura was the one Japanese food all of us would eat.

Though it's only been a few hours since our father left, the kitchen and living room are spotless and smell of Lysol. The washing machine and dryer both chug and whirl in the garage, and a warm cloud of Tide-perfumed air billows in. On the door of the refrigerator is a crisp new duty roster.

Everyone: Make bed. Gather/sort laundry. Police own area.
Abner: Mow and edge lawn. TODAY!!
Buzz: Fix window screens: TODAY!!
Bob: Put away army men: TODAY!!
Bosco: Clean bathroom: TODAY!!
Kit: Clean living room: TODAY!!
Bernie: Float.

"Float" is nurse talk, meaning that my jobs will never start and never end. Beneath that is another chart divided by days that tells who is on KP that night. This part ends with the warning NO COLORECTAL RESPONSE! which is more nurse talk for not disappearing into the bathroom as soon as it is time to do the dishes.

"Look alive in there!" Moe yells into the boys' room.

I grab the local Okinawa edition of *Stars and Stripes,* expecting the top half of the paper to be filled with a photo of the runway explosion, to read some explanation, no matter how lame, for what happened. But the fire that could be seen throughout the entire island is not mentioned anywhere. I switch on the radio.

This is Air Force Sergeant Alan Renfro, your Jock on the Rock here at Armed Forces Radio 650. The time at the tone will be fourteen hundred hours. BEEEEE. Skies are mostly clear with winds from the northeast at approximately ten knots an hour. Sounds to me like perfect weather for a . . . "Stoned Soul Picnic"!

I rush to turn the radio off but am contaminated by the opening lyrics.

Hurry on down for a stoned soul picnic—

I snap it off and leave to find the Spic 'n' Span.

Moe somehow infects Bob, Bosco, and the twins with that secret TDY clubhouse experience, and they dive into their chores without protest or recusing themselves to the bathroom. Only Kit is immune. Without asking permission, she disappears when the convertible of cool teens pulls up.

"Eileen Root, you get your fanny back in here!" Moe calls after Kit, but Kit sails on out to the waiting car as if she hasn't heard. "Oh, well, she doesn't know what fun she's missing," Moe says, dismissing her middle daughter.

A second later: "The egg man!" From the front window above the kitchen sink where she is scrubbing cockroach corpses out of the broiler, Moe spots an Okinawan man pulling a cart after him. He passes by our house. "Why isn't he stopping?"

"Because you're always asleep." Bosco always has the answer.

"I am not always asleep. I'm awake now, aren't I?" Moe grabs her purse.

"Moe, you can't go out like that!" Bosco yells, but Moe is already out the door. My little sister and the twins gather at the open door and watch as Moe runs out to stop the egg man. Across the street, a couple of wives and the tribe of redheaded children are in the front yard. The twins' faces tense as Moe slows when she sees the two women. They are both in shirtwaist dresses, hose, and polished flats, and their hair has been ratted and sprayed into dos that bubble up around their heads and flip at the ends. Moe is barefoot. The purplish ropes of her varicose veins pop out beneath the housecoat she wears under her belt of many bags. The wives and pale children glance up like baboons on the veldt at our mother's approach. Bosco and my brothers plaster themselves out of sight against the wall. Abner leans forward and jerks Bob, still standing at the open door in his Mighty Mouse underpants, back into the shadows. They wait and watch. Moe pulls her housecoat around herself and marches forward.

"Hey!" she calls out to the wives gawking at her unprecedented morning appearance. "The eggs any good today?"

Caught off guard, they stare at Moe as if they don't understand English.

"Eggu *ichi-ban!*" The egg man steps forward to reassure Moe, and she turns all her attention away from her fellow wives to the wizened man smiling in front of her.

"Well, then, give me two—no, make it three dozen. *San-ju-roku? Ne?*"

"*Hai! San-ju-roku!*"

"*Go-shobai-wa ikaga desu ka?*"

"*Arigato, kanari ii desu.*"

The wives go from staring to gaping at Moe as she converses with the egg man, whose smile bursts into a larger and larger grin with each word of Japanese our mother speaks. He plucks eggs from the baskets in his cart and wraps them artfully in cones of newspaper, a dozen to a cone, which Moe clasps to her bosom as she holds out her wallet for her new friend to take what he needs. There is a flurry of hand waving as Moe gestures for him to take more for his fine eggs and the egg man wipes away the offer.

"What's she saying?" Bosco asks me, when Moe's last comment in Japanese causes the egg man to beam even more broadly.

"How should I know?"

The egg man looks up at the wives to make certain they've heard before he bows deeply.

"I guess it was a compliment."

The egg man takes three eggs from his basket, balances a

bonus egg on top of each cone, and pulls his cart away, waving at Moe until he is out of sight.

"Fresh eggs," Moe says to the wives. "So much better than those old cold-storage things we get at the commissary, right?"

The wives nod, and Moe walks back to our house holding the eggs like Miss America cradling her red roses.

"When did you learn Japanese?" Buzz asks, as Moe fills the egg holders in the door of the refrigerator and mounds a bowl with the rest.

"We lived in the country for four years. Most of them on the economy."

"Yeah, but you never spoke Japanese before."

"Never needed to buy eggs before. Well, omelets tonight."

With Moe coaching Bosco through the art of tucking sheets into hospital corners and the twins turning Bob loose with a can of Pledge and a mandate to "rain liquid death" while they attack the lawn, we quickly achieve a level of hygiene adequate to avoid being RIF'd.

"Let's book on out of here," Moe says, snapping off her rubber gloves. The twins bounce their eyebrows up at each other, and I, too, wonder where our mother absorbed hipster GI talk.

In short order, we are coasting north on Highway One toward the less-developed end of the island. Moe is at the wheel. She swings her right arm out at every stop to protect Bob, in just the same way she's done with every child, always the youngest, who sat up front next to her. The convoys of military vehicles thin out as we leave the base behind until the view is nothing but green hills on our left and the Pacific Ocean on our right. Then the land narrows to a slender neck as we pass between the Philippine Sea and the East China Sea. The farther north we head toward the wild north end of the island the more jungly the hills become. The water beside us even shifts from a placid aqua to a white-frothed Prussian blue.

Bosco keeps looking out the window, then over at Moe; she cranes around to check on the twins relegated to the Way Back seats that face the rear window before she catches my eye and almost smiles. She exudes contentment. This is how the world is meant to be, riding in Frenchie beside water sparkling with sunlight, her mother at the wheel, laughing and singing. Even the twins seem to be holding their breath, not wanting to wreck the moment by giving each other monkey bumps or noogies or wedgies or X no-backs or he-who-smelt-it-dealt-its.

Moe starts to sing. At first I think it is my old friend "Mairzy Doats." But Bosco and Bob join in. Of course, Bosco has learned what the real words are, and I learn for the first time that mares eat oats and does eat oats and little lambs eat ivy.

"What's so funny?" Moe asks, glancing at me in her rearview.

"Nothing. I just never knew the real words before."

"Words aren't important as long as you get the tune right."

We pass a farmer riding a horse the size of a burro. His feet almost drag on the ground as he leads a water buffalo by the rope tied to a ring in its nose. Moe sticks her hand out the window and waves. Farther on, another farmer spreads sheaves of rice along a guardrail to dry. We all wave this time, and the farmer waves back.

In the courtyard of a red-tiled farmhouse set back from the road, half a dozen children in zoris play stickball. A Ryukyuan boy in a Cub Scout uniform complete with knee socks whacks a tennis ball with a two-by-four.

"Home-oo run-oo!" Bosco yells out the window.

"Home-oo run-oo!" the kids scream back at her.

Bosco leans back, very pleased with her communication.

The slender curving trunks of papaya trees heavy with green fruit clustered at their crowns run like the slats of a fence along the narrow road. We cross a bridge over a river gushing toward the ocean. Several Okinawan housewives have spread their washed clothes across a clump of sago palms. One of the women, so old she bears the faint blue traces of the old-style tribal tattoos, has her kimono top pulled down to her waist and is sloshing handfuls of water under her armpits and over her leathery breasts.

"I see she's not wearing a bra." I say it to test Moe. Her face lights up and she turns to Bob next to her on the front seat. "Take the wheel."

"Oh, boy!" Bob grabs the steering wheel.

"You're letting him drive?" Abner, alarmed, aggrieved, asks from the back. Moe squirms around, turtling both arms into her blouse.

Bob turns around to stick his tongue out at Abner and the car bumps off the road. I lunge forward to steer us back on. Moe pops her arms back out of her blouse. In her right hand is her Playtex long-line bra.

"Guh-*ross*!" the twins scream in unison.

"You said it, bebbies!" Moe laughs, tossing the big white bra out the window. It flutters behind us for a moment like a white bat before landing in some weeds beside the road. "The natives got it right." She catches my eye in the rearview. "*You* got it right, Bernie. It's too damned hot for all that cross-your-heart nonsense. Bosco, don't look so worried. The old gray mare isn't kicking over the traces, just adjusting her halter a little."

Although Bosco does look worried and even admonishes Moe to "give a hoot, don't pollute" and Buzz and Abner go on for miles about over-the-shoulder-boulder-holders and flopperstoppers, it is as if the instant Moe took her bra off, we could all breathe again.

"Bob, you are doing a beautiful job," Moe says to my little brother, who has kept his hand on the wheel even after Moe took over. "You can be my right-seat guy anytime." It's been a long time since I've heard the phrase "right-seat guy." That was who my father was, back in Japan, when he was copilot, the right-seat guy, for Major Wingo. A memory of Major Wingo brings back a handsome Nordic face. Curly blond hair. Mouth wide open, laughing, his arm around my father, who looks up to him. His nickname tickles my brain. Corny? Connie? The memory floats past.

One by one, the houses with red-tiled roofs and the fields of pineapple, sugarcane, and sweet potatoes disappear, and the hills close in on either side of the Oldsmobile. Fan palms, bamboo, scrubby pine, and banyan crowd in, their roots twisting like vines over everything, an insistent wall of green that casts the road into shadow.

We drive in silence until the low rumble of an American engine approaches coming the other way. A troop truck crests the rise we are climbing and bears down, head on, toward us. There is not enough room on the narrow road for two giant American vehicles. Moe pulls over. The squat olive-drab truck slows down as it nears us. The truck's windshield catches the sun and turns to a shield of polished silver. The canvas flaps are all up on the sides of the truck. Two rows of soldiers in camouflage, ten on each side, sit in the back. The truck creeps past us at a glacial speed. The soldiers on the side closer to us turn as they pass. Their faces are covered in a camouflage pattern that matches the caps on their heads, their lips painted black as panthers'. Sweat and streaks of muddy makeup darken circles around their necks. None of the soldiers smile. They look blank, exhausted. One soldier catches my eye and raises his hand in a peace signal.

"Lurps," Buzz whispers to Abner.

"No shit, Sherlock."

"They're Marines," Bosco whispers to me. "Long Range Reconnaissance Patrols. They do training maneuvers up there on the north end of the island where it's all jungle."

I nod. Moe stares for a long time after the truck as it rumbles south before she starts the engine and we bump back onto the road.

"You're in the boonies, now, cherry!" Buzz whispers to Abner in a creepy redneck twang. "Hell, yes, soldier. You're in-country. You got your flak jacket on? Take your weapon off safety, maggot."

"Yessir, sarge, sir." Abner plays along, nodding, eyes wide with new-recruit terror as Buzz fishes one of Kit's batons out of the clutter on the car floor and thrusts it into his twin's hands.

"You got the M-sixty, grunthead. Remember, bursts of three."

The twins go into their alternate reality. Abner braces the baton out in front of him and pretends to cover the countryside.

"Left! Eleven o'clock!" Buzz shrieks. "Gear in on him!" Spit flying, Abner jerks off an imaginary round of machine gun fire on the baton.

"Ammo up!" Abner cries.

Buzz digs a roll of paper towels out of the bag of picnic supplies and Abner feeds this "ammo belt" into the baton.

"Call in the Eighty-Mike-Mikes!"

"Send in Willie Pete!"

"White phosphorus launched!"

"Frag the Second Louie!"

"Wasted him!"

"Righteous, my man!"

"You smoked Charlie!"

Moe slams on the brakes so hard the drums lock and squeal and Bosco and I slide forward off the vinyl seats. Moe has her arm out, blocking Bob from hitting the dash. She stops dead, swivels around, and fixes the twins with a death glare.

"Was that"—she gestures toward the truck, disappearing over a hill—"was that a joke to you boys? Do you think that is all a *joke*? Did any of those *boys* in that truck look like *they* think it's a joke?" Moe, breathing hard, continues to glare at them until Abner lowers the baton.

Both twins face out the back window. Abner mutters, "Jeez, you don't need to freak out. We were just goofing around."

"Look at me when you talk to me! *Look at me!*"

Hissing gasps of exasperation, they both turn back around.

"Never, ever joke about . . . about *that* again. Do you understand me? . . . Do you *understand* me!"

"Yes, ma'am."

There is a long moment of silence that Bob breaks. "I like the jungle," he observes idly.

"That's because you don't know a goddamned thing about the jungle, Bob."

We dart glances back and forth at Moe's solemn swearing.

Moe turns the station wagon around and we head back, our outing over. A few miles later the twins are happily pounding and poking one another again. Bosco and I remain silent, Bosco searching the horizon ahead for the calamities she is certain wait to overtake her family.

Mildew

$\mathcal{M}$oe's mood doesn't brighten until we are spinning along the coast again. Buzz and Abner pull out Kit's baton and, holding it out of Moe's sight, lay down covering fire as we are swept into the traffic jam that is Highway One.

Back at Kadena, the knot of demonstrators at Gate Three has swollen by several hundred. The new protesters are not the polite suit-jacketed crowd that was there the other day. A Japanese man in Trotsky glasses, his hair in a spiky brush cut, marches back and forth in front of the demonstrators, yelling into a bullhorn and beating his fist in the air in time with his message. Like many of the other new demonstrators, he has a look of pasty-faced fanaticism that I recognize from the ringleaders of the protest movement at college. This time many of the signs are in English.

NUCLEAR NO! U.S. BASE GO! U.S. DISMISS B52S FROM OKINAWA.

"Do you think they mean 'remove'?" Bosco asks.

Moe tries to edge Frenchie through the crowd that has surrounded our car, but the protesters abruptly link arms and slide in front of us in snaking, zigzagging rows. The man on the bullhorn continues ranting, his voice cracking now with hysteria.

"Moe?" I ask, as the crowd swarms around us, the windows becoming a shark tank with wet mouths and greasy foreheads smashing against the glass. Demonstrators pound on the back window.

"Mom!" Bob's shoulders pull up to his ears with each breath he sucks in. "Mom, are they going to hurt us?"

"No one is going to hurt us, Bob. Now calm down, you'll make your asthma flare up." She rolls down the window. Dark heads press into the opening, and I lunge over the seat and grab her hand.

"What are you doing? You can't!"

"Bernie, don't be a ninny. Most of these people appear to be from Tokyo. Japanese are only dangerous to strangers. All we've got to do is to stop being strangers." With an iron grip, she rolls down the window enough to speak out. *"Mihnasan, konnichiwa."* Her voice takes on a ridiculously high, childlike, fluting quality and sounds exactly the way it did when she would make Fumiko and I laugh with her imitation of the way Fumiko spoke when we first met her. *"Ii o-tenki desu, ne."*

The demonstrators back away from the car.

Moe bows her head and extends a cranelike arm out toward the gate with a grace that recalls Fumiko welcoming us into the little house in Fussa. *"Ima itte mo ii desu ka?"*

The ringleader with the bullhorn bows and clears protesters out of the way. Smiling and bowing her head, eyes downcast, Moe drives through the gate.

Abner and Buzz watch the demonstrators bowing good-byes.

"That was weird," Abner observes.

"That was very weird," Buzz agrees.

On-base, we move from a chaotic, congested world crowded with small vehicles and small people into a world where armored personnel carriers and broad-beamed six-footers roam an orderly, expansive landscape of boulevards, runways, and fields, most of them ringed with white-painted rocks.

Among the most expansive of the many rolling spaces on-base is the parade ground. This afternoon, however, it is packed with people and booths. A banner fluttering above it all reads KADENA KARNIVAL: 23 YEARS OF RYUKYUAN-AMERICAN FRIENDSHIP.

"That wasn't here when we left, was it?" I ask.

Bosco, her sleeve pulled up over her hand, continues rubbing her window even though the smudges are on the outside. "Oh, they have one every time there's a big demonstration."

"Can we go, Mom? Can we? Can we?" Bob whines, his terror at the gate already forgotten.

"Bob, we went the last four times they had a carnival."

"Yeah, but I was little then and my memory doesn't go that far back."

"Come on, Mom."

A general pro-carnival movement sweeps the car.

"Aw, what the hell," Moe announces, with typical TDY spontaneity.

An Okinawan woman wearing a yellow hard hat several sizes too small waves us into a portion of the parade ground that has been turned into a parking lot.

As we walk to the carnival a half-track tank rumbles past carrying a wagon lined with hay and loaded with kids. Three Ryukyuan children in sun hats that frame their round faces like wilted petals wave at their parents, taking photos at the side. The rest of the passengers are American kids, mostly occupied with stuffing hay down one another's backs.

"Hey, I wanna ride!"

"We gotta get tickets."

Moe transforms all the cash in her purse into loops of tickets. The twins snag several coils and, with Bob running after them, disappear in the direction of booths where other gangs of boys are hurling hardballs at lead-bottomed Coke bottles and popping off balloons with BB guns.

"I'm good at this." Moe and I follow Bosco as she runs toward a booth with a moatful of plastic carp sluicing around it. Moe trades tickets for a fishing pole and Bosco starts angling. Pole clasped in both hands, she swings the hook at the end of her pole in incremental twitches as the carp rush past, missing each time. Five tickets later, she hooks a fish and wins the Asian version of a Kewpie doll, a pink-cheeked, red-lipped nymph with a wave of molded-plastic hair cresting above her bulging forehead. Bosco is delighted. "I told you I was good at that."

The window of the concession booth is covered with hand-lettered signs reading: FRY CHIKEN $1. FRY FRENCH 50 CENTS. YAKITORI $1. YAKISOBA $1. SPAGHETI $1. SQUID $1. My squid ends up being the best of the items we sample, although Bosco, with a decided predilection for the noncrispy, is quite happy with flabby fries drowned in watered-down ketchup.

I wonder what the Damsels would think of me, circling a parade ground in a hay wagon pulled by a tank while I slurp a Coke and snitch French fries as a Marine band plays Sousa marches in the distance. It is Americana in a concentration known to few who have not experienced the overseas military base.

We hop off at a remote corner of the grounds where military vehicles have been pressed into service as carnival rides. A decommissioned jet rests on the back of a trailer that a serviceman drives back and forth, creating, no doubt, the impression that the boy within is piloting a Winnebago with bad brakes. Grenade launchers have been modified for the event, and for two tickets a child can hurl a pineapple into the pulpy mass already fermenting at the end of the field.

"Oh, my God!" A stricken look comes over Moe's face and she sprints toward another field where a Huey churns the parade-ground dust into a small tornado as it hovers overhead. A crew of Green Berets straps half a dozen kids into rescue harnesses dangling from the helicopter. On a signal from one of the Green Berets, it ascends and circles over the grounds. The kids waiting surge forward, jockeying for a better position in line for this most coveted of all rides. Elbowing their way most forcefully are the twins. Moe jerks them out of line just as a Green Beret points magic fingers in their direction.

"But Mo-om, we're next!"

"Next to be dangled like feed sacks from a helicopter? Not while I'm alive, buddy!"

Back at the "midway," the twins and Bob win a couple dozen Kewpies and turn them all over to Bosco, which makes her ecstatic. With no current means of bringing home all A's, Bosco needs other ways of keeping score. "I'm the girl at Kadena Elementary with the most Kewpies of anyone." Moe buys us all Byerley sodas from a local bottler. The outsides of the glass bottles are powdery from overuse. My diet cola has the delicious hypersweetness of the cyclamates now under suspicion back in the States.

For no apparent reason, Abner snatches Bob's drink away. Abner and Buzz pass it back and forth, taking sips until the soda is almost gone and Bob is mad with impotent fury, at which point he launches himself at Abner, a tornado of skinny flailing arms. Abner holds him away with one arm and casually finishes his soda with the other. Spit flies from between Bob's clenched teeth, his face red and sweating.

"Abner!" Moe yells. "Let your brother hit you before he has a heart attack."

Abner releases Bob. "Give it your best shot, twerp."

Bob winds up like all his cartoon heroes. "This one's coming out of Kentucky, sucker, and it's got your name on it!" Bob lands his puny punch in the middle of Abner's muscled chest and Abner drops like a sack of concrete. Bob cackles with glee.

"Thank you," Moe tells Abner, who is twitching very realistically on the ground.

Around a corner from the booths are the sideshow attractions, all run by locals. Bob drags us into a crowd gathering in front of a low stage. Two speakers the size of shoe boxes broadcast a tape of tinny-sounding Okinawan music. A samisen-like instrument plunks in the background as a singer screeches. An Okinawan man in a tattered, iridescent, electric-blue jacket and an Elvis-style pompadour bounds onstage and picks up the microphone that has been resting near the tape player.

"Wear comb! Wear comb!" It takes a second to process what I've taken to be a very curious personal grooming tip and adjust for the lack of the letter *L* in this part of the world.

"Prease to wear comb my rovery assistant." He swings an arm out to the back of the stage where an Okinawan girl in a sequined bikini, her long black hair pulled up into a ponytail on top of her head, teeters up the steps. She has the chunky, muscular build of a teenage gymnast and, in spite of her waist-free prepubescent figure, the unmistakable air of a working girl with one too many nights on the streets of Koza.

We clap mechanically.

"Take it off! Take it off!" A clump of GIs in slacks and plaid shirts hoots and whistles. Lovely Assistant drops into a crotch squat and squirms around a bit, perched on the tops of her heels. The GIs go wild. Abner and Buzz glance at each other, embarrassed, mesmerized. Moe's eyebrows furrow as she ponders whether she needs to take maternal action and drag her young children away.

The assistant springs back up and wobbles to a basket of Ping-Pong balls at the edge of the stage while Okinawa Elvis puts the microphone back down next to the tape player so we can all enjoy more samisen music played at Conelrad alarm volume. He claps, grunts out a loud "Hah!" and Lovely Assistant begins firing Ping-Pong balls, which he catches in his wide mouth and taps in until his cheeks bulge with half a dozen balls. With much eye-popping and bobbing of the Adam's apple, he "swallows" the balls and his cheeks deflate. A few seconds later, in obvious alimentary distress, Okinawa Elvis dashes from one end of the stage to the other, frantically searching for a private corner. Throwing his hands up in hopeless resignation, he squats down and proceeds into an orgy of red-faced grunting and straining that leaves the twins hanging on to each other, crippled with laughter. Bob is even more amused. Moe has her hand pressed against her mouth, stifling a smile while shaking her head with maternal disapproval. Bosco watches, worried, as if she is going to be required to administer CPR or the Heimlich maneuver or, in some way, rescue someone.

Finally, Elvis bops himself a good one in the pompadour and, like a chicken laying an egg, a white Ping-Pong ball pops out. Bob is now beyond delirious, beating on Moe, who laughs openly with him. With a rapid succession of knocks on the pompadour Elvis poops out the rest of the balls and holds them over his head.

"Look, look." Bosco tugs on my sleeve and points. "He spit the balls into his sleeve before he held his arm up."

"No kidding, Bosk. You mean the guy didn't actually eat and shit out six Ping-Pong balls?"

Ka-ching! Ka-ching!

Onstage, Elvis swings a waist-high machete about, clanging it to great effect against the power pole next to the stage. Lovely Assistant rolls out a round chopping block the size of an ox-cart wheel, drops it in the center of the stage, and carefully positions a yellow Okinawan watermelon at its center. She steps aside and pivots on her high heels several times, as she gestures toward the melon and then toward her machete-swinging boss. With stylized movements and expressions that recall the thundering stomps of sumo wrestlers and the tooth-baring grimaces of Kabuki actors, Elvis raises his machete. The next instant seems to disappear because no one sees the machete descend, no one hears the slurpy *thump* of the melon being split open; the canary-colored fruit simply rocks open without being touched.

"Wow." The twins' jaws drop in unison.

"He didn't even touch it," Bob mutters.

"He did too. He just did it really fast and the knife is really sharp. Big deal. He sliced open a watermelon."

"Bosco, you think you know everything. You don't know everything. He could split your head with that machete."

"Oh, big accomplishment."

"Eat me, twerp. Oh, man, what is he doing now?"

With the same lightning strokes, Elvis hacks the melon into pieces, which Lovely Assistant hands out to the crowd. Abner snags a piece and passes it to Moe. All the melon gone, Lovely Assistant lies down on the chopping block, holding another melon on her bare stomach. Elvis shreds a silk scarf, raining down filaments of pink and white on her upturned face to show how sharp the blade is.

"Ewww," Moe whispers to me. "I think I'd seek another line of work."

Screaming a strangled Kabuki shriek, Elvis rears back with

the machete, swings forward, and stops. He does it several more times, like a man splitting kindling homing in on his target. With each aborted chop, the crowd grows tenser. Finally, a mighty *banzai!* and the melon splits into two perfect halves. Lovely Assistant bounces up, not a scratch on her firm belly.

As Elvis and the assistant steeple their hands in a victory arch above their heads, another Ryukyuan woman comes onstage. Wild and tribal, she reminds me of the old woman we saw bathing in the stream today. The bikini bottom beneath her stretch-marked Buddha tummy seems like a loincloth, the top sagging beneath her deflated breasts an odd accoutrement as optional as the snake-fang necklace hanging above it. Her brown arms and ankles are cross-hatched with scars that make me think of the pineapple pickers and their curved knives. Draped around the woman's shoulders is a small python.

Elvis holds Lovely Assistant's hand as she totters down the steps. The python rouses itself and undulates across the older woman's collarbones, slithering under her armpit in a stream of ductile motion.

"Prease to wear-comb Mama-san!"

A smatter of puzzled applause.

"Bring back the LBFM with the melons!" The GIs crowd around and slam shoulders into their witty buddy. The twins, pleased to get the melons part, laugh. Bob laughs for his own reasons entirely.

"What's an LBFM?" Bosco asks. I shrug.

The microphone squawks. "Mama-san know all ancient art Okinawa. Mama-san make snake magic!" He holds his arm out in an I-give-you motion. *"Mama-san!"*

Mama-san walks to the center of the stage with a splay-footed gait, her thick bare toes prehensile as they grip the plywood boards, the python surging around her belly. The GIs whoop when it detours south, coiling around her crotch.

"Is this really something you kids should be watching?" Moe asks.

"Yes!" Bob yells back, unable to take his eyes off the snake. "This is science, Mom."

"There are no bikinis in science," Bosco informs him sternly.

Mama-san tries to take the microphone, but Elvis won't relinquish it, so she pulls his hand to her mouth and chatters away in a Ryukyuan dialect no one seems to understand except for the announcer, who jerks the mike back. Mama-san, the python now hobbling her ankles, toddles after him, her stream of Ryukyuan punctuated by a series of pelvic thrusts. No one, least of all the guffawing GIs, needs a simultaneous translation. Eyes creased with delight, Mama-san grins broadly at their bawdy *har-hars*, opening a dark, toothless hole.

Elvis, jealous of her cheap laughs, puts the mike back down next to the tape player. Mama-san sways along to the plinking, screeching music. Waggling her butt lasciviously, she reaches down between her legs, grabs the python behind its head, and drags it up to her face. The snake flicks its tongue over her face. Mama-san holds the python's head to her lips and kisses it. The GIs groan. She starts licking the reticulated head, then, abruptly, astonishingly, she stuffs it into her mouth.

The groans turn to enthusiastic cheers. "Whoo! Whoo! Mama-san numboo one! Numboo one!" They imitate the baby talk of the Koza bar girls.

Mama-san's face resembles a picture in a schoolbook of an astronaut being subjected to G-forces that turn lips and mouths into rubber. The snake's thick body protrudes from her mouth and hangs slackly as if it has gone into hibernation. She holds its long body in her hands. I can hear the effort of her sucking breath through her nose with the snake pressed against it.

"Take it all, baby!"

"Up to the hilt, Mama-san!"

Behind us, one of the local girls with the GIs announces, "You gotta take me back. I work now."

"Naw, you short time stay me."

"I stay you gotta pay bar fine."

"I ain't payin' no fuckin' bar fine."

At the F word, Moe starts herding Bob and Bosco away. "Okay, kids, come on, let's go. This show is over." All of us except Bosco walk with our heads turned back to watch Mama-san as she slides the snake in and out of her mouth.

"Okinawans have big mouths," Bob concludes.

Abner whacks him and dances away. "You got a big mouth, dipshit."

Bob charges after Abner, with Buzz darting in and out, smacking them both and yelling his zombie battle cry, "Hasten demise!"

Bosco watches her brothers. "Boys are such savages. Their muscles won't leave them alone."

I'm gonna wait till the midnight hour.

"Oh, my God, what is that?" I ask. What it is is the first non-sanitized music I've heard since arriving. I drag Moe and Bosco toward it. Wilson Pickett's first-line promise has magnetized every black serviceman in the area, and we join the stampede rushing past the ring toss and fishing pond, heading toward a stage set up at the end of the line of booths. A sign on the drum kit announces that the band is the Tomadachis.

"It means 'friends' in Okinawan," Bosco informs me.

The singer is a handsome kid, half black, half Okinawan, who has plucked the best from both gene pools, including straight black hair and a growling vibrato. He has three high school buddies backing him up, and they are thrashing "Midnight Hour." I break into a little backup-singer line-dance action, a few hand rolls garnished with a cuff-link adjustment at each end.

"The wicked Pickett," the singer announces as the guitarist hits the final chord. His accent is a seductive blend of singsong Okinawan and gutbucket soul. "He's the king of them all, y'all."

Nah-nah-nah-nah-nah.

I squeal and punch Bosco. "All *right*! 'Land of a Thousand Dances.' Dance pop quiz."

When the singer tells us that we gotta know how to pony like phoney moroney, I make Bosco high-trot along with me like we've just stepped off the set of *Hullabaloo* or *Shivaree,* the essential dance primer shows of the mid-sixties. Then I show her how to snap her spine when the singer orders us to "do that Jerk." A couple of black GIs step in front of us, and we all Watusi like his little Lucy, hey!

By this time the singer is feeling pretty good, y'all; he's spotted us and starts throwing out every dance he's ever heard of: Twist. Frug. Pearl. Hully-Gully. Alligator. The Skate. Shingaling. Stroll. Slop. The Boogaloo. Dirty Dog. He orders us through everything except a minuet. What moves I don't know from my devotional viewing of *Shivaree* and *Hullabaloo* and a lifetime of hovering at the edges of Teen Club dances, one of the black guys does. Whoever gets it first models for Bosco and me, and we mirror the motions. Dancers around us pick up on our minimarathon, and the GIs and their Koza dates Jerk and Boogaloo along with us as we survey a compendium of how America's young move.

Nah-nah-nah-nah-nah-nah-nah-nah-nah-nah-nah-nah-nah-nah-nah.

*Nah-nah-nah-*NAH*!*

The Tomadachis work with the crowd, going into an even longer extended version of Cannibal & the Headhunters' ode to kinetic ecstasy. As always happens when the music is good and the beat insistent enough, I am set free from my usual prison of self-consciousness, and everyone within a 360-degree radius becomes a partner. I dance with a Koza bar girl, a Kubasaki high school kid with acne and a big Adam's apple, a good-looking GI in baggy Hawaiian-print shorts, and several black servicemen.

You gotta know how to Monkey like funky barunkee.

I grin back at the singer, who laughs with us at his idiotic improvisation, and drop into a deep-bobbing Monkey, climbing the vine with ferocious arm swings that Moe clucks and smiles at. Just to make her laugh even more, I break into an impersonation of Lovely Assistant complete with an excessively low crotch drop.

"You are wicked." Moe can barely contain herself. I pivot

away so she can fully appreciate my backfield in motion and come face-to-face with Kit. Her white shorts, white teeth, and sleeveless yellow ribbed T-shirt set off her tan to perfection. Her hair, pulled back with a broad white ribbon like Alice in Wonderland, flips up perfectly at the ends. The rest of her crowd of half a dozen or so in polo shirts and Weejun penny loafers exudes, though to a lesser degree, Kit's aura of blond American perfection.

I am at the bottom of the vine, my butt almost scraping the packed earth of the parade grounds, just starting my monkey climb back up the vine, when Kit spots me. Surprised, Kit doesn't hide behind her usual disdain. In her look is crystallized so nakedly all her thwarted longing for a normal family, a normal big sister, that I too am caught off guard and can't respond with my usual dismissal. She turns away before her friends can associate her with what I suddenly realize is a crude copulatory performance. I straighten up slowly, disconnected utterly from the music, and walk away until it sounds as tinny as the samisen plinkings coming from the other end of the midway.

"Bernie! Bernie, wait up!"

Bosco, Moe trailing her, runs toward me.

"Why'd you leave?"

I shrug.

Kit and her crowd have taken our places, closed their magic circle, and are reprising the "Land of 1,000 Dances" catalog, except that Kit renders each one a bit too literally. For the Pony, Kit appears to be, once again, the leader of the wild horses, stomping and pawing at the ground, pausing to toss her hair from side to side and sniff the air. Her Monkey involves armpit-scratching and some bowlegged staggering. Her Skate brings Hans Brinker to mind. Her Mashed Potatoes is an enigmatic tribute to the tuber. But the Jerk. Kit's Jerk is another dimension.

Bosco's eyebrows crease farther and farther down as she watches. "She looks like she's being electrocuted."

"Don't make remarks about your sister," Moe orders sternly. But when Kit launches into a pantomime of the death of a killer robot, Moe is startled into a burp of laughter that she corks quickly with her hand. "You couldn't say that rhythm is Kit's big gift in life."

"Bernie is our family's dancer." Bosco parrots the party line loyally. We watch silently as Kit Boogaloos down Broadway as if a sea chantey were playing in her head. "You're tons better than she is."

Still in some obscure pirate mode, Kit takes to hopping around as if she had a peg leg. The boys in the penny loafers and crew cuts gaze adoringly. The girls copy her moves even as she segues into an imitation of a hay baler.

"You know what, Bosk? It really doesn't make any difference. It never has. Never will."

Moe stares hard at me. "Bernadette Marie Root, don't say that."

"It's the truth, Moe. It doesn't bother me. It's just true that Kit is beautiful, and it's true that beauty'll get you a lot more places in this life than a sense of rhythm, and one of those places is going to be an all-expense-paid trip to Tokyo, and that's just how it is. I really don't care, but I have had about enough of Kadena Karnival."

We run into the boys, standing in a long line outside a large surplus tent old enough to have been used during the invasion of the island. A handmade sign over the entrance flaps reads OKI-NAWA AMINALS.

"Come on," I call out, "we're going home."

Bob becomes the emblem of seven-year-old outrage. "No! We'll lose our place in line. I want to see the aminals!"

They all glower at me and look to Moe to intercede. She does. "Come on, Bern, let's see the aminals."

Two airmen in khakis raise the flap. "Next ten." To the grumbling of those behind us in line, we take cuts and meld with the group ducking their heads to enter the tent. The air inside is stifling and smells of mildew, canvas, hay, and manure. A string of bare bulbs lights the tent, which is actually a series of tents strung together.

"Look!" Bosco calls out, gazing at a pen. "A rare Kerama deer."

The creature is inexpressibly lovely, a sort of fairy deer about the size of a small Afghan hound. Her big-eyed face comes to a delicate point in a nose she twitches at us with what Bosco interprets to be a plea for rescue.

I leave Moe with Bosco, who is begging her to figure out a way to buy the deer away from its cruel owner. "I could keep her with Hickory," Bosco pleads.

The boys are in the next tent crowded around an exhibit of banana spiders the size of dinner plates, centipedes big as pull toys, and some more than usually monstrous cockroaches. Several tanks contain lionfish, sea snakes, stonefish.

"Which one'd kill you more deader?" Bob wonders. "Do you think a banana spider could beat a sea snake?"

"No, twerp, it'd drown."

"But if it *could* breathe underwater."

"Bosco?" Abner looks to his sister for a definitive ruling.

Bosco steps up and takes the kind of deep breath that is always a preamble to her reeling out something from the photo memory vault. "Sea snakes inject a neurotoxin that can paralyze a one-hundred-and-sixty-pound man within twenty minutes, leading to a cessation of all autonomic responses and thus to death. So, yes, I think we can safely assume that a sea snake could beat a banana spider. But the most deadly of them all is the stonefish, whose barbed scales inject an even more potent poison."

"We should dig a moat around Kubasaki Junior High and fill it with stonefish and sea snakes."

"Yeah," Abner agrees with his twin. "Then milk the venom from the sea snakes and get a blow gun and shoot darts at Kevin McCloskey and Deirdre Simons—"

"—and Andy McGrath—"

"—Dwight Levitz—"

"—and the whole football team—"

"—and Andrea Sue Deeks—"

"—and the whole pep squad—"

"—and Mr. Pentinotti—"

They gaze at the deadly fish with the deep, homicidal longing that flowers so extravagantly in the unpopular twelve-year-old boy, until a new influx of customers surges into the tent and we are all squeezed into the next section.

This tent is larger than the others but even hotter and has a different smell, a smell of unwashed bodies and a sharper, more acrid odor I can't identify. A bass rumble of male voices spiked with staccato notes of Okinawan fills the crowded tent.

"I can't see!" Bob's high, piping complaint slices through the thrum of harsh voices.

"Hey, the kid can't see."

The mass of khaki and olive drab parts and Bob strolls through, with Moe pushing us all ahead so she can stay with her youngest child.

"Ma'am." A GI who looks barely older than the twins bobs his head to Moe. She smiles sweetly at him and he strong-arms some of his buddies out of our way. We are pushed to the edge of a large round Plexiglas enclosure with a divider down the middle raised to chest height on a plywood platform. Sitting on either side of the divider in the enclosure is a wooden case with one side hinged and snapped shut. The young American men and older Okinawans close back in, crushing us toward the platform. A local man with a broad white sweatband pushing his spiky hair back into a jagged crest passes among the GIs who tower over him. They slap money into the man's hand, and he scribbles frantically on a small pad.

Moe squeezes in next to me. "What is it? What's the exhibit?"

"Got me. GIs with bad haircuts?"

Bob stands on tiptoe, searching the enclosure, empty except for the wooden boxes. "Hey! This is a gyp! Where's the deadly animals?"

The crowd guffaws. Some of the GIs look at Bob as if they might have cute little brothers back home that they miss. The Okinawan man in the headband springs up onto the platform elevating the Plexiglas enclosure and snatches bills held above our heads from the men behind us. When he has collected them all, he smiles warmly at Bob.

"You want see deadree animar?"

Bob nods enthusiastically, beaming as the crowd claps and holds up bottles of Orion beer to toast him.

"You want see deadree animar?" the man asks the entire crowd this time, and we all scream back, "Yes," my family pleased that everyone thinks our little brother is cute.

"Big sister, I didn't expect to see you here." The voice is so close to my ear I feel each warm breath the words are carried on. It is Ron, the OSI guy from the cave. Kit stands behind him, her eyes avoiding mine. Ron's grin is satisfied, as though he knows all the secrets I have now and all the secrets I will ever have in the future. "How come you ain't come back to visit me? I promise you, big sister, you *want* ol' Ron to like you. Ask Kit here, she tell you." His fake black accent gives me the creeps.

"You're too late, Ron. My father already knows everything."

"I know that. Knew it all along." He leans in close to me so that Kit cannot hear. "Not *you* we got to worry about now, is it?" I pretend I don't know that he's talking about Kit. That Kit is the one we have to worry about.

"You want see deadree animar?" the sweat-banded man in the center of the ring asks a third time.

The crowd roars again.

"Okay. Okay." The Okinawan raises his hands, palms up, above his head, pretending to be beleaguered.

Ron strokes my neck as if he were gentling a high-strung horse. "You wanna see some deadly animals, come see me, big sister."

I swat his hand away. He laughs.

The man inside the ring straddles the divider and walks to the wooden cases. A scribble of claws scratching on wood comes from one box. The man leans down and reaches each of his hands out toward the latch on each box, pauses, and leans down toward Bob. "This whuh you wan? This whuh you get."

The edge of menace in his voice alarms Bob, who turns to Moe. She squeezes past the men pressing in on us and pulls Bob close as the crowd howls for the man to get on with the show.

Just as Moe turns to me to say, "I don't like this," the man flips the door latches on both boxes and lifts them up. A snake lands in a writhing clump on one side of the divider. On the other side a streak of fur, claws, and teeth coalesces into an animal with a thick brownish-black coat that is part ferret, part weasel, and part cat.

The tender jumps out of the enclosure.

The snake spirals into an upright coil. A small hood swells on either side of its head.

"Habu! Habu! Habu!" The men pick up the cheer.

The frenzied animal on the other side of the Plexiglas divider moves like quicksilver, tacking frantically about in front of the snake.

"Mongoose! Mongoose! Mongoose!" This cheer is much louder.

At the same instant, Moe and I realize what is happening. She grips Bob. "Where's Bosco?" I glance down to where my sister was standing a moment ago. She's gone. Ron is grinning behind me. I elbow my way past him but still can't find Bosco.

"Where is she?" Moe has to scream to be heard over the crowd bellowing for whichever creature they've bet on. I put my palms up to signal that I can't find her.

In the enclosure, the habu has coiled itself up and is swaying back and forth like a cobra, tracking the mongoose stalking it on the other side of the divider. The tender leans over and teases the crowd, teases the animals, by almost lifting up the divider separating the snake and the mongoose, then slamming it back into place.

"Find her! Find Bosco!" Moe orders me, shoving aside the GIs.

"Pit 'em! Pit 'em!" Southern accents call out for the tender to pull the divider. He holds up his hand and the crowd grows silent. I lean in close to the enclosure as I search the crowd on the other side for Bosco and recognize the odor I hadn't been able to place earlier. It comes from the fear-soured shit of the animals.

With a dramatic flourish the tender lifts the divider and the mongoose charges the oscillating snake. The snake strikes but hits only a blur shadowing the mongoose. The two animals square off. The mongoose dodges to the right, then feints left. The habu mirrors his every move, snapping its hooded head from one side to the other, pivoting to keep the mongoose in sight as he darts about, trying to slip behind the snake.

Its head swiveling imperiously, its long tongue flicking in and out, the habu tracks the mongoose. The sinuous swing of its head momentarily hypnotizes the mongoose. He freezes on tensed, catlike legs as the habu rears up above him, its neck hood swelling until it looms over the mongoose as inevitable as night.

I finally spot Bosco on the other side of the ring, her face mashed against the Plexiglas wet with her tears and snot. I yell to Moe. Moe orders me to get her.

The mongoose unfreezes and skitters back and forth, back and forth, with a dizzying relentlessness until he breaks out with blurring speed to attack the habu's back. Reeling, the habu jerks around, slamming its hooded neck against the mongoose's bared fangs.

Though greatly outnumbered, the habu supporters outyell the mongoose fans. I fight my way toward Bosco as the mongoose fakes an attack on the habu. The habu lunges forward too precipitously. In the split second that the habu is off-balance, the mongoose switches back and strikes. I grab Bosco and try to pull her away from the Plexiglas, but she clings to it, her fingers locked spasmodically.

The mongoose clamps his teeth onto the back of the habu's neck. The snake convulses, twisting furiously to find the mongoose with its fangs. The mongoose rides with the thrashing contortions. The tent falls silent. The habu's body roils about as the mongoose methodically ingests the snake's head. Bones delicate as toothpicks crunch in the mongoose's jaws. It is the only sound in the tent.

"Stop this!"

A current, the current that has flowed between each of us children and Moe since birth, sparks. From each corner of the tent Bob, Buzz, Abner, Bosco, and I all turn to Moe with a tropism as unthinking as flowers following the sun. Even Kit connects, and we are again what we always have been, one organism bound from birth.

We all look at Moe, and when she begins breathing again, so do we. The bones of the habu continue to snap. Moe stares at the spectacle as if seeing it for the first time.

"This is what you consider fit entertainment for children? This? One creature eating another alive? No child should see this. Any of this." She swings her hand wide in a gesture that takes in the old woman giving a python a blow job, children dangling from a Huey, GIs cursing bar girls, runways with B-52 bombers taking off every three minutes. "You should all be ashamed of yourselves."

A path clears in front of her, in front of all of us as we make our way to her side. Only Kit does not go to her.

"Kit?"

"I'm staying." Kit moves closer to Ron, who puts his arm over her shoulders.

Moe marches back to Kit, clamps an iron grip on her wrist, and jerks her daughter forward. "Like hell you are. You're coming home."

Kit looks to Ron to decide the matter. Ron lifts his arms as if giving his permission, and Moe wins the struggle simply because Kit can't stand the embarrassment and Moe no longer cares at all.

Kool

Lucky's chirrup wakes me. A haze of predawn light fades the absolute blackness of tropical night. I listen to Lucky on the ceiling above me, she listening for the telltale rustle of a cockroach. From outside comes the scrape of the aluminum leg of a lawn chair across concrete.

Moe is lighting one Kool off another as I slide the patio door open. "Did I wake you up?"

"No. Lucky did."

The chair I pull up next to hers is light as a basket.

"C-one-forty-one," she says, lifting the red ember of her cigarette to follow the lights and afterburner of the cargo plane sailing through the darkness. Two B-52s follow. Moe seems so absorbed in their flights that it surprises me when she speaks. "I want you to try out for that contest." Moe's voice is authoritative. She has her old spunk back. I wonder what drains the energy from her in my father's presence.

"Kit's contest? The dance contest?"

"Bosco's right, you're ten times the dancer your sister is."

"But it's her contest."

"It's not *her* contest."

"She would flip out if I entered."

"Why? Why should you not enter? Why should you simply abdicate? Cede the playing field? Bernie, you've done that your whole life because that's what you've seen me do for most of your life, at least since we left Japan."

"What happened, Moe? After we left Japan?"

Moe hisses out a mentholated sigh. "Aw, Bern, you don't want to talk about that."

"Yeah, I do."

"Why? That water is so far under the bridge, they're drinking it in China now. The important point is that I set a bad example for you, always giving in on everything, and I don't want you to give in on this. I want you to enter that contest."

"It's ridiculous to even discuss this. Kit is going to be the most beautiful girl who tries out, and the most beautiful girl always wins."

"Bernie, I don't like that kind of talk. You have your own charm, your own appeal. Besides, when you dance something happens. You come to life. The music moves through you and you get this kind of radiance."

"Moe—"

"No, I'm serious. You get a glow on you like it's Singapore Sling night at the club."

"Really?"

"Really."

For a second I almost believe her. "Moe, even if I—you know—tried out and some miracle happened and I—you know—won, I still couldn't leave you. I mean, Jesus, if, *if*"—I snort to indicate what a preposterous idea this is—"if I did win, Kit would be *so* pissed off. With Dad gone, you could never handle her. It'd be RIF City."

"That is my problem. Bernie, listen. I was only slightly older than you when I finished nursing school and got on a troopship for North Africa. I left your widowed grandmother all by herself back in Lafayette, Indiana, running a corner grocery store selling cold cuts for nineteen cents a pound and sleeping on a chair at the cash register because she couldn't afford to hire anyone to give her a break. But I left, and you have to leave. I had my life. I took it from my mother. You have to take yours from me. Maybe you have to take it from Kit too. You have to at least try."

"There's no way. There's not even any good music to dance to on this island."

"I'll get you music. I'll sing for you myself if I have to. Look, I've gotten music for Kit and either bought, sewn, or had costumes, gowns, and uniforms made for every cheerleader tryout, every homecoming court, prom, and pageant your sister has ever been involved in. And I'll do it for her again for this dance contest. But this time I'm also going to do everything I do for your sister for you too. *Capisce?*"

"She's going to be pissed."

"*Machts nichts,* bebby." It's great to hear Moe's snappy World War II nurse talk again. "You were not put on this earth to make Kit Root happy." She sucks in a giant inhalation. "You were put on this earth to make *me* happy!"

For just that second, her laughter drowns out the distant roar of the jet engines.

Benjo

Koza's main street at high noon smells even more of diesel fuel, cement dust, and *benjo* ditches than it had at night. A gritty film of coral dust covers everything and is the reason that even the tiniest scratch becomes infected. There are no GIs in Koza during the daytime. Club My Place. Club Champion. Club Pink Pussy Cat. The Okay Joe. The Manhattan. The Harlem. Aces High. Blue Lady. All the clubs are empty. Papa-sans in string T-shirts and rubber zoris either lean against their darkened doorways leisurely smoking Violet brand cigarettes or wash down the sidewalk in front of their clubs with skinny hoses.

Moe, marching out ahead of Kit, Bosco, and me, glances around at the snarl of shops packed one against another. She stops in front of a fish store to check the slip of paper in her hand with the name and address of a sew girl written on it. Behind us fish are piled silver on green palm leaves, and Okinawan housewives in Mother Hubbard aprons buy thin slices of scarlet red tuna. Next door at the Pink Shoe Shoe Store, schoolgirls in middy blouses and pigtails cluster at the window, pointing to dusty displays of plastic shoes. Bar girls running errands bump past us as Moe gets her bearings. While we wait, Bosco plays her favorite game, Find a Funny Sign.

"Look, there's a good one." She points to a traffic sign that advises CARE FOR PEDESTRIANS!

I find the Memory From You curio shop, the Sexy Boy Hari Cut BarBar shop.

"There's the best one!"

I follow Bosco's finger to a banner fluttering outside Lee's Chinese Bazaar, a two-story structure so new the joint compound is still streaked with dark gray where it hasn't dried yet. Brass trays, vases, pitchers, plaques, candleholders, candle snuffers, ashtrays, bells, birdcages—mountains of fake ivory knickknacks are arrayed behind Lee's windows. Dozens of arrangements of tropical flowers—birds of paradise, orchids—are lined up against the shop. The banner fluttering above it all reads GLAND OPENING.

"Chinese don't have an *r* in their language," Bosco explains as I study the sign. "At least not in Mandarin."

"Gland Opening. Can't beat that," I rule. "That's a definite winner."

Bosco's face lights up and goes east and west in a rare grin.

Moe stops a housewife with a string bag full of huge white daikon radishes and points to the paper, asking for directions.

"You'd think she'd notice the woman has no idea what she's saying." Kit, who started out in a bad mood, is moving rapidly toward a full-blown snit. The woman is very pleased with Moe's efforts to communicate and answers in an incomprehensible stream of rapid-fire Okinawan.

"I'm sorry." Moe reverts to English. "I only know *skoshi* Japanese and no Okinawan. We're looking for a sew girl." Moe pantomimes a needle pulling thread. "Sew girl."

"Oh, Jesus Christ on a crutch, now we have to wait for this little Up with People mission."

"You sound just like Daddy." Bosco says it in a surprised, complimentary way, as if Kit were trying to impersonate our father.

The Okinawan woman plucks the address away from Moe. "*Hai! Hai! Hai!* Sew gurroe." Motioning for us to follow, the woman heads out at a smart pace, shuffling along in her zoris without lifting her feet, as if her ankles were on hydraulics.

Bosco runs after her, but Kit doesn't move. "You know what? I'm just gonna go back and wait in the car. I don't even care anymore."

"Kit, come on. We're gonna get lost."

"You go. You're the one wants it so much now."

"Kit, please."

"Go! Just go!" The schoolgirls at the Pink Shoe Shoe Store turn when Kit raises her voice.

"Look, I'm only doing this because Moe wants me to."

"Why does that not surprise me?"

"We both know you'll win. Come on." I point toward Moe's and Bosco's disappearing forms. "We can barely see them anymore."

Kit cuts her eyes away from me. "How do you always manage to do this?"

"Do what?"

"Make me the bitch?" Kit hurries off toward Moe, leaving me speechless.

I catch up to Kit, Moe, and Bosco just as our guide turns down a narrow alley crammed with stalls. At a stall lined with clothes hanging from pegs on the wall, the owner uses a long bamboo pole to reach a fluffy pink dress and hand it down to a mother who holds it against a little girl wearing a white straw hat with the brim curled up, held on by an elastic band under her chin.

Shopkeepers crowd around us. "Bargain for you, rady!" "Fitty percent off!" "Best price! I make you best price!" "Come here my shop, beautifoo rady."

Our guide with the string bag hectors them in Okinawan and they melt back into their stalls. She ducks into a T-shirt shop. It is claustrophobically small. The walls are patchworked with military insignias. Fanged death's heads, dragons, screaming eagles, crossed axes, crossed sabers, flags, and bulldogs. A T-shirt with a jet streaking across reads RECON: SWIFT, SILENT, DEADLY.

Bosco stares at a T-shirt sporting a voluptuous nude beauty, her slanted eyes twinkling seductively, her nipples unnaturally pert. Beneath the woman is written: LITTLE BROWN FUCKING MACHINE. "LBFM." Bosco mutters the letters. "So *that's* what it means."

"Very good for you, yes?" The owner, a slight man with a thin face, whips the T-shirt off his wall and drapes it across his forearm, presenting it to Bosco like a sommelier with his finest vintage.

"Come, come." The lady with the string bag beckons frantically as she opens a door and points up a flight of stairs. "Sew gurroe. *Go!*"

Moe bows in front of the woman. *"Domo arigato."*

The woman bows several times. Each time, Moe bows lower.

Waiting on the stair above us, Kit rolls her eyes. "What is this, early menopause?"

"We are ambassadors of our country," Bosco informs Kit.

"*Now* who sounds like Daddy?"

Moe bounces up the stairs and we follow.

"What is this place?" Kit asks, when we reach the second floor.

On both sides of the short hall are doors made of plywood and held closed with galvanized steel hasps. We have no idea which way to turn.

"Five," Bosco says. "The lady said *go;* that's five in Japanese."

"My little Nancy Drew." Moe strokes Bosco's hair, then knocks on a door with a metallic adhesive number 5 on it.

A voice barks out a harsh command in Okinawan. Moe hesitates. The command is repeated. She pushes the door open.

The sew girl sits behind a card table with an ancient black Singer decorated with gold scrollwork set up on it. She looks like a pixie, with a broad face and large ears that stick out beneath her spiky pigtails. Her bed is a mattress on the floor neatly covered by a peanut-butter-colored sheet. A pair of pink flats with the imprint of the sole of her foot pressed into the lining sit precisely beside the bed. She is doing handwork, stitching downy pink feathers onto the hem of a diaphanous shortie nightgown much like the one worn by the perky-breasted woman on the sign above Club Pink Pussy Cat. Hung about on nails hammered into the walls are an electric-blue vinyl *Barbarella* space-suit number with transparent breast cones, a crotchless silver lamé teddy, several pink satin Playboy-bunny-type outfits complete with cottontails and bow ties and ears dangling from the hanger, and some geometrically intriguing creations outlined in the stripper's favorite, rows of breakaway snaps.

Moe appears untroubled by these work samples and greets the seamstress in Japanese, but the puzzlement on her elfin face only deepens.

"Some Ryukyuans only speak Okinawan," Bosco points out.

"Or something resembling actual Japanese," Kit adds under her breath.

"Well, okay then." Moe pushes Kit and me forward. Though a white-plastic table fan swivels its head around the room, the air doesn't seem to move.

"My daughters are in a dance contest. Dance?" Her purse swinging from the crook of her arm, Moe illustrates her point with a little demonstration of the Twist that looks more like she is pantomiming a desperate attempt to regain control of a runaway bus. The seamstress blinks and Moe gives me a shove. "Show her, Bern."

The look I give Moe asks her if she's lost her mind.

"This is too weird." Kit starts for the door.

Before she can reach it, I break into a feeble Jerk.

"*Ah so desuka!* Ah go-go! You want ah go-go?"

"Yes!" Moe beams, delighted at this communication. "Not the—uh, you know . . ." Moe trails off, gesturing toward Gate Two street, Turkey Alley.

"No fuckee-suckee," the seamstress adds cheerfully. "Okay, okay. Onaree ah go-go." She ducks down and pulls a box of magazines out from under her table. Most are Japanese; all are limp from wear. She plucks out the most worn of them all from the stack. It is a *TV Guide* from June of 1965 with the *Hullabaloo* dancers on the cover sporting the full go-go: spaghetti-fringe minidress, white boots, swaying mane of tousled blond hair. The seamstress stabs energetically at the prancing blonde. "Ah go-go! Ah go-go!"

Kit returns, magnetized by the image. The girl on the cover could be her. She takes the magazine. Kit is, if anything, prettier than this *Hullabaloo* dancer. "Yes." She doesn't stop staring at the cover. "Yes. But shorter. More *sukoshi.*" Kit holds one arm against her side, then chops at the spot on her thigh where her palm comes to rest about four inches below her crotch.

"Oh, now, I don't think so." Moe chops at a spot a foot lower. "Here is good. *Jyoto.*"

"*Hai! Jyoto!*"

Getting into the spirit, the sew girl jumps to her feet, whipping the long curl of a tape measure from around her neck to lasso Kit under her arms and take a swift bust measurement, which she writes down in a little notebook with the stub of pencil she pulls out from behind an elf ear. Turning her head to the side, she hugs Kit to her as she passes the tape measure behind her back and pulls it loosely around her waist. In practiced zips, she pulls the tape from Kit's armpit to her waist, cervical to lumbar vertebrae, shoulder to shoulder, then down her leg, stopping at the spot mid-kneecap that Moe designated. Winking at Kit and turning to block Moe's view, she pulls her tape measure down the four inches below her crotch that Kit asked for and marks that figure down as well.

Kit points to the magazine cover. "I want that material and that fringe."

"Okay! Okay! *Hai!*" The seamstress starts bowing us toward the door.

"You haven't measured Bernie." Moe pushes me back into the room and holds up two fingers. "*Ni* girl-sans. Two. Go-go for number-one daughter too."

"*Hai! Hai!* Okay." The seamstress giggles as she snaps her tape measure off again.

As I raise my arms so she can loop the tape around my breasts, Kit heads for the door. "I'm gonna go wait in the car."

Oxygen

Have you ever been experienced?

I am onstage, close enough to see a trickle of sweat escape from under the chiffon scarf tied around Jimi Hendrix's forehead, and, even in my sleep, I realize it's a dream. The seat is great, but the sound quality—scratchy, monaural—is something of a disappointment. I would have thought that the acoustics in dreams would be better.

I have.

The incongruity of Jimi's sublime guitar playing being amplified through a bucket is so jarring that the dream begins to fade away. What finally wakes me up, though, is the question: What is good music doing being played on the beautiful, the beautiful balloon of Okinawa?

Fully awake, I walk down the darkened hall, open the door to the boys' room, and find that it has been transformed into the phosphorescent minerals room at the museum. The draped sheets of their bunk beds are neon-blue slabs floating in the illumination of a black light. The sports pennants on the wall are glowing blue triangles. I bump my head against the B-17, and it jerks about crazily on its line.

Buzz and Abner, hunkered down on the floor, are a pair of disembodied blue-white grins above blue-white boxer shorts and blue-white crew socks squatting beside a record player on the floor. The record player has belonged to all of us. It started life as my Christmas present when I was seven back at Yokota, and had just seen service earlier that day with Bob shouting along to his favorite Burl Ives song: *"Watch the donut, not the hole!"*

The twins are surrounded by puddles of jewel-colored albums, emerald, amethyst, sapphire, topaz. The one spinning on the turntable is ruby red.

Have you ever been experienced?

"Where did you get that?"

The spectral grins snap shut and Buzz's and Abner's hellhound eyes find each other in the dark. Abner cracks first. "Will you promise never—"

"—ever, ever—"

"—to tell anyone, 'cause—"

"—OSI would fry our asses—"

"—to a rich, crispy golden brown, 'cause—"

"—they're all bootlegs!—"

"—pirated from Taiwan. We get the jump crews to buy them—"

"—for us for thirty-five cents. Thirty-five cents—"

"—for an album! Of course all the jump crews are—"

"—giant stoners! So they never get the ones we ask for, like—"

"—Jan and Dean—"

"—the Monkees—"

"—the Ventures—"

"—*Lulu*—"

"I never asked for Lulu, queerbait."

"I heard you, Ab. You asked for Lulu."

"I asked for *Zu*-lu, butt munch. It's a really cool movie, and it's got that choice soundtrack with all the natives ululating and that big uprising scene where they—"

"To sir-hir-hir, with love!"

Buzz interrupts Abner's stirring defense with a surprisingly acceptable falsetto.

A solid *thwock* lands in the darkness. In the solar plexus, I guess from Buzz's explosive gasp.

"Do you have any dance music?"

Buzz and Abner shrug and hand me a stack of albums. The covers are made from the same flimsy speckled cardboard that Taiwanese electronic equipment is packed in. The photo on the front of Jimi's album is so poorly reproduced and bleached out that he's paler than Queen Elizabeth. A lyric sheet flutters out of the sleeve. I hold it close to the light to read the spidery print and try to recall a Hendrix song entitled "Hey Ho!"

Hey, ho! Wear you joking . . .

It is only when I read *with that gun in your hand* that I realize they're transcribing "Hey Joe."

"That's how all the Koza cover bands learn the songs."

I shuffle through the albums: Cream, Grateful Dead, The Doors, Vanilla Fudge, Jefferson Airplane, the basic axe in the heart for Motown and any remotely danceable music. "Dance music?" I repeat. "I need dance music."

"Strawberry Alarm Clock?"

"No. When I say dance music, I mean the kind of music humans might dance to. You have no actual dance music."

"What do you mean no dance music?" Abner lifts the tone arm and puts a swirling magma-red-and-black album on. "This is great dance music." The immortal Cream power chords play.

It's getting near dawn . . .

Abner goes into a dreamy whiplash just as if he'd been to a concert and seen some psychedelically debilitated terpsichorean hanging from a monster amp like a streamer blown by the breeze of a fan.

". . . *urreeek!*"

"You're gonna wreck it!" Abner lunges for Buzz's neck.

Bob sits up. "Could you guys please not kill each other while I'm trying to sleep? Hey, that's my record player. Why are all those records see-through? I want see-through records! You guys got see-through records! I'm gonna tell!"

Abner stops trying to strangle his twin. Buying bootleg albums from dope fiends is a RIFable offense. They both creep over to Bob's bed and stand above him, grinning. "What color are our teeth, Bob?"

"Blue."

"What color are teeth, Bob?"

"White."

"This must mean—"

"Oh. I'm having a dream. Okay." Bob pulls his Deputy Dawg quilt up to his chin, rolls over, and goes back to sleep.

Buzz turns back to me. "If you don't think that's dance music, then I guess we don't have any."

I'm relieved. I'll play out the farce of entering Kit's dance contest, embarrass myself to a few bars of "Fever" or "Come On-a My House," then see Kit off at the airport. As I'm handing the bootlegged albums back, another lyric sheet flutters out. The scrambled words are so psychotic, they jump out at me. Somewhere in the back of my mind, a tambourine starts beating and a lead guitar plays in time to the rhythm embedded in the nonsense syllables and the song comes to me. Excitedly, I wave the sheet at Buzz. "Do you have this one?"

Buzz swirls the circles of color at his feet and plucks out an album the red of a cherry Charms sucker. A second later, the notes, half calypso, all pop, plink out sounding somehow right on a nursery room record player, and I am on my feet dancing before the first jangle of the tambourine. The first line on the lyrics sheet, *Hey Roderigo! Dates when no raking!* becomes *Hey where did we go, days when the rain came* in Van Morrison's irresistibly danceable anthem to a brown-eyed girl.

It is like oxygen after the last few weeks of "Up, Up and Away." The twins goof along with me, pretending to make fun of the kind of guy who is not them or any guy they would ever be, but a stupid kind of guy who would seriously dance. Who would dance like a toy monkey on a pole and pick lice out of his brother's head and eat them in time to the music as they sang out words from a Taiwanese lyric sheet.

The transcribed lyrics my brothers shout out bop with poetic hilarity that makes me love their author. When Van lamented that it was so hard to find a way, the little transcriber in Taiwan, no doubt leafing furiously through his well-thumbed Chinese-English dictionary, heard that *Sew hearts fight a highway*. Van's casting of his memory back there, Lord, was refracted on the lyric sheet into *mammary backstairs roared*. In the parallel universe of Taiwanese lyric transcribers, making love in the green grass behind the stadium turns into *making love in the Negroes beehive*. Then it's break time for our industrious transcriber, who returns with a mug of his favorite hot brew only to discover that Van shares his passion and stadium becomes *Stay tea! Yum!*

But, clearly, our friend, scribbling furiously in the back room at a factory spinning candy-colored albums into the world, had an insider's knowledge of the drug culture ravaging the West, for Van's brown-eyed girl is revealed for what she truly is in his transcription: *Brown HIGH Girl! Sha ra ra ra ra ra ra ra ra ra ra! Ra tea tah!*

Jergens

Okinawa's weather clock is off. It is ten in the morning and the sky is still as gray as the endless reinforced concrete buildings we drive past on Highway One. Moe at the wheel, grim as the weather, is still upset from the screaming fight she had with Kit, who refused to drive to the Kokusai Hotel with us for the dance contest. I can't say exactly why I agreed to come with Moe. All I know is that if Kit hadn't almost forbidden me, I would never be doing this.

Moe's mood darkens when we hit Naha traffic. Three-wheeler trucks and diesel-belching buses stream around us. A chunky woman in a pink dress and zoris riding a moped cuts in front of our car. Moe slams on the brakes and her right arm snaps out reflexively.

"Moe."

Moe notices that the back of her arm is pressed tightly against my breasts and drops it. The scent of her Jergens lotion lingers. She slaps the steering wheel as traffic halts altogether. "Perfect!" Construction workers in black rubber boots and yellow safety helmets perched atop rags covering the men's hair begin jack-hammering concrete next to the car. She grips the steering wheel tightly.

"I don't see why you couldn't have worn the costume. Kit is wearing hers."

"I brought it with me. I'm not walking around Naha in it, so can we drop the fucking costume."

"Is that the kind of language your father and I are paying to have you learn?"

"Sorry. *Fornicating* costume."

"That's nice. That's lovely."

"You're mad at me because I don't want to show my ass in some stripper outfit?"

"No one is showing their ass and it's not a stripper costume."

"That's what you think."

"Bernie, I'm just trying to help you."

"You're only about fifteen years too late."

Daughters always know where to put the knife in.

Naha traffic finally starts moving again. Moe presses the accelerator. The station wagon surges forward and dies. A hornet swarm of cars honk as they swerve to avoid us. Moe stomps futilely on the gas pedal several times.

"Stop pumping! You're flooding it!"

The honking grows more shrill. Moe's hands drop from the steering wheel and tears stream down her face. She looks back at the traffic blocked behind her. "What do they expect me to do? I am doing the best I know how. What the hell do they expect me to do?"

I scoot to the edge of my seat. "Mom, move over. Let me drive."

"How did we end up here?" I know she is talking about more than being stuck on a crowded street on a tiny Pacific island with a swarm of angry Asian motorists in miniature vehicles bearing down on us.

"I don't know, Mom," I say gently. "Scoot over. I'm going to drive." I lean forward, raising my butt off the vinyl, and Moe slides behind me while I take her place at the wheel.

Moe blows her nose, huffs out several breaths, then laughs. "Take a tip from me, Bern. Don't have two teenage daughters at the same time you start getting menopausal. It's just a hormonal disaster waiting to happen."

The snap is returning to her garters. I get the car started and head toward the Kokusai Hotel.

Brut

"Jew or tickuh?" I stare at the Ryukyuan woman standing at the entrance to the Kokusai Hotel ballroom for a second until I realize that she has asked, "Your ticket?" I hand it to her. She gives me a number.

Moe glances at the number. "Seven. That's lucky."

"Yes, I can hardly believe my good fortune."

Moe tucks her chin into her neck, admonishing me for my snippiness, and we step into the ballroom.

I search the room for Kit but can't find her in the small knot of girls, their mothers, and friends gathered beside the stage. The walls of the ballroom are stippled with pieces of tape anchoring bits of crepe paper, gold and green, the colors of the Kubasaki Dragons. I imagine the couples from the American high school dancing here at their prom. The shrill scratch of a barely amplified record needle settling into its groove plinks into the ballroom.

Bobby Moses sits regally onstage in an impeccably tailored suit of dark blue sharkskin with the slightest hint of maroon iridescence. His hooded eyes evaluate the contestant, who stands onstage facing him with her back to the audience. She wears a plain black leotard that she outgrew last summer over her pear-shaped body.

The first notes of "Hello Dolly" shrill out of speakers too small for the large room. The girl whirls around and high-steps forward. She heaves the bell of the pear to the right as she kicks out on the first "Dolly," and Bobby looks down to make a note on the clipboard in his lap.

"Where's Kit?" Moe asks.

I shrug. Bobby Moses nods and waves Pear Girl off the stage. Next up is a tap dancer in a red-white-and-blue sequined vest and top hat who clacks her way through "I'm a Yankee Doodle Dandy." Bobby Moses watches the girl's shoes intently, as if she might be pounding out an important message in Morse code that he has to translate. When she finishes, he makes another mark on his clipboard and doesn't look up until the tap dancer stumbles off the stage. Numbers three and four execute jazz-styled numbers that both feature a fair amount of minstrelly hand flapping and the sort of backward tiptoeing generally used to garnish an ice-skating routine.

Number five is a clog dancer done up in a burlesque hillbilly outfit with fake blond braids sticking out from beneath an undersized hat with a giant daisy drooping down over cartoon freckles. She smiles and reveals a blacked-out front tooth. As soon as the fiddles begin to twang, the clogger sets up a powerful counterpoint, banging her feet on the stage until puffs of dust rise all around her. Her knees pivot up and out like pistons beneath layers of petticoats and a short dirndl skirt.

It's a lively, attention-grabbing routine. I think that, if I were Bobby Moses, it would be a good choice for an intermission act. She stomps to a decisive finale and finishes up on one knee, arm outstretched à la Al Jolson in Bobby Moses's direction. Bobby nods, studies his clipboard, calls out, "Number six."

"You should put this on." Moe hands me my costume.

"Kit Root?" Bobby calls out, when no one takes the stage.

"I'm going to go now," Moe tells me. "I don't want to look like I'm cheering for one of you over the other. I'll wait downstairs in the lobby." As I take the costume, my heart starts to pound so hard that blood throbs in my ears. Even though I'm still telling myself I won't go through with it, I'm so nervous after Moe leaves I'm afraid I'm going to throw up.

The quarterback-looking boy who was in the backseat of the convertible the other day runs up to Bobby. "There's gonna be a short delay while we"—he points to another couple of guys busy hooking up a trunk-sized amplifier to a reel-to-reel tape player— "set up for Kit." He wears a red-and-white striped shirt and pressed chinos that make him look like one of the Beach Boys.

"Testing. Testing." The boy speaks into a microphone he's attached to the big speakers and tells us, "Uh. Hi. I made this tape. It's, like, a medley or something." He grins at the group of Kit's fellow cheerleaders and other members of the Kubasaki High School varsity who've come to support Kit. They grin back. "So it's all stuff that Kit is going to dance to." The boy pats his flat stomach, then holds his hand out. "So, without further ado, I give you Kit Root!"

Her crowd applauds, the first applause of the afternoon. The other contestants look around, peeved, their expressions asking if clapping and fancy sound systems are allowed, and, if so, why didn't they get their own clappers and sound systems?

Bobby Moses shrugs.

The clapping dies down, but no music starts. The quarterback squats in front of his huge TEAC setup, clicking knobs so that the big spools of tape squeal and whir one way and then the other. He mumbles something, realizes he can't be heard, and picks up the microphone again. "Short delay here, folks. We'll get it started in—" He flips some switches, turns a knob, and the pulsing intro to "Fever" floods out from several sets of speakers suspended by chains from the ceiling, saturating the ballroom.

The quarterback yells into the mike, "Kit Root!" The door to the ladies' room bursts open and my little sister strides in on a wave of sound, beauty, and supreme confidence. The sew girl's dress does what it needs to, which is to hide as little of Kit as possible and make all of her look as if she just stepped off the set of *Hullabaloo.* The thin straps of the shiny lilac sheath rest perfectly on her tan shoulders. The darts are placed at the precise angle to offset the tilt of her breasts. The waist nips in, then out, flowing effortlessly over her curves.

You give me fever.

Peggy Lee's throbbing voice fades to a whisper and dies away altogether. Whoever made Kit's tape did a professional job, giving her exactly enough time to take center stage and allow her lilac jewel of a self to possess every inch of the ballroom and make it seem sordid by comparison.

The two jazz dancers gaze at Kit onstage, mesmerized, as she stands utterly still and demonstrates what the word "charisma" means. The clogger and the tapper, however, mutter audibly about unfair advantages and why couldn't they have gotten to use a good sound system? I envy them their belief that a few pieces of electronic equipment are all that stands between them and the adulation Kit inspires. Having studied it up close for Kit's entire life, I can promise them that they can buy all the TEAC speakers in the world and they'll never touch what Kit had from the moment she was born. It is so obvious who is going to win that the clogger and tapper and their mothers stomp out in protest before Kit even dances a step.

These boots are made for walkin'.

Kit breaks into a crisp march dramatizing Nancy Sinatra's petulant threat to *walk right out on you!* She slams down the heels of the white boots with each step in a way that makes the silver fringe jump in a startled, unsettling fashion.

Fighting men who jump and die!

Kit segues into a tribute to the Green Berets, saluting each direction of the compass and then marching on. The marching and saluting evolve into an energetic pantomime of skeet shooting for the duration of a brief snatch of "Bang Bang (My Baby Shot Me Down)," which climaxes with Kit taking one in the heart and spiraling to a chest-clutching death. Spontaneous applause ripples through the crowd at the dramatic rendering. Bobby Moses remains as unreadable as he's been throughout.

Kit breaks up the pace by throwing in the preternaturally perky "Sweet Pea." Holding her hands to her mouth like a megaphone, she lip-syncs Tommy Roe's plea, *Oh, Sweet Pea, come on and dance with me.* As Petula Clark warns her darling not to sleep in the subway and Kit acts out both a finger-twitching "no" and sleeping, I begin to suspect that I am either poisonously jealous or mentally ill. I turn and gaze upon a school of rapt faces swimming in delight at my sister's routine and wonder how so many seemingly normal humans could be enthralled by a performance that I find excruciating in ways only prisoners of war usually get to experience.

And, Honey, I miss you and I'm doing fine.

Kit acts out the tree and how big it's grown. I hear sniffles behind me and decide that I am poisonously jealous *and* the world is mentally ill and there is no further reason for me to hang around. Kit does not need one more person to applaud when she is crowned the winner.

A second before I can leave, Bobby Moses catches my attention as he shifts his great bulk and the metal chair creaks beneath his copious buttocks. Far more attention-grabbing, however, is the expression on his face as he watches Kit dramatize Honey's tragic demise. For a second he studies my sister, his big sumo-wrestler head cocked to one side, his eyebrows rammed together so tightly in puzzlement that welts of fat ripple between them. Bafflement is quickly overtaken by irritation, then outright disgust. It is a panorama of expressions that so exactly matches those I am disguising it's like looking in a mirror. I take comfort in knowing that I might not be the only person in the world outside my family immune to my sister's charms.

Kit balls up the pretend hanky she'd been dabbing her eyes with, pretends to toss it into a pretend wastebasket, then raises her arms high in very real triumph. The second she came onstage, the crowd has been waiting for this moment. Resounding applause echoes through the ballroom. Kit milks it, blinking back tears and touching her trembling lips as if to ask, For me? Could all this naked adulation possibly be for, for . . . me? Each lip touch brings forth fresh outpourings of adoration until Bobby Moses, nodding impatiently, signals with a gesture like he's whisking gnats away that he has seen enough. More, in fact, than enough. The quarterback jumps up and escorts Kit off the stage with both hands on her shoulders as if he were placing Miss America's cape around them.

Onstage, Bobby Moses appropriates the microphone, and the instrument brings him to a life I had not witnessed before. I expect him to lead the crowd in another round of applause, maybe bring Kit back for an encore. Instead, he asks, "Number seven? We got a seven out there? Wherever you are, seven, get your bupkes up here unless you enjoy seeing an old man flattening his hemorrhoids on this farshtinkener metal chair. The last time I saw a chair this uncomfortable, the guy in it was *begging* for them to turn on the electricity. Number seven, get your tush up here." His loquaciousness after the earlier silence is so striking it's almost as if he needed a microphone more than vocal cords.

Kit pauses in her stately departure and looks back over her shoulder at me to ensure what she's already certain of: that I will not take my turn. I expect to see a smug smile of triumph. But that is not her expression at all. My sister's perfect features carry another emotion: pity.

Pity?

At the exact moment when I am completely ready to surrender to my sister without so much as shaking one tail feather, everything shifts.

Pity?

In that instant, the most significant fact about Bobby Moses's lack of enthrallment occurs to me: He—not the Kubasaki High School drill team, not the Homecoming Court, not the cheerleading squad, not the football team—Bobby Moses is the person who will be selecting the winner. Secure in her victory, Kit sails past me, her fans closing in behind like seagulls in the wake of a great ocean liner.

Pity?

My arm holding the number swings up over my head as if jerked aloft by a puppeteer holding a string. "I'm seven."

"You're seven? Mazel tov. Did it take you this long to count that high?" To the crowd he adds, "She's not just acting dumb, folks. This is the real thing." The small laugh he gets jolts him to his feet. He points at me. "There's a girl who has to take off her sweater to count to two!" The laugh grows. Bobby starts pacing the stage, holding his hand out to me as he goes. "But seriously. Doesn't she have a pretty little head? For a head, it's pretty little." Big laugh. Bobby stops, stares at me. "Well? What's it gonna be, seven?"

"I have to—" I hold up my dress and run off to the bathroom.

"Just like a dame. If a broad'd been in charge of D-Day, she'd never have figured out what to wear and we'd all be sitting here in our lederhosen. No woman will ever go to the moon. She wouldn't know what to wear!"

The old-fashioned *bah-duh-bing* rhythm of Bobby's jokes follows me into the bathroom. It is a Japanese-style squatter with a toilet hole flush to the ground flanked by a pair of footrests. Bobby Moses's patter is a distant buzz as I pull on the sew girl's dress for the first time and a drop of sweat trickles down my side. I turn to the mirror and see that I look utterly ridiculous. On Kit, the dress made you think about what remained covered. On me, you notice that far too much is showing and that most of that is doughy and freckled. It's impossible. I didn't even bring the right shoes. Kit had danced in some silver pumps that worked perfectly with the dress. All I have are my water buffalo sandals. They clash so badly with the dress I kick them off.

Bobby pounds on the door. "You fall in?"

I can't answer. At least his question wasn't amplified over the PA.

"Gimme a knock, something. One if by land, two if by sea."

I'm trying to figure out if I can shimmy out the small frosted-glass window above the water tank when the door opens and Bobby Moses sticks his hand in. His initials are monogrammed on the cuff of his mint-green shirt in a rococo swirl. The gold ring on his pinkie finger sports a horseshoe band of diamonds. "Give me your music. I'll cue you up." I give him the pirated Van Morrison album simply to make his hand go away. It withdraws, then, a second later, the door opens. Bobby stands there examining the candy-apple-red album.

Necks crane behind Bobby to get a glimpse of me. Bobby comes into the bathroom. "Nice place you got here. Which cut?"

Cut?

"Which side."

"Uh, side A?"

"What *song* you want to use?"

"'Brown Eyed Girl,' but I—uh . . . I don't think I'm going to do this after all." My voice is a strangled bird chirp.

"What? *What?* You're not going on? No. Incorrect answer. No. Not going on is never an option. Very unprofessional." He gives me a sour look and shakes his head, as if to clear away the improbability of my remark. "What's with this not going on? You got your ass down here. That's the biggest part of going on. You're on. You're on already. Out. Out. Out." He herds me out of the bathroom.

In the ballroom he gives my album to the quarterback, takes my hand, and pulls me to the stage. The quarterback puts the red album on the crappy little record player. The opening chords of "Brown Eyed Girl" sound as if they're coming out of a jack-in-the-box, as if Van Morrison in a pointed hat and clown collar will pop up and start singing.

Doo! Bobby picks up the mike. "Not that windup piece of shit. Use the good sound system. The one that other chick, number six, used."

While they hook up the turntable to the speakers, I stand at the foot of the stage in front of the crowd. They have the look of gawkers at a car crash. I don't want to know if Kit has come back in, so I stare intently at my bare feet. I hike my shoulders up so more of my chest will be covered and notice that the dress doesn't so much ride as it flows up, the silver fringe becoming a waterfall shimmying back to its source. In fact, every breath I take causes the rows of silver fringe ringing the dress to fly out in tentacled ecstasy. Stationary, the dress and I don't do much for each other, but the instant I move it comes alive.

The music starts and Bobby, who's taken his place onstage, snaps his fingers. "Hey, this swings. Seven, let's see what you got."

As I walk up the steps, Bobby signals for me to remove my glasses. I leave them at the edge of the stage. Suddenly the crowd of Kit worshipers becomes a distant Impressionistic painting. The only person I can see clearly is Bobby, who is grooving openly to Van.

When Van sings *Hey where did we go?* all I can think of is the little nerd in Taiwan transcribing lyrics for pirated albums and writing *Hey, Roderigo!* and I can't keep the smile off my face. Bobby grins a Happy Buddha grin back at me, hunches his shoulders, and snaps his chunky fingers like a beatnik listening to bongo music. Like a Vegas swinger at the front table at a Frank Sinatra show. That is enough for me. I turn from my sister's booster club and focus on Bobby and the music. I snap along with him, then start making the fringe dance. I twitch my butt west and my shoulders east and the fringe bounces around, hitting all points of the compass and looking cool at each one. I undulate and the fringe ripples like wind moving through the habu grass. Then the music takes over and I throw my whole body and every fiber of fringe into a snap with both hands over my head in a big hallelujah. Bobby starts bobbing from side to side and I pick it up and amplify it into a giant sway that pops the fringe into an exclamation of joy.

At this point, I'm so far into the music that it ceases to matter how many of my sister's friends are praying that I will infarct and die before the next pirouette.

I become the brown-eyed girl, hair in a do rag, switching her sassy hips. Bobby loves it. He rolls his meaty hands around each other the way Moe used to when she was in her calypso phase. With that one motion I am back in Yokota, back in Pink Coke land, with Moe and Fumiko. It's just us three and we're all in it together.

I spin, stop on a dime, hitchhike to the edge of the galaxy and back again. I'm the python swaying in the old Okinawan woman's hands. I'm a wisp of smoke. I'm all seven of the veils.

I laugh when Van sings about the stadium that became the transcriber's plea, *Stay tea! Yum!* Out in the fuzzy crowd a few guys laugh back. I stare right into their faces as if we're partners, dancing together. I do a few swirly hand claps. They clap back. I work in a high-voltage patty-cake and they play along. Heads start bobbing, hands clapping on the beat, shoulders hitchhiking back and forth. Kit's people, they're dancing with me. And then, right at my feet, right at the edge of the stage, is Kit, close enough that I can make out her expression.

It's not pity anymore. Something on the far end from pity now strains my sister's pretty face, compressing her eyes into a hard squint, and I know then how good I am. For the first time in her life, my sister sees me as a threat, and I pounce on the moment like the herd runt who's waited her whole life for the big dog to show just one sign of weakness. When I finally see it, I go feral. I no longer want to beat Kit; I want to rip her throat out. I only want to be good to show how bad she is.

Gravity lets go of me and I channel nothing but rhythm. As Van fades out I have a good chunk of the crowd skating from side to side with me, clapping out each stroke. I am so drunk with this moment that I applaud them when the song ends.

Like the referee in a heavyweight fight, Bobby Moses bounces onstage before the song clapping can fade, holds my hand in the air, and declares me the winner.

Kit glares at me as shocked and outraged as Cinderella if the glass slipper had turned out to fit one of the ugly stepsisters.

Joy

"So, you live here on Okinawa, Mr. Moses?"

"Right off Highway One, Mrs. Root. On the beach near Camp Hansen."

"Well, okay. About this trip—"

"Look, Mrs. Root, let's not beat around the bush. You want to know who I am before you send your daughter off to Tokyo with me. Here's a copy of my OSI report. I probably don't have to tell you them guys is thorough. They can't find anything on me, there's nothing to find."

"Oh, well, that's not necess— You were wounded in the Battle of Sicily?"

"Wounded? No. Dysentery."

"I was with Third General Hospital."

"No kidding. Were you of the Hebraic persuasion before you married?"

"No."

"You musta been the only shiksa in the outfit."

"I joined the unit late. Most of them were from Mount Sinai. Who was your nurse?"

"Minnie . . . Minnie—"

"Minnie Mandelbaum! Minnie was your nurse?"

"Minnie the Doucher. That's what we called her. She was such a douche bag. Pardon my French."

"Minnie could be a pill."

"Pill? Mrs. Root, the Doucher was the whole frigging pharmacy. With a castor oil chaser."

"Mr. Moses—"

"Bobby, or I'm gonna start calling you Mrs. Major."

"All right . . . Bobby, where exactly will you be performing?"

"Like it said on the flyer, Mrs. Root—"

"Moe."

"Okay, Moe. Moe? And you got a daughter calls herself Bernie? So, let me see. We got Moe and Bernie. Sounds like a coupla old Jews sitting around talking about prostate problems. . . . You have a very nice laugh, Moe. Very nice indeed. What is that scent you're wearing, Joy? Gotta be Joy. Only one thing smells as good as Joy and that's Joy. Nakashima! Who do I have to blow to get some service over here? Whatcha drinking there, Moe? Tumbler of Windex? Why do all Okinawan cocktails look like they came from Jupiter? Yeah, get the lady another one of whatever that is, Chivas for me, and another Shirley Temple for the kid."

"And where is it you will be appearing?"

"The gigs? Right. We'll be playing all the O clubs in the Tokyo area. Some noncom."

"Enlisted?"

"No enlisted. Officers only. Tachikawa, Johnson, Yokota—"

"You're playing Yokota Air Base?"

"No, Yokota Home for Wayward Girls. Of course, Yokota Air Base."

"We were stationed at Yokota."

"No kidding. When abouts was that?"

"'Fifty-six to 'sixty."

"Oh, yeah, back when we were still the conquering heroes."

"I suppose."

"Suppose? No, I promise you, Moe, that was the greatest time and place in all of recorded history to be an American. The real hurt of the war was off. We pumped all that money into their economy during the Korean War. They were still grateful. Maybe a little pissed off we dropped the big one on them, but still we hadn't come in and done what they would have done. What they *did* do in Nanking, Manchuria, the Philippines. They knew they got off light. Was your husband flying reconnaissance back then?"

"How did you know—"

"You're checking me out, I checked you out. Moe, let's cut to the chase here. I would have to be the biggest yutz in the world to mess in any way, shape, or form with the daughter of an Air Force officer. Just let me assure you, Mrs. Root, Bobby Moses is no yutz. Besides, if it is any comfort, I'm queer."

"You're—"

"As a two-dollar bill. My father wanted a boy. My mother wanted a girl. They're both satisfied. What can I say? Your little girl could be spread-eagled naked on my bed and I'd be more interested in the pansy pattern on the quilt than in her."

"Oh. I see."

"Nakashima, you asleep over there? Let's keep 'em coming."

"Bobby, I really think—"

"What? You worried I'm gonna be compromising *your* honor now?"

"No, of course not. It's just that—"

"Okay then. *L'chaim.*"

Clink.

"Next year in Jerusalem."

"Moe, you're a gasser."

"The docs at Third General used to say that."

"Moe, I can see where your daughters got their looks. Maybe *you're* the Root girl I should be taking with me."

"A go-go girl with varicose veins. That's just what the world is waiting for."

"Moe used to sing with the USO."

"No kidding."

"Bernie, it wasn't the USO. It was just a bunch of us who got together and messed around. Played for unit dances. The Replacement Depot. Little piddly things."

"The Repple Depple? You sang at the Repple Depple?"

"Well . . . yes."

"No! Of course! You're Nurse Mohoric, Songbird of the Third. I heard you!"

"Now, Bobby, how on earth would you remember that?"

"Hell, yes, I remember. I shipped in in 'forty-four. Green as gooseshit. Stepped off the boat and watched them load up the coffins of the guys I was replacing. Only thing kept me from wigging out was you singing that night. Of course. I shoulda spotted it right off. Voice of an angel. *Face* of an angel. Kid, your mother had it. You coulda gone pro. What was that you sang, Moe?"

"There were a few."

"'Don't Get around Much Anymore.' That was the one. Knocked my socks off. Sang it the way Duke woulda wanted it sung. Hey, Naki, this thing in tune?"

"Bobby, I think that piano is only for the paid performers. Are you sure you should— Why, Bobby, you play very well."

"So sing already."

"I don't— I can't remember the words."

"Come on, come on, if I'm gonna make a total ass of myself least you can do is help out."

"*Heard they crowded the floor.*"

"Moe! Six kids and you still got it!"

"You liar."

"Moe! Take it!"

"*Don't get around much anymore.*"

"*Somewhere over the rainbow* . . . Moe, you knocked me out with this one. Sing with me."

"No, Bobby. I . . . I can't. I don't sing that one anymore. Ever."

"Moe, you look a little pale. Forget 'Somewhere over the Rainbow.' Here, how 'bout this?"

By the time Bobby and Moe work their way through "That Old Black Magic," "Don't Sit under the Apple Tree with Anyone Else but Me," "In a Small Hotel," "I'll Be Seeing You," "As Time Goes By," and finish with "Mairzy Doats," Moe is bombed and I am on my way to Tokyo in one week.

Smoke

The Okinawa weather, always hot, turns sultry and still in the week before I leave. The afternoon rains, when they do come, pour down as if they are holding a grudge against the island, leaving it limp and steaming. Kit all but vanishes after the dance contest. For the last four days, I've only seen my sister very late at night when she comes in and Moe yells at her for staying out until all hours and not telling anyone where she is. Kit doesn't say a word. She has completely stopped talking to me or Moe. Kit doesn't answer, even when Moe slaps her and screams that she will not tolerate this behavior. Even when she cries and begs Kit to behave or she'll get us all RIF'd.

On the fourth night, when she comes back to our room, I pretend to be asleep, then lie in the darkness as she bangs around until dropping into bed. Kit has been exuding a progressively more dangerous combination of odors. The first night it was just cigarette smoke and stale beer. Then bourbon. Then pot. Tonight, a fragrance emanates from her that is dense and resinous. After she falls asleep or passes out, I creep from my bed and watch her. Though Kit seems deeply asleep, her body remains tense and her eyelids twitch a frantic Morse code. I consider not going to Tokyo with Bobby in three days, but the prospect of being around Kit when she is awake and hating me even more than usual is unthinkable.

I lie in bed for a long time, listening to Lucky chirping in the darkness.

On the fifth night, Moe and I sit out on the patio late, hours after Bob, his nose peeling, his eyes a permanently inflamed chlorine red, the twins reeking their new boy odors, and Bosco, sore all over from attempting to teach Hickory the Horse to jump, have gone to sleep. The webbing on the aluminum chairs creaks when we shift around, trying to catch any breeze blowing up the long hill from the East China Sea.

Moe stubs her cigarette out and turns to me. "If anything happens that you don't like, and I do mean anything, the tiniest hint of funny business, you are to go directly to the Dependent Liaison Officer on any base. Or to the chaplain. Or any senior-grade officer, for that matter. You have the MATS number. If you need to call, for anything, just take that number and go to—"

"You already told me all this about eight thousand times. I'm not a total child, you know." The more frantic Moe gets, the more I have to hide my own nervousness.

Moe sighs. Her chair scrapes as she settles back into it. "My mother did the same thing to me before I shipped out. By the time I left, I was so glad to get away from her, I didn't even think to be scared, getting on a troopship, zigzagging across the Atlantic. I guess we mothers are good for that anyway."

"Driving their kids crazy? Yeah, you're doing a pretty good job."

"Hey! At least I'm not crying and hanging on you and telling you that you'll never see me alive on this earth again."

"Did Granma do that? Don't get any ideas."

Moe snorts out a warning to me not to get too sassy. For the first time that night, a good solid breeze swoops up the long hill. Moe holds her nightgown out. "Ewww, that's more like it."

I stand, turn around, and hike my nightie up to make Moe laugh at me airing my backside.

We are both holding out our nighties for the breeze to loft into them when a car pulls up out front. This is what we have been waiting for. We drop our nightgowns and creep around to the side of the house, where we stand hidden in shadows and watch as a midnight-blue Porsche glides to a stop, silent as a manta ray. The passenger door bursts open and Kit steps out in a haze of smoke, like an angel rising to heaven on a cloud. She stumbles, barely catches herself, and loudly curses the garden hose.

Ron leans over and hisses out the window. "Hey now, don't be waking the neighborhood."

Kit flips him a bird and staggers into the house. Ron watches for a moment; then the Porsche disappears in the darkness. I wonder how he can afford a Porsche on an airman's salary and don't like any of the answers.

Several planes take off in the distance far below us before Moe speaks. "Well, we know now why OSI hasn't thrown us all off the island."

"He's just a file clerk. There's only so long he can lose reports. Look, Moe, I don't have to go."

"No! You are going and that is the end of that discussion."

"She's going to get us RIF'd."

"No one is going to get RIF'd. Your father will be home soon. If I have to guard the door with a shotgun, I won't let your sister out until he gets back. Then he can deal with her. I know I never could. She'd never let me. Your father would never let me. That was their mistake. My mistake was ever letting them keep me from trying."

The next day the very worst happens: Kit and the Corvette are gone. That night, Moe and I sit up until the sun rises, our ears straining to catch the telltale rumble of a Corvette engine, but Kit does not return. Bosco, horrified by Kit's outlaw behavior, slides open the screen door shortly after dawn.

"Kit's not here yet, is she? She hasn't brought Daddy's car back, has she?" Bosco is already hyperventilating, and I realize that, if I weren't here, Bosco more than likely would be the one sitting up with Moe.

"Because Kit's not in bed," she goes on. "She's not in the bathroom. She's not in the kitchen. She's not here, is she? She's took the 'Vette and went to the north end of the island, didn't she? They're going to put her picture on TV, and we'll get RIF'd." Bosco pauses only long enough to gulp several breaths before wailing, "I can't leave Hickory. If Kit gets us RIF'd, we have to bring Hickory! I know I said when I got him that I knew we could only keep him while we were here and they would never let us bring him into the States anyway, but I don't care. He has to come, and"—Bosco makes a colossal effort and calms herself—"and if he can't, then I'll get a job here—probably cleaning stables—and I'll stay with him."

"Bosco, go get some cereal."

Bosco looks at me, stricken by my betrayal of her, of her love for Hickory the Horse. She runs into the house, sobbing madly.

The sun slices into Moe's gray eyes. "This is not good."

"I know."

For the rest of the day the three of us wait anxiously, surreptitiously monitoring the television. Bob and the twins bang in and out the screen door all day, consume vats of Kool-Aid, Fritos, and bean dip from a can, and never notice that their sister is missing. Moe and I whisper, trying to keep Bosco from hearing, as we debate what to do. By late afternoon, Moe is in favor of calling the APs.

"You call the Apes and the first thing they're going to do is notify Dad's CO. The second thing they'll do is put her face on TV. The third is ship us off-island."

"That wouldn't be the biggest tragedy this family has endured."

"Dad will flip."

Both of us fall silent at this prospect, which is when we notice Bosco snuffling softly into a sofa pillow.

"Mary Colleen Root, I told you, no one is getting RIF'd."

"It's not that." She pulls her face away from the sodden pillow. "I don't want my sister to be a white slave."

"What are you talking about now?"

"That's what happens to girls who go to the north end of the island. I heard Heather Jameson tell Donna Strickland. The GIs take the girls, sell them, and they're shipped out to Bangkok that night. When their parents finally find them, most of them are dead from being sexed too much."

"Where do you get this?"

"I didn't want to tell you because then you'd worry even more. But that's what happens. That's the part they don't put on TV."

"That's it. This discussion is over. I'm calling the APs."

I pull the phone out of Moe's hand. "Don't. I know where she is. I'll go get her."

"You know where she is? How long have you known?"

I don't answer.

"And you haven't said anything? For crying in a bucket, Bernadette, I know you two have your differences, but she's your sister, for Christ's sake! We're all in this together. How am I supposed to keep this family in one piece if you won't even—"

"I'll get her! I said I'd get her!"

I get lost a couple of times on the coral roads, my headlights tilting crazily off high banks of bamboo and habu grass that stab black spears into a navy-blue sky. It is completely dark by the time I reach the cave near Naha. The red Corvette is in the parking lot, next to Ron's Porsche.

I slip on the steep trail, scraping my knees. Finally, I see a slit of light marking the cave's entrance, grab the gnarled roots of a pine, and pull myself up toward it.

Smoke vents out the cave opening and mists the scene inside. A battery-powered tape player fills the cave with the echoey drone of a sitar. Three girls lie beside the fire, their bodies curved around the flames they watch with hypnotized stares. A couple of GIs sit behind two of the girls, remembering occasionally to massage a shoulder when they can break out of their own trances. The only actual movement is provided by Kit, who stands just beyond the circle of bodies, swaying to the music and watching her hands undulate in front of her face.

No one notices when I step in. In the shadows, two couples make love. I think I see Ron's pale shoulders in a far corner.

Kit's glassy-eyed stare fixes uncertainly on me. "What are you doing here?" she asks with detached pique, as if she were addressing an unpleasant vision in a dream.

I grab Kit's elbow and start for the exit. "Come on. We're going home."

Kit comes to life as if my touch had shocked her. "Get your motherfucking hands off me." She jerks her elbow away, staggering when the movement pulls her off balance. The girls on the ground look up at us as if we were appearing on a distant screen.

"Look, Moe is worried. She's going to call the Apes."

"The Apes?" Kit giggles for too long before she finally points to the guys on the ground. "They *are* the Apes." The two GIs snort silly little laughs and go back to staring at the fire.

I move back in with a no-nonsense "Come on, let's go."

With a swiftness that surprises me, Kit grabs my arm and bites down.

"Oops." Kit presses her finger against the Cupid's bow scar above her lip and tries to stifle a laugh, as if she might have just passed gas instead of sinking her teeth into me.

"You bitch," I say, more for the snicker than the teeth marks on my arm.

"Me? *I'm* the bitch?" The opium takes the edge off Kit's question so it sounds innocent and injured. "Oh, of course, I forgot, Kit is always the bitch. Let's not mention anything about Saint Bernadette stealing the only thing I ever wanted in life away from me." Kit's tone is strangely airy. She whirls in slow circles.

"I didn't *steal* that contest, Kit, I *won* it. Big difference."

Kit stops. "Contest? Not the contest, bozo."

"Well, what the hell are you talking about?"

Kit closes her eyes and twirls slowly away from me. As I watch her actually moving in time to the music, I realize how stoned she is. This might be the only chance I'll ever have to make my little sister talk to me. My tone is gentle. "Kit? Tell me, okay? What are you talking about? I stole the only thing that matters from you?"

Kit's pupils are tiny black leaves floating in a pond of aqua blue. She seems to forget who I am and answers in a small voice, "Mommy."

"Kit, what do you mean?"

"You know what I mean, silly." She undulates forward and slaps her palms against my chest with the slow-motion lassitude of seaweed swept by an underwater current.

"What, Kit? Tell me."

Her words spool out in a long, slow drift.

"You know, you two are always glued to each other. You always were. You were always sick or crying about something, or hurt. You hogged her. You still do. The way you two sit out on the patio and laugh and smoke."

"You could always come out and sit with us too."

"Right, and have the conversation stop the way it always does when I walk in." Kit seems less glazed now and more like a drunk on the verge of blubbering. "You know, there are people in this world who like having me around. Lots of them."

I should argue, tell her that I like having her around, but she would know it's a lie.

"You and Moe and Bosco, you're just this bizarre little closed club, and you decided a long time ago that I don't fit in."

"Kit, you always had your own little closed club."

"What?"

"You know what."

"Me and Dad?" Kit's head rolls sleepily forward on her chest and she snorts in exasperation. "You're kidding, right? Tell me you're kidding. Tell me that my egghead sister isn't that blind and that stupid."

I don't want to get into this, especially not in front of a bunch of cheerleaders on opium, but Kit seems suddenly, aggrievedly, coherent.

"You really haven't noticed that Dad hasn't spoken to me since I got tits? No, really not since the twins could throw a decent fastball."

I try and come up with a time in recent memory when our father has spoken to Kit and am stunned to discover I can't come up with one. Kit studies my face. "You *are* an idiot. You're an idiot, and now you're going to Tokyo. You stole that too."

"Kit, it wasn't yours for me to steal. I beat you. Bobby picked me."

"Right. So now you're going over there and you're going to find her, aren't you?"

I can't imagine what layers of resentment the opium has roiled for Kit to arrive at this deduction. Even though I know exactly who she means, I ask, "Find who?"

"Fumiko."

"Why not? Why shouldn't I?"

"Does the fact that she ruined our family matter to you at all?"

"How, Kit? How do you think Fumiko ruined our family?" I stand so close to Kit now that I can smell the sweet, smoky odor of opium on her breath.

"*Think?* I *know* and you know. You just won't ever admit that a big part of it's your fault."

"My fault? How did you cook that up in your deluded brain?"

"Fuck you. Fuck the three of you. You ganged up on me. On Daddy. Fumiko was more important to Mom than her own husband. You let her in and she ruined our family. We were happy before. Our parents talked. They laughed. We all laughed. We had a family. Then she ended it. Now we don't have a family."

"What are you saying?"

"You know what I'm saying. She screwed our father and wrecked our family, and you and Moe let it happen."

For a second all I hear is the crackle of the fire and the accelerated thump of my heart. It is both unthinkable and the only explanation for what happened to my family.

One of the girls giggles. I glance down and from her dreamy, unseeing stare realize that her amusement has as little to do with anything Kit and I have said as it does with the GI absentmindedly twiddling her nipple.

"Kit, come on, let's go home."

"No. I'm never going back there. Why should I? Why should I ever do one fucking thing you ever say?"

"Because if you don't, your picture is going to be on television and we'll get shipped off this island so fast your head will spin. And then, Kit, you won't be head cheerleader or prom queen your senior year of high school."

Kit is too ripped to drive, so we both get in the Corvette and make the trip back to Kadena in a stony silence that is only broken when we pull into the carport.

Kit seems not just cold sober when she speaks, but lucid in a way she has never been in her entire life. "There's no difference between you and me, you know. Not to them."

I turn off the ignition. "What are you talking about?"

"It all comes down to the same thing in the end. If you're a bad girl, they punish you by making you invisible. If you're a good girl"—Kit opens the door, pauses—"they reward you by making you invisible. That's your reward, ghost girl. You're a pale, silent ghost who nobody notices when she's here and nobody notices when she's gone."

Kit stands, slams the door, and walks away.

Brylcreem

Of course, Kit doesn't come to the airport, the commercial one in Naha, to see me off, but everyone else does. Moe wears a cotton shift bright with a red-and-yellow hibiscus print that we bought together at a stall in a Koza alley. The bright flowers and Moe's rosy cheeks help me dismiss Kit's accusations from the night before. The ghost-girl stuff is harder to forget. I try and remember a friendship I've ever kept up after we moved and can't think of a single one. For that matter, it's hard to recall the names of any friends I ever made to begin with. In the end there was always Moe, just Moe and the sibs.

The twins have disappeared. Bob and Bosco cluster with a group of Okinawan children around a man demonstrating a toy that looks like a Ping-Pong paddle with a wooden ball hanging down from it. As he twirls the ball, the chickens on top of the paddle start to peck.

A murmur of Japanese calls our attention to the main entrance. Okinawans crowd around the glass doors. On the other side, a driver opens the door of a black Lincoln Continental and offers his white-gloved hand to help Bobby Moses out.

I glance at Moe watching Bobby get out. The tropical sun glitters on his Brylcreemed hair and sharkskin suit. For one second, I am certain she is going to tell me I can't go and we were both insane to even consider the possibility that a major's daughter would ever play Joey Heatherton to this fifth-rate Borscht Belt comedian's Bob Hope. Instead, Moe digs an envelope out of her purse and hands it to me.

"You probably won't see her, but if you do—"

I don't have to read the envelope to know the name on it: Fumiko Tanaguchi.

Lavender

"You're back there in the cheap seats," Bobby says, as we step onto the plane. "I'm up here. I need the room." He heads up to first class and the Japan Airlines stewardess, impeccable in a blue suit, white gloves, and a pillbox hat atop her French twist, smiles, bows, and points to my seat in coach.

As soon as we take off, I slide Moe's letter out of my purse and stare at the envelope. Moe's loopy, old-fashioned handwriting twines across the front, spelling out *Fumiko Tanaguchi*.

"*Yoroshiku Onagaishimasu.*"

A stewardess in a dove-gray kimono stands beside me in the aisle offering a wet washcloth with a pair of tongs. The warm, damp cloth is lightly scented with lavender. Once I have wiped off my hands and face, it seems natural to simply set the damp cloth on Moe's envelope until the flap unsticks. I carefully remove the letter. Just as she always made an effort to speak slowly and clearly to Fumiko, Moe has obviously tried to keep her scrolling handwriting as plain and simple as the words she uses.

Dear Fumiko,
   I should have written this letter eight years ago. Probably I never would have if Bernie hadn't been going over.
   What I want to say is, although you took most of the blame, it was not your fault. I never really felt like it was, but you know why I couldn't write. We all just got caught up in a big mess that none of us could control. Maybe Mace was wrong for his part in it. I probably should have spoken up. About that and a lot of other

things. I don't know. We don't discuss it. I have thought of you so often over the past years and so wish I had stayed in touch. You were a good friend to me and to my family. I hope it is not too late for us to be friends again.

Sincerely yours,
Moe

I fold the letter and slip it back into the envelope.

It was not your fault.

Far below, the Pacific Ocean sits like an old friend who's waited a long time, eight years, for me to come back. Who remembers, as I remember that first crossing, twelve years ago.

October 1956

*B*y the time the S.S. *President Wilson* finally landed, I had been living on ice chips for ten days, and my father had to carry me to the upper deck for my first glimpse of Japan. A tug towed our ship into Yokohama Bay. As we slid past the black hulk of a sunken Japanese battleship staked upright in the black water of the bay, my father stared at the wreckage, absorbed to the point that his arms slipped a bit from under me and I had to cling like a starfish to hold on to him. Words I had heard before and not understood—"bombardier," "B-29," "saturation bombing"—connected then, both with the ruined ship and with my father.

When we docked, I was shocked to discover that Japan was like the world on the small screen of the brand-new television set we'd watched *Hopalong Cassidy* and *Howdy Doody* on back in California. There was no color in Japan; everything was black and white. The dock far below was a canvas of gray cement swarming with interchangeable cartoon people all drawn in black: black hair, black eyes, black clothes. Boys in black school uniforms with high Prussian collars pushed black bicycles. Women in black kimonos held umbrellas of oiled paper turned a slick black by the drizzle. Girls, their hair in black braids, wore black skirts, black jackets, black shoes, black backpacks. Men in black caps dug black dirt from the black earth with black shovels pushed by black rubber-booted feet.

"All right, troops." My father addressed Moe, Kit, and me. "We are entering a foreign land. Don't ever forget that you are ambassadors of the United States, of the United States Air Force, and of this family. I expect you to act accordingly."

Even as I was calculating how I would fit this ambassadorship in with my schoolwork, Kit pulled away from Moe.

"Eileen! Wait!"

My sister, already running down the gangplank, looked back at Moe only long enough to let it register that she had heard and had no intention of obeying. Moe, lumbering down the slick steps, glanced at my father for help with reining in my sister. He just grinned at Kit's bravery as she plunged ahead into the throng milling about on the dock. We hurried after her. Kit's blond hair had been bleached platinum by long days in the saltwater swimming pool, her cheeks and lips were a berry-stained pink, her eyes blue as a Siamese cat's. She was a dazzle of healthy American Technicolor in the gaunt and colorless world we had landed in. The crowd on the dock melted away from my sister as if a glowing ember had fallen onto a sheet of black ice.

A Japanese girl, her hair in pigtails, her cheeks chapped red, stepped forward, touched one of my sister's long blond curls, sucked her breath in, and called out on the inhalation, *"Utsukushii!"* I didn't need a translation. I'd heard the word constantly since Kit had been born. Beautiful.

"Hey! Wild Root!" The tallest man on the dock waved at us. He wore a peaked cap with a major's oak clusters.

"Coney!"

Coney. I'd heard that nickname for as long as I could remember. The major and my father went through aviation cadet training together at Kelly AFB. Then the war. Then Korea. I knew Coney Wingo was a Texan who'd gotten his nickname after a particularly wild ride. I'd always imagined the famous Major Wingo in a big hat and boots with pinto-hide chaps, but even in his uniform he looked like a cowboy, a head or two taller than all the Japanese who surged around him, his handsome face open as a prairie sky. He certainly sounded like a cowboy.

"My right-seat guy is here! Now hear this, now hear this: The Mace is *on-base.* Hey, buddy, we gonna fly us an *ay-ro-plane!* Yee-*haw!*"

My father let me slide to the ground and the men shook hands. Coney whacked my father with his free hand so hard that droplets of drizzle flew off my father's belted blue raincoat. As the men pounded each other, my father stopped being my father and turned into the stranger he became with other fliers. His happiness made him a stranger. He was happier in that moment of meeting Major Wingo than I could ever remember seeing him.

"And this little dazzler can't be Eileen, can she?" the major asked, kneeling down right in a puddle so that his face was in front of Kit's. Kit tilted her head to the side and said yes, she was Eileen. I backed away, terrified of receiving such attention from the big major.

Coney put his big hands out and wrapped them both around one of Kit's. "Well, I'm Major Wingo. That should be easy, right? A Wingo who flies, who's a pilot. That sound 'bout right to you?"

Kit smiled the special smile she reserved for strangers and officers.

Major Wingo didn't seem inclined to stand up from the puddle he'd knelt in until Moe waddled up. The major rushed forward then to relieve her of the heavy shoulder bag she carried.

Moe glanced around behind the major. "Is LaRue here?"

"No. Some Wives Club deal she couldn't get out of. We'll get together at the club later. She can't wait to see you all. Just can't wait."

His car was a big forest-green Pontiac with an Indian head on the hood and plenty of room inside. Major Wingo got behind the wheel and took his hat off. His hair was the golden clear color of beer and seemed to have sunlight falling on it even on that rainy day.

"Now *this* is more like it," Major Wingo said, when our father took the front passenger seat next to him. "Got my right-seat guy back. The old team, together again, eh? The world-beaters. The barn burners."

My father grinned a movie-star grin that dazzled me.

We headed into traffic and Major Wingo pulled into the

wrong lane. When a stream of cars hurtled toward us on the right side of the road I grabbed Moe and shrieked a mousy little shriek that made the men laugh.

"Leave it to the Japs to get it backasswards and drive on the wrong side of the road," Major Wingo explained.

That and everything else about this country seemed wrong. There were still no colors. Even the cars were only either white or black. It was crowded and chaotic. I wanted to go home but could no longer think of where that might be.

I snuggled up closer to Moe, who sat in the back between Kit and me. "What about the rest of the luggage?" she asked, looking back toward the harbor.

"The billeting officer'll pick it up for you. I wanted to show you to your new quarters myself."

"VOQ?" my father asked.

"Forget that Visiting Officer noise. No, I promoted a place on the economy for you. Had to cut a lot of red tape, but I swung it."

"Nothing on-base?" My father's disappointment was evident. "Even Wherry housing? Capehart?"

"Nada. Damned lucky to get this."

"So, we're in the ville, huh?"

"You'll love it. Little village, Fussa. It's right outside Yokota. What'd you come halfway around the world for, live in a cinderblock house and mow a lawn? Who needs that bull puckey?"

The frightening thought that we were going to live off-base in this colorless world plunged me into despair, and I complained about the one corner of my life I might possibly have any influence over. "I'm cold."

In the front seat, neither man acted as if they had heard me. They talked about the men they had flown with, and everyone was either a meatball, a hambone, a feather merchant, a brownnoser, or—the worst of the insults—a frigging ground pounder, a desk jockey.

"Hey, what about Blueblade?"

Major Wingo didn't answer.

"You know? Shapiro?" my father asked again. "Remember

that time he was in Alpha wing with us and he made that half-ass wingover outside of Pusan, took out his Norden, and he's reefing back on the column control but can't—"

"Didn't you hear?" Major Wingo stopped my father. "Shapiro augured in."

"Aw, Christ. No."

"Yeah, hotdogging in an RB-forty-seven. Came in low, doing three hundred knots at least. Maybe more. Horsed it back and couldn't hold the G's."

"I'm cold," I repeated.

"Aw, Christ. Once a fighter jock, always a fighter jock." The men in the front seat watched the wipers clear drizzle off the windshield.

"Mace, the girls' jackets are with the luggage and they're cold. We're all cold."

My father acted like he hadn't heard Moe either; then he asked Major Wingo, "Hey, skipper, what are the chances for some cabin heat in this bucket?"

"Check with the crew chief."

My father twisted a knob, and a blast of nauseatingly over-heated air dank with the odor of the wet wool of the men's uniforms shot into our faces. Kit put her head down on Moe's lap and in a spasm of territoriality I did the same, squeezing my sister onto one thigh and one thigh only. The men's voices clotted together with the roar of the heater, then faded into a blanketing drone.

I woke up with the inside of my nose and throat seared from the hot air and listened to the men's voices while Moe and Kit snuffled and whimpered in their sleep.

"Root, I appreciate this. I know you're high-enough time to be sitting in the left seat, commanding your own bird, but I promise you, put your fifty in with me and you are on your way to Command and Staff. I'll get Cartwright to cut the orders himself."

"You don't have to ask LaRue's old man to do any favors for—"

"Never done a damned thing in my life I 'had' to, Wild Root; this one I *want* to do. I *want* to do this for my right-seat guy. You just help me fly those fifty missions and your ticket is punched for anywhere you want to ride it to. We go back, Root. We've covered a few pages in the logbook together, right? I owe you, and Coney Wingo always pays up. Hey, did you hear? Dugan'll be here next week."

"Patsy Dugan! I thought that rumpot was stooging around in goonybirds out of Wright-Patterson."

"He was. I got him."

"Wingo! You got the Mick."

"Yeah, now that you're here the old team's back together. The Bong Bunnies fly again."

"The whole team? You got all the Bunnies? Don't tell me. You couldn't have—"

Before my father even finished his eager question, Major Wingo was grinning and nodding.

"Naviguesser! You got our naviguesser back!"

"Better believe it. Pulled Coulter right out of Offutt."

"No! You snaked Dub Coulter away from LeMay?"

"Correction, Wild Root, the general *gave* Coulter to me. He personally reassigned him to my crew."

Suddenly, the laughing jocularity left my father's voice. "Wait a minute, Wingo. You're saying the head of Strategic Air Command personally assigned Coulter to you."

"That's the name on his orders."

My father's tone suddenly turned serious. "Jeez, Coney, what kinda pop stand you running here?"

I saw Major Wingo's big handsome head swivel and shut my eyes quickly, so that all he saw behind him were three sleeping faces. Even so, when he spoke his voice was a low whisper I had to strain to hear.

"We're only going to talk about this once, Root, and that's one time too many. You got it? I report directly to LeMay himself. Green Door briefing at SAC. LeMay reports to the Joint Chiefs of Staff. That's it. That's the entire chain. I've got ten crews in the squadron. We're lead crew. We never appear on any budget, any operational chart, zip. Oath on a Bible. OSI gets your firstborn. The whole nine yards."

"Black?"

"As the ace of spades. We're weather reconnaissance. We're navigational training flights. You will never know the exact nature of any mission until we hit the cloud deck. Something goes wrong, you auger in, you survive, bite the capsule, buddy, 'cause no one's comin' for you 'cause the mission never happened and you never existed.

"For every swinging dick in the squadron, every Jap national dragging a hose on the Flight Line, every airman cranking a wrench, everyone—I mean everyone, including Moe and the kids—they got two hard-asses in OSI checking you out. You will never talk about the mission to anyone, not to me, not to Dub, Pats, any of the other crews, not to Moe, nobody. One question, Root, one wrong comment, and OSI will crawl so far up your ass you'll never get them back out. You'll be gone, your family will be gone, and there won't be one thing me or anyone else can do to help you because we're off the books now, Root. It's radio silence from here on in. You with me?"

My father nodded but didn't answer.

"You got any questions?"

After a long moment, my father spoke. "Yeah, Coney, I do have a question. A real big question." His voice was so quiet and serious that the breath caught in my throat.

Major Wingo was impatient, irritated. He clearly had not expected my father to have any questions. "What?"

"Where the hell does a guy go around here to restore his fluid levels?"

"Root, you ring-knocking son of a bitch!"

We drove onto Yokota Air Base and my lungs expanded with the first full breath I'd taken since we left Travis. Everything that was wrong about Japan was right here. The streets were broad and calm. Trees stood in tall, straight columns. The cars were blue, red, green, yellow. An American flag snapped overhead. A barbed-wire fence with a guard at the gate embraced it all. This was home. This was where I wanted to stay.

Kit woke up when Major Wingo stopped in front of the package store. Even though it was still drizzling outside, she insisted on going in with the two men. They ran through the parking lot, knees pumping high, splashing in every puddle on the way like boys playing hooky, with Kit held as high between them as the banner of the winning team.

The instant they left, I turned to Moe. "I don't want to live in Japan. I want to stay here."

"You're kidding. Living off-base is the luckiest break we've gotten yet. They can't get us off-base, the wives. No visits from the base commander's wife, and the president of the Officers' Wives Club, and most especially no visits from"—she leaned in closer and whispered—"the squadron commander's wife."

"But I thought Major Wingo was the squadron commander."

"You got that right, kiddo."

"So, you mean his wife is—"

Moe nodded. We had a special secret name for the wives Moe didn't like. The ones who thought they carried their husband's rank. The ones who spent all day playing bridge at the club and let their kids eat Ritz crackers for lunch. The ones who gossiped and said mean things. We whispered the name together: "A big fat pain in the keister!"

"Yep, LaRue Wingo of Paducah, Kentucky"—Moe put on a funny southern-belle voice—"is *Mrs.* Squadron Commander and never lets you forget it for one cotton-pickin' minute. Or that *Daddy* just happens to be General Chalmers Cartwright who just happens to run the whole show up there in PACAF."

I didn't care about LaRue Wingo's father, General Charmers Can't Write, or about the whole show up there in Pack Ass. All I cared about was that, whoever and whatever they were, Moe and I didn't like them. Like all outsiders, they were the glue that sealed the cracks in the little world we two had created. My homesickness disappeared. Moe was right. It was just her and me, we were in it together like the Army nurses sailing to Casablanca in their jungle of underwear, and we didn't want any wives around ruining it. We didn't want any outsiders at all.

The men swung Kit back into the car, then jumped in themselves.

"Wheels up!" my father yelled.

"Wheels up!" Major Wingo yelled back, pulling out fast enough to spin his car into a slide that cascaded a spray of gravel onto a fifty-five-gallon drum painted navy blue with the word TRASH stenciled on it in white.

"Taxi accident averted, skipper."

"Pilot to copilot. Pilot to copilot, you gonna just sit on that beer till it hatches or are you gonna pop one for your aircraft commander?"

My father cracked the opener into a Falstaff, handed it to Major Wingo, and opened one for himself.

Kit kicked on the back of Major Wingo's seat, begging him to make the car slide again.

As Major Wingo reached behind his seat to tickle Kit, who was giggling wildly, a jeep sped toward the parking lot exit on our right side. An instant before I screamed, my father calmly announced, "We got us a little departure hold there, Captain." At the last possible moment, Major Wingo saw the jeep and slammed on the brakes.

The wet brakes shrieked but didn't hold, and we careened crazily toward a collision with the jeep. At the last second, the jeep bumped into a culvert to avoid the Pontiac, but Major Wingo's big bearish body seemed frozen in an arc that pulled us back toward a concrete embarkment. My father grabbed the steering wheel, turning it for Major Wingo, and only then did the major pull out of the slide and, finally, stop. Moe and I were thrown back against our seats.

"We would have died if Daddy hadn't stopped him," I panted into my mother's ear.

"Par for the course for good buddy Wingo," Moe whispered. Her eyes were drawn tight in a hard stare at my father's boss and she panted hard, angry breaths. "Par for the g.d. course."

While the men pretended nothing had happened, Kit hung on the back of their seat, her arms around both their shoulders, begging Major Wingo to do it all again.

At the stop sign leaving the parking lot, Major Wingo revved the engine and Moe pulled Kit down and made her sit.

"Throttles forward." Major Wingo pretended to push some imaginary plane lever.

"Throttles forward." My father did the same thing.

"Boot 'em in the ass!"

"Boot 'em in the ass!"

With Kit kicking the back of his seat with wild delight, Major Wingo jerked his foot off the brake, slamming Moe and me back into our seats as he peeled out of the parking lot, shimmying onto the wet road.

"Mace, you've got two kids back here," Moe said, struggling to keep the anger out of her voice.

Major Wingo and my father exchanged looks like two boys reprimanded by an overly strict teacher. Then they laughed and my father opened more beers.

It was twilight by the time we reached Fussa and color was seeping back into this alien world. The main street was a mosaic of glass signs in jewel colors—sapphire, lapis lazuli, ruby, turquoise, emerald—all set off by red lanterns painted with black slashes of calligraphy. At a corner where a hot pink crab opened and closed his neon claws and a yellow-and-red fan spread wide, then shut, we turned down an alley. Our house was pressed in the middle of a row of small shops and houses, each one glowing like a lantern with soft light shining through paper screens.

Major Wingo stood at the door and yelled for a long time before a young Japanese woman in a kimono printed with poppies and pussy willows slid it open, then bowed. The woman seemed dazed as if we'd awakened her. Her hand wobbled as she pushed the door open further for us to enter.

Moe was at the head of our group and she didn't move, so we remained standing in front of the house. At the edge of my vision, I could see the doors of neighboring houses slide back. As heads peeked out up and down the alley to stare at us, I shriveled with embarrassment. The one who stared the hardest, though, was this strange woman bowing in the doorway of what was supposed to be our house who kept looking at me as if I were an old friend. Although she seemed to fight to keep her head down, every time I glanced in her direction the stranger's obsidian eyes were fixed on me.

"This is your maid, Fumiko," Major Wingo said. Moe glanced at my father, who shrugged to say he didn't know any more than she did. "She comes with the place," Major Wingo explained. "It's standard."

The idea of an outsider, a Japanese outsider to boot, breaching my one outsider-free sanctuary in life appalled me. I was certain that Moe would put a stop to this horrifying prospect. Moe had been an Indiana farm girl who stirred bluing into tubs of boiling sheets with a stick on wash day; she had been a student nurse who mopped the floor of her ward with carbolic acid under the stern gaze of Sister Aloysius; she was a mother who taught me how to make hospital corners on beds, who used vinegar and water and old newspapers to clean windows. Moe was simply not the sort who would ever have a maid. I was certain of that. Moe whispered something to our father.

"Don't worry," Major Wingo said. "She only speaks a few words of English and understands even fewer."

This outsider, this Fumiko, glanced at Moe, then bowed, ducking her head.

"We can't afford a maid."

Fumiko peered up at Moe, then again at me. Again, she looked at me as if we were old friends, as if we were in this together, sharing a joke, and she could barely keep a smile off her face. I glanced around to make certain that Kit wasn't standing behind me. This was exactly the kind of instant acceptance my beautiful little sister always inspired.

"She's ten thousand yen a month," Major Wingo said. "That's—what? Thirty a month. LaRue has a maid, a houseboy, a sew girl, *and* a nanny." Major Wingo's laugh echoed hollowly in the quiet alley.

"Thirty dollars a month? No one can live on that."

"War reparations. Japanese government kicks in some," Major Wingo explained to Moe. "Housing's still real tight. Better than it was right after the war when eight million of them were living in parks and sleeping under pieces of tarpaper, but, shit, if there ain't houses for American Air Force officers, you can bet there's not enough for them. So long as Fumiko works for an American officer, though, they'll put her up at the maids' dorm. Doubt she has anywhere else to go. But it's your decision, Moe. It's all the same to me."

Fumiko straightened up and watched my mother's face warily, searching for a clue to her future, then looked at me and lifted her eyebrows as if she and I were hoping for the same decision.

"Mason?" That Major Wingo used my father's real full name showed how serious and awkward this situation was.

"This really is Moe's call."

I prayed that Moe would tell them it was impossible. We Roots just didn't allow strangers into our houses, our lives. But then Moe gasped, put both hands on her stomach, and poked it, fingers prodding several different spots as she counted. "One, two, three, four, five! Oh, my God, there are at least five separate appendages poking me, which means . . ."

"Twins?" My father's question hoped there could be another answer.

"Twins," Moe confirmed, and in that moment of seeing herself washing two sets of dirty diapers in a house she wasn't certain even had running water, my mother became exactly the sort who would have a maid.

"I would love to have Fumiko's help."

At the sound of her name, Fumiko shriveled back into a bow and whispered "Madam," which came out as "My dam."

Instinctively, I resonated with Fumiko's fear, with the immense effort of not only speaking but speaking in a stranger's language.

Kit looked up at our father and laughed. "She said damn. You said damn was a bad word. She said a bad word."

I liked to think it was because of Kit's tone of amused mockery, but probably it was because I was the one being carried by an American officer wearing a blue hat with a silver eagle affixed to it that Fumiko stared, transfixed, into my face instead of my sister's, then touched, of all things, my widow's peak, sucked in her breath, and exhaled the word *utsukushii*. Beautiful.

"*Domo arigato.*" Fumiko's hand was a white crane slicing through the air, the sleeve of her kimono a wing trailing behind, as she bid us enter. Major Wingo didn't come in. He said Fumiko would get us all squared away, he had to make like a cow patty and hit the trail.

Then Moe, my father, Kit, and I followed Fumiko's hand into our new home.

Sweat

We are stuck in the line to go through Customs at Tokyo's Haneda Airport. Bobby bounces impatiently from foot to foot as we wait for the inspector to poke through a mountain of cardboard boxes being imported by a squat Okinawan man in a porkpie hat who buzzes around the inspector, chattering and pointing animatedly to his goods. The inspector has the white peaked hat and imperious demeanor of a Banana Republic dictator. Bobby slaps his passport against his fleshy palm and groans as the inspector opens yet another box of shell figurines. Standing next to him, I notice that his Brut cologne is losing the olfactory war with body odor.

"Aw, Jesus, what's he think this schmoe's smuggling into the country, sand? It's the same thing every time. They strip-search you when you come in, but when you leave you sail right out. That's the Japs for you. Believe evil only travels one way: *into* their country. Far as they're concerned nothing bad has ever come *out* of this country, and that includes World War Two."

Bobby catches me glancing at his passport, reading the name Moishe Rosenblatt printed on it. "What? You think Jackie Mason is Swedish?"

At last the customs inspector gestures for us to move forward. The boxes of shells clatter as the Okinawan pushes them away with his foot while bowing to the inspector.

"Great!" Bobby asks the inspector, who doesn't understand a word, "You sure you're done with the Shell King here and his criminal empire?"

While Bobby tries to kibbitz with the inspector, I glance

around the airport. The first time I catch sight of Fumiko, my heart lurches. By the fourth time I'm certain I've spotted her, I relax, reassured that the only place I will meet her again is in memories. Memories that always start with that little house on the alley in Fussa.

Honeysuckle

*H*aving this Fumiko stranger in our tiny paper house all the time was bad enough. What was even worse was the horror of school at Yokota's Bob Hope Elementary. On my first day, I was herded into a Quonset hut, a giant can cut in half lengthwise, where catatonia seized me upon being strafed by the merciless gazes of twenty-eight children and my new teacher, Miss Ransom. Miss Ransom wore ballet slippers and shirtwaist dresses. At thirty-five, she had signed on with the Department of Defense school system to add adventure and a husband to her life. Moe quickly learned and just as quickly told me that my teacher was a regular fixture at happy hour at the officers' club—mixed drinks a quarter, beer a dime—where she made new friends with the flight crews that rotated in and out of Yokota on TDY.

I learned for myself that Miss Ransom usually smelled of incompletely metabolized vodka and cigar smoke, and her nerves were not all they should have been. Trying to teach twenty-eight students, too many of them the children of old boyfriends, pushed Miss Ransom to her limit. The addition of a twenty-ninth, myself, who refused to speak and cried if you looked at her crosswise, pushed Miss Ransom beyond that limit.

"Let's all draw a picture of the new girl crying," she invited the class, the morning after three-for-one Manhattan night at the club, which, unfortunately, coincided with the commencement of my third straight week of blubbering.

Kit's new-girl experience was radically different. She woke up early every morning and dressed herself in the outfit she'd color-coordinated and laid out the night before, eager not to miss a moment of fun at her new kindergarten, where both boys and girls chased her around the playground and tried to kiss her.

I, on the other hand, prayed nightly for illness. I prefered that it not be a deadly one, but if death was the only way out of Bob Hope Elementary, I was willing to accept it.

"You just have to *be* a friend to *make* a friend," my mother counseled, as she braided my hair while I sat on a high stool in the kitchen, snuffling, begging to stay home. That I had no more clue how to *be* a friend than I did how to *make* one, that the process was so foreign I couldn't even ask a question about it, filled me with desolation. The song of the canary Moe had bought to cheer me up only emphasized how un–cheered up I was and depressed me even further. We'd named the bird Chisaii after Moe had gotten out the English-Japanese dictionary and found the word for "small." As Chisaii warbled, I mourned for the lost paradise of those days of the past summer before we moved, when Moe would put on her Harry Belafonte album and we'd calypso through the housework, Moe swinging her hips saucily as she pushed the Electrolux, me operating the feather duster, both of us singing loud enough to be heard over the roar of the vacuum cleaner.

Daylight come and me wanna stay home!

"Don't make me go. Don't make me go. Please, please, please, don't make me go," I begged. "I'll clean up the whole house for you."

But Moe didn't need me to help her with the dusting anymore. The intruder, Fumiko, helped her now. Fumiko was always there, silent, smiling, nodding, taking the broom out of my mother's hands when she tried to sweep, chirping in her hateful Japanese and touching her own stomach to remind Moe that she was pregnant. Then Fumiko would shoo Moe toward a chair, where she plopped down heavily, and bring her a cup of tea. The realization that the stranger had taken my place undid me.

"You're a crybaby." Kit, standing next to the stool, did not make this observation in an unkind way; she simply stated an obvious fact. I kicked her in the mouth with the toe of my new school shoe hard enough to make her lip bleed. Chisaii's warbling grew abruptly louder in the split second of stunned silence that fell after the kick. Then, in rapid succession, Moe slapped me, Kit broke into a full wail, and Moe grabbed her belly, sucking in sharp breaths.

Moe's face paled and her fingers clawed spasmodically at the countertop. Fear paralyzed my breathing and the canary's hateful singing grew far too loud. Then Moe breathed again and, without losing a beat, I took up my refrain. "Don't make me go. Don't make me go. Please, please, please, don't—"

Moe slapped me again and shoved me out the door. In the alley, I turned to see her squinching her face up in pain and grabbing the mound of her stomach while Fumiko helped her back to bed.

On the long bus ride to school, Kit sat in the back row with all the little girls vying to be her friend. I sat up front, right behind the driver, and stared out the window at construction workers wearing white headbands and black rubber boots with the big toe separate from the rest and thought they were the luckiest humans in the world. I wished with all my heart I could trade places with any one of them.

At the end of that interminable day, after I'd memorized the spelling words before anyone else and written an extra-credit report on marsupials, and cried at recess, and cried at lunch, and cried when Miss Ransom called on me, I rode the bus home alone because the base commander's daughter had invited Kit to her house. When we finally arrived at Fussa, I rushed through the drizzle that hadn't stopped since we arrived. I turned down our alley and, running, ignored all the strange sights and sounds, holding my breath against the stink of the *benjo* ditches until I was back in my home, away from all the outsiders, and could breathe again.

"Moe!" My voice cracked. It was the first word I had spoken since leaving that morning. "Moe?" I rushed into the house past the flat bowl laid with river stones where Fumiko had arranged three purple irises, impaling their crisp stalks on a barbed weight. I pushed back the paper-paneled door to my parents' room and found Moe lying in bed. Fumiko was there, setting a cup of tea on the nightstand. She melted away when she saw me glaring at her.

"Why are you in bed?" My tone was accusatory.

"I'm just tired, that's all, poops. Come here."

My parents had a real bed because my father refused to sleep on the futons that had come with the house.

"I'm sorry I slapped you this morning." Moe put her hand on my cheek. Her hand was cool, far cooler than it should have been.

"Two times," I reminded her.

"I'm twice as sorry."

"It hurt." I didn't have to try very hard to leak out a delicious, self-pitying tear.

"I know, baby, I know."

Moe pulled me into bed and snuggled with me. I closed my eyes and inhaled her smell. The tears were gone in an instant and I remembered what I wanted to show her.

"Look!" I wiggled my front tooth with my tongue. "It's almost out." The tooth had been loose for over a week and was hanging on by a thin thread of gum tissue. I wished the worthless baby tooth would fall out; it stabbed me every time I took a bite.

With no warning, Moe winced as if a loud noise had hurt her ear. "Could you go outside and play?" Her question came out in little gasps. "I need to rest. Please, just go outside."

Fumiko pulled me away; I hadn't even heard her approach. I jerked away from her soft grasp and looked to my mother to save me, but her eyes were closed. Worse, Moe reached out her hand to Fumiko and squeezed it tight while she sucked air in through her teeth. I slammed out the back door.

Behind our house was a yard of beaten dirt ringed by a barbed-wire fence. The top of the rusted fence was crowned with a collapsed heap of honeysuckle. Beyond the fence spread the field of a farmer who drank tea from a tiny brass pot. He wore a conical straw hat, and on rainy days added a cape, also woven of straw, so that he looked like the roof of a very small thatched cottage moving about his small field. We worked silently on opposite sides of the barbed wire. He on his farm, I on my perfume factory.

I'd started the perfume factory because all my toys were still with the rest of our belongings on a cargo freighter weeks away from arriving. Fortunately, Moe always had bottles. I'd emptied out the brown stoppered bottle the nose drops from my last cold had come in from the dispensary on Mather Air Force Base. Also the bottle of cough syrup, Eileen's leftover St. Joseph's baby aspirin, and the last bit of emerald-green Prell shampoo. The bowers of honeysuckle in my new location inspired me, and every day after school I escaped into the drizzle, outside, away from Fumiko, to collect flowers and turn them into the perfume that would make me so famous they'd have to let me out of Miss Ransom's class.

Absorbed in the business of capturing the white flowers' sweet smell, I forgot everything: Moe's pain, Fumiko's unwelcome presence, even Miss Ransom. I stuffed a bowl with the blossoms and pounded them to a gray slurry ready for bottling. I was filling the Prell bottle when I noticed that, for the first time since we landed, the misty drizzle had stopped and the sun was warming my back. It must have been out for a while because, when I looked up, the clouds had burned away and in the distance far beyond the farmer's field a mountain was visible for the first time. It had the same conical shape as the farmer's straw hat. A ruff of pink clouds hung about the peak's snowy summit, making it look like something especially good from the bakery, a bun with pink frosting and powdered sugar.

As the sun came out, I saw for the first time that Japan was a scrumptious country. The dark earth of the farmer's field and its layer of green vines were the exact colors of an Andes mint. The scattering of dried weeds called to mind the toasted coconut crispness of Chicken Bones. But the earth—the earth was the luscious almost-black brown of hot fudge. And the pink clouds around the mountain; the more I stared at them, the more they looked like cotton candy. Like Brach's cherry nougat. Like pink Neccos.

Lost in a candy reverie, I was startled by Fumiko's voice whispering at my ear, "Fuji-san." I turned, ready to run, to hide from the stranger, but her face was right at my level, stopping my escape. For the first time, I was forced to inspect it closely. Astonishingly, I found that, like her country, Fumiko's face was candied, an apple dipped in a shiny caramel glaze with patches of red at the cheeks and lips. And her hair and eyes were not black, but the same almost-black hot-fudge brown of the earth. "The name of mountain, we call Fuji-san."

"You speak English. Major Wingo said you only spoke a few words."

She laughed like one of the bunnies in *Bambi* and covered her mouth. "*Skoshi*." She held up her thumb and forefinger, barely parted. "Very little bit."

It took me a moment to understand that an adult could speak like a child, turning *v*'s into *b*'s and *l*'s into *r*'s so that "very little" came out as "berry rittoe." Her babyishness made me feel grown-up and strong. She dipped her head in a deferential way that reinforced my feeling of power and pointed her graceful, crane-like hand toward the mountain.

"Fuji-san most holy mountain of Japan."

Even before I could translate "horry" into "holy," in my child's anthropology, I concluded that the people of Japan wore conical hats and carried conical umbrellas in honor of their holy mountain's holy shape.

"The tooth of you mouth?" Fumiko pointed tentatively to my loose tooth. "You wish it go away?"

I nodded. "It pokes me."

"When I am a little girl"—hearing her say "rittoe gurrow" made me feel like a big one—"my mother . . ." Fumiko pursed her lips and I supplied the word she pantomimed.

"Blow."

Fumiko was delighted by my remarkable intelligence. "*Hai! Doso.* Broe. My mother broe." She spread her hand to indicate a vanished tooth, then inclined her whole body toward me to offer the question: "I broe?"

I nodded, not certain what I was agreeing to.

"Close eyes." Her hand slid over my eyes and Fumiko blew the smell of talcum powder and rice crackers and of the jasmine flowers in her green tea into my open mouth. I was thinking what silly, infantile people these Japanese were when Fumiko pulled her hand away. Light cracked across my eyes. I was about to ask why she hadn't taken my tooth out like she said she would when I tasted the salt of blood and looked into her hand. My small white tooth rested in a foamy pink slush in her palm. I couldn't wait to tell my mother about this marvel, our maid's magical power to blow teeth out of a person's head. Fumiko pulled a handkerchief out of the sleeve of her kimono and pressed it against the empty spot in my gum.

She cleaned my tooth and held it up. "In Japan when tooth come out, you throw up in . . ." She steepled her hands together and I barked out, "Roof." "*Hai! Hai! Domo arigato*, roof, and you make wish. Tooth is *presento* to . . ." She pointed up.

"Gods?" I supplied.

Her smooth brow creased; she shook her head, held my tooth up next to her mouth, and pretended to gnaw it. "Like Mickey."

"Mouse?"

"*Hai!* More."

She stretched her hands apart and I guessed, "Bigger? Rats?"

"*Hai!* Rats. *Presento* for rats." She put the tooth in my hand.

The pedant and xenophobe burst awake in me. "We do something better in America. We put it under our pillow and the tooth fairy comes and gives you a dime."

"Fumiko!" My mother's voice alarmed me, as did the startled look that widened Fumiko's eyes before she hurried off, sliding swiftly out of her sandals at the doorway without missing a step.

I looked at my tooth and imagined Fumiko wishing for and receiving one of the chalk-faced dolls in a red kimono with golden threads that I'd seen propped up in dusty shop windows. I would never have wasted a wish on a doll. I would have asked for an insect-collecting kit with actual syringes and formaldehyde or that game I'd seen in the PX where a light went on if you knew that the heart was a muscle or that the formula for water was H_2O and touched metal probes to the right answer.

It was exciting to discover that in Japan little girls' wishes were granted. Back in America my wishes—for a blond cocker spaniel like Lady in *Lady and the Tramp*, for blond hair, for a friend, not to have to move, not, in fact, to ever have to leave my house again—were always ignored. Even when I prayed three rosaries to the Blessed Virgin.

I was not about to give my tooth away for ten cents or throw it to the rats. Not when I had the most holy mountain in Japan right in front of me. I dragged the high stool into the backyard, shoved it next to the fence, climbed up, cleared away the honeysuckle vines, and carefully placed my tooth on the top of the fence so that it was in a direct line with the scoop of the crater at Fuji-san's crest. Then I shut my eyes and whispered my wish from the bottom of my heart.

The next morning, when a boil large enough to keep me home from Bob Hope Elementary appeared on my backside, I switched my allegiance from the Blessed Virgin Mary to Fuji-san.

Released from the terror of school, I snuggled into the futon that made me feel as if I were camping out, breathed in the clean grass smell of the tatami mats covering the floor, and listened to the sounds in the alley. Children chattered words that clacked and exploded as they walked to school. The night-soil man, his honey buckets balanced on a yoke over his neck, thumped past. A noodle vendor tootled some notes on his flute and called out hoarsely, advertising his wares. The wooden *getas* of housewives clattered past. I listened to my father and Kit.

"Oats for my wee bonnie lassie." My father banged the wooden spoon he used to serve oatmeal against the side of Eileen's bowl. I imagined her, long curls tied to one side with a blue bow, watching my father, her small teeth parted in open-lipped admiration.

"No milk, okay, Daddy? Japan milk is yucky."

It was true. The commissary sold an odd mixture of reconstituted powdered milk "filled" with coconut oil, but Moe still made us drink it. "Just brown sugar and butter."

A bit later, I heard my father buttoning Eileen into her red coat—"Hold still, you wiggle worm"—and then they left, my sister begging my father not to ride in front with the taxi driver but to sit in back, right next to her.

I waited for the best sound of all, Moe singing, her voice prettier than any of the records she sang along with. But Chisaii was the only one singing that morning and, once the sun rose high enough, even he stopped.

I woke up again when the front door slid open and Fumiko's soft tread padded past my room as she hurried to the little room by the back door where her work apron hung on a nail, next to the sink and above her bucket.

"Good morning—" Fumiko chirped out from the hallway, then hesitated. My mother had told her to cut out this "my dam" business and just call her Moe like everyone else. So Fumiko now simply avoided direct address altogether. I heard the whisper of Moe's door being opened.

A moment later, Fumiko yanked my door open. She was pulling her apron off. "Stay in you room. I get taxi for Moe."

By the time I decided to disobey, Fumiko and a ropy little driver in a battered sea captain's hat were helping my mother into a cab. Moe had her beige trench coat on over her flannelette nightgown.

"Moe!" I cried out. When she turned, her chestnut hair looked too dark against her pale face.

"Be good, poops," she said, and Fumiko and the driver helped her into the cab. Beneath my feet, prints of her feet were stamped in blood on the tatami mats.

She grabbed Fumiko's hand. "Stay with Bernie." Each word cost Moe an effort. Fumiko nodded, closed the door of the cab, stepped back, and stood beside me. We stared down the alley long after the cab had vanished.

Eventually, Fumiko tried to herd me back into the house. "Mama be okay."

I jerked away from her. "She's not your mother. She's *my* mother!"

"*Hai! Gomen nasai!* So sorry."

Having an adult grovel before me cheered me up enough that I broke into blubbering wails. As I cried, Fumiko unwound her kimono sleeves, which she kept bound up when she worked, reached in, and pulled out a small leather coin purse. From the purse she extracted three dull silver ten-yen coins and pressed them into my palm. They were as light as old leaves.

Without a word, Fumiko led me down the alley and out onto the main street of Fussa. Housewives in wooden *getas* and dull gray kimonos, holding string bags, stopped dead on the brick sidewalk to watch as Fumiko pulled an odd round-eye child through streets where few Americans appeared.

We passed a restaurant with a glass case in front displaying platters of golden-battered tempura and bowls with noodles hanging, frozen, from chopsticks, all made out of wax. We passed a newsstand. Chains lay across the magazines. All the covers faced the wrong way and most seemed to feature the same kittenish Japanese woman, her hair either pulled back in a French twist or tucked under a jaunty Peter Pan hat cocked over her eye at a rakish angle.

The fanciest shop in town had a life-size cutout of a smiling Japanese woman in a purple kimono printed with cherry blossoms outside. The cutout woman held a sign that read in English, WELCOME TO OUR REXALL DRUG STORE. In her other hand she extended a handwritten sign, also in English, that asked, YOU DON'T FEEL WELL? TRY A MILTOWN. I wanted to look at the watches and face creams arrayed in glass display cases around boxes of Rinso White soap powder, but Fumiko tugged me on.

We turned into another alley, this one lined with cheap noodle houses with navy blue banners slashed by white ideograms hanging at the top of the open doorways. Fumiko led me to a small shop where blue plastic buckets, pink plastic dishpans, white and turquoise plastic beach balls, and pink swim floats in the shape of horses hung outside.

The shop reeked of dried fish. A lady barely taller than I with a bad perm and several gold teeth rushed to greet us, her *getas* banging on the wooden floor. She and Fumiko bowed several times and spoke in high-pitched voices that grew progressively higher. Fumiko's twittering bird tones sounded fake to me, as if she were imitating a little girl, because the timbre of her voice was so much deeper when she spoke English. When they finished, Fumiko gestured for me to give the woman the leaf coins. I handed them over and the woman appeared delighted, as if I were an exceptional child who had accomplished a deed exceptional enough to merit the flashing of all her gold teeth and happy choruses of high-pitched hosannas. *"Ano kodomo-wa honto-ni riko desu!"*

Containing her amazement at my performance, the shopkeeper spread a piece of paper and filled it with candies she fished out of glass jars with a pair of lacquered chopsticks. The pile of sweets grew. I marveled that my leaf money could purchase such a hillock. Just when I thought she was finished, the shopkeeper looked at me, reassessed the depth of my genius, burst into another hallelujah chorus, and added yet another candy to the pile. Finally, she gathered the paper and twisted it into a little hobo sack. She wrapped that parcel in powder-blue tissue, covered it with a thick piece of paper printed with doll faces, then tied the whole bundle with pink ribbon. I joined Fumiko in bowing our way out of the store.

By the time I undid the layers of wrapping and was chewing on a piece of candy covered in paper that dissolved into an amazing edible slime, I had forgotten about the footprints. As I discovered jawbreakers striated with a hundred thin colored layers, powdery bubble gum, spicy-sweet ginger chews, and my favorite, the chewy white caramel Milkies, my purpose in Japan had revealed itself to me: to collect as many of the leaf coins as I could and purchase as much candy as possible.

Fumiko stayed at our house that night. After my father

refused her offer to fix dinner for us, she retired to the cot he'd set up for her in the little room where she hung her apron.

"Beanie-Wienies à la Dad!" My father announced the evening's menu as he opened several cans, sloshed them into Moe's big cast-iron skillet, and proceeded to add squirts of all the condiments on the shelf: ketchup, mustard, pickle relish, soy sauce. "And the secret ingredient!" He dumped half of the can of Falstaff he was drinking into the mixture.

"Moe bakes them," I informed him, deeply unsettled by this slapdash improvisation. "With brown sugar. That's why they're called baked beans. And she also gets one of those cans of brown bread from the commissary and heats it up; then we have cream cheese."

"Well, this is the way I make them." My father stirred the beans over the blue flame of the rickety two-burner propane stove. He finished off the beer and punched triangles into the top of another one.

"It's the wrong way. Moe doesn't do it that way." My eyes prickled and I tried hard not to cry.

"I like them Daddy's way."

"All right! One vote for the old man!" He raised his can of Falstaff to Kit, who hoisted her glass of milk back at him with a party gaiety that only amplified the overwhelming fact that Moe was not there.

"Two Beanie-Wienie Supremies coming up! Sit down."

"I can't."

"Oh." He remembered my boil and slapped down a plate in front of me and one in front of Kit. Streaks of yellow mustard swirled through the soupy beans. The vinegary smell of hot pickle relish combined with the sight of the greenish chunks peppered through the slurry of beans knotted my stomach and caused me to make heaving, choking sounds.

"Do not! Repeat, do not throw up!"

I began to cry.

"Jesus Christ on a crutch!" My father tossed the wooden

spoon into the skillet and a projectile of beans splashed out. "Not the goddamn waterworks."

"She's a crybaby." Kit's voice had the same even, nonjudgmental tone it had carried when she'd made this observation earlier. My father caught Kit's eye to communicate that he agreed with her.

Kit glanced at the clock and cried out, "Sumo time!"

The screen of our television was as small as a porthole on the *President Wilson*. The tubes gradually warmed until grayish images appeared: two sumo wrestlers butting against each other like rams. Sumo wrestling was the only program we could get aside from plays where Japanese people, their faces painted white, sang to each other in shrieking voices so high they sounded like an old-fashioned radio being tuned to a distant, wavering station. The one other program we could receive starred a hero called Geiko Kumin who rode around on a motorbike with a towel tied around his neck. I liked that one a lot, but they kept changing the time when it appeared. Kit, on the other hand, liked sumo wrestling entirely because our father did.

On-screen a referee with a beard like a billy goat, dressed in a white gown with a small box tied to his head, waved a curious square fan to signal that the match was over. The two wrestlers parted, bowed, danced lightly down the steps and out of the arena. Two new wrestlers took their places.

"Daddy, it's Thunder Thighs and Easter Island!" Kit called out our father's nicknames for the wrestlers as they stepped into a ring made by a circle of fat rope, each one wearing an apron held up by coils of rope thick as dock cable with zigzag streamers hanging down. Their gleaming black hair was pulled up into top-knots. One of the wrestlers wore an Ace bandage wrapped beneath a dimpled knee. When the aprons came off, they stood in their blubbery abundance wearing nothing but loincloths that wedged into the cleft between their massive buttocks. This was the only part of sumo wrestling that appealed to me, the chance to see naked butts.

The opportunity was maximized during limbering-up exercises when the giants, posteriors to the camera, squatted, stomped the ring with thunderous concussions, and balanced first on one mammoth haunch, then the other, stopping occasionally to toss handfuls of salt about.

"They're purifying the ring," my father explained.

Easter Island was impassive throughout, not responding to Thunder Thighs's repertoire of theatrical expressions.

"He's going to win," Kit said, pointing to the comically ferocious Thunder Thighs.

"I'll take that bet." My father held out his palm and Kit pretended to slap imaginary money across it. "Easter Island's gonna cream the big man. He can hold his mud. Thunder Thighs's just a lot of hot air."

"Says you," my little sister sneered back.

My father grinned at my sister's perfect imitation of him. "Hey, who taught you to talk like that?"

"I take Easter Island too," I said, but my father and Kit didn't look away from the set, and no one put a hand out to receive my bet.

The wrestlers crouched and approached each other several times, but the referee waved them back. Finally, they stampeded forward. Pushing and lunging, they grabbed at the black loincloths that disappeared up their butt cracks to heave each other around.

"Come on, Easter!"

"Come on, Thunder Thighs!"

"Go, Easter Island!" Only after I yelled out did I realize that my timing was off.

"He already won, dodo."

Even though my father had explained that the object was to force the other guy either to step out of the rope ring or to touch the ground with anything but his feet, I always missed the deciding moment.

"Yay, Easter! Creamed him, I told you!" My father gloated.

"Hah! You buy the beer." Kit, leaning her whole body against the opener, happily punctured another can of Falstaff and handed it to my father.

"When is Moe coming home?" I asked. "When can I see her?"

"Visiting hours are already over today."

"When are they tomorrow? Can we go tomorrow?"

"Look, Bernadette, your mother needs a little R and R. She's resting. She's not supposed to see anyone."

I sensed the menace that lurked behind my father's casual tone.

"She's supposed to see me." I hated the whiny one-blink-away-from-tears wobble of my voice and tried to swallow it down. But Kit had heard the telltale warble and was already rolling her eyes as I asked, "Did you see her? Is she going to be okay? There was blood—" By then I was sobbing openly. My father patted my back and told me not to get so worked up. Mom would be fine. But she wasn't Mom to me; she was Moe.

I went to bed and, lying on my stomach, read the Wizard of Oz book I'd had my father bring me from the base library. I waited for the series' usual narcotic effect, strong as the one that overtook Dorothy when she walked across the poppy fields, to sweep me away. But it didn't. The story of *The Laughing Dragon of Oz* was hollow and heartless, as out of kilter as my world had become the instant Moe left. Worse, it was about a *boy*. I checked the spine of the book and noticed the two traitorous letters following Frank Baum's name: Jr. In the foreword that I'd ignored in my haste to achieve escape velocity, I learned that the real L. Frank Baum had died in 1919 and his imposter son, the incompetent pretender, Jr., had authored this bit of counterfeit pulp.

Then the full implications of such treachery truly settled in and my heart raced and I had to open my mouth to breathe: If even the great L. Frank Baum could die, never to write another book, leaving his child, inadequate and unprepared, behind . . .

From down the alley, the insect whir of the pachinko parlor clattered and droned. I remembered our last move, when we drove from Wichita Falls to Mather Air Force Base and took a detour to see the Grand Canyon, where I'd plucked up all my courage and peeked down into that endless emptiness. I had the same feeling now, thinking about my life without Moe.

I slammed the book shut, ripped open my pink *All About Dinosaurs* book, and began to read, racing after the words until they formed a vision of a peg-toothed brontosaurus munching its way through forests of ferns so compelling that my heart slowed and my stomach unknotted.

It was dark and the alley was silent when the car's headlights shining through our paper screens woke me up. The roar of the engine cannonaded through the sleeping paper-and-wood alley. I slid back the paper screen at the window just a crack. Just enough to see Major Wingo behind the wheel of his Pontiac. My father stepped into the alley. Major Wingo leaned out the window and said, "Mace, Tachikawa Hospital called. It's Moe."

My father was dressed and in the car in less time than it took me to start crying. Kit, snoring loudly beside me, never woke up.

I stood at the open window for a long time, long enough for the cold to seep up through my feet and chill my whole body, crying, yearning for the Pontiac to return with my mother.

My bedroom door slid back but I refused to turn around until Fumiko hissed at me several times. She wore a gray sweater over her navy blue kimono and had *tabi,* white cotton socks with a separate pocket for her big toe, on her feet. She waved for me to follow her.

The kitchen was warm and smelled like my idea of heaven, cooked sugar. On a plate on the table, sections of candied tangerine were arranged in a pinwheel. Fumiko gestured for me to eat one. My intense love of all things sugared overcame my equally intense antipathy toward fruits and vegetables, and I put one of the sections in my mouth. The lightly caramelized coating crackled slightly as it gave way beneath my teeth and then blended with a squirt of sweet citrus juice.

Melted sugar bubbled like lava in the black skillet, then

sizzled and hissed as Fumiko slid in the unglazed tangerine sections. She arranged another plateful and set them down before me on the table, where I stood and ate with an automatic intensity. As long as my mouth was flooded with sweetness, I could keep the terrifying awareness of Moe's absence at bay.

"Doing wah-wah—*ne*?—Fumiko mutter aw-mose die."

I couldn't make any sense of Fumiko's words. I wondered if she was using the baby word for water, wah-wah. Seeing my confusion, Fumiko gestured for me to wait. "Momento, *kudasai*." A minute later she returned, paging through a small red Japanese-English dictionary. The little red book ushered Fumiko and me into a realm where my pedantic bookworm tendencies blended perfectly with her incomprehensible eagerness to communicate and console. I couldn't understand why she seemed to like me so much in spite of how fiercely I pushed her away.

With Fumiko pointing to the English words beside the kanji characters and me prissily reading out their meanings, I translated her words into "During the war, my mother almost died." I had to know this story of a mother *almost* dying.

"What happened?"

"Wah-wah short time, *ne*? *Takusan, takusan, takusan,* uh . . ." She searched the dictionary until she found the word written in kanji characters, pointed to it, and I supplied, "Bad." Pushing the little dictionary between us like the planchette of a Ouija board that pointed to the words you needed to know, I deciphered not just what Fumiko had said but what she meant: "The last days of the war were the worst."

At that moment of my desperation and Fumiko's inexplicable desire to comfort me, with the scent of caramelized sugar soothing me, we both became unguarded children and communicated in the telepathic way of children. Though Fumiko's actual speech was still childish and ungrammatical, something magical happened between us. The missing articles, *l*'s turned into *r*'s, mangled syntax, all disappeared and, combined with the children's Japanese I'd overheard in the alley and a little help from the dictionary, Fumiko's story formed itself directly in my imagination.

"The last days of the war were the worst," Fumiko began. "Late in 1944, the bombing was so heavy that my mother and my little brother and I were evacuated from our fine house in Tokyo. The government sent us to a village where we didn't know anyone. My mother wrapped the baby and carried him on her back, and we pushed our futon and our pots and pans and my mother's kimonos in a cart to a cave. Yes! We lived in a cave! We chased out the bats and the snakes, but the smell of their shit remained.

"Our cave was near a village built on rocky soil where no rice would grow, so the villagers grew wheat and millet. Japanese who have no rice are mean and bitter people. The men were either woodcutters or charcoal burners. The women tended tiny vegetable gardens, braided straw into sandals or rain capes, and sent their children into the woods to hunt for herbs, nuts, and roots. We hunted with them and brought back roots and weeds that gave us diarrhea.

"The villagers took advantage of us. For a small fish, for some millet mixed with wheat and mock barley, for some nuts and a withered eggplant, they would demand one of my mother's kimonos. For a chicken and a dozen quail eggs, they took her wedding kimono stitched with golden thread and carefully preserved with camphor. When all my mother's kimonos were gone, she made soup with grass that tasted like dirt and left us even hungrier than we were before we ate it. At first, my brother and I cried for food; then I was too tired to make any sound. When she nursed my brother, my mother cried because there was no milk left and it felt as if he were pulling electricity from her empty breasts.

"My brother died, and overnight my mother became an old woman. Her hair dangled in wisps around the shoulders of her dirty cotton kimono. Worst of all, she no longer made any effort to keep her knees properly closed when she sat down. My mother! Before the war she used to tie my legs together with a silk sash, so that even in sleep I would resist such vulgar postures.

"She looked like a scarecrow. This frightened me worse than the air raids, which turned the mountain ridges pink. Worse even than thinking about myself dying. One morning, she could not make herself stand and lay all day on the futon and whimpered in the same sick kitten way my brother had before he died. I knew what I had to do.

"At sunset, I crawled out of the damp cave, faced Fuji-san, and made my offering. If she would spare the life of my mother, I would give her my own.

"The next morning, I awoke to find a pair of legs in dust-covered soldier's boots standing beside my futon. I barely recognized my father in his uniform with his cap and greatcoat. My mother was bowing before him, her head on the ground until my father threw off his backpack; then my mother unwound the moss-green gaiters around his ankles, a white puff of dust blowing into her face each time she unwrapped a round.

"My father didn't say much. He gave each one of us a chunk of rock sugar from his satchel. At first I was too shy to take it from his hand, so he put it in my lap. I will never forget the taste of that sugar. My mother put hers in her mouth and, her lips paler than her teeth, she smiled. I knew that Fuji-san had taken my offering. My mother would live."

By the time Fumiko finished, a milky predawn opalescence lightened the little house and a liquid warbling of notes was flowing from Chisaii's cage.

I asked, "But if Fuji-san took your offering and your mother lived, why are you still alive?"

But Fumiko put away the little red dictionary and acted as if she couldn't understand my question. It didn't matter, though; she had already told me what I needed to know.

I left her and went to my perfume factory. In the backyard, my breath clouded in the cool, damp air. I stood next to the barbed-wire fence. On the ground were the bottles of honey-suckle perfume I'd concocted, already turning to slime.

Fuji-san was hidden behind a scrim of misty gray. The farmer came into his field. His straw raincoat and rain hat reminded me of the cruel villagers. Over his shoulders was a pole with buckets on either end. He unhitched one of the buckets, carried it to the pale green shoots piercing the black earth, crouched over, and ladled a bit of the dark soup onto each plant's roots.

As he scuttled away down the row, the sun burnt through the clouds above Fuji-san. The mountain was pink in the morning light and rays of gold streamed out from behind her. That was when I made my deal with Fuji-san: If the sacred mountain would return my mother to me, she could have the life of my sister.

Kit had not even woken up that morning when my father came home and told me that I had two new baby brothers and that Moe was fine. Tired but fine. My father, always so impeccably groomed, had several odd, whitish streaks on his cheeks that it took me a second to realize were the salt of dried tears.

When my father went inside to tell Kit, I stayed in my perfume factory and the smell of honeysuckle rose around me so sweet I could have drowned in it as Chisaii's song burbled forth, each note a perfect shimmering bubble floating through the waves of fragrance, up toward Fuji-san.

Polyvinyl

"No burusheeto, *capisce*? Imperial Hotel. No burusheeto. Don't jack me around or I'll snap your little Nip neck." Haneda Airport traffic surges around us as Bobby badgers a small driver standing outside a cab. His white gloves, spindly arms, and short-sleeved shirt make the man look like Mickey Mouse. He bows and nods several times.

"Imperial Hotel, how much?"

"Yes, Imperial Hotel." The driver bows and nods enthusiastically, opening the door of his white Datsun Bluebird.

"Yeah, sport, Imperial Hotel. How much?"

"Yes. I take you Imperial Hotel." He motions for us to get into the Bluebird.

"Uh-uh. How much?" Bobby rubs thumb and forefinger together. "*¿Cuánto cuesta?*"

"*Hai! Hai!*"

"I don't think he understands."

"Don't believe that. They all understand a lot more than they let on."

An airport traffic policeman with a white strap across his chest approaches us.

"You know, we really ought to move," I suggest.

"How much, ace? You want the fare or not?"

I glance away, embarrassed, wishing to distance myself from this crude American. When I look back, the driver is writing a figure on a piece of paper.

Bobby snaps the paper away. "You crazy, boy-san?" Bobby winds the air around his ear, crosses his eyes, flaps his tongue, then points at the driver. I am thoroughly mortified. The driver laughs, crosses out the figure, writes another.

"You got a deal, bubeleh. Let's load 'em up."

Tokyo is unremittingly gray and has a cluttered, unfinished look, like a vast machine that has been disassembled for repairs and then forgotten. It smells of polyvinyls poaching in the sun. We pass factories and smokestacks, a deserted racetrack, muddy baseball diamonds. Gray canals crisscross beneath gray congested roads under a gray sky. I search for trees and find none. Even the rows of new buildings, many still under construction, seem leprous, shedding chunks of stucco in the rain, leaving wire lath exposed.

"'Sixty-four Olympics really crapped the place up," Bobby comments dolorously.

His bulk presses against me in the backseat of the Datsun, the smell of Brylcreem and Brut overwhelming even the dense residual odor of cigarette smoke.

"Used to be, you'd drive in through nothing but rice paddies. Mile after mile of rice paddies. I tell you, when I first came here, Tokyo was the greatest city on earth. Right after the war, it was wide open. I defy you to name a bigger party town than Tokyo right after the Occupation."

Bobby stabs his finger at me as if I had disagreed with him.

"Vegas? That's what you're thinking, right? Vegas? Did Vegas have the Mikado? A thousand hostesses. A thousand! Each one hotter than the last one. High-class pussy. You didn't know whether to shit or go blind." Bobby rubs the air, erasing the argument he is making. "Forget it. You hadda be there."

"I was."

"You 'was.' Right, 'you was.'"

"I was."

"Okay. Where did you hang out? Latin Quarter? Bohemian Club? Papagayo's? Club Eighty-eight? You must have hung out at the Eighty-eight, am I right?"

"No."

"No! You were here before the Olympics and you didn't go to the Eighty-eight? The Bohemian? Papagayo's? Where did you hang out?"

"Bob Hope Elementary."

"Bob Hope Elementary?" Blood rushes to Bobby's face. "You're joking."

"No, that was the name of my school when we lived on Yokota."

Bobby's head looks like it's been boiled. "They named a school after that prick? So you think Hope's a big hero."

"I didn't say that."

"Never wrote a line of his own material. Not a word. King of the Cue Card, we call him. They lose that Magic Marker and Hope is dead. Dead! That's your comic genius. That's the man you idolize."

"I never said I idolized him. Actually, I think he stinks."

"*Now* you say that. Bob Hope. Biggest prick on the circuit. Ask anyone. Joe E. Brown. *That's* who they shoulda named a school after. Ah, well. Whatever, while you were studying how to be a putz there at Bob Hope U, you missed one swinging scene."

Bobby calms down and falls into a nostalgic reverie as he recalls the swinging scene I missed with my ill-advised decision to attend elementary school.

"Luigi's, my man Lou. He knew how to run a club. All the heavyweights fell by. Ava Gardner. The Duke. Sinatra. You think I'm lying. I see that look."

"There's no look."

"I shit you not, the Chairman of the Board was *in* Lou's. All the biggies, if they were in Tokyo, they were in Lou's. I'll take you. Be an education."

The driver makes a sharp left that avalanches Bobby onto me.

"Hey, you kamikaze? You try to kill stupid *Ameko?*" Bobby makes his hand into a Zero on a suicide mission flying right at the driver's head. "You kamikaze us, right? You Kamikaze Joe!" I look out the window, away from both my own and the driver's embarrassment.

At the next turn, Bobby lunges forward. "Hey, Kamikaze Joe, you fuckee-fuckee me? Why you take Yamato-Dori? Stay on Two. *Ni! Ni! Ni ichi-ban!* You take Yamato-Dori fuckee-fuckee me!" Bobby emphasizes his point with a scream of pain and a hand on his wallet. "You kamikaze us, right? You Kamikaze Joe! Kokkasukka!"

When I figure out that Bobby has just called our white-gloved driver a cocksucker, I scoot down in my seat, the greasy plastic cover sticking to me from my own sweat, and calculate what our chances for survival will be when the driver slams on his brakes and tosses us into the eight lanes of traffic hurtling past.

"No fuckee-fuckee!" the driver yells back. "No fuckee-fuckee! Yamato-Dori *ichi-ban!*" He points to Bobby—"Kokkasukka!"— and laughs maniacally when Bobby balls up a giant fist and pretends he is going to throttle him.

For the rest of the trip, Bobby keeps the driver in stitches by alternately slumping contentedly into his seat and then bouncing forward, fist balled, face a Kabuki mask of rage, yelling, "Kamikaze Joe! Pearl Harbor! *Banzai!*" To which the delighted driver screams back, "Kokkasukka!"

At the Imperial Hotel, a doorman holds the door open and three bellboys carry in our luggage, then wait while Bobby and the driver go through the whole routine until he has the doorman and the bellboys yelling "Kokkasukka!" Watching it with my lips twitching in a frozen grin, I try to remember that many, many people find Danny Kaye amusing.

In the end, Bobby slides two ten-thousand-yen notes out of the silver horse's-head money clip he pulls from his pocket and stuffs them in the front pocket of the driver's Dacron shirt to cover the one-thousand-yen fare, all the while pantomiming anal rape.

"Well, whaddaya think?" Bobby turns to the hotel and spreads his arms out wide. The Imperial Hotel looks like a combination of a very large ranch-style house and a Mayan temple. "Best hotel in Asia. Am I right?" He looks to the doorman and bellboys for confirmation. "Imperial *ichi-ban!* Yay! Hotel Okura number ten! Boo, Okura!" The bellboys join in, enthusiastically booing the rival inn. They have to raise their voices to be heard above the sound of a jackhammer tearing loose the west wing of the hotel.

"Is this hotel being torn down?" I ask.

"Frank Lloyd Wright designed the Imperial. Only thing for miles that survived the 'twenty-three earthquake."

"It looks like they're tearing it down."

"Sinatra never stays anyplace else when he's in town. Total class all the way. Wait until you get a load of the lobby."

"Look." Workmen load a section of the front wall onto a truck. "Parts of this hotel are actually being taken away." I point to the departing facade, but Bobby and his instant entourage have already gone inside.

The lobby resembles a particularly stuffy British men's club shortly after a blitzkrieg air raid. An entire wall is missing, the gaping opening covered by large sheets of plastic that fail to keep out the construction noise or dust.

At the reception desk, three Japanese men in black suits beam smiles of welcome. One of them runs around to the front of the desk and drops into a sumo pose. Bobby grabs a rubber band out of his pocket, quickly pulls his hair into a topknot, and squats down. I back away as swiftly as possible, running into some high-backed chairs occupied by geriatric Japanese gents in traditional kimonos all craning around to watch. The clerks attack Bobby and pepper him with swift chops that he seems not to notice. He grabs one of the clerks, tucks the man's head under the haunch of his arm, and grinds his knuckles into his laughing captive's spray of black hair.

This is not the first time Bobby has stayed at the Imperial.

Still laughing, the noogied man runs back to the other side of the desk to check Bobby in and hand him two keys. The bellboys confer with the clerk, then hurry off. I watch my blue Lady Baltimore luggage with the giant daisy decals disappear.

Bobby pulls me close as we walk toward the elevator. "Keep an eye peeled. You never know who you'll run into. All the biggies stay here. Ava. Frank. Shirley MacLaine stayed here while they were shooting that—what's the name of that picture she shot here? Had that pantywaist Bill . . . Bob . . . you know, that chowderhead with the . . ." When I can't supply a name, Bobby squints his eyes in annoyance and brushes the air above his own head to indicate a crew cut. "You know—"

I shrug. Bobby rolls his eyes, exasperated by my lack of knowledge of the biggies.

A sign next to the elevator reads:

We offer pardon to guests of fresh and highly refined culture. We are determinate to render with thoughtfull-ness and consideration thorough services. Especially, we want to be a host at dinner of your house.

An architect's rendering of a high-rise hotel labeled NEW IMPERIAL jutting into the Tokyo skyline high above the phantom shape of Wright's original is more informative.

"Had to pull some strings to get us in." The arrow hand on the old-fashioned floor indicator above the elevator swings down to L and the doors open. "They're carting the whole megillah away to some museum. You can tell your grandchildren you were one of the last got to stay at the real Imperial."

The prospect of grandchildren seems particularly remote as the elevator shudders when Bobby steps on, then again as the jackhammers start up and the ancient lift sways and creaks its way upward.

On the third floor, I start to follow Bobby off but he stops me, jabbing his finger upward. I check my key: 903. "Oh." I step back into the elevator feeling vaguely embarrassed, as if Bobby had just been forced to parry my unwanted advance.

"You're in the new section, kid. Enjoy." The doors slide shut, framing Bobby on a black-veined marble floor, an immense mirror in an ornate gold frame behind him, a crystal chandelier sparkling above his head.

On the ninth floor, signs direct me out of the original building. I wind my way through a maze of increasingly narrow corridors.

Room 903 turns out to be a single bed framed by a tiny border of open floor. I squeeze past the bed to a narrow window. By standing at the window's extreme left edge, I can see a corner of the olive-green moat that circles the massive stone barricade surrounding the Imperial Palace. A shrill ring alerts me that the room contains a phone. I find it in a niche set into the wall.

Bobby doesn't waste time on preambles. "Meet me in the lobby in fifteen minutes. Wear something classy."

When I zigzag my way back down to the lobby dressed in a paisley polyester pants suit created by the Koza sew girl, Bobby rolls his eyes and smacks his forehead. "*Oy vey.* Who taught you from class? Come on." He has Kamikaze Joe waiting outside. The taxi is now a *haiya* car, a car-for-hire.

"*Depaato Mitsukoshi Nihonbashi,* Joe."

"*Hai! Hai!*" Joe explodes the syllable, apparently delighted with his mission. Without a glance in the rearview mirror, he aims the Bluebird into a solid wall of traffic and slithers in.

We drive past repeating sequences of pachinko parlors, fruit shops, and stand-up bars studded against blocks of reinforced-concrete office buildings and apartments. The streets are jammed with other Datsun Bluebirds, with Toyota Publicas, three-wheeled trucks, diesel buses, and delivery boys on bikes with boxes strapped to the handlebars; through them all zips a droning swarm of Honda motorbikes.

The Ginza is dominated by an enormous electronic board that displays how bad the pollution is alongside another readout giving the decibel levels of noise from traffic and construction machinery.

At the department store, Joe hits the button that automatically opens the back door of the Bluebird to let us out. The sidewalk is jammed with an unbroken stream of pedestrians whose black and white clothes move past in a gray blur. Like Joe, Bobby plunges in and, somehow, the gray waters part. I follow in his wake toward the entrance of the *depaato.*

"You need a pick-me-up?" Bobby asks, when we reach the safety of the entrance. He points to a lady holding a face mask attached by surgical tubing to a green tank marked O_2. A man with a navy-blue plastic valise tucked under his arm and a cigarette jammed in his mouth hurries up and tosses a hundred-yen coin in the woman's bowl. He sucks the cigarette down to his yellowed fingertips, tosses it aside, takes the mask, and breathes deeply while the attendant turns a knob until oxygen hisses through the tubes.

"They got 'em all over the city. Tokyo air's like sucking on a Mack truck's exhaust pipe. Go on. It's a kick in the head." After the third deep breath, the man starts hacking wildly. The attendant removes the mask and holds it out to me.

"Uh, no, thanks."

Bobby shrugs like it's my funeral and we surf into the store on a wave of Tokyoites. A team of young women wearing pillbox hats and pink Jackie Kennedy suits along with the ubiquitous white gloves beams at us as we enter. A chorus of *Irashimase* spoken in the silvery tinkling tones of forest sprites greets us, along with a puff of perfume. It has the light, powdery smell of the cologne Fumiko used to spritz herself with before she left us in the evenings.

One greeter runs up to Bobby and begins buffing his nails, which are surprisingly small against his puffy fingers. With his free hand, Bobby fluffs his hair and pretends to put on lipstick. Once the manicure girl starts giggling and a crowd forms, Bobby plucks at imaginary undergarments, tugging down a girdle, tucking in bra straps, adjusting stocking seams. By the time he hikes breasts up over a push-up bra, schoolboys in black caps with book-satchel straps across their chests are pounding on each other in helpless mirth.

Bobby finishes by licking a forefinger and smoothing down each eyebrow; then he twinkles the polished nails at me and asks in a falsetto, "Don't they look just divine?"

Suddenly, the crowd, several dozen dark heads, all turn to me. Clearly the straight man, I attempt what I hope is a smile.

Bobby buys four manicure sets from the girl and tips her several thousand yen. I lose track because he leaves several times, then, with the girl and most of the crowd waving bye-bye, he turns and comes back with another thousand, acting like their ever-louder farewells are demands for more money.

On the elevator, Bobby hands me one of the sets. "That one's for Moe. Oh, yeah, the sister. Jesus, the sister." He rolls his eyes exasperated and puts another one on the stack. "Now I suppose you got a grandmother. Okay, one for Grannie." He gives me the last one. "Okay, I'm out. You happy now? I'm flat. This means you gotta do this hand." He holds up the nails that haven't been polished. "I'm outta balance."

The elevator attendant puts down the rag she is using to polish the gleaming brass on the automatic panel and asks in a high-pitched voice, "Wichi furoru?"

"Dresses. You know. . . ." Bobby does a little girl holding up her skirt, grinding a toe into the floor.

"Ah-so. Doresu. *Hai!*"

"Yeah, dressoo."

Within moments of debarking on the fifth floor, Bobby is holding court for three salesgirls, while a fourth takes the manicure sets away to be wrapped. "Dressoo," he instructs them. "For girl-san here."

"*Hai!* Ooruokeejondoresu? Oorushiizundoresu? Kakuterudoresu? Infoomarudoresu?"

When we don't respond, the salesgirls confer for a second, then add even more uncertainly, "Wedingudoresu?" And then, almost horrified, "Matanitudoresu?"

"What the hell are they saying? Doesn't anyone around here speak English?"

The twittering voices, shy, self-conscious, are like a scent I first inhaled a dozen years ago. They bring back an entire world in one sniff. I feel as if I am back in my perfume factory, talking with Fumiko, and can understand everything she says when no one else can.

I translate for Bobby. "They want to know if you'd like an all-occasion dress, an all-season dress, a cocktail dress, an informal dress or, or"—I roll my eyes and take a deep breath—"a wedding dress, or"—I can barely make myself say the words—"a maternity dress."

The three tiny salesgirls bow and nod, gleeful with gratitude for my translation.

"Wedding? Maternity? That's rich." Bobby pantomimes an enormously pregnant bride holding a bouquet lumbering up the aisle. His lumbering is quite good, and one of the salesgirls has to cross her legs, she laughs so hard. Then Bobby wipes away the comic moment and gets back to business.

"Cocktail," he dictates. "But classy, you know. Your best stuff. No hippie shit."

"No ah hi-pee shee," they echo in their wood sprite–chipmunk tones, fanning out to cover the racks of dresses. Within minutes they return, each one bearing a stack of dresses.

"No, no, no." Bobby waves away the trio of floral-printed numbers one salesgirl displays. "I didn't say I wanted to *upholster* her, for Christ's sake. Classy. I want something like Frank Sinatra's doll would wear to Caesars. Class, *capisce?*" Bobby touches all five of the fingertips on one meaty hand together and holds them up in front of the salesgirl's face. "Class, you got it? Class?"

Much breath is sharply inhaled. All three salesgirls nod like chickens on speed, pecking out their understanding, then scatter again to return with new selections. Bobby riffles through them and selects a plain black shift, which he holds up against me and pronounces perfect.

The dress turns out to be only a canvas against which Bobby paints in highlights, adding a jade panther pendant, a silver-and-amethyst butterfly brooch, a cloisonné bracelet, a topaz cocktail ring, pearl-drop earrings. I object when Bobby has the salesgirl fasten the pendant around my neck, saying I could never accept such a present.

"Kid, we're going to Lou's, not some be-in or love-in or happening or some other hippie hoedown. You go to Lou's, you look classy or you don't go. Put the earrings on her too," he directs a salesgirl. And so, feeling as if I have less control than the winning horse at the Kentucky Derby over the color of the roses it gets draped in, I let Bobby turn me into whatever version of Frank Sinatra's doll or Bob Hope's Joey Heatherton he has in mind.

The *depaato* has a beauty salon where Bobby leafs through a thick book showing swan-necked Japanese women in styles that go all the way back to Jean Harlow's marcel wave. While I sit in a swivel chair—the new black shift and Bobby Moses jewelry collection covered by a striped cape—Bobby confers with the stylist. She wears a white lab coat, a bow clipped above the pouf of her bangs, and a name tag that reads CHO-CHO. Bobby makes emphatic fingertips-touching reference to "class" a dozen or so times.

For several minutes, Cho-Cho turns the pages of the book and Bobby dismisses hairdo after hairdo. "If I'd wanted a poodle, I'da bought a poodle." "No, she's supposed to dance, not herd sheep!" When they both start smiling, nodding, and tapping rapidly on a page, I begin to worry.

"You can't cut it," I warn.

"Don't worry."

"And no bangs."

"Bangs are for tourists."

I relax. No permanent damage will be done.

"Get beautiful, kid," Bobby says by way of farewell, before leaving.

Cho-Cho bows and extends her hand in the direction of my glasses. "Prease."

I surrender my glasses and the world smudges away. It is further softened when Cho-Cho massages my neck and brushes my hair tenderly. With no warning, all the long wakeful nights of waiting for Kit to come home catch up with me, and I drop into a hard sleep.

I wake to the crack of Cho-Cho whipping the plastic cape off. She twirls the chair around, hands me my glasses and a mirror, and I behold a hairstyle piled atop my head in a color that the world has not seen since Mae West invited Cary Grant to come up and see her sometime.

"You bleached my hair!"

Apparently Cho-Cho takes my tone of stunned horror to be hushed admiration and beams until her eyes narrow into happy parabolas floating above her cheeks flushed from the exertion of making me look like a female impersonator. "*Utsukushii, ne?*" she asks me.

I am unable to say anything other than "Yes, it's beautiful."

Bobby loves the new look. "Okay, now you're ready for Luigi's."

I am silent on the ride to Luigi's.

"Hey, remember I told you about the Pagoda Club?"

All I can remember at that point is I am now a bleach blonde.

"Joe, swing by the Pagoda Club. I wanna show the president of the Bob Hope Fan Club here what real living looks like."

Joe has no idea what Bobby is talking about, so, after several slow detours, Bobby guides Joe through a succession of smaller and smaller streets until we arrive at a structure shaped like a pagoda. A tall chain-link fence surrounds it. Much of the white stucco has fallen away from the pagoda. What is left is stained with streaks of rust.

"Fuck. When'd they close the Pagoda? That there used to be the world's biggest cabaret. They had the girls dolled up in these feathered G-strings that they shuttled around up over your head in these dinky cable-car things. The Flying Beaver, that's what we used to call it. A thousand hostesses all with a number and a buzzer in their bra. You'd be dancing with old number six hundred and sixty-nine and her buzzer'd go off, so she'd hotfoot it off to whoever ordered her up. No sweat, you'd turn around and the next babe'd be even better."

"I thought you were—you know—gay."

"Me? Yeah, that's right, I'm as cheerful as they come."

"No, you know, you told Moe you're queer."

"Did I? I don't recall that. Joe, turn here! Turn here!"

We pull up to the corner on a street densely packed with high-rises. Bobby points to a flight of stairs descending beneath the level of the frenetic activity. "Right after the war, the Latin Quarter was down there. The Russian embassy was up there. And the army barracks were right over there. Nothing in between but *soba* stalls, tearooms, and hookers. Always at least a hundred and fifty working girls outside the barracks gate. The tallest building was three stories high. Hey, the Silk Hat used to be right there. Under that Coke sign. And the Green Spot was there where that golf store is. The Bohemian. Club Enjoy. They're all gone. All except the granddaddy of them all. All except Luigi's."

Bobby's glum mood lifts at the mention of the club's name, and he leans forward to give Joe directions.

A few blocks later, we pull into that rarest of all Tokyo attractions, a parking lot directly in front of an establishment, in this case, a two-story concrete building with a striped awning and a sign: LUIGI'S PIZZA.

I start to get out, but Bobby stops me with a hand on my arm. "Cool your jets, kid." Bobby straightens his jacket, pulls a comb through his mossy hair, runs a finger around his collar, pulling it away from his neck, and carefully realigns his tie, clipping it again with his diamond horseshoe tie tack. Only then does Bobby signal that we can leave.

Outside the front door, he stops and gives the top of each of his shoes a quick polish on his pants leg before striding to the entrance.

Inside, Luigi's is dark, the walls painted black, candles guttering in red glass holders.

"I've been here before." The smell of pizza, smoke, and old beer overlaid with Tokyo's signature scent of car exhaust and damp concrete plugs directly into my eight-year-old brain. I remember sitting at a dark table watching my father and the other guys in his crew, who for some reason called themselves the Bong Bunnies. They could have been frat boys, the Rat Pack, RAF pilots, any impossibly glamorous group of men where style was everything and all dying together perhaps the most stylish, most glamorous move of all. And my father was as young and handsome as all the others.

I remember Major Wingo calling my father Wild Root for his dark hair, oiled and piled atop his head in a glossy pompadour, and my father smoking skinny cigars that he held clamped between his front teeth like FDR. The navigator, Dub Coulter, with big ears and the wet-combed look of a Boy Scout, sat at the table with them. Patsy Dugan, the Mick, pulled quarters out of Kit's ear and told me he wouldn't bite when I refused to approach for the same trick. I can't recall the others who crowded in close and laughed and swore and held empty pitchers high above their heads when they needed a refill. Guys who, off duty, wore loafers with no socks. Who sat leaning way back in the chair with one sockless ankle resting on a knee. Who smoked cigars simply because they looked so cool.

"Of course you were here," Bobby says disdainfully. "If you were anywhere near Tokyo in the 'fifties, of course you came to Luigi's. It was the only place on the whole island you could get a pie. Pizza? The Japs didn't know from pizza. Businessmen used to wrap slices up and stick 'em in their briefcases to take back to the office just to show what this strange food looked like. Luigi, what a genius. He's like the Toots Shor of Tokyo. Liz Taylor was here! The Duke! I was here the night John Wayne put away twenty-four straight whiskeys. The Crown Prince brought his wife here when they were dating."

Bobby stops and studies me for a second. "Could you, you know . . . ?" He pantomimes a ritual I've seen Moe perform.

"Powder my nose?" I guess.

"You know. The whole megillah with the lipstick and the mascara and the this and the that."

"I don't have any of those things. I have this." I pull a menthol-flavored Chap Stick from my purse.

"Never mind. Forget I asked. Just lose the glasses, will you?"

I pull my glasses off, but Bobby rants on anyway.

"Does Joey Heatherton wear glasses? Does Ann-Margret?

Does your idol, Bob Hope, have to put up with this tsuris?" He notices a photo on the wall. "Hey! Stick your glasses on, here's something worth seeing."

It's a photo of two American men dressed in samurai kimonos, each one flanked by a pair of beautiful Japanese women in Western clothing. I touch one of the men. "That's not—"

"The hell it's not!"

I study the young Bobby Moses. He is thin. He is handsome. He has a smile like the smiles of my father's friends, heedless, glamorous.

"What? You don't believe that's me? You think me and the Statue of Liberty always wore the same size?"

"I believe you."

"Come on and lose the . . . " Bobby waves at my glasses and I pull them off and follow him upstairs to the restaurant. It is in the traditional Italian mold with red-and-white-checked tablecloths and bunches of purple plastic grapes hanging from the walls. Only one of the two dozen or so tables is occupied. Too many waiters with nothing to do stand braced at attention against a wall and watch our every move. It's hard to imagine Ava Gardner or John Wayne hanging out here.

"Luigi! Paisan!" Bobby throws his arms open to an American with the mustache of an Italian fruit vendor and the shoulders of a middle heavyweight gone to seed. Luigi wears a suit that shimmers between iridescent maroon and black when he holds up a finger to stop Bobby's advance and turns to attend to the quartet of sallow-faced, middle-aged Japanese men seated at a shadowy table in the far corner.

Bobby's arms wilt.

I put my glasses on long enough to see that two of the four men sport something I've never seen on any Japanese male before, permanents that have turned their straight black hair into frizzy coronas. All four look like used Bluebird salesmen on holiday in Waikiki, wearing gaudy short-sleeved shirts, white shoes, belts, and an assortment of gold pendants, bracelets, chains, and rings. Peeking up in the triangle of bare flesh exposed above the collar of each of the men's shirts are garish swirls of tattoos. One man's pinkie ring glints in the candlelight as he reaches up to take the menu Luigi hands him with a servile, unctuous grin, and I notice that the finger above the ring is a short stub missing two joints.

After Luigi distributes the menus, the men glare at him until Luigi backs away, bowing the whole time. By the time he reaches us, he is sweating. Bobby spreads his arms wide again. Luigi, however, looks past Bobby to snap his fingers at one of the line of waiters waiting at parade rest against a far wall. Luigi points at the four men, tips an imaginary bottle, and the waiter rushes downstairs. Only when the waiter has returned with a vintage bottle and is pouring complimentary glasses for the scowling men does Luigi submit to Bobby's embrace.

"You dago prick." Bobby pounds Lou's shoulder. "You still shtupping your—uh . . . ?" Bobby points to the Japanese woman at the cash register. She does not look happy to see Bobby.

"Katsumi. Yeah, we're—uh, we're married."

"Married! What is this? Number four?" He looks at me. "Lou's been divorced so many times he thinks his wife's name is plaintiff. But they're friendly, right, Lou? Always friendly divorces. Lou gets to keep everything that falls off the truck as they're driving away. You can't buy love, but you sure the hell can pay through the nose for it. Am I right, Lou?"

Lou glances at Katsumi. Behind Bobby's back she nods toward the exit, then points her chin to the four men.

"You are right, Robert."

"I was married once, but I just lease now. Your best table, Lou, for me and my—uh, traveling companion." Bobby bounces his eyebrows up and down, trying to make it sound like there's something going on between us that he's too gentlemanly to reveal.

At the table, Lou stands nervously. Bobby drops into a chair and starts chewing through the breadsticks like a beaver through a stand of redwood. "Lou, take a load off. The staff can handle the overflow."

Lou glances around at his nearly empty restaurant, checks to make sure the four Japanese men are happy, then sags wearily into a seat at our table.

Bobby points to the four in the corner, then asks through a shower of bread crumbs, "When did you start letting them in without ties?"

"Oh, would you like to inform those particular gentlemen about my dress code?"

Bobby ignores the sarcasm. "Luigi's was always a class place. The people come for the class."

"The people come for the class." Lou shakes his head at what he clearly considers an expression of ignorance. "You know what *the people* come for now? They come for squid on their pizza. Squid and seaweed and raw fish. A place opened up just around the corner. They're packing 'em in with tofu pizza. The only things American they like on their pizza are corn, mayonnaise, and Tater Tots. Tater Tots! On pizza! . . . They never really liked pepperoni." Lou's tone is heavy with betrayal. "They only pretended."

"Well, I'm here for a Luigi's Special. Give me a sixteen-incher with the works. What are you having, doll?"

"Lasagna?"

When Lou doesn't move, Bobby stops pulping the breadsticks. "So? What? You want me to go back into the kitchen and toss my pie myself?" Bobby stands and pretends he's going to go into the kitchen. "Because I will. You know I will, you schmuck. I done it before. Who was out in that kitchen the night you opened and your new chef started putting bamboo shoots in the marinara sauce?"

Lou pulls him back into his seat. "I heard you were in town."

Bobby elbows me to make sure I caught this accolade. "So, some of the guys gonna stop by? Should I order for them? That tall Australian jerk with the goiter for an Adam's apple, looks like an ostrich swallowed a potato, he still like your crappy ravioli? Get that mooch a couple orders. And a selection of pies. You decide, Lou. Stick it to me however it feels good to you."

Lou glances at his wife, then drags his gaze back to Bobby. "Bobby, you can't do business here."

"Business? Who's doing business? I thought this was a restaurant. I'm trying to get something to eat here." He yells back to the kitchen, "Could you send some food out here before I eat my *other* leg?"

The four men in the corner glare at Bobby. Lou holds an appeasing hand up to them. "Bobby, you can't do business here."

"Business? What business? I've arranged to have a little meeting just like a thousand other meetings I've had here; you've always gotten your taste, am I right, Lou? I've always taken care of you, right? You give a little, you get a little. Life goes on, right? What's the problem?"

"It's different now. You been gone for a while."

"Lou, you can't let them run your game, man. You can't do this."

"Shut up, Bobby. You're over there in Okinawa, you don't know how it is here now. Okinawa is America. You're in Japan now."

"It was Japan the night you opened. Remember? Fourth of July 1956? You had the red-white-and-blue cake with the sparklers on it, remember? They made the icing out of fish oil?" Lou doesn't join in Bobby's laugh. "Lou, you can't let them muscle you around. You let them muscle you around, you're dead."

"Look, Bobby, you can't. . . ." He cuts his eyes to the four men, leans in, and lowers his voice. "Those are *Tosei-kai* guys. If I let your guys come in—"

"My guys, your guys, they're Japs, Lou. Nips. Fucking *yakuza* humps. They're *all* our guys."

"Not anymore, Robert. Them days are over. Look, I'll send a pie over to your hotel. Where are you staying, the Imperial? Shit, I'll send a dozen. And the lady's lasagna. Bobby, you got to—"

Lou's wife stops him with a furious burst of Japanese, pointing frantically to the stairway, where four more Japanese almost identical to the four in the corner are trying to push their way up past several waiters and busboys. Lou's wife joins them, screeching at the four intruders.

Lou stands. The placating tone is gone. "Get out, Bobby."

Bobby takes his time rising, then stands nose-to-nose with Lou. "Come on, kid, let's get out of here. They make lousy pizza anyway. They always did."

Lou won't look at Bobby as he walks away.

In the unlighted parking lot the four Japanese men who weren't allowed in the restaurant buzz around Bobby, throwing their arms in the air and cursing. One of them carries a silver Haliburton suitcase. Bobby tries to calm them down. He tells Joe and me to take a walk. When we come back around the block, Bobby is putting the silver suitcase in the trunk of the Bluebird. The four men are gone.

In the car, Bobby drops his weight onto the seat beside me like a bag of cement.

"Don't give me that look."

I'm not aware that I'm giving Bobby any look.

"What do you think your father was on when he was flying eighteen-hour missions into Siberia?"

Siberia?

"Tums? Tums and Actifed? Shit, they practically packed speed in every lunch. Now that the flight surgeons aren't passing Dexedrine out anymore like Life Savers, what are they supposed to do?" He flips a bird at Luigi's, then yells at Joe, "Get out of here! Go on. Go on! Can you move this bucket already?"

At least I know now how Bobby is making expenses.

"Those *momzers.* They were falling all over themselves when I played there." He pounds his chest with an open hand. "I played there! I opened for Xavier Cugat. Coogie! They were real fucking happy to see Bobby Moses then!" He leans forward toward Joe. "You were real fucking happy to see the *Amekos* back then, weren't you, *chipatama?*"

Joe's expression darkens enough at the last word that I figure it is a serious insult.

"Whole fahcacting country eating grass and bugs and bark. Killing each other for a bag of rice. Then we came. Biggest meeting of cultures since Rome took Carthage. We were gods. We got the best pussy in the country. You couldn't shove the cunts at us fast enough back then, could you? Now . . . now . . ." Bobby contemplates the gray haze, the relentless traffic, a little old lady in a dark kimono buying oxygen at a corner. "Now this. This. You, you Japanese, no *giri,* no shame. No gratitude. No obligation."

The gray sky darkens and jewel-colored neon lights blink on, one after another, until we are driving through a neon aurora borealis of kanji characters, club names, and tipping martini glasses.

Enchiladas

The next morning, I wake up at six and spend several hours peering out my window at a thin slice of the Imperial Palace. Swans glide around the moat. Even at six, there is a crowd that grows each hour. I call Bobby's room at nine and am informed that his calls are being held. I dial room service and a chirpy voice answers, "Mornie. Rooeen sorbee."

When I tell her I'd like to order breakfast, she asks how I'd like my aches, suggesting, "Scrampoe?" I agree to scrambled eggs. She inquires whether I'd like toes or ningrish mopping we bother with my aches. I choose the English muffin with butter and she repeats my odor of scrampoe aches and ningrish mopping we bother. After adding orch jews to drink, she concludes with a "Tangjewberrymah." I tell her she's welcome and wait for my breakfast.

For the rest of the day, I wander around, staring into a multitude of windows, turning down one street after another that seems identical to the one before it. At five that evening, Bobby calls and tells me to meet him in the lobby in an hour. "Vacation's over, kid. We're going to work."

Bobby is pacing the lobby when I arrive half an hour early, at five-thirty. When he sees me, he whacks his forehead. "Why are you wearing your costume? You carry your costume." He holds out the garment bag he has looped over his forefinger to illustrate. "You carry your costume."

Though it only takes me a few minutes to change and race back down to the lobby with the sew girl's go-go dress packed away, Bobby is apoplectic by the time I return. "At last." He turns to Joe. "Cancel the hearse. She's alive." This time he notices my feet. "Where are your go-go boots?"

"I don't have any."

"Oh, for the love of—" Bobby walks away, muttering curses and throwing his arms up in supplication. "You don't have go-go boots."

"They didn't have any on Okinawa. We looked everywhere."

"Every titty bar on Okinawa's got broads shaking their asses in white go-go boots."

"The biggest any of the shops had were sixes. None of them had any in my size, size ten."

"Size ten? Christ almighty, lemme look at those gunboats."

I hold a foot up.

"Whadda you do, get your shoes out of a clown catalog? Those dogs are special order. Be a coupla weeks before any store in Tokyo could get in something that gargantuan."

"They're not *that* big."

"No, no, they're very petite and delicate. For God's sake, Zelda, you could snowshoe with those things. Okay, what do you propose doing the act in?"

"Nothing."

"Nothing. Nothing as in barefoot? Where do you think you are, Dogpatch?"

"I usually dance barefoot. I danced barefoot at the tryout."

"Tryout! Tryout is over. This is the real thing. You are going onstage as part of the Bobby Moses Revue. You are a go-go dancer. How can you not have go-go boots?"

Shame overwhelms me. "I didn't think it would be that big a deal."

"That's good. That's perfect. And when I go onstage with my dick hanging out, will that not be that big a deal? Where does it stop with you kids?" Bobby presses both his palms flat against his temples as if he were trying to keep his head from exploding.

On the drive to Tachikawa Air Base, Bobby doesn't say a word, though every time he glances in my direction, he does emit an eloquent calliope concert of hisses, wheezes, sighs, grunts, and gasps.

Outside Tachikawa there is the usual assortment of bars, pawnshops, and strip clubs. Bobby orders Joe to pull over at the Good Sex Club.

Joe and I wait in the car for half an hour before Bobby returns carrying a pair of white go-go boots. He tosses them in the open window onto my lap. The boots are easily three, four sizes too small for me.

"Put 'em on."

I make an attempt just to show Bobby that it is physically impossible to shove my clodhoppers into the doll boots. But the tiny boots have a stretch insert running their length that gives enough to actually allow me to jam my foot in. My foot bulges over the sides, and the top of the boot, meant to reach almost to the knee, stops at the middle of my calf, where it squeezes the muscle and all surrounding flesh up into a mushroom cloud that blobs over the top. Triumphant, I turn to Bobby. I don't need to say a word. The boot's awfulness speaks for itself.

"Perfect," Bobby proclaims. "Now you look like a go-go dancer."

"I'm not wearing these."

"Why? You have to be the first woman in the history of the world wears her real shoe size?"

"I don't care. I'm not wearing them."

Bobby blinks several times and studies the roof of the car as if someone were up there talking to him. He nods at his invisible interlocutor, dips his head, holds his hands up, presses them down.

"Bobby?"

Bobby suddenly seems to remember that I'm sitting beside him. "You don't want to wear the boots? You want to go on as part of *my act* barefoot? Good. Fine. Then I hope you have five hundred dollars to reimburse me for your ticket over here and another five to get your barefoot carcass back to Okinawa. Do you? Do you have a thousand dollars?"

"No."

"May we consider this case closed?"

This time I answer with my own calliope assortment of sighs.

At Tachikawa's front gate, Bobby gives his name and the guard raises the black-and-white striped arm across the road, then gives the car a salute that makes me miss my father. Bobby returns the guard's crisp salute with a joke version of his own that includes crossed eyes and his tongue stuck out.

The road widens. It runs through a parade ground that stretches out in either direction with nothing on it but grass and an American flag. Our headlights pick out the borders of white-painted rocks that surround every building, flag, and statue and line every path, parade route, and street. Tachikawa's broad avenues, open parade grounds, and white-painted rocks make me deeply homesick. In the darkness, the rocks that have always before seemed the height of stupid wasted effort now shine like strands of pearl, trails laid out with the best of intentions to guide us past danger.

As Joe pulls up in front of the Tachikawa O Club, Bobby stares at me, then whirls his hand around his head to indicate my hair. "What are you going to do with your—"

"My hair? You already bleached it, isn't that enough?" Bobby doesn't comment, and I feel I must take a stand. "I have no plans for my hair."

Bobby leans forward, talks to Joe. "No plans. She's got no plans for the hair. With the Dogpatch bare feet, the hair hanging down, the makeup by Ma Kettle." He turns to me. "This—*this* is how you intend to go onstage? You know they call this 'show' business, don't you? Not *hide* business?"

I step out of the car and discover that my feet, bound in the tiny white boots, have gone completely numb. Tottering behind Bobby, I am as hobbled as a geisha on wooden *getas*. He waits at a side door. I pray he will notice and let me take the boots off.

"Can you shake your tush there, Zelda?"

"I'll never be able to dance in these."

"Look, Zelda, you wanna get hookworm, do it on your own time. You're on my dime now."

Half a dozen Japanese musicians in matching maroon tuxes and string ties are waiting inside the door. The younger ones have long hair that they wear in greasy pompadours. They all smoke like they've been studying James Dean. The older guys don't seem as sullen as the younger ones. Their leader, Mr. Watanabe, springs forward.

"Bobby, you rate. You bust my bars."

"Ah, Knobby, your balls are bust anyway."

"You want you-shoo-roe?"

"Yeah, the usual. Just hit me a rim shot when I need one."

Knobby translates into Japanese and the musicians stand, pick up their instruments, and start to leave.

"Oh, Knob, I got a dancer. Work out what she wants."

The bandleader turns to me expectantly. "Give me you charts."

"Charts?"

"You know," Bobby intervenes. "Give the man your music."

"What music?"

"What music? Whatever music you were planning on dancing to—unless you were going to accompany yourself on the accordion, in which case I'll just shoot myself now and get it over with. Give him your music."

"You mean sheet music? I don't have sheet music."

Bobby twirls his bulk on his heel and walks away from me, muttering in Yiddish, asking God if he needs this aggravation. If he *needed* to pay for the privilege of having his act completely fucked up. Once he's calmed himself, he turns back to me and with a great show of theatrical patience asks, "Let's say you're working with a band that—oh, my goodness—*doesn't know your arrangements.*" Bobby affects a piping falsetto to emphasize how stupid he thinks I am. "How do you communicate what you want them to play?"

"I don't. I mean, I don't communicate with bands. They play something and I dance."

"And if they play 'Flight of the Bumblebee'? What then, Zelda?"

"They don't. They wouldn't."

Bobby throws his arms up and walks away. "Get a gun. You're murdering me here. Just get a gun and shoot me now, you're killing me anyway."

Knobby steps up. "What song you rike?"

"To dance to? I don't know. 'Midnight Hour'? 'Sweet Soul Music'? 'Knock on Wood'?" The bandleader has never heard of any of them.

"Give me you tempo."

"Tempo?"

"The beat," Bobby translates. "What tempo do you want. Waltz, march—"

"I don't know. Just regular rock 'n' roll."

"Ah, *hai!* Roku roru!" One of the younger band members gives me a thumbs-up. "*Ichi-ban!*" He confers with the bandleader, who nods rapidly, then turns to me.

"Okay. We get with program now. Roku roru. No probrem. Can do, chief."

The band leaves.

"Well, you got your wish, Zelda. The band's gonna play something and you're gonna dance. Now, if only I could get my wish and be struck dead on the spot. Go." He points to the ladies' room. "Change."

He walks away to the men's room muttering, "Gai gezunterhayt." The backward slap of his hand tells me he means this as some kind of Yiddish brush-off.

Behind his back, I flip him off to raise my spirits a little, but it doesn't help much.

I get dressed, then go backstage to wait for Bobby. Flats painted to look like a pyramid and emblazoned with the legend TACHIKAWA ON THE NILE OFFICERS' WIVES CLUB SPRING PAGEANT, 1962 lean against the walls. I remember the Yokota Officers' Wives Club pageants. I remember the year LaRue

Wingo, the squadron commander's wife, was Cleopatra, Queen of the Nile, with a headdress that had a cobra sticking off the front. Moe was one of the slaves who carried her in on a palanquin. The year before that, LaRue was Joan of Arc in paper-clip chain mail and Moe was one of the devoted peasants.

Though Moe would have looked far better in paper-clip chain mail and a cobra headdress than LaRue Wingo ever would, it never occurred to me to ask why she didn't try out for these lead roles. It was understood that the rank of the squadron commander devolved onto his wife, and if she chose to pick the prize plum year after year, no wife who cared about her husband's career would offer any opposition.

As I wait amid the dusty scenery, a feeling of colossal doom washes over me. As a twitchy introvert who was forced to move far more than was conducive to good mental health, I find this feeling of dread is familiar. I would get it every time I walked into a new school, or stepped onto a school bus that didn't contain one person I knew, or searched for a seat in a cafeteria full of strangers while I held a tray of food that always seemed to be enchiladas smelling like body odor.

I'd learned after we left Yokota, though, that no matter how hideous each new experience was it would be over soon. We would move from temporary quarters to base housing and change schools. Or my father would be reassigned or the base would close and we would move. Whatever the reason, the moves came with much greater frequency after we left Japan. I learned that wherever we landed we were just passing through. That no one knew me and I knew no one and that, when we moved, once again no one would know me, so it never mattered. If I could just hold my breath for as long as it took to pass through, it would soon be as if I'd never been there.

A young airman with the tag CLUB STEWARD above his name, DINKINS, bustles up to me and asks where Bobby is. "The base commander's out there and he's tired of dancing with his wife."

"What can I do?"

The steward's face is raw from shaving over blemishes. "The guy who had this duty before warned me about this."

"About what?"

"About Mr. Moses. The way he gets before the first show of a tour. He's fine after that. But the first one can be a real bitch. Pardon my French, ma'am. It's just part of his—well, the last guy called it Mr. Moses's windup. A lot of the performers are like that, even the big names. You wouldn't believe what they had to do to get Soupy Sales onstage. Would you at least come with me?"

He leads the way into the men's room. Bobby, fully dressed in a tuxedo, sits, glowering, on the closed lid of the commode in the last stall. "I hope you've liked your free trip so far, Zelda, because as of this minute it's over."

"Uh, Mr. Moses, sir, I'm Spec Sergeant Dinkins. I'm the club steward here at Tachikawa Officers' Club. You were scheduled to go on at twenty hundred hours. It is now twenty-one hundred hours, and the base commander is wondering why the show hasn't started yet."

"Tell your fucking commander that my watch only goes up to twelve."

"That comment would not be advisable, sir."

"Then tell your fucking commander that I'm taking a crap and I can either do it in here or I can come out there and do it on his head."

The club steward grows pale beneath his abraded pimples. "Could you . . . ?" He moves close to me. His breath is sour from nervousness. "I really need to keep this assignment. They'll send me to Nam."

"Bobby, come on. It's one show. Just do what I plan to do, pretend you're not here."

The gaze Bobby turns on me is equal parts distilled contempt and disgust. "You're *not* here. The name and the face on the poster is Bobby Moses. I was Far East Funnyman three years in a row. I played the Mikado, the Pagoda, the Latin Quarter. I had the Bitchi Bashi girls dancing for me. Now I'm supposed to go out and make those turds in khaki and their fat-assed wives laugh? Laugh? Those numbnuts wouldn't know a joke if it bit them on the ass. I can't cover my dry cleaning for what I'll take home here. I don't know why I ever agreed to play this retard factory to begin with. Zelda, your people suck."

He slaps the cheap metal partition of the stall.

"Look at this crap they give you people. They got better johns in Sing-Sing. You Air Force heroes are so important, why don't they spring for a decent can?"

For the first time, I notice how crummy everything is. Bobby is right, it's a whole world created for and by people like me who are just passing through, whose only lasting monuments to quality, to beauty, sit out on runways.

"I'm not going on. I'm leaving."

Bobby glares and folds his arms like a stubborn toddler. The steward looks at me. They both wait for me to do what I'm supposed to do, talk our reluctant star out of his trailer and onto the set.

"You know what, Bobby? I'll bet if you'll get up right now and come with me"—the steward looks at me with a gleam of grateful hope in his rabbity eyes.

I turn my back on him. "I'll bet Joe can get us back to the Imperial Hotel before the dining room closes. They've got a travel agency right in the hotel. They'll probably be closed by the time we get back, but we can get there first thing tomorrow morning and book a flight out. We can be back in Okinawa by tomorrow afternoon." I become more exhilarated as I talk. The notion of simply leaving is a revelation to me. I think Bobby is a genius as I reiterate the simple brilliance of his plan. "Let's just leave."

Bobby stands. His shoes, polished to a mirror gloss, wink in the light as he walks out of the stall. I am enveloped in a comforting cloud of Brut as he stands next to me, hikes his foot up onto the sink, and smooths the razor-sharp crease on his pants. He straightens his cummerbund, bow tie. Adjusts his French cuffs and cuff links to the perfect angle, then faces me and asks, "Have you lost your tiny little mind? Bobby Moses has never—I repeat, never—disappointed an audience. Wherever two or more fans gather in his name, Bobby Moses goes on, you got that? Now get backstage and wait for your cue and—" He stops dead to study my hair, my lack of makeup, my costume, and the sort of expression used to sell Rolaids comes over his face. He starts to speak, realizes the job is too monumental, and dismisses me with a mournful shake of his head.

Backstage, Bobby paces, grumbling to himself and throwing punches. The steward watches, pointing occasionally to the audience on the other side of the curtain but not daring to penetrate the nimbus of rage whirling around that night's headliner. Abruptly, Bobby stops and glares at Sergeant Dinkins. "Who's doing my intro?"

The steward holds up some index cards. "I prepared these for the commander to read."

Bobby snatches, reads, tears up the cards, and hands the steward one he pulls from his pocket. "Tell him to use this and tell Knobby to play my signature."

Backstage, waiting for Bobby to go on, the dread is worse than before, when I had no more hope of reprieve than I did that my father would refuse a new assignment. The steward disappears and I shrink as far from Bobby as I can, since he acts like I have made a pact with the devil to destroy his career. The instant, however, that Knobby strikes up "East Side, West Side," which is, apparently, the Bobby Moses signature, some switch flips and Bobby is transformed, throwing his shoulders back, holding his ursine head high.

A swell of applause greets the base commander, who reads, "It is my great honor to introduce you to, directly from a six-week sold-out run at the Tropicana in Las Vegas, America, Mr. Bobby Moses!"

Where, a second before, Bobby's tuxedo seemed to hang on him, he now fills it to bursting as he bounces onstage, leaving me alone in the dark.

"It's great to be back here in Tachi. It's been a couple years since I toured Japan. I decided I had to come back." Pause. "I needed a bath." The drummer hits the cymbals. "This country. I love this country. They don't see many guys big as me outside a sumo ring here. Every time I sit down, they start burning incense, putting tangerines at my feet. I'm like a god to these people: the Happy Buddha."

Bah-bing! The drummer hits a rim shot.

As the crowd laughs, Bobby grumbles, "They don't get it. They just don't get it at all."

"And the food. They're killing me, I'm telling you, they're killing me. It's not easy for a guy my size to get enough to eat here. I spent a week in Kobe getting massaged and living on beer. Only time I wasn't hungry. Then they found out I wasn't a cow and chased me out of the barn."

Bah-bing!

"They don't get it. Just don't get it at all.

"This is an island country. You know that, don't you? All you can get is fish. I eat so much fish here I'm starting to breathe out of my cheeks. I came on-base early, I was really looking forward to getting some good old American grub. I stopped by your mess hall there, and I don't want to say the cook's bad but, we were all praying *after* we ate."

Bah-bing!

"He thinks there's only one flavor: charcoal. Must have trained in the army. Everything he made was olive drab. The biscuits were so hard you had to rivet on the butter! Then the cook comes out, sees no one's eating the biscuits, says, 'Ulysses S. Grant's troops would have been grateful to have those biscuits.' Private Jerkoff sitting next to me—yeah, Jerkoff, he's Polish; family changed their name at Ellis Island, used to be Whackoff—Private Jerkoff says, 'Yeah, Sarge, but they were fresh back then!'"

Bah-bing! Bah-bing! Bah-bing!

"This is the same recruit can't understand why they call him private. He's sleeping in a room with eighty other guys! Jerkoff don't get it. Just don't get it at all."

Bobby and I wait for the drummer to punctuate the last joke, but he don't get it. Just don't get it at all. I creep closer to the curtain and almost pull it aside to peek at Bobby, but I don't. I know that if I have even one glimpse of the audience waiting on the other side of the heavy velvet, I will never be able to step out from behind it.

"Not that Jerkoff wanted to get drafted. Tried like hell to dodge it. Draft board told him to come in for his physical and bring a urine sample. He figured he'd con them and got everyone he knew to pee in his bottle. At the physical the doctor came out, told him, 'Your old man has diabetes, your girlfriend is pregnant, your dog is in heat, and you're in the Air Force!' He don't get it. Just don't get it at all."

Bah-bing!

"Hey, great, the drummer woke up. Welcome back, pal. My buddy, Jerkoff, was in the barbershop, the captain was in the chair next to him. The barber tries to splash some aftershave on the captain. Captain won't let him. 'Don't put that crap on me. My wife'll think I've been in a whorehouse.' Jerkoff looks at the barber, tells him, 'Go ahead. Put it on me. My wife don't know what a whorehouse smells like.'"

A wave of masculine laughter rolls back, giving me enough courage to peek out. I focus on the wives sitting beside grinning husbands. Their faces are like the faces of the wives back at Yokota, smiles tight, eyes searching out the gazes of other nearby wives, and when they meet they shake their heads in tolerant dismissal. The blood surges in my ears and Bobby's voice is lost in the rushing sound. My brain snaps off until Dinkins's face appears in front of mine.

"You missed your cue."

I give no indication that I understand the meaning of the word "cue."

"You're on. Go on." He holds the curtain back. It is the wives' hair that has undone me. Rolled, teased, bubbled, sprayed, most have clearly been to the base beauty salon in preparation for their big evening out. There is nothing I can do that is remotely worth anyone's ratting their hair.

Bobby spots me. "And now, here she is, ladies and gentlemen, direct from her sellout tour of Itchy Pussy, Okinawa, the Amazing Zelda!"

The remembered smell of enchiladas fills my head and I clump out, my feet having turned to blocks of ice in the tight boots. I catch sight of a wife's face and quickly rip my glasses off, tossing them behind me. It is only when I enter the radiated zone of the spotlight that I become aware of the song the band has chosen to play: "I Dig Rock and Roll Music." For a frozen second, my limbs twitch about until I finally find the thready pulse of a beat that is all hands and feet, leaving my pelvis completely uninvolved. With nothing else to hang on to, I end up doing an imitation of Kit's drill-team maneuvers, and the experience becomes no more, but certainly no less, horrible than any of several hundred new-girl meals I've eaten alone in school cafeterias around the world.

The band finishes with a Gypsy Rose Lee strip-show-style flourish that inspires the exact sort of bump-and-grind pantomime that I know Kit would have thrown in. It is all so sexless and pathetically amateurish that Bobby is able to milk a smattering of pity applause as I teeter off.

"Let's hear it for the Amazing Zelda! You gotta remember, folks, this is her first time doing this go-go thing. She used to be a bubble dancer. Then, one night, her career blew up in her face."

The laugh that echoes backstage sounds tinged with relief as Bobby incorporates the awfulness of my "performance" into his act.

"Zelda'd be a great dancer except for two things—her feet. When I hired her I asked her how much she expected to make a night. She says, 'Fifty dollars.' 'Why, Zelda,' I say, 'I'll give you that with pleasure.' Zelda tells me, 'With pleasure'll be seventy-five.'

"For her first night's pay, I gave her a gorgeous negligee. For her second night's pay, I gave her some jewelry. For her third night's pay, I tried to raise her first night's pay."

Bah-bing!

"She don't get it. Zelda just don't get it at all. Zelda's a college girl. Yeah, you know, back in the States. They got the hippies and the happenings and the this and the that. I asked Zelda, 'You into all that?' She tells me, 'Right on, man.' I say, 'How 'bout this free love?' Zelda tells me, 'Yeah, man, I believe in free love. But you, Bobby—you I'm puttin' on the installment plan!'

"Great. The sexual revolution is in and I'm out of ammunition! Zelda thinks she's too young for me. I ask her where she's been all my life, she tells me, 'Teething.'

"Zelda's one of them women's libbers. She was out there with her sign yelling, 'Free women! Free women!' This drunk comes by, asks her, 'Do you deliver?' Zelda bonked him with her sign. She don't get it. Zelda just don't get it at all."

Bah-bah-bah-bing!

Bobby finishes up with some pokes at the band, a few jokes about wives, a few about husbands, a real crowd-pleaser involving squat toilets and the constipating effects of a rice diet leading to the shape of the Japanese eyes. By the end of the act, Bobby has his jacket off, his tie loosened, he's sweated down to his cummerbund, his Brylcreemed pompadour has melted onto his forehead, and the audience is eating out of his hand.

The applause rolls on. "Zelda? You back there? Come on out. Your public wants to see you. Zelda, blow up your bubbles. Get your tushie out here." I totter into the spotlight. Bobby raises my hand, then lowers it, pulling me into a bow along with him. The audience applauds me for being a good sport. I smile, happy because the night is over.

"You've been a great audience. Come on back and see me. Tomorrow I'll be playing an early show at the Johnson Service Club, then later at the O Club. After that, catch me at Fuchu NCO Club. Thursday we do a matinee at Showa. Call the O Club for times. That night it's back to Johnson for the NCO Club there. Tops Club, Falcon Service Club, O Club. We'll even be playing the Airmen's Club there. Club Zanzibar, Club Lamumba. Club Spearchucker, something like that. Whatever, just send help if they throw us in a big pot. We finish up the tour at the Yokota O Club. Call for dates and times.

"God bless you. *Sayonara.* Don't let your meat loaf. Get out of here, they need the room. General's coming to show stag films. Be careful, and if you can't be careful, name it after me!"

Night Soil

On the drive back to Tokyo, the glow from each small paper-windowed house or shop is linked to the next with no intermittent darkness. Even the blackness above is lighted by the twinkle of a million fireflies. The land exhales the complicated odor of night soil being transformed back into life.

Bobby, silent since we left the club, presses against me both with his weight and the weight of his unspoken criticisms. I know I was horrible. Since I danced like Frankenstein, it takes me by surprise that his first comment is, "You missed your cue."

"Oh. Yeah. I was—"

"You left me standing out there with my dick hanging out. Don't do that again. You make me look like a yutz. Very unprofessional. Also, you never sit down until after the show. Your costume looked like you slept in it. You need more eyeliner and you always wear false eyelashes on my stage. Period. End of discussion. While you're at it, you might as well get some falsies too."

"What about the dancing?" Much as I try, I cannot control the wobble in my voice. I bite down hard on the inside of my mouth to keep from crying, a trick I learned after first grade with Miss Ransom.

"The dancing could be not so . . ." He puts his arms straight out in front of him. Apparently, Bobby thought I looked more like the Mummy than Frankenstein.

"I guess you wish you'd hired Kit instead of me."

"Kit? The sister?"

I sniff out confirmation.

"Right, Kit. Kit I need like I need a hole in the head. That little chickie-boombah is a statutory count waiting to happen. Too sexy. Too pretty. Plus, she's got worse rhythm than Mamie

Eisenhower. You—you're okay. The wives, you don't make them jealous. The husbands, you make them think about shtupping the babysitter. Everyone's happy. With your sister, suddenly I'd be Fatty Arbuckle. No, kid, you're okay. You work a little on the entrance, the exit. A little less—" He does his Mummy imitation again.

"I could do better if I didn't have to wear the boots and had some decent music."

"The music!" Bobby pulls a roll of sheet music out of his pocket. "We got lucky. Knobby let me have the charts for that cockamamie song you requested. He bailed you out, kid."

"'I Dig Rock and Roll Music'? I hate that song."

"Great. She hates that song. Listen, Zelda, unless you got the charts to something you *don't* hate stuck up your ass, this is your song." He thrusts the music into my hands. "You should come prepared. It's the hallmark of the professional."

"To say nothing of the Boy Scout."

Bobby recoils. "So now you're riffing on me? You got a schtick? Stick to dancing, kid, it stinks less than your jokes."

Within minutes, Bobby goes from snorting, shaking his head in disgust, and cursing me, Joe, Japan, and the United States Air Force to buzzsaw snores.

They make an interesting counterpoint to the lyrics to the most hideous song in all the world, which now refuse to leave my head.

I DIG rock and roll music!

I wonder if Kit and Bobby would have killed each other by now and almost wish I had stepped aside to find out.

Toast

At four that morning, I am in Bobby's palatial room watching five waiters set up three tables of food. When all the silver domes have been whisked away, revealing steak and eggs, waffles, pancakes, spaghetti, French toast, hamburgers, French fries, several pieces of a pie-looking confection, tempura, and sukiyaki, Bobby nods.

The waiters leave and Bobby applies himself with a ritualistic devotion, pausing only long enough to observe, "I only eat one meal a day. Wastes too much time otherwise."

I glance around. A couple dozen of my rooms would fit into Bobby's suite. Frank Lloyd seems to have modeled his hotel after one of the grand colonial British establishments. Much teak and brass gleam. A porcelain button next to the bed is labeled VALET. The open bathroom door, however, reveals a room of completely Japanese luxury, with a huge round tub next to an unenclosed shower for bathing before parboiling.

"Dig in. Here, here's a plate."

"I'm not really that—"

"Better get your stomach on the night shift. Show people always eat late." He lifts the lid on a tub of strawberry jam. "Shit! They always forget the extra jam. You like jam? They import this from England. Here." He piles several heaping spoonfuls on a piece of toast already limp with butter and hands it to me.

It is the best piece of toast I have ever eaten.

"Get you some of these." He spears a quartet of sausages and passes me the fork.

We munch in companionable silence. With Bobby absorbed in shoveling in spaghetti topped with fried egg, I take a moment to study him. I search his face, trying to find the handsome man I'd seen in the photograph at Luigi's. Bobby feels my attention and looks up.

"What?"

"Nothing."

"Nothin', shit. You're wondering if I got a blowhole under my shirt. You know, Zelda, I made a choice in this life. Either my mouth's gonna be happy or my dick is. So which one do you think I listened to?"

When it becomes apparent that Bobby actually wants me to answer, I shrug.

Bobby wags a melon ball on the end of his fork at me for emphasis. "Let me give you a hint. My dick don't talk." Satisfied that he's made his point, he pops the melon ball into his mouth.

"Well, I guess I'd better . . ." I wave vaguely in the direction of my room.

"You're not gonna stick around?"

"No, I think I'll . . ." Again the vague wave.

"You can stay here if you want. Plenty of room." He pats the bed.

"Thanks, but I'd better . . ." The wave.

"Aw, stick around. We don't have to screw if you don't want to."

"Uh. Okay. That's good to know."

"Jesus, Zelda, you look like your ovaries just dropped or something. You can't blame a guy for trying. Lot of the big comedy acts—" He pumps his right index finger in and out of the closed fist of his left hand. "You know, Burns and Allen. Stiller and—what's the horsy-faced broad's name?"

"They're married."

"Oh, right. But Hope. Your idol Bob Hope, he puts the boots to every dame he tours with. It's in their contract. Okay, forget it. Quit looking at me like I'm that lech in that crazy movie about the baby boinker, Humdinger Humdinger or whoever."

"*Lolita.*"

"Yeah, what a load of crap that one was. Hey, don't give me that face. I gave it a shot, you shut me down. Case closed. You give a little, you get a little. Life goes on. Right? No harm done."

"No. No harm done."

"Okay, then, if you're gonna leave, leave already. I'm thinking of getting a little paid companionship in here before it gets too late."

Bobby is on the phone before I close the door behind me.

Vitamins

After Tachikawa, we play a succession of service clubs: Showa, Fuchu, Washington Heights, the Navy bases at Yokohama and Yokuska, a couple of Marine and Army bases, but mostly the Air Force clubs. I learn to read the insignia on the men's shoulders that distinguish a chief sergeant from a master, a technical sergeant from a staff. I count the stripes. Anything below three is an airman. At the first club after Tachikawa, Johnson Air Base, we leave early and Bobby sends me into the BX with a hundred dollars and orders to spend every cent of it on cosmetics.

Before each performance, Bobby insists that I trowel on the makeup. Pretty soon I look like a blond Priscilla Presley, with my bleached hair ratted up into a hydrocephalic bubble, my face and lips whited out, my eyes slashes of black liner and llama sweeps of false lashes. I hobble out night after night, an American geisha in my foot-binding boots. Bobby adjusts his act for what he perceives as my new heightened level of sexiness.

I chased Zelda all around the hotel room last night. Problem is, when I caught her I couldn't remember what I'd been chasing her for. I ain't gettin' any, just ain't gettin' any at all.

At the enlisted men's clubs the airmen who also aren't getting any they don't pay for roar their approval for this line. At their clubs, the audience is almost entirely young men, young men who mostly would blend into any shop class in America. Individually, they are heartbreakingly sweet, sneaking up to reveal a desperate homesickness and to tell me I remind them of a sister back home. Together, however, they are a snarling pack of testosterone-maddened dogs, grinding their crotches and making jerk-off motions in my direction. The only females I ever see at an airmen's club are paid professionals, locals working as waitresses or B-girls. The more raucous the club, the higher my father's rank is when Bobby tells them to back off.

You know you're getting old when your telephone cord is kinky and your sex ain't. I'm a father figure to Zelda. She keeps asking me for money! I ain't gettin' any, just ain't gettin' any at all.

The clubs for noncommissioned officers staff sergeant and above are considerably more sedate. There are wives in the NCO clubs, many of them Asians, who seem to be enjoying an American diet. The food the chubby wives are, apparently, enjoying is a little better at their clubs. You can order a steak instead of just pizza and hamburgers. Some drinks come with umbrellas. The tablecloths are fabric.

I took Zelda there to this great restaurant. She orders everything on the menu—the caviar, steak, wine. I ask her, 'Zelda, does your mother feed you like this?' She says, 'No, but my mother don't want to take me home later and screw me.' I ain't getting any, just ain't getting any at all.

But it is the officers' clubs that make Bobby nervous and testy. "Hell, yes, I'm nervous," he admits, as we drive to the gig at the Johnson O Club after he has told me for the fifth time that I'm killing him, that it is my sworn duty in life to assassinate Bobby Moses. "One word from some tight-assed bird colonel whose wife gets a bug up her butt, and I never tour Japan again."

When we play an officers' club, Bobby wears a little more Brut than usual, has his nails buffed, hits his roots with the Grecian Formula, slicks a little more Brylcreem into his hair, brings an extra tux shirt to change into at intermission.

I catch his nerves, spackle on an extra layer of pancake, and double up on the Maybelline for the Keene big-eyed-baby look he prefers.

The days take on a shape. I sleep as late as I can, then wander around the Imperial Palace for a few hours, feeding the swans.

Around one, Bobby gets up and we go shopping. After the first expedition when he outfitted me to meet Luigi, I won't let him buy me any more gifts. This doesn't prevent Bobby from purchasing presents for every member of my family.

The day after we play Johnson Air Force Base, Bobby takes me to the Akihabara district to visit an endless array of discount shops where the phenomenal outpouring of Japan's electronics industry is on display at a high-decibel level. Bobby buys a foot massager for my father and, the newest thing, a cassette tape player for the twins.

We spend the next afternoon in the Takashimaya department store. We start at the rooftop playground, where Bobby sits down and immediately starts snoring like a hibernating grizzly until a little boy wearing knee socks, shorts, and a sun hat with an elastic strap under his chin tiptoes away from his grandmother to touch the "sleeping" *gaijin*, whereupon Bobby turns, roaring, on the child, who runs away screaming in tears.

Downstairs, Bobby buys a play tea set and a chalk-white Japanese doll for Bosco. Bob gets a chemistry set, a kit for making a kite the size of a picnic table, and a happy coat.

We troll the Imperial Hotel's arcade looking at cloisonné, ivory, coral, wood block prints, dolls in glass cases, binoculars, and pearls until Bobby settles on a sweater and matching purse both beaded with a cat design for Kit. Along the way, he orders two dozen lighters inscribed *You Just Don't Get It At All! Bobby* to give away to club stewards and ranking brass.

But the person Bobby really likes buying gifts for is Moe. At shop after shop, he holds up a bolt of raw silk, a pearl pendant, a slide projector, gold-rimmed sake cups, embroidered hankies, and asks, "Will my buddy Moe like this?"

At each possible selection, I shrug and Bobby puts the item down.

"What does Moe like?"

The only thing that comes to mind is strawberries. "She told me she really craves strawberries."

Bobby makes the sort of sour face he makes when something does not coincide with his idea of class and turns back to the jade mother and baby elephant he has been contemplating.

At the end of our shopping outings, we stop in at a *mikuru* bar for a "snack" of cake, pastry, cookies, and coffee, since Bobby maintains that he only eats the one meal a day. Then we head back to the hotel to start getting ready.

Around six, I meet Bobby in the lobby. Joe drives us to the first of what are usually two shows at whatever base we're headed for that evening. While Bobby comes more fully awake during these drives until he reaches a state of edgy irritation that can spike into homicidal rage, I withdraw into the just-passing-through catatonia I perfected on endless bus rides to the inevitable new school.

At every club, Bobby pulls out my "charts" and the band plays some version of "I Dig Rock and Roll Music" that ranges from hideous to coma-inducing. The song, if it could be called that, is impossible to dance to, and by the second night I give up trying, realizing that my main purpose is to smile, serve as the butt of a few lame jokes, and demonstrate the possibility, however remote, that Bobby Moses might, in fact, be getting any at all. He really likes it when I pretend to get mad at his jokes and sleazy-sad innuendos. Once I accept that the essence of my segment of the act is to trot a selection of secondary sexual characteristics onstage, it really stops mattering how poorly I shake said characteristics around.

I go onstage each night secure in the knowledge that on the other side of the catatonic state is amnesia. By the time Bobby holds my hand and we take our bow, I have forgotten almost everything about my "performance." The one element I cannot submerge is what Bobby has taken to calling my "signature." "I Dig Rock and Roll Music" plinks uncontrollably through my head at odd times during the day.

The end of the night becomes the best part of the day, sharing a gargantuan meal in Bobby's room. Even though Bobby makes such a big deal of "showing" me to my room that the staff, and eventually even Joe, think we're sleeping together, after the first night the thought becomes exactly what Bobby makes it in his act, a joke.

In the middle of the second week, we take the bullet train north for a two-day tour at Misawa Air Base. The air is cool and the light has a wintry, spectral quality to it, as if it were bouncing off snow even though there is none. I think of a photo of my father and his crew taken during a TDY outside an inn somewhere near Misawa. Snow covers the ground. Sake bottles line the railing of the porch. All the men's faces are flushed. They are in a line, with one kimono-clad hostess between each flier. The men grin, legs stuck out to the camera, doing the bunny hop. The wives had a fit about this photo. LaRue Wingo made a great show of tearing up her copy during a bridge game at the club with all the kids supposedly in another room watching a magic show.

A jet thunders overhead at an alarmingly low altitude heading due east. My father called Misawa a "staging area" and once returned from a TDY here that lasted three weeks with tiny totem poles for each one of us carved from walrus tusk and stamped MADE IN ALASKA and a bottle of American children's vitamins in the shape of characters from the Flintstones that looked like candy and tasted like chemicals. No one even thought about asking how he'd gotten American vitamins and Alaskan totem poles at a Japanese base.

Near the entrance to the officers' club in Misawa is a map. I trace a line almost directly west from the dot marking Misawa and my finger hits a knot of black lines where the borders of Korea, Red China, and Russia all snarl together. It is odd that, for all the years we lived in Japan, I never realize until that moment just how close we were to Russia.

Lacquer

Back in Tokyo, we move out of the Imperial. Bobby has arranged it so that our last three days of shows will all be on Yokota. "A buddy of mine's fixed it so we can stay at the BOQ." This same buddy gets an airman from the motor pool to pick us up. Bobby stuffs wads of thousand-yen notes into Joe's pockets, and we drive to Yokota.

We enter Yokota at Gate Three. The guard waves the motor-pool car on, and, just that easily, I am back in my childhood. All the bases I've ever lived on blur into this one, the prototype. Driving down Yokota's wide avenues plied by Chevys, Fords, Dodges, I remember seeing the base that first time when we were in Major Wingo's big overheated Pontiac. My heart leaps as we pass the base chapel, as plain and nondenominational as a Quaker meetinghouse, where I made my first communion, where the bishop of Tokyo patted my cheek to confirm me. The smell of gas fumes as we pass the base service station reminds me of how my father would always tell the Japanese attendant, "Fill it up with ethyl." The sight of the base library, a long prefabricated metal building, fills my head with the sound of rain beating on the tin roof and the oily smell of the kerosene heater.

"The bowling alley's right up there."

Bobby snorts when the triple-peaked roof of the bowling alley appears. "So you really did live here."

"I really did live here."

Though Bobby complains about his room at the BOQ being a "cracker box," mine, although smaller, is vast compared to the one I had at the Imperial. I don't miss the view of the emperor's swans at all. The instant Bobby leaves to meet friends, I'm out the front door.

At the Base Exchange, I show my ID card, but the guard won't let me in because I'm wearing blue jeans. I point out that I bought the jeans I am wearing at the Kirtland Air Force Base Exchange and that I can see a rack of blue jeans in the women's clothing area. Yes, the guard agrees, you can purchase jeans at the BX, but you can't wear them into the BX.

I come back wearing an obscenely short skirt and am instantly admitted. I buy a package of Georgia peanuts and a Nehi grape soda from a vending machine, then wander through the comforting array of American products. Levi's jeans. Breck shampoo. Dial soap. Right Guard deodorant. Craftsman tools. Weber grills. Huffy bikes. Louisville Slugger bats. Voit tetherball sets. Cases of Coke. Bags of Fritos. Bottles of Tabasco sauce.

Behind the BX a row of Japanese-operated shops marked CONCESSIONS sell silver, lace, china, wrought iron, porcelain, dry cleaning, and haircuts. The Look Optical Shop promises *Your Order Will Receive Our Best Attention.*

The parking lot of Yokota Commissary is as full as if a typhoon were about to hit. Kota Kabs cruise, watching for wives at the exit followed by Japanese bag boys pushing one or more carts loaded with groceries. Next door, the Yokota BX bulk sales booth does a brisk business. A tower of six-packs blocks both side windows. Pyramids of half-gallons of vodka, scotch, and rum sell for $1.80. I stare at the parking lot and remember the rainy day Major Wingo spun doughnuts here that would have killed us if my father hadn't grabbed the wheel.

Officers in pressed khaki and shoes black and shiny as patent leather march purposefully past heading toward Wing Headquarters. Wing Headquarters looks like the administration building of a large state university. American and Japanese flags fly outside. I walk on toward the officers' club.

On the street a car slows down and creeps alongside me until I look over and glimpse the Kota Kab logo on the door. I smile with relief at the driver of the two-toned black-and-white Chevy Bel-Air. I am certain that I rode in that very cab. I peer at the driver and wave in recognition. Yes, I'm certain this is the cab and that is the driver who used to take me to ballet lessons at the Youth Center, where I hid in the bathroom for several months until the teacher asked Moe why I'd never shown up. I remember the look of the MPC, military payment certificates, in my hand as I passed them to this driver. There were no coins, just those bright bills colored turquoise and magenta that the military used to thwart black-marketeers. Then I realize that the driver behind the wheel is my age and could not have been driving a Kota Kab ten years ago. Embarrassed, I wave him away and hurry on.

At seventeen hundred hours a scratchy recording of "The Star-Spangled Banner" blares out through speakers planted all over the base. Every car stops while all the flags on base are lowered.

When the national anthem stops, I trudge across the large field in front of the Richard Bong Theater where Santa's helicopter, in a whirl of dust and bits of cellophane from cigarette packages that had been shredded by relentless mowing, used to touch down.

As I walk toward the base theater, I recall the last movie I saw there, *Pardners,* with Jerry Lewis and Dean Martin. This was months after Martin and Lewis had ceased to be pardners, and my step when I'd approached the theater that day was burdened as Kit and I walked up to pay our fifteen cents apiece to view the celluloid eulogy.

In front of the theater is a plaque dedicating the Richard Bong Theater to the memory of Richard Bong. I stop to read the plaque and learn that Richard Bong was the Army Air Corps "Ace of Aces," dying in 1945 at the age of twenty-five and winning the Medal of Honor for "voluntarily and at his own urgent request engaging in repeated combat missions including highly aggressive sorties. His aggressiveness and daring resulted in shooting down eight enemy airplanes during this period."

The Bong Bunnies. So this was the man, this lover of the "highly aggressive" sortie, that my father and his friends had named themselves after.

I check out the poster for that day's feature, *The Happening.* Anthony Quinn's and Milton Berle's faces are contorted in expressions of comic panic as a gang of extras in hippie wigs that appear to have been borrowed from Raggedy Ann and Andy close in on them. A swirl of script advises, *Go with the flow, man!* Berle and Quinn are dressed as mafiosos, a fashion style very similar to Bobby's. The hippies are barefooted. I vaguely recall avoiding this film more than a year ago when it passed almost instantaneously through theaters in the States.

I hurry on to West Area. My longer grown-up stride causes me to miscalculate and my alma mater, Bob Hope Elementary, takes me by surprise. The pines that were saplings when I attended now tower over the two-story building. I step over the picket fence encircling the school and walk in the front door. Even in summer, it smells of the damp lacquer umbrellas of the locals who clean and cook, of the wet woolens of the children, of the kerosene burned to heat the drafty buildings. At the end of the dark hall, silhouetted against the bright light pouring in through the double doors, I spot the unmistakable hourglass of Miss Ransom's shirtwaist dress and understand the psychology of the abused child who still longs for the bad parent, for I bound toward her as if I had been Miss Ransom's treasured pet.

"Miss Ransom!" I run to the end of the hall where the figure is turning and face a stranger.

"Excuse me?" She holds a stack of paper monkeys curled into the letters of the alphabet and still smelling of singed plastic from the laminating machine. She is barely older than I am.

"Oh. I thought you were someone else. I used to go to this school. You don't happen to know a Miss Ransom."

"Ransom?" She shakes her head no to that name and the other three I mention. Her glossy eyeliner has collected in a ball at the inner corner of her eyes. "'Course, this is my first year here. I think it's everyone's first year here, actually. The students'll have to tell us where the toilets are."

"They're back there. Next to the office."

"I was only kidding." The new teacher pushes the bar opening the big metal doors. I go back out the way I came, flag down the next Kota Kab that passes by, and tell him to take me to Fussa.

When he stops, I'm sure the driver has made a mistake. We are in a miniature version of Tokyo. But after he repeats Fussa three times and points to the earth beneath us, I step out of the cab. At first, it seems that the little town I once lived in has vanished completely, but between the canyons of high-rises, I find alleys lined with *benjo* ditches and crammed with paper-screened houses, pachinko parlors, and small shops where the owners wash the sidewalks from blue plastic buckets. I can't find our alley, though, nor is it possible any longer to see Mount Fuji, but that is not what I'm looking for. I scrutinize every female face that passes and see Fumiko in all of them and in none.

Polish

"So, Zelda, who'd you look up?"

"No one."

Bobby has called me into his room while he finishes his preparations for the night's show. I'm already made up and have done my hair. I sit on his bed in my bathrobe and paint my nails with the clear gloss Bobby uses, while he combs and recombs his hair. His tux is in a garment bag and he's wearing a sport shirt and slacks. He angles his head to the mirror, scrapes at his part where the roots are growing in, decides he can make it another night without a touch-up, and pats his hair back into place.

"No one? You were gone all afternoon and you didn't look anyone up?"

"No."

"You did live here four years, right?"

"Right."

"And that's a long time for the Air Force."

"Yeah."

"Okay, so this is like your hometown. So, you're in your hometown and you don't look up anybody?" Bobby is doing what he does when his preshow jitters kick in, sprinkling himself with extra Brut.

"Do you have to wear so much aftershave?"

He stops and holds the bottle up.

"This is Brut. Your idol, Bob Hope, wears Brut."

"Bob Hope is not my idol. He's a tired old hack who tells jokes that aren't funny to captive audiences of GIs." A suicidal glee overtakes me. I can't stop myself. "Because he's such a has-been that no one who has a choice would ever come to one of his shows. And Bob Hope doesn't wear Brut. Nobody but a—" I want to say "loser" so bad I can taste the word but manage to stop myself. "Bob Hope doesn't wear Brut."

"So you been hanging out in Hope's dressing room a lot."

I mumble an answer.

"What? I didn't catch that."

"You don't get it. Bobby, you just don't get it at all."

"Hey, that's my tag line! It took me thirty years to come up with a signature. Find your own!"

"It's all yours, Bobby." I stand up to leave.

"Touchy, touchy. What? That time of the month? You wanna borrow a couple Midol?"

I explode a gasp of exasperation and head for the door.

"Hey, wait! I know what it is." Bobby beams with inspiration. "You're nervous 'cause we're playing your hometown!"

In fact, Bobby is right about one thing: I *am* getting my period. But he is so wrong about everything else and has been so wrong from the moment I first set eyes on him that I can no longer stand it. Like an aneurysm exploding, something bursts inside my head.

"Are you a complete moron? This is not my *hometown.* A hometown is where you go back and they remember you from when you were a kid. This is like being Jewish and going back to Krakow or something. All the buildings are the same, but everyone you ever knew is dead or PCS'd, which amounts to the same thing. For me, Yokota is a fully populated ghost town. I can't go back and visit my old teachers or my old neighbors or even the guy who sold me *Mad* magazines in the BX when I was nine or the girl who sat next to me on the bus in second grade. She's gone. They're all gone. They've been transferred three, four, five times since then, and they wouldn't remember me any more than I'd remember them. This is not my hometown. Military brats don't *have* hometowns."

"Moe said you might feel that way."

"Moe? When did you talk to my mother?"

"Me and Moe, we got a lot in common. Your father's lucky he spotted her first. Me and Moe, we see eye to eye."

The thought of my mother being eye-to-eye or any-organ-to-any-other-organ with Bobby Moses unsettles me deeply.

"Don't make that face. Your mother is a very attractive woman. Very Catholic. Very married. So, we talked a few times. She's a good mother. She wants to be sure her daughter's safe. So, you're sure there's no one."

"There's no one."

"*Mazel tov,* you're the man without a country. You're sure there's no one?"

The twinkly way he keeps asking this question annoys me even further. "How many times do I have to tell you? I don't know anyone here and no one here knows me and that's the way I like it. I'm just passing through."

"Just passing through, huh? Moe said that was your problem."

"Moe said—"

"Just passing through. No friends. No roots. You sound like a prune. Yeah, that's you, Zelda. You're a prune in the duodenum of life. Just don't be surprised when you get shit out. Go. Get dressed. We got a show to do."

Bobby is jollier than I have ever seen him, as if my asking if he were a complete moron and insinuating that he and his idol are gigantic losers has brought us closer together. I leave Bobby probing a nostril with a pair of cuticle scissors, snipping at the thicket of hair within. I want to kick the door, after I slam it behind me and hear him laughing on the other side as if he has some juicy secret I don't know anything about.

Kool

We are the entertainment that night for the annual Costume Ball at the Top 3 Enlisted Officers' Club. The emcee announces the start of the costume contest. Everyone takes a seat at tables ringing the dance floor to applaud the work of a platoon of sew girls as the contestants parade across the low stage in their costumes: a caveman, an astronaut, Marie Antoinette, a couple of Marilyn Monroes. By popular acclamation, however, the plainest pair of costumes takes the big prize of the evening. A middle-aged couple, Master Sergeant Randy Cox and his wife, Betty, take the Best Costume prize for stapling themselves into sacks of brown butcher paper. They wear matching terry-cloth bedroom slippers and their calves are bare. On the front of Cox's sack is his name, COX. Written on the front of his wife's is COX'S OL' BAG. As the Coxes rustle offstage to a big round of applause, the emcee brings Bobby on.

Since there is no backstage, I stand at the far end of the room and wait to go on. From a distance, as Bobby's tux shimmers electric blue under a lone spot and Julius Caesar and Pocahontas laugh at his lame jokes, Bobby looks like the real thing.

"So this Japanese dame has a white baby. Just goes to show ya, Occidents can happen."

Bah-bing!

"Hey, you guys with Japanese wives, what's her favorite day? Erection day, *hai!* Am I right?"

I wince with embarrassment for all the Japanese wives, but both jokes get big laughs.

"Oh, look, Katsumi there in the Cleopatra outfit doesn't get it. She's asking Marc Antony what the joke is. Oops, he's waving her off. Erection Day nebber hoppen. Velly solly, Chollie! Poor Katsumi, she don't get it. She just don't get it at all!"

Marc Antony's pals are slugging him good-naturedly when Bobby announces me. The band breaks into an especially cheesy version of "I Dig Rock and Roll Music," and I walk through the tables toward the stage.

I would never have recognized her, sitting at the farthest edge of the semicircle of tables. It is the coat I recognize because it was Moe's coat: a beautiful A-line dove-gray mouton with a shawl collar. Where Fumiko once seemed beautiful to me in a Japanese way, she now seems beautiful in a Western, an American way. Unlike the odd sexlessness of most Japanese women, their hair tied in pigtails with Minnie Mouse holders, their breasts flattened, giggling and covering their mouths, Fumiko is a grown woman. She sits alone at the table smoking a cigarette with the defiant seductiveness of Ava Gardner and holding an envelope with my mother's handwriting on the outside.

Onstage, a conspiratorial twinkle lights Bobby's eye. Moe obviously gave him a copy of the letter to Fumiko.

Before Fumiko can look up, I glance away and force myself to walk to the front of the room, unable now to hear the awful music for the blood rushing through my head. Onstage, the knowledge that there is one person watching who knows me paralyzes me. To survive this moment, I draw upon years of standing alone in the center of miles of varnished gym floor, listening to team captains argue over who will have to take me for their teams. I initiate a spasmodic jerking of my limbs that finally ends when Bobby sweeps onstage.

"Okay, ladies and gentlemen, that was the Amazing Zelda doing her impression of a hippie fighting her way out of a bathtub!"

I try to leave, my gaze firmly trained away from Fumiko, but Bobby holds my hand in a death grip.

"You gotta forgive her, folks, there's someone in the audience Zelda hasn't seen for a long time. Let's bring her up with a big hand, Miss Fumiko Tanaguchi!" All the costumed clubgoers turn to look at Fumiko and clap.

Fumiko comes to the stage. I submerge more deeply into myself than I ever have before. Bobby stands between us and holds up our hands. The crowd applauds like we're two contestants on *Queen for a Day.*

"All right, already. Enough with old home week. Go hog someone else's spotlight." Bobby shoos us off the stage, and we find our way to the exit.

Outside, the sultry night is alive with the drone of cicadas. I am grateful for the darkness, for the insect noise. I can think of nothing to say.

Fumiko pulls a pack of cigarettes out of the coat pocket, lights one up, and inhales. She smokes Moe's brand, Kools. "Hey, whassamatta you? You no rike see Fumiko?"

Fumiko sounds like a Koza bar girl, a *pan-pan* girl. She is not the shy delicate young woman I remember. On each word Fumiko speaks, on the hearty brusque manner she affects, are the fingerprints of all the GIs who have passed through her life for the past eight years.

"No, no, I'm happy to see you."

"Hey, you not so shy no more." She shakes her shoulders, miming me dancing. "What hoppen?"

"You're not so shy either." I mimic her: "What hoppen you?"

"Oh, you wise guy now, huh? At first I think you Eye-reen."

"Me?"

"Yeah. You hair. You"—she makes a pouty face—"I think, must be Eye-reen. Bernie? Nebber hoppen."

"Well, it's me." The cicadas' screech seems to grow louder. "I guess Bobby gave you Moe's letter."

"You read retter?"

It is an effort to have to discuss such a personal matter with a complete stranger, a stranger wearing my mother's coat.

"Not really."

"What 'no rearry'? You read, you no read."

"I read it."

"Okay, so why rong face? You mad?"

"I'm not mad."

"Don't shit me, I'm you favorite turd."

I really, really, *really* do not feel like discussing any of this in the middle of the Top 3 Club parking lot. "Isn't it kind of hot to be wearing a coat?"

"Hot as hair. I just want you remember."

Fumiko takes the coat off. She wears a tight shirt that shows off her broad shoulders and high breasts. She strokes the coat, silver now in the purplish illumination from the crime light high on a pole above the parking lot.

"You remember coat?"

I remember. Moe had worn it on the ship coming over. She'd worn it all through the last months of her pregnancy with the twins. She gave it to Fumiko after Fumiko showed up for work one snowy morning wearing nothing but a pink cardigan sweater.

"How you mama? How Moe?"

"Good. Pretty good."

"How my baby?"

She means Buzz. With his eyes swollen into slits by his chubby cheeks and his spiky black hair, the joke was that he was Fumiko's child. It doesn't seem funny to me now, and I can't keep the stiffness out of my voice. "Fine."

"You mad me?"

"No."

"You mad at anybody, be mad at RaRue."

"LaRue? You mean LaRue Wingo?"

"Sure. She the one to brame."

"You know, I realize that Moe wrote in her letter that . . . whatever happened might have happened anyway. I guess that's what Moe thinks. So I don't blame you, okay? I don't blame my father. But I'm sure the hell not going to blame LaRue Wingo. I'm really tired. I'm going to go now, and—"

Fumiko grabs my arm as I start to leave. "You think . . . me and you father? Me and Captain Root?"

"Look, I really don't want to—"

"Nebber hoppen." Her fingers dig into me. "That nebber, nebber hoppen." Tears stand in Fumiko's eyes, making them into ovoids of black obsidian so dark that any emotion could hide within their depth. For one instant they are unguarded, and I see clearly that I know nothing about this woman. Fumiko exhales loneliness scented with menthol as if she'd drawn it from her cigarette.

"Why you think me and Captain Root? Captain Root? No! Nebber, nebber hoppen. Captain Root too . . . too . . ." Frustrated, Fumiko flutters her hands about her head and mutters in Japanese, searching for the word. "Too . . ." She genuflects and makes the sign of the cross. "You understand? Why he want to? He marry Moe. Why go out for hamburger when you got steak at home? You berieve Fumiko? I rying, I dying. You berieve Fumiko? . . . Prease."

Fumiko looks up at me, and the hearty brusqueness of a thousand dates with a thousand servicemen falls away like a mask. All the Americanness leaves her face and Fumiko is, once again, the young woman who touched my widow's peak in that mysterious way then welcomed our family to the little house in Fussa with a movement graceful as a crane in flight. She is the person who blew my loose tooth out. Who made candied tangerines when I thought my mother was never going to come home. Who sang *Day-oh* with Moe and liked me better than Kit from the very first moment, and I know her completely.

"Yes." I believe Fumiko. I believe the truth I always knew.

Bar-girl English still comes out of Fumiko's mouth, but once again I can hear the words she means to speak instead. I know that her answer to me is, "I'm glad, Bernie. Glad that you believe me. That makes me happier than I can say."

I hear this in my head. What Fumiko actually says is, "Fumiko *takusan* grad. You *ichi-ban* asshore buddy."

But I don't hear that. Once again, I can hear what Fumiko means. The magic that found us when we first spoke together in the shadow of Fuji-san wakes again and I can fill in all the blanks, add in articles, make subjects and verbs agree, intuit meaning from the tilt of Fumiko's eyebrow, the semaphores she flags with her hands.

"Fumiko, if you and my father didn't—you know, weren't involved, why did they stop talking about you? Take out all your photos. Pretend like you never existed?"

"Why not? I was your maid, not your sister."

"You were more than that."

"You should ask Moe this question."

"I'm asking you."

"You don't remember? You were there."

"Remember what?"

"If Moe hasn't told you, I can't tell you. Moe knows that you will remember what you need to remember."

"Zelda, there you are! I been looking all over this farshtinkener club for you. They loved the reunion bit. Let's do it again tomorrow."

Bobby puts his arm around Fumiko. "What I tell you?" He points to me. "Number-one girl-san." He taps his head. "College girl. Big brain. Me *presento* you from Moe."

"Moe *steky-ne?*"

It is jarring to hear the bar-girl English return as they discuss how beautiful my mother is.

"Moe *takusan takusan steky.*"

Bobby pulls Fumiko closer. "You pretty goddamned *steky* yourself. We go Club Tokyo together?"

"*Anone!* Fumiko have job-u go, *ne?*"

With a flirty laugh, Fumiko squirms out of Bobby's grasp, grabs my hand, and pulls us both away.

"*Do shi'te.* What'sahurry?"

"*Dekinai,* Bobby-san. No can stay. Go job-u."

"Job-u, right. What's his name? How 'bout you-me job-u?"

Fumiko pulls me away as she flags down a Kota Kab.

"The club. Ten. Tomorrow," is all Fumiko tells me, before she jumps into the old black Dodge, but I know what she means. She issues orders to the driver in harsh Japanese. He pulls away quickly.

Bobby lumbers to my side. We watch the red taillights disappear.

"Hey, Moe didn't tell me the old family retainer'd be such a babe."

I don't answer.

"Don't forget, we got the big one tomorrow. We play the Yokota Officers' Club. You gotta shine for that one, Zelda. Gotta really sparkle. Yokota O Club, that's like the Tropicana of service clubs. Am I right or am I right?"

"You're right, Bobby," I say, and remember the time when it was true.

Onion Rings

I'm early the next morning. In a far corner of the parklike grounds in front of the Yokota Officers' Club, I wait at the foot of a Japanese bridge arching over a pond stocked with koi fish grown to an immense size. The fish crowd the edge of the pond, sucking greedily at the cracker crumbs I sprinkle on them. Japanese lawnmen push mowers around the topiary shrubs and stone lanterns. Wives loaded down with towels and beach balls, surrounded by swarms of children, pass by on gravel paths heading to the pool, where swim lessons are in progress.

Before I reach the high fence surrounding the pool, the morning breeze brings the scent of chlorine, Coppertone, rubber swim caps, and warm wet cement and I am swamped by nostalgia. I remember the dressing rooms where Moe and LaRue and the other wives, heads cocked to one side, would tuck their hair into thick white rubber swim caps with rubber flowers bunched above one ear like a droopy corsage. Where they shimmied into bathing suits with zippers and stays and breastpieces that held the shape of a bosom even without anyone inside them. I would stare at their nipples, some as small and pink as pencil erasers, others as big and dark as Oreos, the bellies with silver stretch marks, the beard between their legs, and try to figure out the mesmerizing/repellent power of those bodies.

"Take a picture, kid, it'll last longer." LaRue Wingo's voice had echoed off the tile floor when she'd caught me studying her breasts, turned up at the tips like sultan's shoes, her figure as voluptuous as Marilyn Monroe's.

"Yeah, it's not polite to stare." Kit turned to LaRue and the squadron commander's wife nodded her approval.

Moe pulled me to her away from the laughing women and, with Kit and the twins, we went out to the pool. My father stood in the middle and made Kit and me take turns swimming out to him. Kit was a good swimmer, but the trip across the vast pool took all my strength and courage. Halfway to my father, I inhaled a mouthful of water and my father had to pull me out. I felt as if I'd swum the English Channel.

I reach the gate, open it, and behold a pool hardly larger than one you'd find at a motel.

A little boy genuflects at the edge, his arms steepled over his head, ready to dive to the instructor waiting in the water. He is a skinny spider monkey like Bob, his stretch-waist swimsuit ballooning above skinny legs. The wives sunbathe on lounge chairs. They are all overweight. None of them reminds me of Marilyn Monroe.

As I walk back past the arched bridge and koi pond, I recalibrate my expectations and only partially succeed. I remember the Yokota Officers' Club the way exiles remember Batista Cuba, as a nightclub of sophisticated, forbidden delights with a heavy emphasis on rattan. I can't stop myself from feeling like an exile returning to Havana. The big letters YOC on the side of the building remain an acronym for glamour and sophistication. I can't keep my heart from leaping as I walk into the shade of the porte cochere, just the way it did walking in with Moe and Captain Root.

No club should be viewed in daylight, and the Yokota Officers' Club seems more forlorn than most. Inside the rattan has been replaced by molded plastic furniture. The rugs are worn, the paint is dingy. Only the smell is as I remember it: old beer, cigar smoke, floor wax, perfume, hair spray; filet mignons, onion rings, spiced red apple rings. Signs point the way to the Samurai Ballroom, the Terrace Café, and the Sho-Ichiban Restaurant.

Some magnetism left over from visits long past tugs me toward the Samurai Ballroom, the main dining room where my family always ate, but it is only open for dinner. The Sho-Ichiban is also closed. At the entrance to the Terrace Café, a full colonel sits high up in a shoe-polishing booth, reading a copy of the *Yokota Afterburner* and having the mirror finish on his shoes buffed by a white-haired Japanese man. The shoeshine man's face has a wonderful burnished quality, like Moe's big brass tray that she has polished beauty into over the years. His white hair is thick and spiky as a lion's mane around his face. The sharp chemical smell of the black shoe edging he carefully paints around the sides of the colonel's soles triggers a memory and the name Yoda Hayashi jumps into my mind, along with a memory of the man when his hair was more black than white.

The colonel stands and presses some coins into the old man's hand, and the man turns to bid him farewell. I read his name tag: YODA HAYASHI, the name I remembered. He sees me staring at him and smiles. Does he remember me? I beam at him, ecstatic to find this one link to a vanished world. A fraction of a second later, I realize it is impossible that this man, who's watched thousands of dependent kids pass by his stand, would remember one very shy girl who's now mostly grown. I adjust my smile from one of grinning recognition to the generic tilt of the lips used for any stranger, nod my head, and go into the café.

The Terrace Café, once a fifties fantasy of bamboo and rattan, has been remodeled and now sports the blandly pleasant look of a chain-motel coffee shop. Several tables overlooking the pool are occupied by groups of wives who gossip over Cokes and iced teas, occasionally glancing at the children splashing outside. Another half dozen tables around the edges of the café are occupied by operations officers eating early lunches. I find a table in an uneasy area between the two groups.

A Japanese waitress, her attention on flipping an order pad to a clean page, comes to my table. "Jew wan sontheen?"

Stitched above the pocket of her pale blue Dacron blouse is the motto *Ladies and gentlemen serving ladies and gentlemen.* Like housing developments named Deercreek, the motto seems more wistful memorial than description of current reality.

"Filet mignon and onion rings."

"No fray. Ion ring. Hahburger. Hah dog."

"Just the onion rings."

My elation at remembering the name of the shoeshine man fades when nothing else seems familiar. The onion rings that were once as good as tempura are now machine-punched loops frozen months ago in a factory in New Jersey.

I sense the wives turning their attention toward me. A glance, a few overheard words, gazes that sweep in my direction then quickly away, followed by laughter, knowing and excluding, suddenly recall the strict hierarchy of LaRue Wingo and her crew of harpies. For a moment I know exactly why I should hate "RaRue." In the next second, the memory vanishes and I am back in a second-rate coffee shop with a bunch of women eyeing me with hostility because I am young and single, and they know their next child will permanently explode their waistlines and marble their legs with varicose veins.

The pressure of those gazes suddenly lifts when a flight crew swaggers in. A cocky major with a red crew cut leads the pack. All the men wear nylon flight suits that zip up the front and are creased at the crotch from parachute straps. Zippered pockets line the legs, arms, chest. In those pockets are matches coated in wax for survival in the event of an emergency water landing, hard candies to relieve thirst during unheated high-altitude flights when the water will freeze, a Benzedrine inhaler to keep eardrums from blowing out in unpressurized cabins, a compass, and a serrated knife for hacking away fouled straps before ejection. I once overheard whispers about cyanide capsules. These items jingle like a gunfighter's spurs as the men enter and cause all the wives' heads to turn.

The operations officers, ground pounders, paper pushers, desk jockeys, the men whose careers stand or fall on Brasso, Kiwi shoe wax, and efficiency reports, all stop eating and watch the fliers strut in, talking too loudly, unshaven, smelling from whatever mission they just completed, from the hours of sweating or freezing in the nylon suits. The wives shift in their chairs, turning away from the chubby-legged children in the pool toward the fliers. The five men take a table, order Cokes and coffees, and don't try very hard to hide the pint bottles of bourbon and scotch they tip into the drinks. The redheaded major with the smirky grin holds his mug up in a toast to the ladies. A wife, the prettiest one, a petite brunette wearing a lacy cover-up over her bikini, holds her glass of iced tea up in an answering toast.

A phrase LaRue Wingo used to use when TDY crews like this one would enter the club echoes back to me: "exchange program." It meant nothing to me when I was one of the children splashing in the pool outside the window.

The crew and the wives size each other up. The wives who stare the longest are most likely to have dropped their husbands off at the Flight Line that morning to take off on TDY missions bound for—who knows?—maybe the exact base this crew has come from. Maybe at this very moment the husbands are heading for the O Club at that other base where the wives of this visiting crew are huddled over Cokes and iced teas. Exchange program.

And then Fumiko walks in. Instantly, all the male attention turns away from the wives and toward her as she crosses the coffee shop coming to me. For a second I am proud that the best-looking woman in the room is my friend. Then I catch sight of the wives' stretch marks and varicose veins that are just like the ones Moe bears and the pride vanishes. I jump up, intercept Fumiko before she reaches the table, and head for the cashier.

As we leave the coffee shop, the shoeshine man stops us. He points excitedly to me and speaks to Fumiko in rapid Japanese. The words "Moe" and "ojosan" jump out at me several times. Fumiko nods and answers with a brisk and smiling, "Hai! Hai!" She repeats the same words: "Moe, ojosan." Though the shoeshine man bows and beams at me as I walk away, I assume that the words I heard are random syllables.

It is not until I am outside that I recall ojosan means "daughter."

DDT

The wind has shifted direction, and the smell of JP-4 fuel drifts over from the Flight Line.

Fumiko catches up with me and grabs my arm. "Hey, why you piss off me?"

"I'm not pissed off at you." But I am and have no desire to deal with any of this.

"Don't shit me."

"Yeah, I know. I'm your favorite turd."

"Okay, you terr me Moe? Captain?"

"He's a major now."

"Onaree major? He fry after reave Yokota?"

Her question surprises me. "No, he never flew again."

"Moe? She sing?"

This question surprises me even more. "Not really."

"No fry, no sing."

There is such sorrow in Fumiko's voice that my irritation disappears. "What happened then? If it wasn't you and my father, what happened? We were happy, we were a family, my parents loved each other; then it all ended. We left Japan and nothing was the same again."

"You were there. The night ebbrything ober, ebbrything end. You were there."

"Fumiko, I was ten years old. I don't remember."

"Ten? Ten not so rittoe."

"Fumiko, tell me."

"Okay, but you hear stupid *pan-pan* girl talk or you hear what Fumiko mean?"

"I'll hear what you mean."

"Okay, but I terr you part story, Moe part story, got to terr arr story."

"Yeah, fine, of course."

"No, you say 'yeah, fine,' but story rong, berry berry rong. Have to terr when Fumiko rittoe gurroe, so you know why ebbry-thing hoppen. Rong rong story."

"No, I want to. I want to hear all of it."

"Okay. Come."

Fumiko leads me through the gardens surrounding the club to an area far behind the pool that had always been off limits. As children, we were told it was off limits because it occupied a low spot where water ponded, and no amount of the DDT that was sprayed every evening in thick pine-smelling clouds over the entire base would ever eliminate the mosquitoes whose bite could make your brain swell up and turn you into a vegetable.

An old gardener, stooped with age, greets Fumiko by name and unlocks the gate blocking the path. We enter the thick stand of pines, supposedly guarded by what Bosco would have told us were ravenous *Culex tritaeniorhyncus* mosquitoes. The path leads to a small, exquisite teahouse hidden away in the forest. As she slides back the paper-screened doors, Fumiko explains that the teahouse is reserved for special parties, for generals, visiting senators, members of the Diet. It is understood that Fumiko has entertained at these parties.

Nothing in the teahouse betrays that centries ago the Black Ships ever landed to taint Japan with Western ways. Fumiko leaves her shoes at the entrance. Her steps become shorter; she shuffle-glides with hydraulic ease across the smooth wooden floor, leading me to a room at the back of the teahouse.

The floor of the room is covered with tatami mats. Polished cypress and soft white shoji walls are offset by a cloisonné vase with a few pussy willow branches artfully arranged in it. The light filtering through the paper screens is dim and gently diffuse. One wall opens onto a garden. The scents of jasmine and cedar hang in the air. Fumiko rolls her hand over and, her pale wrist leading, gestures to a low table. We kneel at the table, sitting on our heels.

Fumiko composes herself. Her brash American manner drains away and she sits silent for several minutes. When she speaks, the bar-girl English is gone. She sounds again like the timid young woman who slid the door open on the little house in the alley.

"You risten Fumiko or risten what Fumiko mean?" Her voice is as high and babyish as it was that first time.

"I'll hear what you mean. I promise."

And I do. When Fumiko begins, I stop hearing the words she uses. I hear again what she means as she tells me her long story, a story that started many years before my family ever sailed into Yokohama Bay.

Breath

"Imagine," Fumiko tells me as she begins her long story, "what cannot be imagined. Imagine Japan conquered. You believe you can imagine this, but you cannot. You cannot because we Japanese even twenty-three years later still cannot imagine it."

I can't understand why she's starting this far back but will myself to stay with her, to hear the meaning of her story.

"The days before the war officially ended were the hardest. When my mother learned my father had died on Okinawa, she lay down in the cave and prepared to die. But death does not come to someone strong enough to wish for it. She continued to eat the yam roots and mushrooms I grubbed from the earth and the barley and radishes I stole from the villagers' gardens, but they only fed her body for her spirit had died.

"From then on, my real mother, my beautiful, elegant mother, existed in my memory alone. There she stood in her dressing room back in our house with the blue tile roof in Tokyo, in front of a tall thin mirror framed in dark mahogany, her long hair parted in the middle and flowing to her knees.

"My mother was a warrior when she dressed. Her long, square sleeves sliced the air as she bound the slippery mass of silk of her kimonos and under-kimonos about herself, tightening the strings around her waist until her face went pale from the pain and the room filled with the smell of camphor used to preserve her kimonos. When she finished, my mother was perfect. Do you remember the fragrance of the apricot blossom? My mother was more perfect.

"The stranger that I led from the cave on the last day of the war wore a dirty *monpe* bulky as a baby's diaper with her tattered cotton kimono tucked in at the waist. She had cut her long hair. Stubby ends stuck out like the fur on a macaque's head and were tied back from her face with a piece of white rag. On her feet were black rubber boots with a pocket for the big toe like the gardener back at our home in Tokyo wore. She sat with her legs splayed apart.

"I didn't know what the day was then, but now all Japanese know this date: August fifteenth, 1945. The villagers gathered in the yard of the chief, who brought his radio outside, the only radio in the village, and nestled it on a grimy cushion of violet silk.

"I was fourteen and did not understand why all the villagers who had been so hard and cruel for the past years now fell silent. The voice coming from the radio was thin and whiny and spoke in Japanese so old-fashioned and high-blown that, any other time, these farmers would have jeered. Instead, they all stood in the boiling sun with their heads bowed gentle as lilies.

"The Emperor told us that we must endure the unendurable. That from then on he was no longer a god. That we must call the enemy the Allied Army of Occupation. A howl rose from the villagers. They wailed and sobbed, gasping for air, tears running down their faces. I had never seen grown-ups act this way, and it scared me.

"Though my mother kept her head bent even lower than anyone else's, her shoulders were shaking, not with sobs but with laughter she was fighting to contain. I asked her why she was laughing and everyone else was crying. She dug her bony fingers into my thin arm and pulled me so close that her words were wet on my ear. When she told me the war was over, I could not contain myself. The long nightmare would end. We would go home. My beautiful mother would return.

"I was infected with the laughter my mother was hiding. Unlike her, however, I could not contain it. When they heard my giggles, the villagers raised their heads and stared at me in horror.

"My mother slapped me so hard tears flew from my eyes, she

jerked my arm until I thought she had pulled it from its socket, but still the villagers glared. My mother said that what happened next was my fault, because I laughed when the Emperor said Japan had lost the war. But I think it all would have happened anyway.

"Late into the night, all the men of the village stayed at the headman's house. One had a cousin who was in the navy. He'd been on Okinawa when the *Amekos* invaded the island and raped all the women with penises big as beer bottles. Ten females, twenty—old women, girls, infants torn from their mothers' backs—none were enough to satisfy them. And the dark ones were even worse.

" 'That is the nature of conquerors,' said another man, adding, 'Remember Nanking.' He held up his hand, which was missing the thumb he'd blown off when his rifle misfired during the sack of Nanking. Nothing more needed to be said, though the thumbless man did remind the group that the women of Nanking were not Japanese, not real humans, so no true offense had been committed.

"The problem before them that day was that since their young men, soldiers of the Imperial Army, were the finest men on earth, what had happened in Nanking was, obviously, the best that could be expected of conquerors. When the barbarians' Allied Army of Occupation arrived it would be infinitely worse, especially for women. Something had to be done. Fear made the hot night grow cold.

"Each day brought new rumors. The *Amekos* were in Tokyo burning homes and looting temples. The *Amekos* were in the prefecture raping Buddhist nuns and grandmothers. Each day the conquerors came closer to the village.

"After weeks of debate, they agreed on what had to be done. Early the next morning, the packing began. By the end of the day, all the daughters of the village, all the young wives, were gone. We, my mother and I, of course, had no one to send us off. Nowhere to be sent. For the first time, I noticed the women's chattering because it had fallen silent as if all the birds had died.

Late that evening, the old women who were left came to our cave and invited us to stay with them. One had the audacity to wear the stork-and-water-lily kimono she had traded my mother for one small packet of weevil-infested barley. They told my mother that there would be bowls of rice and hot baths for us. That in the end we were all Japanese. Our hearts beat as one. We must sacrifice for the good of all.

"I thought my mother would snarl and hiss and throw the old bitches out. Instead, she lowered her eyes and answered in a soft voice that, yes, we would come. Just as the old women broke into cracked smiles, my mother added *if*—and they stopped. 'If my wedding kimono is returned to me.' They agreed immediately.

"That night we tied up all the belongings we had left in a *furoshiki:* the comb carved from cypress that still carried the scent of my grandmother's hair, a dozen ten-yen coins. I started to put in the handful of barley that we were saving for our meal the next day, but my mother told me to leave it behind. That we would never eat barley or taro or yams again. Only rice, the silvery-white rice that makes a Japanese feel Japanese. I felt I had been saved from death, but my mother was sadder than I had seen her since she tried to die, and I was frightened again.

"My fears melted as the old women placed bowl after bowl of rice in front of us. In the village *sentoo,* they scrubbed me and my mother and joked as if we had all been friends throughout the war. As if they had never turned their dogs on us for taking a yam. It was only when I was soaking in the big wooden tub filled with water heated to an almost unbearably delicious heat that I noticed my mother staring at me with the same expression she used to wear in our fine house in Tokyo while setting out new candles, incense sticks, flowers at our family altar. She had the same look when she rang the bells and turned a page in the Book of the Dead. This book had thirty-one pages, and on each page were the names of the family's ancestors who had died that day. It frightened me to see my mother looking as if she were reading my name in our family's Book of the Dead.

"Each day, we stayed with a different old woman and her

family, who fed us as much as our stomachs could hold. Seeing how little the women had, how their shoulder blades stood out like plucked wings, I felt sorry for them and regretted stealing their food. For three days, we were all friends; our hearts beat as one. On the fourth day, a boy from the next village ran into ours. Panting and out of breath, he told us the *Amekos* had been spotted. The village elders nodded and began burning wood to make fuel for their one vehicle, an ancient truck that ran on charcoal.

"In the house of the village chief, the old women patted rice flour on our faces, outlined our eyes with soot, and reddened our lips with crushed berries. When they were finished, they left us alone. My mother brushed the hair away from my face and stared into my eyes. 'You are beautiful,' she told me, but in a sorrowful way that made me think she wished I were ugly. She told me to shut my mouth when I asked her where we were going. She told me the answer to that and to all the questions I might have in the future was that my belly was full, I was clean, new clothes covered my back, and my mother had fulfilled her obligation to me in the only way she knew how. She ordered me to repeat that to myself no matter what happened.

"Then the women came back in and told us to go out to the truck. The women, our hostesses, would no longer meet my gaze. The village chief gruffly ordered us into the back. I felt his shame and knew that whatever was about to happen to us would be worse than anything that had gone before, because none of them had felt shame for what they had done to us until then.

"We sat for a long time in the back of the truck while the men worked to make it start. At last the truck shuddered to life. Belching backfires and rattling, we drove slowly down the narrow country lane. The chief rode in front with the driver. The rest of the men followed on foot, easily keeping up. When we came to the road that led to Tokyo, we stopped and waited. Rivulets of soot-darkened sweat ran down my mother's face. She wiped them away with the loose ends of her *furoshiki*. After many hours, we heard the clatter of chopsticks against the metal *obento* boxes the men had brought their lunches in. When they finished, they handed the leftovers to us without a word and went back to squat in the shade.

"Late in the afternoon an Army truck the color of river moss came, crushing the bamboo stalks that lined the road. The villagers stopped the truck. I had seen photographs of *Amekos*, but they were much uglier in person. One of the village boys had once thrown an old tomcat into the pond with stones tied to each of its paws. Days later, swollen with gas, it floated to the surface. That was what these *gaijin* looked like to me, like humans bloated to hideous proportions, their faces, puffy and pointy at the same time, bleached of life.

"The headman went to speak to the driver, who told him to wait. Then he called a soldier out of the back of their truck. When the men of the village saw the soldier who raised the flap and stepped out, they gasped. He looked Japanese and even spoke an odd sort of Japanese, but he wore the uniform of the enemy and followed their orders. After he and the headman exchanged formal greetings, the headman begged to be excused for a moment.

"His face pale, the headman huddled with the other men to decide what to do. Though terrified, they were relieved because they now understood how their country could have been defeated: The *Amekos* had the power to steal souls. The man who had just spoken Japanese to them was, obviously, the ghost of a loyal defender of Nihon captured by the *Amekos*, enslaved now for all eternity. This was both much worse and much better than they had imagined. Though they understood how Japan could have been vanquished, they knew then that they were battling not just for their families' lives but for their souls.

"The headman, stiffened by cries of *Gambatte*, 'Try hard, persevere,' returned to the ghost boy. My mother and I could not hear what they said, but the headman repeatedly gestured toward us. The ghost boy translated his words and the other soldiers laughed. The headman, so polite and supplicating when he spoke to the ghost boy, ordered my mother and I out of the truck in the harshest of tones, as if it were our fault that the exchange was not going well.

"We stood in front of the men of the village as well as the *Amekos*, who had climbed out of the back of the truck. I stared only at their feet, the huge feet of monsters. I did not have the courage to look at them. I was proud of my father and all Japanese men for keeping these monsters away from us for as long as they had.

"The headman and the ghost boy spoke. The headman told the ghost boy that he was making the unworthy offering of me and my mother if the exalted Army of the Occupation would spare his village. The ghost boy translated and the Americans' laughter filled the air, a different kind of laughter than I had ever heard before. As unconscious as the grunts of pigs, this laughter proved to me that *Amekos* were not human. The ghost boy told the headman that they did not want us. I stole a glance at my mother. At her ugly, spiky hair. If she were still pretty they would have wanted us.

"The headman insisted, saying we were pathetic, wretched excuses for women unworthy of the smallest modicum of their attention but women all the same, equipped as all women were, and the esteemed Allied Army of the Occupation would do them a great honor by taking us with their blessings along with one *sho* of sake and three *kin* of rice. The village men brought forward the small barrel of sake and three precious, hoarded bundles of rice wrapped in straw.

"The men of the village were confused and shamed when, in return, the *gaijin* hauled immense burlap bags out of the back of the truck and slung them contemptuously at the feet of the headman. It was rice, not the silvery-white rice of Japan, but a great quantity of rice nontheless. Four to five *koku* of rice. Enough rice to feed the entire village. The *Amekos* didn't need our rice, and they didn't need my mother and me.

"As the village men prattled among themselves, a sound soft as a dove cooing fluttered about me. It took me and the ghost boy several moments to realize that my mother was speaking. For the first time since my father left, she spoke in the high, fluting voice of a wellborn Japanese woman.

"'Take us with you,' she asked the ghost boy. My mother told him that our home was in Tokyo and all we wanted was to return to it.

"As we left the village men kneeling in the dust, my mother sat rigid, looking straight ahead, holding the folded bundle of her white wedding kimono on her lap, stroking the golden threads. After a long time without speaking, she whispered to the ghost boy that she would like to be cremated wearing the wedding kimono. When one of the other soldiers asked what she said, the ghost boy shrugged. When my mother wasn't looking, he wound his finger around his ear to tell the other soldier that she was crazy.

"But with each kilometer the Army truck put between us and the village, with each kilometer that none of the soldiers paid us any attention, my mother's fear lifted. The *gaijin* confused me. They put their thumbs in their ears, waggled their fingers, and stuck their tongues out, trying to make me laugh. Then they peeled silver paper from slabs of a sweet brown food, handed one to me, and gestured for me to do as they were doing. The soldiers happily ate their slabs. When I smelled mine, I wished that they would have given me one that wasn't rotten, but I ate the sweet food that they called Hershey. When it became clear that they were not going to do what the villagers had assumed they would do, my mother became positively gay, her spirits brightened as much by having her opinion of the villagers' stupidity confirmed as by knowing we were safe.

"As we approached Tokyo, a shiver passed through my mother so forcefully that, sitting next to her, I could feel it. It was her spirit, missing since my brother died, returning to her body. She put her arm around me, hugging me tightly, and I thought I would faint from the pleasure of a touch from her that was not a slap or a pinch.

"'We're going home,' she whispered, as much to herself as

me. Home to the fairy city. We had left a magic castle of paper and wood homes. The joy in my mother's face made me forget my questions about how our fairy city could have survived the long weeks when the sky above Tokyo glowed pink as the city burned. She told the ghost boy where our neighborhood was. How many important people lived there. She hummed 'Sakura' under her breath, the first song I ever learned. It was as though we were starting all over, returning to the time when I was a little girl and my father dressed in a suit every morning to eat breakfast and my mother wore an obi twelve feet long wrapped about her waist.

"From the opening at the back of the truck we could not see what lay ahead, but as we drove into Tokyo we saw what lay behind. Devastation and ruin. The B-29 raids which had turned the sky pink had left behind only gray and black. No tree, no green blade of grass survived. No blue tile roof. No paper house. The truck rumbled off the road again and again because it became impossible to tell the road from the rubble of shattered roof tiles and the ash and cinder of burned paper and wood houses. Here and there, a piece of charred black timber poked out of a gray flatness that went on for as far as I could see.

"We passed hundreds, thousands, of homeless survivors, their faces pinched by hunger, living in shelters of cardboard, rocks, tarps pulled over bomb craters in the middle of the street. Everywhere we looked were shattered blue roof tiles, just like the tiles that had been on our house, tiles that were supposed to fool the god of fire, making him think the home was a blue lake. By the time we reached Shinjuku Station, far to the west of our neighborhood, my mother's spirit died again and for always. Her arm sagged away from my shoulders.

"When the truck stopped at the station, a mob of women as vulgar as Koreans swarmed the back, reaching up to the men, yelling, 'Fuckee-fuckee.' 'You fuckee-fuckee me.' The ghost boy asked if we wanted to get out, but my mother didn't answer.

"When even the threat of returning to the village could not make my mother speak, the ghost boy looked at the other soldiers and asked what they should do with us. Someone said, 'There's always the International Palace.' They all laughed. Then one of them said they had to make a drop-off there anyway. And, after they threw the last of the bags of rice to the crowd, that is where they headed. As we drove away from Shinjuku Station, I watched a skinny man in a dirty uniform kick a woman in the head and grab away the rice she held cupped in her hands.

"'Japan is dead. There is no Japan.' Though she stared straight ahead at the canvas side of the truck, my mother spoke my own darkest suspicion.

"We drove east to Funabashi. The International Palace was an ugly old Imperial barracks building where a line of American soldiers, boys like the ones in the truck, waited outside. The ghost boy handed me our *furoshikis* and told me in Japanese to take my mother inside. That they would know what to do with us because he sure didn't.

"There were no walls inside the barracks. Sheets hanging from the ceiling divided the long, narrow building into hundreds of cubicles. It stank of the DDT the Americans sprayed on everything, especially our hair. The sheets fluttered constantly as one barefoot soldier came out, collected his shoes at the back exit, shined while he had been occupied, and another came in from the front and took his place.

"An old woman with a face like a dried plum, her teeth the color of old tea, stopped us at the door and asked if the Recreation and Amusement Association had sent us. Everyone called her Mama Pan-Pan, she told us, because she was the most famous madam in Tokyo. When my mother only stared as if Mama Pan-Pan weren't there, I answered yes, we had been sent by this association she mentioned. Mama Pan-Pan looked at us, shut her eyes tight, and cursed her fate, having to run the largest brothel in the world with the worthless trash, pathetic amateurs, that the government sent her.

"As she showed us to a cubicle she asked if my mother spoke. Before I could answer, Mama Pan-Pan said it didn't matter. The men who came to the International Palace weren't looking for conversation. The futon on the floor took up almost all the room. There were rust-colored stains in its center.

"'They won't let you work,' the woman told me. 'The Americans are strict about that. No children. You can't stay. MPs catch you here, they'll shut me down. You can come in the morning to collect what she's earned. Early. Before dawn.'

"A woman bellowed for towels and Mama Pan-Pan told me I had to leave. I didn't want to know what my mother would be doing in this place, but the sheet dividing my mother's cubicle from the next jumped and billowed, a man grunted, and I could not pretend I did not know. I left my mother there and the next morning when I returned, Mama Pan-Pan handed me the wedding kimono and said that the MPs had already cut my mother's body down from the metal beam from which she had hanged herself and taken it away to be burnt so it wouldn't spread disease.

"Since there was no body to bury in the gold-embroidered wedding kimono, I traded it for a box of powdered milk and eight cans of C-rations. When the cans were gone, I joined the pack that scavenged for scraps behind mess halls, that stole provisions that had been stockpiled by the Imperial Army. I slept in subway stations, parks, and bomb craters, covered with burlap rags, terrified of the ones who would slice your throat for a radish.

"We did what we had to to stay alive. The moat around the Imperial Palace was so clogged with used condoms that a man came once a week with a big wire scoop to clean them out. For a pack of Old Gold cigarettes, women gave themselves in jeeps, in stairwells, in front of the Imperial Palace itself. They didn't care who watched. I swore I would never be a *pan-pan* girl.

"But months of hunger drove me back to the International Palace. I told Mama Pan-Pan I was ready to work. She laughed in my face and asked me how old I was. Ten? Eleven? I lied and told her I was sixteen. A gleam lighted her eyes. Something could be done with me. There was a major with certain 'particular' tastes very dangerous for an American officer to have. She bound the small buds of my breasts, dressed me in a pink kimono, put my hair in pigtails, painted my cheeks with a rosy powder, and took me to Rocker Four, a five-story club that had sprung up amid the rubble on the Ginza 4-chome intersection.

"Rocker Four was the showplace of the *Shawa Dakai*, the Dark Society that ruled the sprawling Tokyo underworld. Every day two thousand hostesses converged there from all over the starving city to extract as much money, chocolate, soap, rubber, beer, sugar, cigarettes, salt, C-rations, and powdered milk as they could from the GIs who flocked to the club. The club was surrounded by three-wheeled cabs, rickshaws, and charcoal-burning trucks. An Army bus pulled up and Japanese women all trying to look as American as they could streamed out. Their hair was frizzed by bad permanents. They painted their lips with waxy lipstick made of fish oil cooked up in pots over bonfires and wore short skirts made from kimonos that had been handed down for generations before they were ripped apart and stitched into American clothes. The most beautiful girls, those who made the best tips, had the shortest skirts to show off the biggest prize a hostess could earn, nylons. Baggy, webbed with runs, worn out at the heels, it didn't matter; the few who had nylons wore them proudly. Gum was the one American item they could afford and all the hostesses chewed it. The most daring had cigarettes and they smoked them the way they'd learned from the GIs, letting them droop insolently at the corner of their mouths, never bothering to tap the ash off.

"The women laughed and talked too loudly in the American way as they filed into Rocker Four, attracting the attention of a group of Japanese veterans. By this time it was unusual to see more than a solitary veteran walking the streets in public, so many had died, so many had killed themselves. Most had simply found ways to hide. The leader of the group, a one-legged man, wore a great cape and walked on crutches, his single leg swinging in the middle like the clapper of a dusty black bell. Three or four other old soldiers followed in grimy caps that laced at the back of their heads, their uniforms reduced to dirty, patched memories of uniforms.

"The one-legged man stopped and hissed curses at the women, calling them *gaisen*, a terrible insult, someone who sleeps with *gaijin*. The other veterans joined him. Most of the women stopped their loud talking and lowered their heads in shame. I suppose I lowered my head as well because I noticed a legless man sitting on a dirty square of cardboard trying to light the butt of a cigarette he'd plucked out of the gutter by magnifying the milky rays of sunlight through a piece of shattered lens from a pair of glasses.

"Mama Pan-Pan strode over to the veterans, called them *kusojiji*, old farts, and told them, 'You are the army that lost the war. These women are the army that will win the peace.' She added *Kuso shite shinezo*, that she hoped they would die shitting, and pulled me past the veterans and the hostesses and into the club.

"The first floor was reserved for American privates, new recruits, all the teenagers General MacArthur had selected for the Army of Occupation instead of old battle-scarred veterans who might seek revenge. With the young GIs were Japanese farm girls who'd either come on their own to escape starvation in the country or, more often, been sold to Mama Pan-Pan by their families.

"On a low stage, lighted from underneath, a Japanese woman in red-white-and-blue shorts and sailor top, red-sequined tap shoes on her feet, danced the Charleston to the music of a Japanese combo wearing red-striped vests and straw boaters. Mama Pan-Pan told me to stop gaping and jerked me to a door guarded by an MP. The military policeman stepped aside and let us into a private stairway. Mama Pan-Pan hurried me up metal stairs that clattered loudly beneath her wooden *geta*.

"On the next floor were the street prostitutes, still young but never pretty. The lower-grade NCOs could go up to the second floor. The higher-grade noncoms went to the third floor, to be greeted by the pretty street prostitutes and prostitutes who used to work in houses before the war. The fourth floor was reserved for junior-grade officers. The young and pretty prostitutes, former hostesses at bombed-out clubs and bars, and make-believe geishas were allowed on this floor.

"The fifth floor was for field-grade officers only, major and above. Real geishas worked there. All the women wore nylons. The entire floor smelled of Chanel No. 5. There were no bad perms. Women pulled gold Revlon compacts and Max Factor Cherries in the Snow lipstick out of small beaded bags stuffed with gaudy military payment certificates and packs of Lucky Strike cigarettes. The band on this floor wore tuxedos. A tall man with silver hair and stars on his shoulders glided around the dance floor with a Japanese woman in an evening gown the color of milky jade, her bare back covered by yards of silken hair held back at one ear with a gardenia.

"A gardenia? To walk out of a world where legless men lighted their cigarettes with pieces of glass into one where a woman's hair was held back by a gardenia was to glimpse life after death.

"Mama Pan-Pan took me to a private room and arranged me like a doll in a glass case, fluffing out the hem of my kimono, tightening my obi, pinching my cheeks, smoothing my hair. She told me I'd be back pawing through trash behind the Nomura Hotel if I dared to move before she returned. If the officer she was bringing did not want to take out an 'only' contract on me for his exclusive use, she could do nothing with me. She didn't want me around drawing attention to the underage girls she had who could pass for older than they were.

"I stood motionless in that room in Rocker Four long enough for the three-hour incense stick smoldering in the corner to burn down to a pile of ash before Mama Pan-Pan held the door open and stepped aside so that an officer wearing a blue Air Force uniform could enter. In spite of all I had seen and lived through, I could not raise my eyes, and my gaze remained fixed on his black shoes, which shone as if they had been lacquered. The shoes circled me like a pair of panthers. My skin prickled as they slunk behind me. Mama Pan-Pan raised the back of my kimono to show my legs.

"'She's older than eleven.'

"'Okay, maybe twelve.'

"'Maybe thirteen.'

"'Thirteen? Nebber hoppen! Twelve! Cherry girl! She cherry girl from country! All general want this cherry girl. They gonna be mad Mama Pan-Pan give you. I give General Harry.'

"'Anderson? Anderson likes them young?'

"'He pay *takusan* for cherry girl like this one. Like doll. You don't want, I go get General—'

"'No. Wait. Okay. Bring her to me at the Dai-Ichi. Just don't let anyone see you. How much for the whole night?'

"'No night. You take Only Contract. One week. Two hundred dollar.'

"'Two hundred dollars! Are you insane? I could buy every girl at the International Palace for a month for that. I'm not taking any Only Contract.'

"'Yeah, sure. Okay. You go International Palace. Stand in line. Everyone see. You be number thirty that day. Cherry girl you be number one of whole life. Only one first time. You got money. What about nice Ford convertible you bring from States? Inside you hide enough lighter flints to pay for car.'

"'Who told you about that?'

"'Who tell Mama Pan-Pan? Who *not* tell Mama Pan-Pan? Everyone have lighter. No one have flint.' Mama dragged me toward the door. 'Okay, I take cherry girl General Harry—'

"In three quick strides, the sleek black shoes overtook her. 'Screw you, Mama Pan-Pan. Here.'

"'No screw me. Screw cherry girl.'

"The bills, the Military Payment Certificates, pink, turquoise, violet, beautiful play money with the faces of Greek gods and goddesses, passed from the officer to Mama Pan-Pan. *Screw cherry girl.* I'd once seen a girl, younger than me, still wearing the white middy blouse and navy-blue skirt of her school uniform, squashed against the stone blocks of a wall near the moat around the Imperial Palace by the khaki-clad body of an American soldier as he pumped against her. When he let her down, a trickle of blood ran along the inside of her leg to blossom crimson at the top of her white anklet.

"After the officer left, Mama took me to the Dai-Ichi Hotel, told me a room number, and pushed me up the stairs. The officer opened the door and took a girl he thought was twelve into his room, into his bed. What had to happen happened. I was glad I was not really twelve, and I was glad the officer did not have a penis like a beer bottle. I was like a kitten to the officer, a doll, a playmate. I walked on his spine. I rubbed almond oil into his fingertips and learned to use the Gillette razor to shave his beard. We played badminton with cotton balls on the big western bed. I squealed when he brought me presents from the PX: Baby Ruth candy bars. Tootsie Rolls. Tinkerbell bubble bath. Superman comic books. We shared the same secret: I wanted to be a child as much as he wanted me to be one.

"At the end of a week at the Dai-Ichi, the officer was in love with me. It didn't matter that I wasn't twelve. Because of the years of living on grass and roots, I had only the beginning traces of the things that made him hate and fear his wife back in the States: breasts, hips, hair between my legs. I didn't even bleed yet like a woman.

"When Mama Pan-Pan came and demanded another two hundred dollars, the officer told her to fuck herself. Mama cut her price to one hundred. The officer told her she wasn't getting another dime out of him. She said she would go to SCAP. He told her to be his guest. He was very sure that General MacArthur, the Supreme Commander of the Allied Powers, would be very interested to know that she was pimping children to American officers.

"After that, he moved me to a room on the seventh floor in the Hotel New York across the Sumida River, where lots of other 'onlies' stayed, though the officer forbid me to talk to them. He put a lock on the door, something that was very rare in Japan at that time, and each morning locked me in.

"A month before Christmas, the base emptied out part of a

hangar and filled it with toys for the children of the Occupation officers. The officer brought me a Betsy Wetsy doll with a hole between her legs so she wet her tiny square of diaper when I gave her a bottle. With Betsy Wetsy, I didn't even mind anymore when the officer screwed me. If that was what women had to do to have babies, it seemed a small price to pay. In short, I was happy. I had nearly starved to death in a cave. After that, the room seemed a paradise. It was warm, the officer brought food. I came to love the officer. It seems a strange thing to say now; it didn't then. He gave me my life back. Yes, I loved him.

"It was the officer himself, though, who destroyed his own secret desire. The rewards the officer brought me for being a child—hamburgers, T-bone steaks, orange juice, doughnuts, milk—were what ended my girlhood. Over the next months, I grew like a bamboo shoot. My breasts became sore, then swelled. Hair sprouted. I bound my chest and used the officer's Gillette Blue Blade razor to shave the hair. The one thing I couldn't disguise, however, was the smell. No matter how many Tinkerbell bubble baths I took, the smell would always return. I started to notice how thin the children begging in the street below my window were. I remembered how the cold wind cut at me.

"I tried to talk to the officer like a baby in a high, sweet voice, but my words came out desperate, pleading. I tried to giggle, and tears flooded my eyes. I tried to run gaily after the shuttlecock but tripped on my long limbs. Nothing I did fooled the officer. After he found the dark rose of my bleeding on the futon, I was not surprised when, one morning, without a word, he left but did not lock the door behind himself.

"For a week, I stayed in the room eating the last of the Hi-Ho crackers and smoked oysters. When the owner of the hotel came to tell me I had to leave, he didn't recognize me. He asked what had happened to the other one, the young girl. I said I didn't know. I packed every scrap that was left in the room, even scavenging through the trash to salvage the officer's used razor blades. I tied them all in two *furoshikis*. I strapped Betsy Wetsy on my back, *ombu*-style, like a real baby. I knew I could make more from selling old razor blades than I could from selling my body.

"Outside, I found that my lungs had grown weak from months of breathing heated air and the icy wind sliced into them. I walked to the Shinjuku Station, where the largest black market, Hikari Wa Shinjuku Yori, The Light Shines Forth from Shinjuku, was set up near the main entrance of the subway station. Thousands of homeless sold pots, pans, kettles, plates, cooking oil, tea, *geta*, bayonets, uniforms with brown bloodstains, bullets, grenades.

"Fortunately, I knew enough to first find a representative of the Kanto Ozu gang that ran the market just as, in centuries past, they had run the festival vending stalls at temples and shrines. The underling I saw took me to meet the boss of all *Ozu-gumi*, Kinosuke Ozu himself. Ozu had a face as small and leathery as a shrunken head. Luckily, Kinosuke Ozu was *tekiya*, he lived by a strict code of chivalry like the samurai. In honor of my father's sacrifice on Okinawa, he did not make me pay the usual tribute fee.

"Ozu gave me a wooden pallet that I placed next to a man who was selling boxes of American Beauty spaghetti and ornamental combs that he claimed had belonged to Chiang Kai-shek's concubine. On my pallet I placed all the *presentos* the officer had given me except for Betsy Wetsy. Men fought to purchase the Gillette Blue Blade razor blades the officer had thrown away, and by the end of the day I had made enough to purchase five boxes of shoelaces from a crate containing hundreds, all stamped 'Supreme Commander of Allied Powers. For Use By US Military Only. All Other Use Forbidden By Law.' I bought them. I would have bought anything. In those days, it didn't matter what you put out to sell. Since the Japanese people had nothing, they would buy anything.

"That night, as I slept in the subway, a soldier tried to steal my shoelaces. I screamed, but no one helped me. Luckily, I had been eating hamburgers for the past months and the soldier had been scrounging in garbage dumps. After I drove the soldier away, I had to pay a boy to guard my shoelaces while I ran outside to throw up. I thought it was the strain of yelling in public that had upset my stomach, but it wasn't.

"Over the next seven months of snow, wind, rain, and sun my face became almost as leathery as Kinosuke Ozu's. It was July and sweat was streaming down my cheeks when I accepted that the officer's child was growing within me. Most Japanese women who found themselves pregnant with a *gaijin* baby made a quick visit to the abortion clinic. Or, if they didn't have two thousand yen, they killed themselves. I thought they were stupid. Though I knew keeping the baby meant I would be cast out forever by decent Japanese, I didn't care.

"The birth was not easy. There was bleeding, scarring. This would be my only child. Though the midwives insulted me and my baby by taking their surgical masks off when they came to my bed and talking loudly in the hall about *omajiri*, comparing my baby girl to a thin gruel no one likes and joking about who would do Nihon a favor and throw the *omajiri* baby out with the trash, my own eyes told me how stupid they were. My baby was more beautiful than any child I had ever seen. The gold of my skin had combined with the pink of the officer's and my child looked like a rose in candlelight. For this, I named her Hana Rose. She had even been marked with the most beautiful of treasures, the Mount Fuji hairline. The more I was scorned, the happier it made me. I had a treasure no one wanted to steal.

"I walked out of the hospital that night and, for the first time since the war, found Tokyo bright with light. So much had been rebuilt. I stopped to notice the new city that was being born from the rubble. Lanterns and small fires blazed at every house, every shack, every lean-to we passed. It was the final night of O-bon. In front of the few surviving old houses, in front of the astonishing number of new houses built from concrete blocks to look like concrete blocks, families feasted before the house altar. I smelled pickled plum, cherry blossom tea, garlic and leek dumplings, tofu with five sauces, all the favorite foods of the families' dead ancestors being honored. Mixed in with the food smells were the fragrance of incense and the alcohol-and-ash smell of play money that had been sprinkled with sake and then burnt.

"I sat in a pocket of darkness and nursed Hana Rose, whispering to her that all the festivities were to welcome her, to welcome all the new life being born in Japan. I leaned in so close that my nose was in her mouth and I inhaled her breath. It smelled like caramel. Joy surged through me at that scent and the city tilted and fell away, leaving me and Hana Rose alone in our own perfect corner.

"At length, I began to walk again. It was late. The people had gone to sleep, many leaving their offerings on the altars outside. I went from altar to altar and ate all the foods I had eaten as a girl: *udon, edamame, umemaki, aburaage, bukatakimi, anago tempura, onigiri, nasudengaku.* I ate and ate, filling the long years of hunger past and stockpiling for the future, Hana Rose's future. I swore she would never pull electricity from empty breasts the way my little brother had. Hana Rose would always have the milk that made her breath smell like caramel. When I was thirsty, I drank tea from pots hundreds of years old that had been buried in the family's backyard to save them from bombardment and theft, pots that the dead who were being honored had drunk out of. I drank, and the ancestors' thirst was slaked. Only the dead and I understood that it was right for the living to eat and drink so that the newborn might be nourished.

"We walked all that night. Without planning, we ended up in Awashi, the neighborhood where I'd grown up. The streets had been cleared and rebuilt. I found our old house. Two American military guards slept beside the gate outside the grounds. A station wagon was parked in front of the house. It had an eagle painted on the side clutching arrows in its claws. A basketball hoop had been bolted to the flagstaff where my father once put up a blue carp for me on March third, Girls' Day, because I cried to have a flag like boys flew on their day. I wanted Hana Rose to see her grandparents' house before I took her to the shack I lived in near the station. I promised her that we would soon have an *apaato*. I had almost saved enough.

"When I returned to The Light Shines Forth from Shinjuku market with Hana Rose tied to my back, all the other vendors shunned me because my baby had the despised pink skin of the conqueror. Hana Rose and I laughed about that. When they dragged their pallets away from mine, all it did was leave more room for customers to cluster around, since, whatever my competitors sold, I sold for a few yen less.

"I was always the first one at the station before dawn and the last one to leave at night. Then, with Hana Rose sleeping on my back, I would take my three-wheeled cart to visit my sources with PX contacts and see what they had to sell that night. Once it was four hundred pounds of pinto beans. Another time it was ten crates of Big Chief tablets. I sold three hundred rolls of Tums pill by pill by telling customers that they cut hunger pains. And they did. Whatever it was, I bought.

"At night, Hana Rose and I snuggled together in the little shack made from a wooden crate that engine parts had been shipped in. I sang to my daughter and traced the outline of Mount Fuji on her forehead, telling her of all the beauty the world held.

"Then, on September nineteenth, Hana Rose and I woke up to feel the chill of a wind blowing down from Siberia. That day, for the first time, I wrote to the officer. I put his name and rank on the letter and gave it to a sergeant I bought four boxes of Listerine mouthwash from. In my letter, I told the officer to write me in care of the Shinjuku stationmaster and send money for his daughter. I sold Listerine by the sake cupful for twenty times what I had paid to men desperate to drink anything with alcohol in it.

"Each day, I asked the stationmaster if a letter had come for me. Each day there was nothing and the winds grew chillier. I worked harder. I had to make enough to rent an *apaato* so Hana Rose and I would be inside when winter came. And we would have been, too, if General MacArthur hadn't declared war on the Underground Government. When the Americans finally figured out what all Japanese already knew, that the real rulers of our country were men like Ozu—gangsters, racketeers, *yakuza* all in league with the police and the politicians—they cracked down on the black markets. Vendors with a box of Hershey bars were arrested and sentenced. A U.S. Army colonel was court-martialed for selling nine dollars' worth of cigarettes. Meanwhile the leather-faced Ozu walked out of jail a free man when the public prosecutor testified that he was too sick to serve his prison sentence.

"While the raids continued, we vendors hid. For weeks, I had no money coming in and had to use my *apaato* savings. Hana Rose and I were not the only ones who suffered. It was impossible to survive without the black market. One man tried, Yoshi-tada Yamaguchi. He tried to feed his family on a salary of three thousand yen, seven dollars a month. 'How can we break the law, even if it is a bad law?' Mr. Yamaguchi asked his wife. He grew weak from hunger but insisted that his family live on government allocations. His wife begged him to let her sell her wedding kimono, the family altar. He refused. It was the talk of Tokyo when Mr. Yamaguchi starved to death. Maybe that is why the police raids stopped.

"Hana Rose and I went back. But it was too late. I could never save enough before winter came. By the end of October, the Siberian winds had blown into Hana Rose's ear and she cried all day and all night with the pain. The market was in full operation again, but she was too sick to take outside. When green fluid oozed from her ear, I began to search for a nursery where I could keep my baby out of the cold until she was well. There were thousands of women in the same situation and all the nurseries within walking distance of the station were full. The ones that didn't immediately slam the door in my face, did so after they saw Hana Rose's skin. The only nursery that would accept her was the Jusan-in halfway to Yokohama in Yanagi-cho.

"I had to change trains three times. The long journey was very tiring for Hana Rose, and the cigarette smoke that filled the trains made her cough continuously.

"Jusan-in was run by Mrs. Miyuki Ishikawa and her husband in their home. This I will never forget: Mrs. Ishikawa came to the door, wiping grease from her chin. The house was warm and smelled of frying pork. Food and heat, that was the most we could dream of in those days. There were children everywhere. Like all Japanese children then, they looked thin and hungry. But Mrs. Ishikawa was a grandmotherly woman in an apron that tied behind her neck. I looked for kindness in her face and believed I found it. She took Hana Rose, held her, and told me how beautiful she was. I did not realize how hungry I was to hear a country-woman tell me what I knew until she spoke those words. Then she told me it would cost two thousand yen a month to keep my child there. I protested that that was almost enough to rent an *apaato*. Mrs. Ishikawa answered that if I had an *apaato*, I should take my child and go. If not, she would have to have a month's payment in advance, and maybe she shouldn't take Hana Rose after all. She was sick. She would make the other children sick.

"I said that many of the children already looked sick, and she asked me what I expected. She took the children that no one in Japan wanted. She started to hand Hana Rose to me.

"The thought of taking my baby on the long train ride back to my unheated shack frightened me. I vowed I would work night and day for the next month, find something, anything, then return to claim my daughter. One month, I told her, one month. And I would come as often as I could to check on my daughter. Every night if that was possible. I took the money out of my obi and paid her. Hana Rose cried when I left, but Mrs. Ishikawa told me to pay no attention. All the children cried, but as soon as the mothers were gone, they stopped crying. I knew this was not true because so many of the children were crying.

"Hana Rose's thin, thready sobs followed me out of the house. I put them out of my mind and worked as I never had before. I bought forty boxes of Ray-O-Vac lantern batteries, twenty to a box, from the back of an Army truck on the condition that the sergeant would deliver them to my stall since they were far too heavy to carry on my three-wheeled cart.

"For two and a half weeks, I could not leave my purchase. I had to sleep beside the boxes of batteries until they were all sold. I couldn't leave them for a second or they would have all been stolen. There was no chance that I could visit Hana Rose. I comforted myself with visions of her in the warm house, surrounded by other babies, being cared for by Mrs. Ishikawa, who thought she was beautiful. Each day, I sent someone to the stationmaster to ask if a letter had arrived from the officer. Long after I had given up hope, I kept on checking.

"At last, all the batteries were sold. By that time, I was very sick. My breath rattled in my chest worse than an old tin teapot rattled its top as it boiled. When I walked, the ground seesawed beneath my feet. It didn't matter. I had enough money. I rented an *apaato*, one room in a new ferro-concrete building filled like a beehive with hundreds of similar cells. But it was warm, sheltered from the Siberian wind, and I could bring Hana Rose home.

"On the train, I put all my strength into my right hand clinging to the strap while the rest of my body hung from it heavy as a sack of rice. By the time I reached Yanagi-cho, I had to tilt my head at odd angles to see around the tunnels of black that had opened up in my vision. With all that, I was giddy with happiness. I hid my smile in the folds of the new quilt—all silk, maroon and gray—I had bought to bring Hana Rose home in.

"At the door of Jusan-in, I called out a greeting and waited. No one answered. No one slid the door back. I called out more loudly. Neighbors on the alley began to poke their heads out and mutter under their breath to each other. I called out one more time. When no one answered, when none of the neighbors spoke to me, I slid the door open. The warm house was cold and empty. All the children were gone. I became a madwoman. I turned on the neighbors, screaming, pleading, demanding to know where my child was. They all knew, yet none of them would tell me. They turned their backs and went into their houses. I grabbed one old woman before she disappeared and she told me to ask the police and that, in her opinion, we *gaisen* had brought this on ourselves.

"There was a neighborhood station around the corner. A tall, skinny policeman in a baggy uniform with a streak of egg yolk on the front would not look in my face as he informed me in a scolding monotone that Mr. and Mrs. Ishikawa were awaiting sentencing for the murder of eighty-five babies, all dead of starvation and buried at isolated spots around the city. They might never have been found out if a servant pushing a cart hadn't slipped on an ice patch and spilled the corpses of four infants. Skeletons, really, he said. Little mummies, they were so emaciated.

"Fearing that I would do something that might embarrass the station, the policeman walked me to the train station and stood with me until I was pushed on the train. On the train, there was no question of falling to the floor. The crowd, though it squeezed the breath out of me, forced me to remain upright though my legs had stopped working.

"Back in my concrete room, I knelt on the floor cradling the new quilt as if Hana Rose were tucked within its folds. I prayed to my mother to be merciful and care for her granddaughter. I begged her forgiveness that I would not be alive to honor her on O-bon. To read her name from the Book of the Dead. I wished that I were not sick so that I might suffer exactly as Hana Rose had as she was starving to death, but I was already escaping from consciousness.

"When I awoke, the American officer was there, making tea on a hot plate in the corner. The stationmaster's assistant had told him where I was. He asked why I had left the Hotel New York. He'd given the owner enough to pay my rent through the winter. He asked why I hadn't told him before he left that I was pregnant. He asked where his child was, if it was a boy. He'd come as soon as he could get TDY. He'd written. Did I get the money he'd sent? One hundred dollars.

"*One hundred dollars.*

"I knew then that I had died after all, just as my mother had died in the cave, just as all of Japan had died on the day the Emperor surrendered. I turned my face to the wall. The officer understood and accepted that I was his fate and he was mine. This made us closer than he and his wife ever would be.

"Once he realized that we were bound together, though neither one of us would have chosen the other, he confessed his greatest secret to me who knew his greatest sin: He was scared. The great air hero was scared of flying. The cockpit of his airplane had become a coffin. He saw the end of each flight in every beginning. The tilting plummet through the sky, the feigned bravado, the ejector seat that jams, the parachute lines that foul. The endless nightmare moment before his soft bag of flesh hit the rock of earth. More than death, however, the officer feared his crew discovering his fear. For an aviator, this fear was more shameful than his desire for the body of a child.

"He paid the rent on my room, then left to meet his squadron in Misawa and return to his wife and child in the States. But he would be back. War with Korea was inevitable. TDYs would be easy and lengthy.

"Then began a time when I walked in two worlds. I was careful to keep my body alive so that I could fulfill my obligations to the dead. The first thing I did with the money the officer gave me was to buy a beautiful altar made of luminous paulownia wood with five steps and many drawers. The first item I placed in the highest drawer was Hana Rose's umbilical cord nestled in a box of fragrant cedar. In the other drawers I placed all the items I remembered being in my family's altar: prayer books, packets of incense, strings of beads, feather dusters, ornate china, bells made of pure brass. Then I set about reconstructing the thirty-one pages of our Book of the Dead. The first name I entered was Hana Rose. Even as I wrote it, the air filled with the smell of camphor from my mother's kimonos as she protested the entry of my daughter's name into her family's book. I advised my mother to heed the Emperor's advice and endure the unendurable, then calmly continued wiping my brush over the ink stone and entering my daughter's name and birth date in the beautiful hand my mother herself had taught me in the house with the blue tile roof.

"When I wrote in the date of my mother's birth and death next, a crow landed on the sill of the window and pecked out my mother's continuing protest at occupying the same book as my bastard daughter. But the pecking stopped the instant I struggled to recall the date my little brother died. At the exact moment the correct day came into my mind, the room flooded with a smell of caramel like Hana Rose's breath when her stomach was filled with the milk my little brother had starved for. I knew by these signs that, at last, my mother was happy, and I rushed to enter all the dates and names that I could remember: my father, my grandparents, aunts, uncles, cousins. With each entry, that ancestor appeared to thank me. Many made their appearance in the form of insects: beetles, grasshoppers, butterflies, moths, cicadas, cockroaches. Some came as the smell of burnt rice, of old chrysanthemums. I meditated for days, trying to remember the names of distant ancestors and the dates upon which they had died. As I struggled to recall when my father's great-uncle, a successful kimono merchant, had died from eating bad oysters, the blades of the fan began to sob mournfully, stopping only when I wrote the proper date of the merchant's death on a practice sheet and meticulously copied it into our family's book. In this way, I became a bureaucrat listening endlessly to the petitions of those demanding favors.

"Each morning, I fetched fresh water for the flowers or bought new ones, a chore that involved riding the train to the countryside, where I also purchased soft candles made of beeswax. Back at my room, I would clean away the old flowers, arrange new ones, set out fresh candles and incense. When all was ready, I would ring the bells, recite the names of all the ancestors who had died that day, then turn the page in the Book of the Dead.

"While I struggled to remember, all of Japan sought only to forget. As the weathered veterans in their grimy caps—feet missing, legs missing, arms missing; hopping about like crows on crutches—disappeared, it became easier and easier to pretend that they had never lived. That Japan had still never been invaded. That nuclear bombs had not been dropped on our country and no one had ever apologized. The only past anyone wanted to remember was long ago, the era of the Emperor Meiji, who had taught his subjects to 'let all Japanese hearts beat as one.' An era when neighbor trusted neighbor and the stifling, comforting bonds of *giri* ruled all relations.

"MacArthur told the world that Japan would be the Switzerland of the Pacific and then established a thousand bases from Kyushu to Misawa. More than 245,000 acres of military installations, more than even Hirohito himself had dreamed of. When the sky filled again with B-29s, people kept their eyes on the ground in front of them and said nothing, the drone of the engines drowned out by the incessant beat of the jackhammers battering away what was left of vanished Japan and replacing it with a new Japan built of concrete. F-80s, F-82s, F-94s roared overhead, training, we were told, to defend Japan from China, from Russia, from Korea. And then, on June twenty-fifth, 1950, the North Koreans crossed the Thirty-eighth Parallel.

"The officer returned. He was stationed in Korea but came to the room every few weeks, still wearing his nylon flight suit, sticky with sweat and terror. He told me about shooting down MiGs over the Yalu River. He was an ace. They might name a theater after him like Richard Bong. As he spoke, I searched his face for some sign of Hana Rose and found none. Even when our ghost bodies were together, the officer was less real than my cantankerous great-grandfather who had died in a typhoon and appeared in the form of a squirrel that bit my finger in Ueno Park when I fed him a rice cracker. I believe the officer came to need that about me: that I was not of this world.

"With each mission, the fear grew. The officer told me everything. He had to speak. He was a man with too many secrets. His job had become finding secrets and keeping secrets. He flew where American pilots were forbidden to fly. Forbidden by their own government, their own president. He could tell no one. Once the mission was over, he could not speak of it even with his own crew. But the officer was a man whose fear forced him to speak, so, in just the way a boy will tell his dog everything, the officer talked to me.

"There was money in the secrets he told me. Many of the women sent to the clubs and bars and brothels to win the peace for Japan made fortunes selling the secrets they learned while giggling behind fans. Though I could have sold the officer's secrets for more money than he would make in a year, I never considered it. He was Hana Rose's father.

"Each year as his secrets grew more dangerous, his need to confess, which had become the root of his need for me, grew more desperate. The officer could no more hold his tongue than a riverbed can stop water from flowing. He could hide the fear from his crew for only so long before he had to come to me to lie shaking and crying in my arms. He asked me to write his name and the day he was born in my book. Then he asked me to enter the names of his mother and father. Of an older sister who had died of scarlet fever. Of his grandparents. Of a favorite uncle who had taught him to shoot a gun. In this way, he tried to make friends with death.

"He made me tell him of the ways that our daughter appeared to me: as a tiny cyclone of dried azalea petals that followed my ankles. Fog on a warm mirror. A dandelion whose white fuzz would not be blown away. Soon the officer too could see Hana Rose's presence in a wind sock on the Flight Line that inexplicably reversed direction, heat shimmers from a jet engine that swirled into whimsical shapes, the sparrow that came to him and no one else. It calmed him to kneel beside me at the altar as I turned the pages, rang the bells, lit incense. Only then would he be able to put on the flight suit I had washed and return to his crew, to the sky where MiGs waited to kill him.

"Money from the war poured into Japan as our factories again made guns and ammunition, steel and plywood. The Allied Army of the Occupation loosened its grip. We no longer had to have our hair sprayed with DDT every week. Schoolchildren no longer had to drink the sludgy green *makuri* made from boiling seaweed twice a month to kill parasites. The black markets all but disappeared. The Korean War ended, but factories remained as busy as ever. Then one day—perhaps it was on the day the newspapers pronounced us to be in the midst of an economic boom and called it *jimmu bumu* after the first emperor—Japan was reborn. The front pages filled with numbers: production of steel, value of exports, employment rates, productivity rates, and the most treasured number of all: Japan now had the eighth largest economy in the world.

"The war was never mentioned. A whole generation sprang up that did not know and could not believe that Japan had ever tried to conquer the world by force and been defeated. They believed that Japan was a small island nation whose only weapon was hard work. That is how it was during the *jimmu bumu* as this new Japan scraped its way from eighth to seventh and then to the sixth largest economy in the world. And that, we told ourselves, was how it had always been.

"On the day Hana Rose would have been five, the officer came with flowers, candles, incense, and both rice-flour cookies stamped in pink with a cherry blossom design and Baby Ruth candy bars for the altar. As we prayed, the room filled with the scent of roses and the flames of the candles danced in a room where the air did not move.

"All the secrets the officer had to dam up spilled out in the small room. He told me about the general who ruled his life. This general believed that a war with Russia, still weak from the war they had fought as allies, but now an enemy, would be like a vaccine, where a small dose of a disease is given to prevent a fatal occurrence. But the general needed evidence to wage this preventive war. For this, they sent planes high over Russia to take photos of missile factories and bases, to decode radar signals. But mostly he sent planes to call forth other planes, so that the general could learn how long and how sharp the Russian bear's claws were.

"All the men on these missions went knowing that their

deaths would be the best proof the general could offer that the bear's claws were so long and so sharp that all of America was in mortal danger. That more bombers had to be built. That a halo of radar stations had to encircle the top of the earth like a crown. Proof had to be gathered. So many men died gathering this proof that the bear was coiled and waiting to spring. Each time a plane was shot down, the officer would tell the wife and children that her husband, their father, had died gathering weather information. Had gone astray on a routine training flight. Then the officer would come to me and lie in my arms and shiver as the truth spilled forth.

"He told of the eighteen-hour flights when his men had to suck hard candy because all the water on the plane had frozen in the bitter cold, and even then his flight suit would be slick with bitter sweat from fear. He told of vibration, so constant, so loud, his bones hummed in time with it. The smells, he didn't have to tell me of the smells, he was saturated in them: diesel fuel, the navigator's grease pencils, the radar men's cigars, the crew chief's Lucky Strikes, the milk souring in the white-boxed lunches, Vitalis, Aqua-Velva, Right Guard—all eventually curdling into the smell of too many men in too small a space. And through it all, the officer had to pretend to be eager for the next mission, for the next chance to strap himself inside ten tons of metal that he knew would become his coffin.

"And then his wife and children arrived. His wife now controlled the family's money, and soon he could no longer pay even for my small room. The officer told me he had found a job for me that would bring me much closer to him at Yokota. I was going to be a maid with the family of one of his men.

"I cared as little about where I lived as I cared if I lived. I was like my mother, waiting only for the proper time to force my body to join my spirit in death. I moved into the empty house and set up the altar in a room that faced Fuji-san. I knew I had found the proper spot to die and went to the pharmacy around the corner to purchase the correct pills.

"I covered the concrete floor of the room with a thick layer of straw, dressed in the crane-and-willow kimono the officer had given me, and knelt before the altar. I opened the Book of the Dead and entered the date of my death. As the sun set, I emptied the bottle of pills onto the altar. With each pill I swallowed, I read the names on one page. The great-aunt who died in child-birth. The nephew stricken by scarlet fever. The cousin who drowned when the battleship *Yamato* sank. There were eighteen names listed for August 9, 1945. My mother's family had lived in Nagasaki. As I swallowed a pill with each name I read, a glow lightened the room. Outside, the setting sun turned Fuji-san the golden pink of a rose in candlelight. Exactly the color of Hana Rose's skin. Exactly. In that moment, I knew Fuji-san was going to answer my prayers to allow me to join my child. I dropped to the straw and slept.

"I dreamed that Hana Rose was cold. That my mother was carrying her. That they were locked outside and only I could let them enter. Hana Rose was crying from the cold. They called my name and I fought to answer. Struggling to pull myself off the straw, I opened the door, and there you were, my Hana Rose."

Marshmallow Creme

"Me?"

I stare at Fumiko, not understanding. Not the words, not the meaning, nothing. The late-afternoon light slants in through the courtyard, illuminating a golden haze of dust motes and pollen above the stone lantern and turning the lacy leaves of a small willow tree into a chartreuse cloud.

"Me?"

"Yes. I saw it as soon as I opened the door. Your father was holding you so that I looked directly into your face. Hana Rose stared out at me through your eyes. I was not surprised when I learned that you had been born several years later but on the exact same day Hana Rose died. And, of course, the Fuji hairline, what you call a widow's peak. How many American children have that? I was so pleased that Hana Rose had chosen her father's people. That she had had bottles and bottles of milk to drink, as if it were water. That she could run without shoes on fields of soft green grass. That she had never had her neck dusted with DDT powder. That she could sleep with her legs untied and sit and eat at the same time, at the same table, as her father and her brothers. Later, what I was most pleased about was that she had chosen Moe as her mother."

"She? You mean me?"

"Yes, of course, you. You were Hana Rose to me only long enough for Hana Rose to let me know that my sorrow was of no use to her."

I see again that first moment when Fumiko slid back the door of the house in Fussa. I recall her touching my despised vampire hairline. I recall who brought us to the little house.

"The officer was Major Wingo."

Fumiko nods. She stands, then helps me to my feet. I am stiff and one leg is numb. I find a bathroom and Fumiko runs to the kitchen. She returns to the private room with a tray holding a teapot, cups, and a dish of tabby-cat-orange rice crackers striped with black seaweed. We drink tea and eat the crackers. The band of sunshine on the wall narrows, then almost disappears before I ask again about the long silence between my parents.

"Do you remember the last mission?" Fumiko asks.

Our father's last mission at Yokota. We had been living in Japan for almost four years. The last mission started for me on a hot day in the summer that I was ten. The day Moe lost her fight to stay in our paper house on the alley in Fussa.

"Mace, I am not plopping myself and my family right in the middle of Queen Bee's hive."

"For Christ's sake. Ignore the woman."

"Ignore LaRue? There's no ignoring LaRue. You either kiss her ass or stay the hell out of her way. She's already got it in for me."

"Attention, Mohoric. LaRue Wingo is a wife. You are a wife. You are auxiliary units. Her function is to support the mission. Your function is to support the mission."

"Mace, don't make me paint you a picture. Not in front of . . ." I felt my father's attention settle on me.

"The Root family is transferring quarters to Yokota Air Base. End of discussion."

"She'll crucify us, Mace, and you know why."

The air, hot and muggy, turned weightless and crackled with a dizzying menace. When my father spoke again, his voice had the low, unanswerable gravity of a doctor giving very bad news. "I want my family on-base in case anything happens."

"What, Mace? What is going to happen?"

"What is going to happen, Mohoric, is that the Root residence is moving to Yokota Air Base."

And it did. After four years of living in a house with paper walls where a whisper in the kitchen could be heard in the back bedroom, we moved into a house with cinder-block walls that stopped light and sound so thoroughly I missed my family when they were one room away.

The day after Kit got the stitches taken out of her lip where the monkey had bitten her, our father announced that he was going TDY. It didn't even occur to us to ask where or for how long he was going to be gone.

The last mission started the way they all did, with Moe pulling the battered B-4 bag down from the top shelf of the closet and throwing it onto the white chenille bedspread. She made a puffy comforter of folded undershirts and shorts on the bottom layer. Next was an extra flight suit, then a khaki uniform starched until the pants could be held straight and made to wobble like the blade of a saw. On the very top, Moe placed a Dopp kit with its travel-size bottle of amber Listerine, the Gillette Blue Blade, the rust-stained stalactite tip of a styptic stick.

At the Flight Line, our father promised me he would throw a bucket on a rope out the window when they flew through the right kind of clouds and bring me home more marshmallow creme than I could ever eat.

"Hey, you jabonies!" Major Wingo, already heading into the deep shadow of a hangar, called out. "Any of you plan on flying a bird today? Well, let's go then. Let's bite 'em in the ass!"

All the fathers left the individual clots of their families then and hustled across the runway, a gray quilt pieced together from giant squares of concrete. The instant the men came together, they ceased to be fathers, husbands. They melded into a crew, taunting each other, boyish and high-spirited. We watched them disappear into the hangar. For a second, the abandoned families were quiet, uncertain, like hangers-on outside the gates of a party we hadn't been invited to.

LaRue Wingo's heavy gold bracelets clanked together in the silence as she brought her cigarette to her lips. LaRue's hair was wrapped in a tiger-print chiffon scarf that bubbled around her head and tied at the neck. Smoke coming out of her nose like from a cartoon bull's nostrils, she announced, "I don't know about any of you shitbirds, but mama-san here's gonna get herself a big stiff one. And for once I mean a drink." Most of the wives perked up and crowded around LaRue, anxious for a party they *were* invited to.

"Moe, you coming?" LaRue yelled.

Moe held her hands out to us. "I've got the kids, LaRue."

"That's why God gave us maids."

"Yeah, well . . ."

"Doesn't your maid baby-sit, Moe? Maybe you should fire her."

It was interesting to me that, at that moment, my twin brothers were able to continue amusing themselves by pretending to wipe the contents of their noses on each other even though it was breathtakingly clear to both Kit and me that Mrs. Wingo had said something so terrible that it made all the other wives glance once at each other then stare at the runway. Something so terrible that welts appeared on Moe's face as if LaRue had lashed her. Kit and I watched Moe's lips twitch like she was going to say something; then, abruptly, she herded us away.

The car was as hot as a pizza oven on the drive home, and no one spoke.

None of us—not the wives, not the children—were allowed to voice our fears. We never mentioned the other crews, the ones who hadn't come home, wives and children gone overnight from our lives with no comment. The expression of even the slightest suspicion could bring a visit from OSI. The words "Soviet" and "atomic bomb," "spy" and "shoot down," were never breathed, never consciously thought by most families, and lacking words the dread found other ways to express itself.

Over the next two weeks, toddlers long out of diapers began wetting their pants. The doctors at the Base Dispensary saw an epidemic of children with stomachaches, headaches, and rashes they could find no cause for and sent mothers home embarrassed about wasting their time with such imaginary complaints.

At the Richard Bong Theater, the older, bolder children of the absent crews took to slouching in their seats instead of standing at attention when the National Anthem played. Teenage boys stole fire extinguishers and left behind smoking piles of foam. They refused to mow lawns, opened fire hydrants, and shoplifted Coleman pocketknives at the BX. The girls pocketed Max Factor lipsticks and wore them when they made out with GIs.

Nor were the wives immune. They bought ninety-six-piece sets of Noritake china and smoky topaz cocktail rings, geisha dolls in tall glass cases, and beaten brass coffee tables they didn't need and couldn't afford.

And they drank.

On a particularly long afternoon at the club, LaRue convinced the other wives that they needed to stage a gala complete with skits and talent acts to both welcome "the guys" home and celebrate the squadron's tenth anniversary. From that moment on, the wives spent most of their waking hours at the O Club, decorating, rehearsing, and drinking. Only Moe refused to follow the prevailing practice: leave her children with the maid, spend all day at the club, and return home very late, very drunk. Consequently, most of the motherless children gravitated to our house and for those weeks a tribe of kids swirled around and through our house. For the most part the interlopers were Kit's friends. Now that the stitches had been removed from the monkey bite and her upper lip was pink and plump, the gang of girls who trailed after Kit banging the screen door constantly and consuming vats of the red Kool-Aid and bologna sandwiches Moe and Fumiko made seemed to adore her even more than before.

It was on just such a day, the new house filled with Kit's herd of friends, that I decided to reopen the perfume factory. We'd left all the fragrances in our lives—honeysuckle, caramelized sugar, noodles, dried fish—behind in Fussa and I missed them. Even the smells of the honey bucket men had come to seem cozy, homey to me. After our first couple of years in Japan, I'd abandoned my work with honeysuckle and turned to the more reliable comfort of books. Moving to the new house on-base with its infestation of outsiders, however, combined with the general TDY jitteriness that twitched through the air like static electricity waiting to spark anyone it touched, had me searching through the bathroom cabinets for old nose-drop and St. Joseph's aspirin bottles.

Out in the yard beside the house, Moe and Fumiko, both in the faded dungarees and old, stained blouses they wore to do housework in, pried screens off windows. Fumiko pressed her thumb over the end of the hose and sprayed a jet of water on the screen that Moe held and scrubbed at with a brush. The smell of the dust rising off the old screens was the odor I would forever associate with that house.

Moe didn't ask what I was doing or order me to "Heave to, sailor, and give us a hand" as I set about collecting what few blossoms there were in the yard. When I mashed what I'd gathered, though, I discovered that the hydrangeas and bougainvillea that surrounded the house were as scentless as paper and I missed our old house even more. I was batting yellow jackets away from a clump of clover I wanted to experiment with when all three of us looked up at the sound of a powerful American car engine rumbling through the still, hot afternoon. We glanced at one another the instant we saw that it was the big Pontiac that LaRue Wingo had been driving ever since her husband had acquired "the 'Vette."

"Run for the backyard!" I yelled as they came to a stop in front of our house.

Moe gauged the distance from our exposed spot to the safety of the backyard. "Too late. They spotted us already."

LaRue was the first out of the car. She wore capri pants, a redstriped boat-neck top, black espadrilles that laced around the ankles, and a picture-frame hat. Two other wives emerged from the Pontiac: Madge Coulter, the navigator's wife, a broad-hipped bottle blonde with Mamie Eisenhower bangs who always had lipstick on her front teeth, and Denise Dugan, the radar observer's wife, who with her pop eyes and skinny frame seemed to have a thyroid problem. They both had on high heels and crisp shirt-waist dresses, the skirts belled out with petticoats. Obviously, they'd come straight from the O Club, where such dress was required.

As the three pristine women approached, their heels sinking into the grass, Moe glanced down at her blouse, wet and streaked with dust turned to mud, rolled her eyes at Fumiko, and pushed her hair out of her face with the back of her hand. Fumiko turned the hose off.

In a frosty tone, Mrs. Wingo announced, "I've come in my official capacity as squadron commander's wife."

Moe froze at the word "official" and the scrub brush dropped, unnoticed, from her hand. "Oh God, Mace . . ."

"No, it's not that," LaRue Wingo said, her voice softening a little, though not much. "The guys are coming home. Tomorrow. Zero six hundred hours. They came to the club to give us the news since that's where all the wives are—except you. You know, we're all down there getting things ready for the blowout home-coming for the guys." Mrs. Wingo laughed a fake laugh.

Moe smiled stiffly and waved at the children thundering around. "Well, the kids, you know . . ."

"That's what maids are for."

Moe opened her mouth to answer, stopped herself, and, her voice tight, said, "Thank you for coming by." Then she turned her back on the squadron commander's wife and walked away.

LaRue's mouth seamed into a tight line. She was clearly not accustomed to anyone, ever, turning their back on her. She left her honor guard and moved in so close to Moe that I could smell the sickly sweet carnation smell of her Bellodgia perfume, mixed with smoke and hair spray. Fumiko stared fixedly at the ground as LaRue harshly whispered, "Listen here, Mrs. Root, I have had to eat a lot of crap to get where I am and you are not going to make me swallow this load." At "this load," LaRue whisked her hand toward Fumiko.

"Mrs. Wingo," Moe answered, "your personal problems are none of my business."

"That is where you are wrong, Mrs. Root. The problems of the wife of your husband's commanding officer are very much your problems unless—"

"Unless what?"

LaRue sagged and a little of the harshness seeped out of her voice. "Don't, Moe. You know as well as I do that the only thing that really matters to Mace is flying, and the only way he's going to stay up there is if my husband and my father say he can."

Moe turned until she stared directly into Mrs. Wingo's face; then she cocked her head to the side and said in a voice spiked with a fake peppiness, "Gosh, LaRue, when did they pin the stars on your shoulder? I must have missed that."

Moe bent over and turned the hose back on.

Mrs. Wingo's jaw muscles bunched up as she glanced over at the other two wives, waiting between her and the car, and stepped closer to Moe. "Moe, don't break the chain of command."

"LaRue, I wasn't the one who enlisted."

LaRue snorted a sound somewhere between a laugh and a dying gasp. "Don't kid yourself. You signed up the day you let him put a ring on your finger. We all did." LaRue tensed again and jerked her head toward Fumiko. "Get rid of her, Moe. This is your last warning. Either you do it or I will, and you won't like my way."

"You're standing on my hose, LaRue. I've got work to do."

"You are an idiot, Mrs. Root." Mrs. Wingo headed toward the car.

"Takes one to know one!" Moe yelled the schoolyard taunt after her, then laughed a giddy laugh the way she did when she was drunk. She held her thumb against the flow of the water and aimed the hose up so that a heavy rain sprinkled back down on her, on me, on Fumiko. Mrs. Wingo hurried to the car and, shooting gravel everywhere when she peeled out of the driveway, roared away.

Water fell down in a high arc that pattered giant drops on the gang of children who now swarmed around Moe, shrieking with delight. Though Moe sang in a loud, happy voice, "Daddy's coming home! Daddy's coming home!" while she sprinkled everyone, her hand was clenched so tightly around the hose that it trembled and her fingers turned white. That and the scared look on Fumiko's face made me very uneasy. They should have been happy that the squadron was coming home, but they both were acting as if something even worse was going to happen. Before we went in the house, Moe pulled me aside. "Don't tell your father I said that."

"Said what?"

"You know . . ." She put on a bratty kid's voice. "'Takes one to know one.'" At that, Fumiko broke into one of her all-out, whinnying laughs. Moe's lips twitched as she fought to keep her own laughter back, then exploded in gusty blasts that went on until I told them both to stop, people were watching and they were embarrassing me.

That night we all had baths. "You don't want your father to come home and think you've all taken up goat ranching, do you?" Moe asked. Steam filled the bathroom. Water slopped over the edge of the tub and ran down the drain at the center of the tile floor and we all, even Fumiko, sang with Moe.

"I'm an old cowhand, from the Rio Grande." "I was born about ten thousand years ago." "Or would you rather be a mule?" "Bluebirds fly over the rainbow, why then, oh why, can't I?"

It was the last time Kit and I took a bath in the same tub. I don't remember many times when Kit and I were happy at the same time about the same thing, but that evening, knowing our father would be home the next day, bringing a bucket of marshmallow creme with him, we sang all of Moe's songs together.

Chlorine

We were at the Flight Line the next morning before the sun was up. Fumiko stayed back at the cinder-block house with the baby. Most of the wives were hungover. They held their hands over their ears when a cargo plane took off, filling the air with the smell of jet fuel, its afterburners lighting the darkness before dawn with orange flames. As the ground rumbled from the strain of the big plane leaving the earth, all the wives took grateful swigs of the "hair of the dog" Bloody Marys that Mrs. Wingo passed around, laughing, delighting in using the same phrases the guys did. All except Moe, who was not hungover but was one month pregnant with the first of three babies she would miscarry before Bob was born.

The clotted look of the pulpy drink that the pop-eyed Mrs. Dugan shoved in her face, combined with the smell of jet fuel, caused Moe's stomach to shimmy. She waved the Bloody Mary away.

The cargo plane took off into orange streaks of gathering dawn, and in the silence that followed, LaRue announced, "Moe's not gonna drink with us." Suddenly each wife's memory conveniently reorganized itself around this slight to the wife of their husband's commander, the wife of the man who filled out their husband's Officers' Efficiency Reports, the document that would decide whether she and her family would be stationed at Hickam Air Force Base in Honolulu or living with her in-laws in Bogalusa, Mississippi, while her husband completed an unaccompanied tour in Greenland. This perspective helped the wives recall Moe's absence from the club over the past three weeks. How they had managed to get over there and decorate the club, make the banners, design the centerpieces, rehearse the entertainment, decide the order of the acts, while Moe had chosen to just stay home. And now this? Refusing to drink with the commander's wife?

"Hey, you'll all survive."

Moe's answer was a joke, a testament to how lightly she regarded herself. But the wives looked to LaRue, who bugged her eyes in a caricature of innocent, injured astonishment behind Moe's back, and conveniently chose to interpret the joke as an insult. That Moe, blithe and unconcerned, didn't care what the wives thought of her was the worst—the source, in fact, of all her sins.

As the sun rose and Fuji-san flushed pink in the dawn, I felt the tense geometry between Moe and LaRue. I wished my mother would make a joke, a good one, or say something to remind the other wives that their children had swarmed over our house for most of the last three weeks—anything to break LaRue's spell. And she might have, except that a line mechanic in a greasy jumpsuit stepped up to our group and asked, "Hey, are y'all waiting for the Thirty-eighty-first?"

Madge, emboldened by the drinks, the newfound wives' solidarity, the weeks of no husbands, and her new closeness with the commander's wife, snapped back, "You can bet your sweet ass we are."

The mechanic stopped, the fuel line he carried drooping beside him. He squashed his cap around to scratch his head, and deep furrows of puzzlement creased his narrow forehead. "Didn't anyone tell you?"

The group of wives froze into a glacier, movement and life stilled.

After a very long moment, LaRue asked, "What do you mean?"

The mechanic recognized LaRue's tone of command and stiffened, looking around nervously, wishing he had said nothing. "Well, you know . . . I just figured someone'd told y'all something. You know, 'cause—"

"That will be all, Private!" The order issued from behind the wives. They turned to find a colonel, full bird, whom none of them recognized, flanked by a couple of APs in white helmets, white belts, and gloves. The colonel nodded and the APs stepped forward, grabbed the mechanic, and led him away. Three letters were embossed in gold on the briefcase the colonel carried: OSI.

"What's going on?" LaRue demanded, the Bloody Marys having blurred her usually acute radar for the bounds of her own power. Demanding was a mistake with a colonel from the Office of Special Investigations.

"That is classified information."

"Where are our husbands?" Captain Coulter's young wife pleaded, a note of hysteria spiking her question.

"That is classified information."

"They are supposed to be here. We got official word."

Again, the colonel answered, "That information is classified." The Apes flanked the colonel as he issued his order: "Go home. You will be notified of any further developments."

There was a stunned moment in which all the wives knew that the thing they were never allowed to name had come to pass. The children caught their mothers' unspoken dread like a virus and burst into tears. The twins wailed. Moe, her face blank, pulled us away.

On the drive home, I scrutinized Moe's every breath, every blink. The sick putty color of her face and the way she was panting through her mouth worried me, but I didn't start to panic until we came to a stop and she didn't throw her arm out to protect Abner and Buzz, who sat next to her in the front seat.

"When is Daddy coming home?" Kit asked. "He was supposed to be there. Lisa's mom said they were coming home today. Why wasn't he there? Why didn't—"

"Shut up, Eileen. Just shut up." Moe's order, issued in a dazed monotone as if she were trying to add a very big number in her head, stunned us all into silence.

Fumiko met us at the driveway. As Moe got out of the car, Fumiko went to her, took both her hands, and guided her into the house as if she were a very old person. I knew when Fumiko told Moe that everything would be fine that our father was dead. Everything was never fine. I went into my new bedroom, the girls' room, and closed the door.

Fumiko came in a moment later and sat on the bed next to me. I looked over and saw that she was holding my hand, but I couldn't feel hers. I lost track of the world around me. Each time my heart beat, everything in front of my eyes sprang up on the spot, startling me as if it had just been created that very instant. The Dolls of the World, my insect-collecting kit, the pennant on the wall from our class trip to Tokyo Tower, my collection of pink All About books. I had never seen any of it before.

"Breathe!" Fumiko ordered, but until she whacked me on the back I couldn't recall what the word meant.

I gasped, then inhaled and exhaled a sob.

"He's not dead." Fumiko repeated herself three times before I could stop crying enough to hear the words. "Captain Root is alive. All the fathers are alive."

"How do you know?"

"I can't tell you that."

"Don't just say something to make me feel better."

"I'm not. They're alive."

"How do you know?"

Outside, a misty spray of rain glazes the leaves.

How do you know? How did she know?

In the hideaway behind the officers' club, Fumiko pours the last of the tea. It is cold and bitter. Moths batter themselves against the paper globes around the light. I realize then what Fumiko saw that day eight years ago that made her answer my question. She saw what she'd seen from the first moment she slid back the door of our little house in Fussa. She'd seen Hana Rose, but she'd also seen herself. In me she'd glimpsed a little girl like herself, a child fundamentally displaced. At that moment back in my bedroom on Yokota when I asked Fumiko how she knew my father would return, she saw the child in the cave whose father was never coming home. Only this time she had the power to stop the anguish.

"You can never tell anyone," Fumiko had told me. "You have to swear."

I stopped crying and sat up on my bed, alert. The secrets you weren't allowed to tell were always true. "I will."

"No one."

"Cross my heart and hope to die."

"They are in Alaska. If they had been shot down, your country would be at war with Russia. They will be home soon."

"But how do you know?"

Fumiko makes me swear one more time that I will never tell anyone.

"Major Wingo told me."

Then I believed. The squadron commander had told her. Of all the children, only I knew that the fathers were safe. Our lives were built on the knowledge that secrets were powerful, and now I had one. A very big one.

"Remember," Fumiko cautioned me. "You can't tell anyone. If you do, I will get in very bad trouble."

"Not even Moe?"

"Especially not Moe. She is too kindhearted. She will tell the others."

That afternoon, Moe announced that she couldn't stand to be trapped in "this tomb of a base house" one second longer and all of us except Fumiko went to the officers' club pool. Fumiko stayed at the new house. Moe wore sunglasses and a big hat and sat still as a statue in the wading pool with the twins and Bosco, who were too young to understand that something was very wrong. The other wives all gathered around LaRue at the Terrace Café and drank and cried. I usually ate French fries under an umbrella and read, but not that day. That day when Moe left the ladies' dressing room balancing Bosco on one hip, the twins following her like ducklings, I stayed behind in the cool damp darkness of the dressing room where Kit and her friends had gathered.

Usually, in public, I followed Kit's lead and we pretended that we didn't know each other, but that day I had a secret. I wasn't going to tell anyone, I'd promised Fumiko I wouldn't, but I had it. I had a secret. Warmed by my nugget of power, I dared to brave the chilly reception I would receive from Kit and her friends clustered at the back of the dressing room.

Kit's platinum-blond head was, as usual, at the center of the girls. Kit and Lisa Wingo sat on a metal bench in front of a row of lockers hugging each other and crying. Debbie Coulter and her little sister, Ellen, had tears rolling down their faces, as did Captain Dugan's daughter, Sheryl.

I stood beside them for several minutes before Kit and her friends looked up. When they did, they stared at me, puzzled by how I could have found my way to the planet of the cute and popular girls. Too late I realized it wasn't enough to simply possess the nugget, I would have to display it. I decided I would flash it, just give the girls a glimpse, certainly not enough to betray Fumiko.

"You don't have to be sad." My voice came out a thin little mouse squeak. The girls looked at one another, checking to see if any one of them could interpret the strange sounds they'd just heard.

"You don't have to be sad," I repeated.

All the girls turned and gave me their full attention.

"Not be sad?" Lisa Wingo sneered. "Uh, dodo, in case you hadn't noticed, our fathers didn't come home today."

"But they will."

It was what the girls wanted to hear more than anything, and, in spite of themselves, they leaned in incrementally closer to me.

"That's not what the OSI guy said." Sheryl Dugan popped her eyes at me in a way that suggested she might have inherited her mother's thyroid problem.

"But he didn't say they weren't."

The circle enfolded me a bit more tightly.

Kit, who had been eyeing me skeptically, delivered her ruling. "Don't listen to her. She lies like a dog."

Without moving an inch, the girls receded.

My breath clotted in my chest and all I could hear was the blood roaring in my ears as if Kit were holding me underwater.

"I do not!" I gasped, bursting back to the surface of their attention. "It's true. Our fathers are alive! If they were dead, we'd be at war with Russia!"

The girls then surged around me, desperate for details. In the space of one second, I became the one they all liked. The one they wanted to be with. I was newborn. I opened my eyes for the first time and found myself surrounded by litter mates, sisters, friends. I filled my lungs with the oxygen of their attention and never wanted to exhale.

"Who told you?" Kit demanded.

The girls looked from Kit back to me.

That part I couldn't reveal. That would have been telling. As long as I didn't say her name, Fumiko would be safe.

"Yeah," Lisa repeated. "Who told you? We don't believe you unless you say who told."

After breathing the oxygen of the girls' attention, I thought I would die without it.

"She doesn't know anything. She never talks to anyone," Kit informed her playmates without the tiniest hint of malice. "This is stupid. Come on, let's go have an underwater tea party." She stepped away, trying to pull her coterie with her.

To my amazement, none of them moved.

"Marco Polo? I'll be it."

The girls looked from me to Kit but didn't move. Kit shrugged her beautiful, heedless shrug that said what would always be true, she'd have fun with them or without them. Kit left; the other girls stayed. I could breathe again.

"Okay, tell us who told you." With Kit gone, Lisa Wingo, her second-in-command, became bossier. Her order had her mother's peremptory tone. It made the words stick in my throat.

When I hesitated, Sheryl said, "Aw, come on, let's go find Eileen."

The girls moved away and I felt myself turning back into the ghost girl that Kit would tell me I was eight years later. That I was invisible and silent. A nauseated, untethered sensation overtook me then as if I were floating at a great height above the other girls and that I would continue floating higher and higher until I disappeared forever out of sight.

"Okay, okay." They were nearly past the last row of lockers. "But if I tell, you have to promise you won't ever, ever, ever tell anyone. Ever."

They each promised, then crossed their hearts and hoped to die. But that wasn't enough. So they triple-crossed their hearts and hoped to fall into a *benjo* ditch and get caught by the Apes and their moms and dads would die, and then I believed them.

I knew they would never tell. I told them where the secret had come from. I told them Fumiko's name. Debbie and Ellen and Sheryl stopped and looked at Lisa. For one second, Lisa looked like a little girl instead of the squadron commander's daughter, as odd comments and overheard conversations about her father and Moe Root's maid clicked through her mind. Then, wiping them away, she declared to the other girls authoritatively, "She's crazy. Fumiko is their maid. Maids don't know anything and neither does she."

Satisfied with that verdict, the girls left, and it was as if I had never spoken, never bartered away Fumiko's secret to become visible for that one moment. They didn't believe me. But, more important, even if they had, they had promised not to tell. So when what happened next happened, I never, not for one second, thought it had anything to do with me.

White Russian

"There you are! Call off the bloodhounds. Christ, I was getting ready to drag the river. Shoeshine guy finally told me where you went." Bobby Moses in full tuxedo, glowing orange from a fresh application of QT, stands at the sliding door. In one hand, he grips my vanity case and the white boots. In the other is my costume. He thrusts all of it at me.

"Zelda, do you, by any chance, remember that we've got a show to put on in, oh . . ."—Bobby makes an elaborate production of throwing his arm out to expose his Rolex watch and trills out with theatrical surprise—"oh, my, ten minutes." His voice is a girlish singsong that gives way to repressed fury when Bobby bellows, "Ten fahcacting minutes!"

Bobby immediately reins himself in, presses his palms together in prayer position, and asks, with the edgy control of a bank robber assuring everyone that no one will get hurt if they just follow orders, "Do you think you could possibly put your costume on and be ready to go on when the spotlight hits that big black space onstage where your ass is supposed to be? Do you? Do you think you could do that for me?"

Bobby presses his fingers to his lips, pretending alarm.

"Or—oh, goodness, Zelda—am I breaking up your little kaffeeklatsch here with my cruel demands that you actually work?"

Fumiko stands. Bobby's presence scrambles the frequency that Fumiko and I communicate on. With him glaring at us, I cannot hear the meaning behind her words. Only the bar-girl English comes through as she tells me, "You go job-u now, *honto. Hayaku.* You go, Bobby. I go job-u now. See you tomorrow. *Sayonara.*" Before I can stop her, Fumiko is gone.

Bobby squints murderously at me. "This joke is over, kumquat. I do not give a flying fuck anymore if your father is General Dwight frapping Eisenhower. This ain't the Top Three tonight. This is the Yokota Officers' Club. We got field-grade out there tonight. Probably a general or two. The whole freaking brass factory."

Shaking his hands above his head, questioning a cruel god about why such a cockamamie shiksa should be inflicted upon him, Bobby escorts me back to the club.

The ladies' room is exactly as it was the last time I visited it eight years ago during the evening of the squadron's tenth anniversary celebration, the evening the 3081st Reconnaissance Squadron came home from my father's last mission. The same bent-wire vanity chairs with pink velvet cushions sit in front of a long dressing table and mirror. The pink velvet covering them and the walls is faded now to the color of a shell on the beach. It is as if this one room of the Yokota Officers' Club has been preserved as a little shrine to the final shining moment of the American raj. To a time when America had conquered the world and was magnanimous in victory.

There is even, tucked away in a dark corner, a framed club calendar from April 1959. My heart leaps to see confirmation of my memory that the Yokota Officers' Club was once a place of glamour and sophistication. Every square of the month is filled in. There was Black Jack Nite, Lobster Tail Nite, Buck and Doe Nite, Free Manhattan and Martini Nite. There were family brunches, jazz concerts, floor shows, kiddie entertainment. Johnny Watson and his Kampai Kings played every night of the week except Monday. Drinks were fifteen cents on Thursday. There was brandied duck, leg of lamb, broiled salmon. Monday was Stag Nite and Tuesday mornings the Officers' Wives Club met.

All that remain now are the smells. Aqua Net hair spray. Revlon Aquamarine hand lotion. Max Factor Cherries in the Snow lipstick. The smells of wives preparing themselves to celebrate the return of their husbands. Chanel No. 5, Wind Song, Emeraude, Bellodgia perfume. The last, Bellodgia, with its memory of the dense funeral-parlor carnation smell of LaRue

Wingo's signature scent, takes me back to that last night at the Yokota Officers' Club.

It was steaming hot that second morning when we went to the Flight Line to pick up our father. We'd gotten word late the night before that the crew was really coming in this time. No false alarms. All the wives except Moe had assembled at LaRue's house at the news of this reprieve and had stayed up all night drinking Kahlua Stingers and playing canasta to celebrate.

"There he is," Moe said, pointing eagerly to one in the group of men in zippered flight suits, fleece-lined jackets thrown over their shoulders, who was breaking away and coming toward us. Our father turned wavy and smeared as he walked through a stream of jet exhaust roiling across the runway. Moe gave me Bosco to hold and ran to her husband. He swept her into his arms, twirling her so that her feet left the earth. They kissed like actors in a movie and I was embarrassed until I looked around and saw that all the fathers were kissing the wives the same way. Then Moe put her head on his chest and he patted her back while she sobbed.

As usual after a long TDY, we were shy with this man in the olive-green flight suit with all the zippers who had become a stranger. All except for Kit, who thrived on strangers and rushed to greet him. He scooped Kit into his arms and touched the new pink scar on her upper lip.

As our father approached us, Bosco buried her head in my shoulder while the twins hid in Moe's full skirt. I waited and watched, searching to see where he could be hiding the bucket of marshmallow creme he'd promised to bring back.

The ice wasn't broken until we were in the car and his flight lunch was being distributed. Moe broke the Milky Way into enough pieces for all of us. The twins got the corrugated packets of salt and pepper. Kit claimed the apple. I snagged the packets of mustard and mayonnaise and held them to my flushed cheeks, amazed, as always, by how cold they were. By how cold it must be in the sky.

Back in our new cinder-block house, sugar greed overcame shyness and I asked where the bucket of marshmallow creme was. My father furrowed his brow. Moe whispered in his ear. He said, "Oh," then he told me the rope broke, but not to worry. That he had an even bigger treat in store. That evening, the big kids, me and Kit, were going to be allowed to go with him and Moe to the welcome-home tenth-anniversary-of-the-squadron party.

When Bosco and the twins started crying about being left out, Fumiko rushed forward and promised that she'd make them candied tangerines while we were gone, and they quieted down. Then our father "roughhoused" with Kit and the twins until Buzz threw up and Moe said it was naptime and there would be no special evening at the club or candied tangerines for anyone who woke our father up.

Kit, too old for naps, went out to find her friends. Because I was the oldest and quietest, I was allowed to read my Frank Yerby novel about a beautiful woman captured by a handsome pirate, while Bosco napped in the girls' room with me. Fumiko left after Moe told her to take the rest of the day off, since she was going to baby-sit the little kids that night.

After the twins sneaked out the window of the boys' room, the house grew quiet and our father slept. As he slept, his smells— the primal male funk of cigar smoke, beer sweat, meat breath— staked out, claimed, and protected our house and in the heat and the happiness of our father being home, I slept too.

I woke up to the sound of our parents fighting, Moe's voice rising above my father's. "I can't believe you're serious. I can't believe what I'm hearing!"

My father's answer was a low bass rumble I couldn't make out, but Moe's was clear.

"No, I am *not* going to drop it, Mace. Do you know what the one thing standing between me and insanity is when you and your buddies take off for God knows where for weeks at a time? Do you know whose hand I grab every time an officer in uniform comes anywhere near the house while you're gone because I'm sure this is it, this is the time, the time you *don't* come home? For God's sake, Mace, there were ten crews in the squadron when we got here four years ago and yours is the last original one left. I couldn't have lived through that without Fumiko."

There was another indecipherable male rumble; then Moe's voice, teetering toward hysteria. "Fumiko is *not* just a goddamn maid. Fumiko is the person who stayed up all night with me when that idiot at the dispensary told me the abscess in the baby's armpit was leukemia. Fumiko is the one who was with me when I got the news about Mama's cancer. Fumiko saved my life when I was hemorrhaging to death. And maybe none of that means much to you, but it sure the hell does to me, buster. So, if effing LaRue Wingo is looking to fire someone, she can just fire that limp-dick husband of hers."

And then I heard my father's voice. "Keep it up, Mohoric, just keep it up. You're doing one colossal job of ruining my career here. Don't, please, don't consider that Limp Dick is my CO. And don't spend a second of your precious time worrying that Limp Dick's father-in-law roomed with Hap Arnold at the Point and is, at this very moment, over there in Hickam practically running PACAF, where one word from his precious daughter, LaRue, and his numbnuts son-in-law becomes squadron commander with ten crews under him reporting directly to Curtis LeMay. No, don't even pause to consider that one word—one word—and I'm flying tractors out of Bumfuck, East Jesus. If I'm still flying at all. If they don't make me a frigging ground pounder, in which case we'll never be stationed anywhere ever again for longer than a year. Is that what you want? You want to be packing up and moving from one shithole to the next every year? Yanking the kids out of school? Leaving their friends? You think Bernadette is bad now, wait until she tries *that* routine for a few years."

Bernadette is bad now?

"That what you want? Then keep it up, Mohoric, just keep it up, because that's what you're going to get."

"Mace, we can't give in to LaRue. She's a bully. We can't let her win."

"Win? What do you know about winning? You're not the one out there fighting. You're not the one putting your ass on the line for eighteen hours at a time wondering when the hell it's gonna get shot out of the sky."

My father's voice turned urgent and quiet. I had to slip off of my bed without letting the springs squeak and sneak to the door to hear. "Listen, Moe, things happened out there. This last mission. Things happened."

"Which means you saved Wingo's sorry ass again, doesn't it? Why do you put up with it, Mace? You actually fly the g.d. plane and he gets all the glory."

"Look, we're not going into details here, let's just say Wingo's putting the whole crew up for Distinguished Flying Crosses. So don't shit that away for me. Please, can you do me that one little favor?"

"She's the one getting the favor."

"For Christ's sake, Moe, LaRue's back is to the wall. I can't believe you don't understand. That you're not on her side. She doesn't have a choice here. She's got to end it. Shit, I wish he'd never sucked us into his little . . . Anyway, she's looking for a way to end it, and either you give her that way or she'll find one that ends my career too."

"Mace, I can't fire Fumiko. Please."

"No please. I'm three short of getting my fifty in. Once I have fifty missions and a DFC, we're home free. I'll make field grade, no sweat. I'm on my way to Air Staff and Command College. We can stop living like this. Pay back the loans. Start putting some aside for the kids' college. Have a good life."

"We have a good life, Mace."

"Case closed, Mohoric." My father has used his official Air Force voice, like a robot's. "As of this moment, consider Fumiko fired."

"Mace, you can't—"

"Zip it. Now hear this. Do not, repeat, do not say one more

inflammatory word to the wife of your husband's commanding officer. Do I make myself clear?"

Moe didn't answer.

"Mohoric, do I make myself clear?"

"Yes."

"I can't hear you."

"I said yes."

"Repeat after me: I will not utter one more word to LaRue Wingo."

Moe didn't speak.

My father yelled, "Say it!" and Bosco woke up screaming. I picked her up out of her crib, but she wanted Moe and only howled louder, her tongue a soft scoop trembling in the middle of her wide-open mouth. I held Bosco close and bounced on my bed to try and make her stop. Her wet diaper soaked my shirt and still Moe didn't come.

Finally, Moe yelled, "All right! Let go of me! The baby is crying, Mace. All right! I will not utter one more word to LaRue Wingo."

When Moe came in and took Bosco out of my arms, her face was white and her lips twitched against the tight seam of her mouth, like it was sewn together and she was trying to pull it apart. She snuggled Bosco up between her shoulder and cheek and clung to her as if the baby were the one comforting the mother.

Neither of my parents spoke on the drive to the club that night. In the chilly silence between them my father worked to make Kit and me laugh. He called us his dates and teased us about going out when we were in third and fourth grade. Kit giggled and I ached to join in their silly jokes, but that would be betraying both Moe, who stared stiffly out the window, and Fumiko, whom we'd left back at the new house not knowing she was going to be fired.

Banners proclaiming WELCOME HOME BOYS!! and 3081ST: TEN YEARS OF VALOR hung across the ceiling of the Samurai Ballroom. Hundreds of tissue-paper flowers in maroon and silver, the squadron colors, fruit of the wives' long hours at the club, decorated an arched entranceway that Kit and I passed through, following our parents. Strings of lanterns gave the windowless room the feel of an outdoor festival. All ten of the crews from the 3081st Reconnaissance Squadron were there. I recalled Moe's words and realized that all the men except for my father's crew were replacements for fliers who had died.

That night there was steak on everyone's plate. For the ladies—for Moe, for me, for Kit—there were filet mignons wrapped in bacon. "The guys" and their sons all had T-bones. LaRue and the wives who'd huddled around her for the past three weeks had planned out the menu right down to the red ring of spiced apple decorating every plate and the Baked Alaska for dessert.

Moe sat between Kit and me. The petticoats that Fumiko had starched with sugar water crackled as I nestled my folded hands down into the cloud of the skirt of my dress. Our father's chair was pulled away from the table just as all the other crew members' chairs were pulled away and turned around so that the men formed an inner circle with their families orbiting around it.

The Wingos were at the head table. Everything about LaRue that night was too big: big eyes with Cleopatra liner, big mouth with lipstick going outside its boundaries like *I Love Lucy,* big hoop earrings, big loud voice. She wore a cape that tied at the neck and had a collar that stood up behind her head like the one the wicked queen in Snow White had worn. Madge Coulter sat on her left side, Denise Dugan on her right. Lisa Wingo left their table, came over to ours, grabbed Kit's hand, and pulled her away without even a glance in my direction. I watched longingly as they disappeared, headed for the secret place where cute well-liked little girls went to have fun.

That night, however, I wasn't the only one left out. The families exerted a weak and diffuse gravity over all the fathers in the squadron. But our father's crew, the Bong Bunnies, the squadron commander's crew, the only one left with its original men, was the most tightly tethered to one another. Patsy Dugan would lift his head on one side of the room and Dub Coulter on the other would look up. After a few perfunctory bites of their meals, they all gravitated toward one another, gathering at the rattan bar where Riki, the barman, poured them with a heavy hand. They laughed into each other's faces and finished jokes someone else started. That night, they were gleaming brothers, each one equally loved.

At the time, I thought this golden state they shared had to do with being a man, with growing up. But it didn't. It was the secret they shared. The ground pounders didn't know, would never know, exactly what they had done while they were in the sky for eighteen hours, but they knew. Only they knew that their families and all the families of America were safe that night because they had put their lives on the line and won. For that day, that mission, they had saved democracy. No other crew could have done it, none ever in the history of man. The golden light they were bathed in that made them look like heroes came from the simple fact that they were heroes.

"Here, baby. Could you get me a refill?"

Because she refused to step one foot closer to LaRue, Moe handed me her glass for another one of the White Russians she was relying on to get her through this evening. Not even my father noticed me when I slipped in behind him and his crewmates at the bar.

Their conversation that night comes back to me like the lyrics to a song recorded at 33⅓ and played at 78. Slowed down now to its proper speed, phrases that had zipped past me then return as I sit in the Yokota Officers' Club and empty a can of spray onto my hair, trying to achieve a hairstyle Bobby Moses will consider classy.

That engine shroud blew and that was it. We were buying the farm.

The farm? Amigo, we were buying the whole frigging county.

When Wingo got on the squawk box and Command goes: Complete the mission, *I tell you Baby Boy here needed hisself a whole new change of underwear.*

So that's what I smelled.

The Titanic. *It was the frigging* Titanic *all over. Eighteen hours knowing there's not a snowball's chance at the other end.*

Stooging around up there with MiGs coming up our ass.

And fucking Dugan telling us he ain't getting the goddamned frequencies.

Fucking Harvard spark jumpers. What'd they want? We invite Ivan in for tea?

Did I get them, though?

You? Man, you wrote down the numbers. Root got them.

Yeah, I wondered what the hell you were doing stuffing all them empties into that wheel well.

But, Christ, when you dumped those Falstaff cans, they must have thought the whole Ninth Bombardment Wing was coming in at them.

Scope fucking lit up like a fucking pinball machine. They turned on everything they had.

And we got 'em all. If there's a frequency they didn't use it's 'cause they don't got it.

Jesus, that landing.

Hot? That bucket was rattling. Amped? That bird didn't know she could rev that high. Wild Root up there yelling at him to horse back on the throttle.

Wild Root, where the hell are you? Get your hands out of Moe's pants and get your ass over here. Root, you poot, how long you gonna pretend you're a copilot? To Captain Mason Root, the hottest rock in the wild blue. I'm drinking to your DFC right now. Ain't no way they don't pin one them babies on you. To Root!

To Root!

Clink.

Don't fly in my sky!

Don't fly in my sky!

Clink.

The men hoisted glasses. Blue cigar smoke twined around

and knotted them even closer together. Only Major Wingo was not tied into their charmed circle. I grabbed Moe's drink and hurried back to our table.

Perched on one of the faded pink velvet vanity chairs in the officers' club, I spray the beehive hairdo that Bobby favors with so much lacquer that my hand turns cold from the propellants. I put the can down and replay the moment of the crew toasting, crowded against each other like players in a huddle, and remember then how Major Wingo was squeezed out. How his men had subtly turned from him and toward my father.

As I outline my eyes with a pencil, I picture LaRue, surrounded by her handmaidens, raising her head and calling her husband to her. I recall how Coney Wingo left the men who were turning away from him and went over to his wife's table. How LaRue whispered in her husband's ear, then raised her finger and pointed in my direction. How her husband had stared at me, nodded slowly, then walked briskly over to break up the charmed circle around my father, so much like the circle of girls that always surrounded Kit, then pulled him away for a private talk that drained the joy from his expression. Remembering how my father had left Major Wingo and marched grim-faced to our table, coming directly toward me, I understand at last that in the Yokota Officers' Club pool dressing room all those years ago, surrounded by those little girls, I had been heard after all.

Though I hadn't, couldn't have, known at the time about Fumiko and Major Wingo, LaRue very clearly did, so that when Lisa repeated the crazy thing Kit Root's sister had said in the dressing room, LaRue had known instantly where this deeply classified information had originated.

As I realize for the first time how I'd handed Fumiko to LaRue Wingo on a platter, I blink and almost poke myself in the eye with the mascara wand. The pink velvet bathroom seems to fade even further as I realize that it *was* me. That with the smell of chlorine and Coppertone filling my head, I was the one who told. That everything that happened after that happened because of me.

After my father walked away from Major Wingo, he came to our table and spoke in a low, pressured voice. "Bernadette Marie, come here. I need to speak to you."

Moe stood up and faced him.

"Don't stick your nose in this, Mohoric. This is OSI territory."

"Uh-uh, this is my territory. I will not allow you to badger my child. Whatever LaRue and Coney's problems are, I'm not letting them take them out on Bernie. It's not right, Mace, you know it's not right."

My father glanced around. Everyone pretended they weren't paying attention. He clamped his hand around Moe's elbow and pulled her a bit farther away so that only I could hear.

"Right. Wrong. That doesn't matter with OSI. This was a black assignment. No one knows anything. No one tells anything. One slip. One near slip and you're gone. You know that. It's what you signed on for."

"I never signed on to have some bitch run my life and torture my children."

"Bernadette Marie, get your butt over here."

Everyone was staring at us. Their gazes paralyzed my legs and tightened my stomach into a hard knot.

"Leave her alone, Mace."

"Shut up, Mohoric, you have no idea what you're dragging me into. I am about two minutes away from getting hung out to dry."

"Quit kidding yourself, Mace. Wingo is going to hang you out to dry whether you torment our child or not."

"Wingo and I have an understanding. Bernadette, come here."

Though I didn't understand at the time why my father was so mad, as I tried to stand my twitchy tummy got the best of me and I vomited what I'd eaten of my dinner.

"I hope you're happy now," Moe said to my father as she pulled me out of my seat and dragged me off to the ladies' room.

When we returned, the band, sitting behind rattan-covered stands decorated with large black metal musical notes, was playing "That Old Black Magic." The muscles of Moe's jaw bunched spasmodically as she stared straight ahead and we walked back to our table. Her face was blanched white except for two bright welts of crimson flaming on her throat. She chewed her bottom lip and then tilted her head upward a fraction of an inch, as if trying to drain the tears that glistened in her eyes back into her head.

"Officers, may we have your attention, please." Madge Coulter's tremulous voice was lost in a shriek of feedback. The bandleader rushed over to tilt the microphone. She started again.

"Officers, may we have your attention, please."

From her table near the stage, LaRue gestured at the roll of paper in Madge's hand and Mrs. Coulter unfurled the tightly wound scroll. It had been dipped in tea and its edges charred to make it appear ancient.

"Hear ye, hear ye, hear ye. Whereas the men of the Thirty-eighty-first Reconnaissance Squadron have been proclaimed the hottest rocks in the Fifth Wing"—all the men from all ten crews cheered—"and whereas the Bong Bunnies have been deemed the studliest of them all—"

The other crews hooted out laughing protests while Dub Coulter struck muscleman poses and Patsy Dugan waggled his ass for the other fliers to kiss. Major Wingo clasped his hands above his blond head like a winning prizefighter and my father grinned a grin that was not his real one. When the hooting stopped and Madge started reading again, Major Wingo and my father glanced at each other, then looked away quickly.

"We do hereby offer this evening's entertainment in honor of the Thirty-eighty-first's ten years of service to the United States of America, far above and far, far beyond the call of duty!"

The men whooped and whistled through two fingers. LaRue, delighted that the words everyone knew she had written were being so well received, grinned with open pleasure.

"And now, to express what we all feel, the Biloxi Bombshell herself, LaRue Wingo!"

As rehearsed, the band launched into the theme from the LP of the new Broadway show *The Stripper.* Major Wingo led the applause. My father joined in, pounding his palms together as a spotlight found LaRue. Though neither of us could see my father's gaze in the darkness, we could both feel it. Moe patted her hands together woodenly. LaRue stood in the spotlight beside her table, her eyes wide as if surprised by this tribute and uncertain how to react.

Moe rolled her eyes in disgust.

LaRue finally strode onto the stage, her wicked-queen cape billowing behind. With a lingering coyness that verged on striptease, she slid off the hood, untied the velvet cords at the neck, and let the heavy cape fall to the floor as if it were being pulled off by an unseen hand. Whoops and catcalls greeted the low-cut, backless, sequined gown she revealed. She took the microphone with a polished professionalism, swirling her hand high above the stand like a witch casting a spell as she unwound the cord.

LaRue sang "Besame Mucho" with a throbbing sensuality, writhing in a pantomime of desire. Though she could imperson-ate a woman with an itch, her imitation of a woman with a good singing voice was far less convincing. Moe winced every time the commander's wife bottomed out, growling over the low notes she missed and searching for the high ones. By the time LaRue hit the refrain, Moe was signaling the waitress for refills of her White Russian and my father's vodka tonic, which she had fin-ished. When the drinks were delivered, Moe slammed them both back like she had a deadline to meet.

She was throwing down another round of refills when LaRue finished with an impassioned plea for many, many kisses, then drooped at the waist, spent, as applause washed over her. Revived by the shower of attention, she stood, arms to the heav-ens, tawny mane thrown back.

Madge bounced onstage, clapping and fluffing up the air in front of her, exhorting the crowd to their last round of applause before LaRue exited to the covey waiting to congratulate her on her triumph. The houselights came back on. Madge replaced the microphone on its stand.

"That was our own squadron commander's wife, the very talented and lovely LaRue Wingo!"

A new wave of applause crested. LaRue looked around at her subjects with actual tears glistening in her eyes.

"Wow, LaRue," Madge enthused woodenly. "I guess everyone wants to hear another as much as I do. You think you got one more for us?"

The band members leaned forward to pull out the sheet music LaRue had provided for her encore.

As LaRue touched her chest, miming surprise and checking to be sure that it was "Me? You want me?" Moe put her glass down, whisked a bit of lint from the front of her dress, and stood up. Odd, usually one drink had Moe wobbling, her cheeks flaming red, but all the alcohol she'd consumed that night seemed to have steadied her. Her face was porcelain, cool and immobile. I prayed she wouldn't open her mouth, but she did.

"I've got one for you."

My gaze skittered nervously to my father, hoping he would do something to end the agony of the attention my mother had caused to descend upon me. He stood at the bar, his drink raised in a frozen gesture. Slowly, as if he could erase what he was seeing, my father closed his eyes. When he reopened them to see his wife advancing unsteadily toward the stage, he belted back his drink in one gulp.

The wives who'd clustered around LaRue pinballed glances of consternation and contempt back and forth.

Moe stopped at their table. "This is supposed to be a show by all the wives for all the guys, isn't it?" she asked the women. "Well, I'm a wife."

She sailed past them, past LaRue and right onto the stage. Madge Coulter held the microphone out like a club ready to ward off my mother's advance. Moe disarmed her in one lurching motion.

I put my head down and melted into a puddle of burning shame. The gazes, the judgments strafing my mother had annihilated me. It was me onstage and I was naked. There was no death so horrible that I would not happily choose it over continuing to exist as the charred cinder of humiliation my mother had turned me into.

A skirl of microphone noise caused me to lift my eyes a few micrometers and see Moe covering the mike with her hand while she conferred with the bandleader. The wives offered their smirks to LaRue at my mother's amateurish mike technique. LaRue received the smirks with an old pro's expression of patient forbearance for the upstart's gaucheries. I thought longingly of the picture of Saint Sebastian in my missal, eyes cast heavenward, his breast pierced by a dozen arrows.

"I'd like to dedicate this song"—my mother's amplified voice was a waterfall gushing out, a flood I would never be able to bottle back up or mop away—"to Fumiko Tanaguchi."

I drowned in her words, and still the waters rose.

"And to all of us who've kept our mouths shut for too goddamned long."

I chewed on the inside of my lip, hoping to open a wound that would allow me to quietly bleed to death without attracting any further attention as Moe began to sing. Blood thundered in my head so loudly I couldn't hear her.

Mercifully, the house lights dimmed. I risked raising my head. A spotlight bleached my mother. At first glance, she appeared only as patches of dark hair and red lips floating in a dazzling radiance. It was an X-ray vision of Moe far worse than if she'd been naked. Still no sound reached my brain, and I could only watch the grotesque pantomime of my mother on a stage pretending to be a singer.

When, out of the corner of my eye, I noticed the men, all from the other crews, moving up, I was certain they were coming, like the angry villagers in *Frankenstein,* to pull Moe down and poke at her with their torches. Their grins, the obvious pleasure they were taking in this mission, shocked me. I was so startled when the men halted at the foot of the stage that, for a second, the blood stopped pounding in my ears long enough for me to hear my mother's voice. I didn't believe what I heard. Moe was singing "Somewhere Over the Rainbow." Of all the hideous twists this night had taken, this was the worst, my mother putting herself up for comparison with Judy Garland.

But Moe didn't sing Judy Garland's song. Instead, when she sang about a land in a lullaby and waking up where clouds are far behind, when she begged to know why, oh why, *she* couldn't fly beyond the rainbow, it amazed me to hear that she was singing about that place where I was blond and had a cocker spaniel and lots of friends and never had to move ever again and be the new girl.

I was embarrassed at Moe telling everyone my dream until I looked around and saw the men in the other crews and their wives, their heads tilted up as if they were about to receive communion, staring at Moe the way the crowds of little girls that swarmed around Kit stared at her. The way sobbing teenagers stared at Elvis.

As she sang, the men saw again the Charles Lindbergh sky of their boyhoods. They saw the shimmering white canvas that would contain the infinite stretch of their bravery, their heroism, their dreams. The wives saw once more the hope of flying into a future of limitless promise and bold adventures. A future beyond mothers, fathers, sisters, brothers, uncles, aunts, cousins, beyond hometowns that suffocated and stunted. As Moe sang they all remembered again the dream of making a home in the sky.

Why then oh why can't I?

The song ended. Moe dropped her head, and there was utter silence. When she looked back up, her face was wet with tears. She cocked her head to the side in a gesture that said, "Well, that's it. That's my song," and the Samurai Ballroom exploded. Hands pounded together, men put fingers in their mouths and whistled, wives from the other crews fished in evening bags for wads of Kleenex to dab at their eyes. They screamed for an encore, but Moe walked off the stage, past my father, and straight out the back door of the club.

The guys from the other crews crowded around my father, asking him how he managed to catch such a songbird. Was she a professional? She sure sounded like a professional. I searched for LaRue, for a glimpse of her face, but her seat was empty.

My father told me to get Kit and go to the car. I finally found Kit, asleep on the damp cushions of a chaise longue by the pool.

"Did you hear Mom sing?" I asked her, as we walked through the parking lot.

"What?" Kit wasn't cranky, which meant she wasn't really awake yet. I took her hand and led her to the car, where she curled up in the backseat and slept on, never knowing that that night our mother had mopped the floor of the Yokota Officers' Club with LaRue Wingo.

Candied Tangerine

The same OSI colonel and the same APs who'd told the families on the Flight Line that the crew wasn't coming in woke us up at four the next morning.

They took us to the BOQ on Tachikawa. We weren't allowed to speak to anyone. We were each permitted to bring only one small bag apiece. We had to leave everything else behind, even Chisaii.

Three days later, our father got his orders. None of us could find out where we were going because, every time we asked, he would answer, "Bunhump, East Jesus."

My parents' anger was too large for the small room we all shared and so buried in the secrets of my father's work that, sometime around then, they lost the habit of talking to each other.

Kit and I turned to the Ouija board to try and find out what the name of our new home was to be, but all it would give us was the first letter, Y, which Kit said was only because I pushed it that way since I wanted to stay at Yokota so badly.

Our new assignment was Mountain Home Air Force Base in Idaho. Months later, when we unpacked, our hairbrush was clotted with dried toothpaste because the tube left open in the bathroom had been thrown in the same box. Another box contained everything that had been on the dining room table that last night. The tablecloth was stained and sprinkled with the dried petals from a vase of snapdragons that had been packed, water and all, on top of it. Dried scrambled eggs were shellacked to the dinner plates Fumiko had used to serve the meal she'd prepared for the twins and Bosco while we were at the club. On the last dirty plate

Moe pulled from that box were shriveled bits of candied tangerine, a hard shell of sugar crystallized around each leathery section. Moe started crying, threw the plate away, went to her room, closed the door, and didn't come out even when we all pounded on the door and said we were hungry.

Our abrupt departure from Yokota was never explained, never discussed. Fumiko's name was never mentioned again. In time it became natural—convenient—to put the two together and blame Fumiko not only for our exile but for everything that followed.

Our father's predictions all came true. Everyone in his crew except him was awarded the Distinguished Flying Cross for the last mission. He never was sent to Staff and Command College. We never stayed anywhere much longer than a year. And he never flew again.

Spiced Apple

I push open the swinging doors of the Samurai Ballroom. For a second, I almost expect to see the banners proclaiming, WELCOME HOME BOYS!! and 3081ST: TEN YEARS OF VALOR that had hung there the last time I stepped into this room. But there are no banners. There's not even any rattan furniture or banquettes covered in raw silk. They've been replaced by Formica tables with steel-frame chairs and booths covered in burgundy vinyl occupied by couples in dress-up clothes.

The wives, hair sculpted into glossy helmets, eyes shadowed in aqua, mascaraed lashes curled up into right angles, perch on girdled butts. Their husbands wear suits they had made in Hong Kong from fabrics that looked good in the tailor shop but haven't worn well, have grown shabby and tight. Lines of fragile tension string between the couples as the wives flick shadowed eyes from their plates to their husbands and the husbands scan the room, checking out the other officers. Nowhere is there any evidence of the swaggering Rat Pack cool of my father and his crew.

Bobby works his way through the crowd, shaking a hand here, pounding a back there. A one-star general is installed at the best table in the room. Bobby pretends to go rigid with fear in front of him, snapping off a salute that vibrates with terror at his forehead as Bobby shoots pop-eyed grimaces around the laughing room. Finally, the general returns the salute to a round of applause. He has the cowboy cocky manner of Coney Wingo and doesn't look any older than my father.

Bobby bounds onto the stage. "Ladies and gentlemen, let's hear it for the general! There's one man who wants to die with his boots on. He's got holes in his socks! His family has always served the country—some of them ten years, some of them twenty. All right, all right, I can see that most of you agree with his proctologist, we've seen enough of this asshole! Come on, let's hear it for the general. A good sport, a good sport."

A table of stag guys at the back leads the crowd in whoops of laughter that verge into braying insubordination, and eyes carom from the general to the men. I recognize the TDY crew I saw earlier in the day, picking up wives at the Terrace Café. Some of the men, including the redheaded major, seem to have succeeded. Several wives sit with them.

The room is with Bobby, laughing, grinning, from table to table. "You know why we're in Vietnam, don't you?" He asks the crowd, and I feel the tug of them slipping away from him like the tide pulling sand from underfoot. But Bobby doesn't seem to notice. "It's the only country in the world where the women come out to meet you in pajamas! It's called Operation Headstart!"

Bah-bing!

He gets a rim shot but very few laughs. The very last thing the diners at the Yokota Officers' Club want to be reminded of that particular night is Vietnam. Bobby, oblivious, plunges on.

"Yeah, I just got back from a tour of Nam. Nice country. They got two seasons there, rainy and dry. I missed the dry season. That was the day before. It was so damp I couldn't tell whether the men were applauding or splashing. It wasn't that bad. Next time I go back I may even sleep on top of the bed. But, seriously, I don't see what all this protest stuff is about. All this burning the draft cards. I just heard the government's got a new policy. If they're old enough to play with matches, they're old enough to be drafted. You've seen some of these guys with the shoulder-length hair. I guess they'd rather switch than fight."

In the silence that follows, forks clatter against plates. I could have told Bobby this bit would bomb. Women in pajamas, long-haired draft protesters, a war in a rainy country where Americans are killed in their beds, it is both too real and completely unimaginable.

"Hey, someone forgot to tell me I'd be playing the Far East Morticians Convention tonight!"

At the back of the room, I touch the lacquered pillar of my hair, press my girdled toes against the go-go boots, and try to activate the nervousness I should be feeling. It is hard, however, to unwind the tentacles of memory that still grip me and recall that, within a matter of minutes, I am supposed to take the place of the stubby, sweating man onstage. I can't stop returning to the image of Moe singing, as if the memory were a room I'd just discovered in a house where I'd lived a long time. Again and again, I sort back through the years of my parents' silence. I shuffle in Fumiko's story, the secrets my father was burdened with, the secrets I knew, the secrets I told.

The Japanese drummer hits a belated exclamation point to Bobby's joke. The tinny clatter of the cymbals echoes hollowly in the room.

"Oh, someone's alive out there. Thanks, Yosh. That's Yoshi Gottaweewee. Yosh don't drink. Don't smoke. Don't curse and never made a pass at a girl. He also sews all his own gowns."

Bobby gets a few pained smiles.

"Okay, you don't like me. You don't like Yosh, let's bring on Okinawa's answer to Joey Heatherton, the Amazing Zelda!"

The band, cued by Bobby, launches into "I Dig Rock and Roll Music."

I walk through the ballroom toward the stage. The familiar red rings of spiced apple sit like bull's eyes on white dinner plates. My strange detachment continues even as I hobble on the tight boots up the three steps to the stage. My heart pounds with nervousness, but I can't force my mind back into the present. I am so distracted that I forget to take my glasses off. At the center of the stage, I look out and see what Moe saw eight years ago: grim faces set into expressions of resentment enlivened only by the hope of witnessing a true catastrophe.

A dim impulse causes me to attempt motion in time to the music. The result is a lurching afterthought committed while my attention is spent studying the faces watching me. They are the faces of my father and his crew. The glamorous RAF boys and their wives eight, ten, twelve years on. The men and women who, like my father, like Moe, in the imperial glow cast by World War II, pledged their lives to deliver the sky from America's enemies in return for a promise to be their nation's heroes. I have seen their futures, I know the disappointment that awaits them back in their native land, and I am overwhelmed by tenderness for these remote men and their girdled women.

I wave at the band to stop bleating out this false proclamation about my "digging" rock 'n' roll. I am a visitor from the future. I am the only one of this tribe, my tribe, who knows that they have been overtaken by history. That none of the promises they based their lives on will ever be fulfilled. I unzip the white go-go boots and my bare feet explode out. By the time I straighten up, I've pulled most of the pins out of my hair. For a second, half a can of hair spray allows the structure to defy gravity, before it falls in shellacked clumps around my face. The very least I can give my tribe is the truth about the country they will return to, the truth about their children, the truth about me.

I turn to the hipster bandleader. "Do you know 'Brown Eyed Girl'?"

Yoshi beams and gives me a thumbs-up. "Van-u Morru-san! *Ichi-ban!*" He fires off a burst of rapid Japanese, opens a case, pulls out an electric guitar. I try not to look at Bobby but catch a glimpse anyway. His face is the color of boiled tomatoes as he repeatedly slices his finger across his throat. Yoshi tunes his electric guitar and the women clap hands over their ears. The men exchange What-is-this-shit? glances.

"Hello." The microphone squawks and I jerk back. "Hello. My name is Bernadette Marie Root. My five brothers and sisters call me Bernie. I am not Okinawa's answer to Joey Heatherton. I am an Air Force brat. My mother is Mary Clare Mohoric. My father is Mason Patrick Root. I went to five schools in fifth grade. The longest we ever lived any place was here. We were stationed at Yokota Air Base from 1956 to 1960. My father flew RB-fifties with the Thirty-eighty-first Reconnaissance Squadron. His crew was the Bong Bunnies."

Led by the redheaded major, all the guys at the back table bound to their feet. "All right! Thirty-eighty-first!" The major hoists a mug high above his head and delivers his panegyric, "Thirty-eighty-first! First in war! First in love!" The rest of the crew raise mugs high and stare at the surrounding tables until those officers hoist their drinks up, as well, in a salute to the 3081st. The young redheaded major clinks his mug against his tablemates'. The toast rings through the ballroom, and all the men slam down their drinks.

"Barkeep!" the young major bellows. "Drinks for the house! The best goddamn squadron in the best goddamn Air Force in the world is buying!" Waitresses scurry around, distributing free drinks. Then the crew turns toward me and each holds his drink aloft while the major bellows out, "To a brother!" Everyone in the club hoists their drinks up for my father and yells back, "To a brother!," clinks, and drinks.

Hey Roderigo! Dates when no raking!

Yoshi holds a flimsy lyric sheet and sings out the words written by my old friend, the tea-loving Taiwanese transcriber. He bends down to plug his guitar into the amp and picks out the lead. The drummer follows Yoshi, picking up the rhythm. The keyboard player slips in where he can. The baffled horn players try to throw in a fill or two. Still, suddenly, it's music. I take my glasses off and the Yokota Officers' Club becomes an Impressionistic painting.

I grin uncontrollably as Yoshi turns Van's new game into a nude game and, before I realize it, I'm dancing.

"Whoo! Whoo!" The young major leads his table in a conga line toward the stage. Tables are bumped, plates knocked to the floor, wives pulled out of their seats and dragged away. "Nothing can stop the Thirty-eighty-first!" they sing to the tune of the Air Force song, almost, but not quite, drowning out Yoshi.

By the time the conga line reaches the stage, nearly all the officers have appropriated partners. The redheaded major, the last of his beer sloshing from his mug, dances with me.

He takes my hand and makes me spin like a ballerina in a music box while Yoshi sings about sew hearts fighting a highway and mammary backstairs roaring.

The stage crowds as all the single officers shanghai waitresses and drag them onstage to dance. A chubby lieutenant bumps into me and I dance with him, laughing even harder as Yoshi bawls out the transcriber's thoughts about making love in the negroes beehive!

The chubby lieutenant, the redheaded major, the petite brunette wife, we're all laughing as we scream out "Stay tea! Yum!" along with Yoshi. Yoshi catches my eye and mimes sucking on a joint as he sings "brown *high* girl!" and I laugh with him, too. All of us, me, the band, the girdled wives, the once-young officers, all the members of my father's old squadron, we're all in on the joke and we're all laughing together.

Sha ra ra ra ra ra ra ra ra ra ra ! Ra tea tah!

Yoshi, thrilled by this response, cues the band and they go into extra innings. The officers dance around me, happy and graceless as drunken bears.

The first shriek of the alarm doesn't register. By the second, however, I have already translated the blast from a code I didn't realize I remembered: *Typhoon. 1E. First Stage. Destructive winds of fifty knots or greater are anticipated within twelve hours. Active duty personnel contact Officer of the Day. Dependent personnel return to quarters.*

Band members all stop playing on the same note. The club manager flips on the overhead lights. The dancing officers seem dazed, like sleepwalkers who wake to find themselves in the middle of a street.

Chairs scrape back all around the room. Some officers help their wives on with their coats; most already have their keys in their hands and are striding toward the exits.

"Crap." The young major puts his empty beer mug down. "I thought it was gonna miss us." He walks off the stage, followed by the rest of his crew. The lights go on. Within minutes, the dining room is empty. As Yoshi waves goodbye and follows the last band member out, I realize what I must do.

"I have to go home."

"Home? You mean Okinawa home?" Bobby rolls his eyes, the preliminary to his what-did-I-do-to-deserve-this-fahcacting-shiksa routine.

Before he can start, I repeat, "I have to go home."

"No can do, kid. We're already in Condition One-E. All commercial flights will be suspended by the time you get to the airport."

I slam out the swinging doors and run down the hall. Near the front entrance I catch up with the crew from the 3081st. They've been slowed down by the fact that the navigator is passed out on the floor. The young major has the wife he picked up at the coffee shop slung over his shoulder, and he's directing his crew in how best to help their fallen comrade reclaim verticality.

"Not like that! You're just spinning him around. You got to pick him up." As the men try to coordinate their efforts, I run up to the commander.

"Hey, look! It's Joey Heatherton!" He tries to dance with me and the wife slides off his shoulder, landing unsteadily on her feet.

I explain to the major that I need to get home to Okinawa and that my father, who flew with the 3081st, would consider it a personal favor if he could help me.

The major studies me blearily for a moment, then bellows out, "Get me a phone!"

A few minutes later, the young major comes back. "Boy, are you a lucky dog. There's one flight out. It's going to Okinawa and the AC knew your old man. Get out to the Flight Line. ASAP."

Outside, that afternoon's misty rain has turned into a downpour. I'm waiting under the porte cochere with the gang of drunk fliers when Bobby ambles up. I make him promise to bring the rest of my stuff with him back to Okinawa.

"So, kid, it's been real."

"Bobby, I'm sorry I'm leaving—"

"Forget about it. So they sue me for breach of contract. So I'm ruined and end up eating outta trash cans."

"Bobby, could you give Fumiko my address? Tell her to write."

"So you decided to stay in touch, huh? The man without a country is going to write a letter, that it?"

"Yeah. Bobby, I . . . The whole"—I don't know what to say— "it was fun."

"We had a few laughs there, Zelda, didn't we?"

"Yeah. We did."

"Jesus, let's not start blubbering. What? You think this is the last time you're ever gonna see Bobby Moses? No such luck. I'll be looking you up. We'll keep in touch."

"Thanks, Bobby, thanks for everything."

"What thanks? You give a little, you get a little, life goes on. Just one thing, okay? Listen, kid, when you're my age you realize that we all pass through this life too soon and, in the end, what have you got? Your friends, right? Fuck it, just don't—don't be a prune, kid, huh?" He looks away, embarrassed by this brief dip into sincerity.

Bobby flags down a cab. As I run out to it, skipping bare-footed through the puddles, he yells at me, "Get some shoes before the freaking hookworms eat you alive!"

I pause in the pouring rain long enough to holler back, "You get it, Bobby, you just really do get it."

"Hey! What'd I tell you about stealing my tag line! Get out of here, get your own tag!"

Strawberries

I pile into the taxi and we drive through a rain that turns the windows of the car into sheets of wobbly liquid.

At the Flight Line, the security guard already has my name on a list and waves us on. We drive to a hangar at the end of the runway. I pay the driver then run through the downpour into the hangar, where rain thunders on the metal roof. The hangar, open at both ends, tunnels fresh, cool air past me. Outside, the rain makes the runway lights hazy and distant. The rotating red beacon in the control tower barely penetrates the downpour.

A Kota Kab pulls up. The back door opens. Fumiko, holding a box, gets out and runs into the hangar.

"Bobby told me you were here." There isn't even an instant when I don't hear what Fumiko means instead of the bar-girl English.

"Fumiko, I was the one who ruined everything." The words pop out. "I was the one who told."

"You were a child. It would all have happened anyway. Does Moe still love strawberries?"

"More than ever." Raindrops glisten on Fumiko's hair, as dark and shiny as it was the day we met. "She misses them. A lot." She holds out the box, a small crate made of slats of pale, sanded balsa wood and tied with a thick apple-green grosgrain ribbon. Through the slats, I see perfect, hydroponically immense strawberries nestled in excelsior as securely as babies in incubators.

"Tell her—" Fumiko stops.

There are words to say, but I don't know them any more than Moe knows the words to say to my father. Hearts beating as one is less a matter of will than of time and place and circumstance.

"You Mace Root's girl?" an officer yells at me, and I see the crew hustling out onto the runway.

Fumiko shoves the tiny crate of strawberries into my hands and like a magic spell lifting, I stop hearing what she means and only the bar-girl words are left behind. "You give Moe."

I say what was there from the first. "I love you."

Fumiko nods, and I can't tell whether the drops running down her face are rain or tears.

"Wheels up, babe!" the officer yells at me. "You're on crew time now! Move it! Move it! Move it!" The last of the crew hustles out to the plane rumbling on the runway.

Fumiko reaches out and touches my widow's peak, then steps away and—*blink*—a time that started when she first slid back the paper-screened door of the little house in Fussa is over. She turns and hurries through the rain to the waiting cab.

Rain

I fly back to Okinawa in a WC-130 Hercules with a crew from the 54th Weather Reconnaissance Squadron out of Andersen Air Base in Guam. Turbulence is ferocious. I am grateful I haven't eaten.

The aircraft commander, a jaunty, long-faced colonel with a deep tan and no discernible lips, bald on top with a fluff of blond on the side poking out around his earphones, swivels around in his captain's chair to face me. He shouts to make himself heard over the drone of the propellers.

I crane forward from my perch on a drop seat bolted to the wall but can't hear him.

He nods, switches on the intercom, and speaks into the microphone that curls in front of his mouth. His words now boom down from the speaker above my head.

"We're the Guama Bombahs."

I grin and nod like a lunatic, eager to express my appreciation for the immense favor they are all doing me. Especially the colonel. Taking an unauthorized dependent along on a weather scouting mission would not look good on his OER.

The colonel sits, ankle resting on his knee, sprawled back in the chair as if he were watching a football game in his living room. The cockpit is dark except for an array of lights on the control panel and the phosphorescent face of the radar screen in front of the navigator. They are charting the edge of the storm wall. "Milk run" was how the colonel had described it. The weather officer passes me and consults with the copilot, who stands beside the navigator, staring at the screen where a yellow fireball spirals against the black background. The only word I can hear as the copilot circles his finger around the open center of the spiral is "eyewall." The weather officer nods and goes back to the rear of the plane to radio information back to ground control.

The copilot, whose dark curly hair is pushed up into a pompadour above a high forehead by his headset, has the look of a young seminarian reading his breviary as he gazes into the screen and quietly answers all the questions only very occasionally interrupting the pilot to ask a question of his own or to forward a request from another crew member.

It is dark, loud, and cold, very cold, even with the two blankets and the pair of wool socks the flight engineer hands me. In the darkness, the search screen with its flame of whirling typhoon is like a hearth on a wet, miserable day where everyone draws warmth, comfort. Copilot; that was my father's job. I imagine him as he was then, his hair dark, long, combed like a movie star's; smoking a Camel cigarette; surrounded by men whose lives depended on his doing his job just as his life depended on them doing theirs. Everyone went through him. Like the Virgin Mary, he interceded for the others with the commander.

I think that my father and his crew must have been as oddly at peace as these men as they fly through the far edges of a typhoon. Maybe even as much as Moe and her group of sixteen nurses packed into a stateroom designed for a honeymoon couple, never knowing when an enemy torpedo would hit, singing in a jungle of damp underwear.

The Hercules shudders along. At dawn, a dim spectral illumination shines in through the fifteen windows that wrap around the front of the cockpit. Empires of cloud—gray, slate blue—rise up outside the windows. The ocean is a block of granite far below.

"Everyone buckled up back there?" The colonel's voice comes over the intercom. "It might get a little bumpy now." I don't see how it could get any bumpier, but I hook my thumb under the seat-belt straps coming over my shoulders as if I were snapping my suspenders at the county fair. "Time to go to work." The colonel directs his last comment to me.

The plane banks with a lurching yawn into the shroud of clouds and the ocean disappears from view.

The yellow bar on the navigator's screen that indicates our heading, which had been skirting the edge of the bright flower of the typhoon, now pierces its center.

The copilot sees my sudden panic. "Don't worry. We're not flying into the eyewall. Not this time. I wouldn't have allowed a civilian on board if we were. Just have to scooch in enough for the Dropsonde operator to deliver his packages."

The operator muscles a couple of two-foot silver cylinders packed with weather-sensing instruments toward the cargo bay. The copilot is close enough to yell to me over the roar of the engines that they have to penetrate into the wall of the typhoon to drop the cylinders, which will transmit information as they parachute down. He tells me not to worry.

"This is nothing compared to our last mission!"

"What was that?"

"You don't want to know!"

"Sure I do!"

"Trying to make enough rain to turn the Ho Chi Minh trail into a mudslide!"

The intercom crackles to life. "Okay, ladies, let's bite 'em in the ass!"

All the men turn to their duty stations. For the next several minutes, the intercom spills out a complex garble of numbers, coordinates, words spelled out with *bravo* and *delta* instead of letters, with each utterance receiving a *roger that, Captain.* Even I stop noticing how the plane is pitching. The tight harmony is sustained until the cylinders are dropped. The garble is like a musical score conducted by the aircraft commander. I wonder what kind of commander my father would have been.

A bubble of euphoria swells as the colonel banks back around and heads south.

"Next stop, Kadena O Club. I'm buying. Wake me up when we get there."

The pilot makes a show of stretching out, tipping his headset so it covers his eyes, folding his arms into nap position. He is grinning broadly. The rest of the crew yell jokes, tease one another about supposed incompetencies, laziness, cowardice, all of which highlight how perfectly brave and skillful they all were together. How entirely extraordinary.

"Is your father—"

The pilot is not using the intercom to speak to me and I can barely make out his shouted words. He puts his hand up and pantomimes a plane soaring through the air, its wings tilting up one way then the other.

I shake my head no. He presses his mouth together tightly and nods with sad understanding.

In half an hour, we've outrun the typhoon. Tattered streamers of dingy clouds slide past windows misty with a rain that has slowed down to a constant drizzle. We have to circle the island several times before landing, the runways are so busy with planes being evacuated.

The landing is effortlessly smooth. My biggest worry is what Moe will say about my bleached hair. It turns out that this is an unscheduled stop. No one else is getting off. They made this detour on their way back to Guam simply to deliver me. The colonel brushes off my thanks. "I'm sure Wild Root would do the same for my kid." His voice sounds soft and faraway after the hours of engine noise.

Outside, the wind socks balloon out at a stiff ninety-degree angle and the heavy drizzle threatens to graduate to a downpour. The sky overhead is filled with aircraft moving out of the path of the typhoon.

It only surprises me for a moment when I see Moe, Kit, Buzz, Abner, Bob, and Bosco standing on the observation deck outside the Kadena terminal. Someone in the Air Force net must have alerted Moe that I was coming home. For one second, before they spot me, I watch my family. They are all alert, searching, even—maybe especially—Kit.

I once asked Fuji-san to take her life for my mother's. I thought her beauty and her charm had been given to be used as weapons against me. I look at her perfect face and wonder at the life I might have had if I'd been the outsider in my own family and I could only draw an easy breath with anyone *except* them. Next summer, I won't finagle my way onto a Space A flight and come back to Okinawa or to anywhere else my family is stationed. I will stay in Albuquerque and find a job. A roommate. Some friends. Kit, the only one of us to have found a way out of our family, maybe Kit will show me how to stop being a prune just passing through the duodenum of life.

Standing on the deck, the wind blowing her dress out behind her, molding it to her in front, Moe looks like a pioneer mother searching a vast prairie for the one missing. As the sirens announcing a Typhoon Condition 1E beep out, Bob scales Moe's body until he is safe in her arms. Kit and Bosco both move closer to her and from the awkward, stifled tropisms of the twins' bodies it is clear they, too, with a typhoon wind whistling, are fighting the urge to cling to their mother.

I put the box of strawberries in front of my face to keep from crying and see myself again in my backyard perfume factory laboring in Fuji's shadow. I inhale the berries' fragrance and realize that what I was bottling, all those years ago, was memory. That honeysuckle was just one link in an endless limbic chain that contains all the smells of my family and of our life together: Baby Magic, support hose, Kool menthol cigarettes, sweat and Chanel No. 5, soggy diapers, talcum powder, Young Pinkoo lipstick, rice crackers, green tea, *benjo* ditches, tangerines and caramelized sugar, Brasso, Kiwi shoe wax, Right Guard, vodka, cigar smoke, kerosene and old books, canned beans and hot pickle relish, lacquered umbrellas and wet wool, DDT, old beer, floor wax and onion rings, black shoe edging, Herbal Essence shampoo, cut grass, Tide, warm cotton and steam, hamburgers and fermented ketchup, coral dust and diesel fumes, coconut hair conditioner, Brut, mildew, canvas, hay and manure, opium, JP-4 fuel, pickled plums, cherry-blossom tea, steamed rice, sweat, grease pencils, fear and Aqua-Velva, chlorine and Copper-tone. Rain. Breath. And now, strawberries.

Each smell is a blossom that combines with all the other smells the same way real flowers would in a real perfume factory where the days of sunshine and growing, the days of storm and drought, the times of plenty, times of want, what the flowers got, what they didn't get, they're all squeezed together under prepos-terous pressure or boiled or tinctured or distilled into a few drops of a smell so beautiful it can make you remember everything.

In a minute or two, I will hand Moe the strawberries and tell her they are from Fumiko. I will tell her I'm sorry I told the secret and took away her best friend and messed things up with our father. She'll tell me the same thing Fumiko did—that I was only a kid and it wasn't my fault. That it all would have happened anyway. That there's never just one thing, and neither one of us will ever mention it again. But for the rest of my life, the scent of strawberries will forever remind me of standing beside a runway on the island of Okinawa with my mother, my sisters, my broth-ers, our clothes filled like sails by a tropical wind, as we all watch the sky and wait for our father to return, one more time, ahead of the storm.

Perfume

Everyone in my family has one thing. Bob can recite, ka-blooey for ka-blooey, every line of every cartoon he's ever watched. Abner can do his age times one hundred in sit-ups. Buzz can put both his ankles behind his head and walk on his palms. Bosco is never wrong about a fact. Kit can walk into any school anywhere in the world and become the most popular girl inside of a week. My one thing is dancing. A long time ago, our mother's was singing and our father's was flying.

Acknowledgments

More than any book I have written, I owe thanks.

Above all, to my family who shared their memories of our gypsy childhood and, most precious of all, understood and accepted my capricious weaving of fiction through our shared past.

To my boys, my angels, George and Gabriel.

To Kris Dahl for twenty years of friendship and representation without equal.

To Ann Close, whose impeccable editorial guidance verges on the clairvoyant.

To Dave Hamrick and Robert Draper, who both went out on limbs of varying lengths for this book.

To my first and dearest reader, Kathleen Orillion.

To the friends and writing companions who have given me such generous portions of heart and wisdom at critical junctures: Bert, Bill, Carol, Casey, Clare, David, Diane, Dick, Elizabeth, Emily, Ernest, Hickey, Jesse, Jim, Jo Carol, John, Judith, Larry, Marcie, Mary, Pat, Rebecca, Robert, Sara, Suzanne, Tim, and last, though he's been there from the first, Tom.

To Glenn Greenwood, indispensable guide to all things brat.

To Pat Conroy for creating the definitive portrait of a military family in *The Great Santini* and to Mary Edwards Wertsch for, in her words, "taking the military family into therapy" in her landmark work, *Military Brats: Legacies of Childhood Inside the Fortress*.

And, finally, to the glorious convocation of brats I've met in our hometown in cyberspace.

A NOTE ABOUT THE AUTHOR

Sarah Bird is the author of four previous novels: *Virgin of the Rodeo, The Boyfriend School, Alamo House,* and *The Mommy Club.* She lives in Austin, Texas, with her husband, George, and their son, Gabriel.

A NOTE ON THE TYPE

This book was set in Caledonia, a face designed by William Addison Dwiggins (1880–1956) for the Mergenthaler Linotype Company in 1939. It belongs to the family of types referred to by printers as "modern," a term used to mark the change in type styles that occurred around 1800. Caledonia was inspired by the Scotch types cast by the Glasgow typefounders Alexander Wilson & Sons circa 1833. However, there is a calligraphic quality about Caledonia that is completely lacking in the Wilson types.

Dwiggins referred to an even earlier typeface for this "liveliness of action"—one cut around 1790 by William Martin for the printer William Bulmer. Caledonia has more weight than the Martin letters, and the bottom finishing strokes of the letters are cut straight across, without brackets, to make sharp angles with the upright stems, thus giving a modernface appearance.

W. A. Dwiggins began his association with the Mergenthaler Linotype Company in 1929, and over the next twenty-seven years he designed a number of book types, the most interesting of which are Metro, Electra, Caledonia, Eldorado, and Falcon.

Composed by Stratford Publishing Services,
Brattleboro, Vermont
Printed and bound by R. R. Donnelly,
Crawfordsville, Indiana
Designed by Virginia Tan